The illustration that follows is described in Ezekiel.

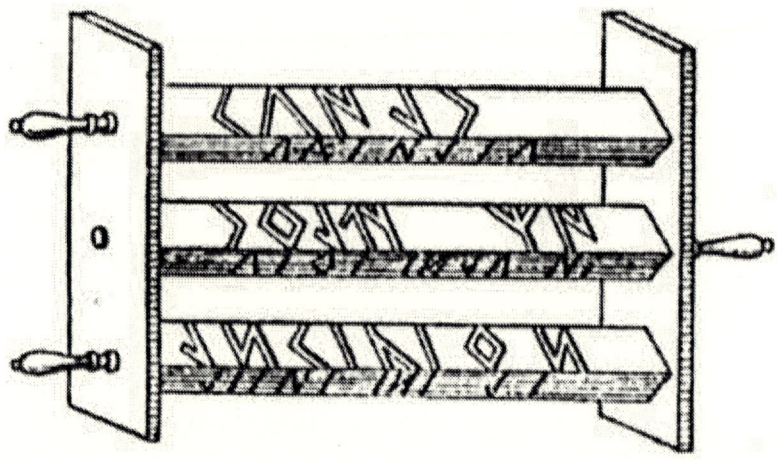

What would they say about *'How the Irish Saved Civilization'* by Cahill and who on?

Diverse Druids:
The Origin of All Religions

Robert Baird

Copyright ©2003 Robert Baird

All Rights Reserved. No part of this publication may be reproduced, stored in a retrieval system or transmitted, in any form or by any means, electronic, mechanical, photocopying, recording or otherwise, without prior written permission of the copyright holder.

ISBN: 1-931468-17-6

Cover Design by Kirk Heydt
First Printing

The Invisible College Press, LLC
P.O. Box 209
Woodbridge VA 22194-0209
http://www.invispress.com

Please send question and comments to:
editor@invispress.com

Diverse Druids

PROLOGUE

History is prologue to the present as thought is to action. Our socially accepted 'norms' or acts often determine how average people think - based on the propaganda presented as fact. These supposed facts of history are revised to suit attitudes of the prevailing paradigm. Reading about Cleopatra in the words of Lucy Hughes-Hallet will make the point clear to anyone; she presents an alchemist or temptress to seem either evil or laudatory depending on many social imperatives in different centuries. The same is true with Jesus and there are many good books written by Rabbis or other scholars to demonstrate that issue, which repeats like cucumbers on a full stomach. Marshall McLuhan made an interesting observation about the person who controls the media for 15 years. He said if he was given that power he would control all society. His recent biographer says McLuhan knew about secret societies who own or control the very media and society we live in.

It is a multi-layered management that many popes, kings and professors have mistakenly thought they were in charge of, but later were seen to be operating according to a larger plan. The Bilderbergs are not the most powerful, or at the top of the mountain but whoever organizes their seminars and information is an important person. Whenever powerful people seek to come to common ground it can easily be seen as a good thing. There is no good reason to reject such efforts that take place every year at hotels owned by the Rothschild family, unless we know what they do. In the absence of facts we must look to history or the outcome of the supposed plans (or lack thereof) that such people agree to implement. Shortly after the Trojan World War in 1200 BC a similar and probably similarly structured meeting (by the ancestors of the Rothschilds) took place off Miletus. They were called the Perpetual Sailors and as members of the Phoenician Brotherhood had been around since Ba'albek and before the Pyramids.

Robert Baird

Those who run the bureaucracy or act as political 'stooges' and 'fronts' for these plans include the likes of Napoleon and Hitler. But the history we are told about, seldom explores how these supposed dictators were put in power and how they were managed or 'handled'. Hitler was a Jew and lived as one in Vienna; according to the report made for the top dog of US Intelligence (is that an oxymoron?), Wild Bill Donovan. This book written by a psychiatrist leaves out all evidence of any spiritual or occult specialties employed by Hitler or his handlers. I assure you Professor Horbiger, Himmler, Eckhart and others were adept in matters of the occult ('oc'= 'not', a cult). This book is called *The Mind of Adolf Hitler: The Secret Wartime Report*, and it makes it very apparent Hitler was related to the Rothschilds: but it doesn't explain who these people were before they took their name from the 'red shield' in front of Meyer Amschel Rothschild's father's hotel just a century before Adolf's father went to study in Vienna. Vienna is the place Salomon Rothschild had run his part of the Rothschild financial EMPIRE.

The U.S. and the whole supposed Free World were anti-Semitic as the movie *Ship of Fools* does indicate. We are scapegoating Germans to this very day. The truth about the Jews is not even known to the Jews themselves. There is no homogeneous Jewish people who came from a genetic group separate from all other white people. Their 'Lost Tribes' and Bible Narratives are an affront to reality or mere propaganda that became managed by Rome. The holocausts include the 'brothers' of the Jews - Ukrainians, Armenians and Irish etc. In fact even in the 20th Century the attempted genocide of the Jewish people was not as bad as what happened to the Ukrainian people perpetrated by our ally, Stalin. The Aryan fiction was used by political forces to create a war. The Jews are the high priests or at least the 'arch-tectons' (architect, and the title of Jesus and Joseph in the early Bible called the *Septuagint*) of the Pyramid. The Father of Biblical Archaeology, W.F.Albright, states that the Bible 'is a Phoenician literary legacy'. Aryan can be shown derived

Diverse Druids

from 'Eire-yann' or the Keltic people (including the Germanic Teutons) whose spiritual center was Tara in Ireland (for at least a millennia in a far longer period of influence). These are the builders of the Pyramid who Moses led out of Egypt as the story goes. The language of Hebrew was the sacerdotal code of these 'arch-tectons' who knew knowledge in the hands of the power-mongers could be harmful. Thus we have the name for the Hebrews who are part of the Jewish 'Brotherhood'.

Genetics is a record that the Empire-builders could not fully eradicate. They did an excellent job ridding the world of knowledge in books or libraries like Alexandria, Bangor and the Mayan lands. Genetics now shows a Haplogroup X marker which allows us to know all white men including many North American Indians like the Sioux, started out near the Caucasus Mountains 30-35,000 years ago. Linguistics and other archaeological tools such as forensic analysis of corpses hooked on cocaine (from Peru) in Egypt (see Balabanova and various TV specials); has made the ongoing history of Empire and man far from palatable or believable. Hellenizing usurpers of previous cultural and technical knowledge was not so much the intent of the Greeks who honored the 'ancient ones' they called 'Keltoi' and 'ogygia'. It was the enslaving barbarians of Rome who enjoyed their 'sport' in their arenas who really refined this prejudice. They had the audacity to call the Berbers - 'Berberoi' or 'barbarians' even before they ripped off their own people by creating Caesar and later as they made Churchianity the true Roman Empire.

Our sovereign nations are founded on concepts of 'Manifest Destiny' (While they give their cronies 'Manifest Subsidy') and such perversion,as allowed the British to colonize India or force opium upon the more sophisticated and cultured civilizations such as China. The Treaty of Tordesillas dictated by Pope Alexander VI was the significant starting point of a plan to expand the Inquisition. I wonder if kids today learn about it in school. I know I didn't. This Pope was a Borgia and related to the De

Robert Baird

Medici's who were then in charge of the finance monopoly that had once been the Templar 'fatted calf'. Could the De Medici's have passed their monopoly on to the Rothschild's? Yes, indeed, if you look to the place Meyer Amschel Rothschild lived and worked as the chief financial guru; you find it was the Hesse family castle. This is the same place where a De Medici favorite 'son' by the name of St. Germain(e) spent a lot of time. At the time of the founding of the Jesuits you will find the Borgias donate their first University, which implemented full scale teaching of St. Thomas Aquinas.

The De Medici matron Catherine was the protector of another Jesuit named Nostradamus. The Alumbrados were the secret society within the Jesuit Order and they may even have founded it in the style of the Priory of Sion founding the Templars and Knights Malta five centuries before. It is reasonable to suspect that Nostradamus was a member of this esoteric inner sanctum. Nostradamus, Aquinas and St. Germain(e) are three of the most knowledgeable alchemists this history has ever known. You will see that alchemy comes from or was akin to Druidism in this book.

When the Pope apologized for two millennia of 'heinous acts' in 1999 while asking for 'forgiveness and renewal' he did not mention the Thomists are still a major force in his Order. He might be a rare person interested in explaining these things to you, but he is not allowed to go into such details (perhaps for legal reasons). You should have facts before you make determinations or start the decision-making process. However, you have not been allowed to know the facts and we have all been kept in the dark far past the Dark Ages created by these people who keep knowledge (power) to themselves. Despite his 'goodness' the Catholic Church and their Anglican henchmen were named as the creators of the near genocide in Rwanda, by an International Commission and the Organization of African Unity. The same thing is still true in Ireland where all culture of old was forced and policed out of the Irish people over the last three centuries after a millennium of war. In fact when the Pope said there is no such place as Heaven or Hell his priests in Toronto suggested to their parishioners that he was old and feeble. The prejudices that run rampant in our civilization are directly attributable to theocratic ecclesiasties. They have done worse things to women ever since Hammurabi decreed a woman is the property of her father until she is sold to her husband.

Theocracy has been a tool of noble or monarchist families and philosophy was often controlled by these theocracies from the time of Plato to Bertrand Russell. How much blame can we lay at their feet for allowing women to be abused to the extent they are? Today more women wear berkas or saris in the house/prison of their father/husband than are free to go topless or wear a mini-skirt. Yet the Kelts often went naked on hot days - so we are told they were 'barbarian'!

There are many secrets and intrigues of old that have simply donned an overcoat of propriety. We will demonstrate the Druids and their 'Red Headed League of Megalith Builders' or Tuatha De Danaan are the likely originators of all religion. This Source of the teaching of Jesus and 'Brotherhood' could be re-energized just as Jesus tried to do before others put words in his mouth after he died. The mummies found near the present day Great Wall of China and those of the Aleutian Islands are just some of the 'giants' we will show were part of this 'Brotherhood of Iesa' (Hesous or Jesus). They were on Malta before they built the Pyramid of Iesa and here we find archaeology shows 2800 years with no weapons. They were Chaos Scientists 13,000 years ago and keen observers of nature (God or Reality) for a long time before they met the older modern man we've found near Lake Mungo in Australia.

Nostradamus was a member of an even more ancient and secret inner sanctum called the 'Sons of the Widow' according to The Secrets of Nostradamus by David Ovason. He also says he was an initiate of the Hibernian Mysteries and an expert in the Green Languages derived from the 'Language of the Trees'. I know this language relates to the

Robert Baird

Bards (BRD in vowelless early tracts or alphabets) whose Troubadours of Cathar times he was born amongst their recent remains, caused by the Crusades of the Dominican 'Hounds of God'. Ovason has a good handle on the Irish part of the equation and the Bardic Tradition. He says the 'Sons' were followers of the Biblical Miriam who he shows is the Masonic Hiram through these cryptic or coded languages. I think there was an earlier widow that Manetho places at the very beginning of the genetic foundation of white people 35,000 years ago. This is when Manetho says Isis founded the Egyptian colony. Manetho pandered to Ptolemy in his history which has played an important part in the Bible Narrative, so that is not the best of sources. A web site with insight to how these codes were part of the Languages of the Birds or Bards (Ogham) is found at: http://users.gloryroad.net/~bigjim/GreenLang.htm

The Bardic 'verbal tradition' is kin to the Qabala, Tao and shamanic systems throughout the world. Scientific American and National Geographic know North America (Jan/Feb 2001 issues) was visited from 30,000 years ago by Europeans. The degree of world trade has not been addressed in any major academic institution I know about, although Prof. Cyclone Covey at Wake Forest and Steve Omar in Hawaii join Fell, Kelley and others in addressing what we will cover to some extent, again. Ovason says the following on page 383 of his book that explodes all the previous poor scholarship dealing with Nostradamus:

"There is even some indication that the mystery schools of Imperial Rome had ordained that Ireland should remain untouched as an un-Romanized periphery on the edge of the map of the Imperium. It was intended by the initiation schools (who go back to a re-organization by Tuthmosis in Egypt and before.) that this map would correspond to the future Christian world. It had been part of the destiny of Rome to establish the ground for the development of the spiritual mysteries of the future - which was to be the new initiation schools of Christianity. (Thus St. Columba said 'Christ is the new Druid'.) Although the Roman soldiery did

Diverse Druids

reach Ireland, they did not take over its cultural life, nor destroy its Druidic priestcraft, in the way they seemed to have destroyed it in England, Scotland and (to a lesser extent) Wales. Thus, something of the great pre-Christian mystery wisdom survived in Ireland, and it was for this reason that it continued as the main esoteric center of European cultural life. This is why Ireland became a refuge for esoteric Christianity (through languages like Uncial they created many Bible myths or dogma and the language Insular they developed grew into English.) - for what we might even term pre-Roman Christianity. What we now tend to see romantically, through the eyes of later poets, as the twilight of the Celts was really the dawn of esoteric Christianity, which has yet to speak in the future of Europe. (Hitler tried to bring this forward in a perverse manner as he called himself 'the torch-bearer of Jesus'.) The ancient Druidic wisdom which had served the soul-life of the North, had already begun to give way to, or integrate with, the Christian Mysteries - to those mysteries which we would probably now call Celtic Christianity."

And the Rosicrucians of the Masonic Lodges have maintained much of the ritual and knowledge even if most of them are not able to decode the rituals, symbols and words they speak. It may surprise some people to see German historian C. Besoldus (1577-1638) claiming that the name Huns came from a Celtic word meaning 'Great Magicians'. Surely this is what the Druids and 'smiths' were able to do. They were even able to create spiritual visions of such force that whole armies would shudder and quake, then run from the field of battle. This book is much more than a statement on the nature of propaganda and yet it can only begin to cover all our human potential might have allowed or might yet allow.

Robert Baird

"Everybody was glad that I was living; but as I lay there thinking about the wonderful place where I had been and all that I had seen, I was very sad; for it seemed to me that everybody ought to know about it, but I was afraid to tell, because I knew that nobody would believe me."

- John G. Neihardt, *Black Elk Speaks*.

CHAPTER ONE:
What (Who) is a Druid?

Introduction

The Britannica even acknowledges that the Judaeo/Christian/Islamic complex owes a great deal to the Magi as they talk about Zoroaster's influence on early Christian thought. We will easily connect them with the Druids. Many early Christian saints are Druidic trained in places like Iona and Bangor where the discipline of the monastic orders had not suffered the degradation of greed and sexual dysfunction that so characterized the continental churchians. St. Columba actually helped save 1200 bards at the Synod of Drumceatt in 575 AD, from a very inauspicious degradation. Some academics have noted it seems he was acting as the Arch (head) Druid. However, in reality these early Christian roots are a segment of political people who were caving in to the power of Rome that Polybius had foretold would happen.

If you can believe St. Columba beat a Druid at the manipulation of the weather you must believe in his ability to control the forces of God in some Divine way. However, there is a science known to the Druids and it is not some Divine Intervention but rather a commitment to purpose and Intent that is required. I do believe St. Columba could affect the weather, as could any Druid. I have been part of human input to the weather.

Simon Magus and the Gnostics are adept contributors to the *Corpus Hermeticum*; and it should be no secret that many Christian Mystery Schools including the Rosicrucians are hermeticists in their design even if few ever get past the ritual. Thus, the Good Samaritan is an interesting study when one considers he was a Gaedhil or Gael with genetic links to the people who colonized Egypt before the glaciers threatened their 'Emerald or Blessed Isles'. There is little known about Lyoness but it would appear the ruins at the bottom of the Bay of Biscay near the megaliths of Carnac in Brittany are part of this lauded legendary place which was one of the 'Emerald Isles'.

Jesus was from an adept family of noble lineage including the adept wise man and metallurgists of Solomon and David. Solomon married into the family of Hiram of Tyre and he also worshipped Ba'al. The Bible is now known to be a Phoenician 'literary legacy' according to the Father of Biblical Archaeology, W.F.Albright. Perhaps the time has come when ecumenicism such as the Cathar 'living love of Jesus' might again be attempted. What does humanity have to lose except the continued wars and power grabs associated with theocracy and their hegemony with the powers that be? Catharism did not end when the Dominican 'Hounds of Hell' burned them all as they went hand in hand singing hymns into the Catholic fires of the Crusade. We can hope I am right about this.

This book is not so much an academic treatise on the details of all world religions as it is an insight to the ethical nature of the earlier civilizations from which all current religions derive. Yes, there is enough to prove the point for open-minded people, who can understand why Lao Tzu went to the west from his native China to meet the Ancient Maters. There will be lots of archaeological and linguistic evidence to make any religious 'believer' re-consider their 'following' if they are so inclined. However, that is not the primary motive in writing this book; even if it becomes the most important aspect for many readers who have not spent time to research what their 'gurus', rabbis or priests tell them.

When the last great social attempt to re-institute 'brotherhood' failed in Southern France, with the Troubadors, who are the bards of their time; there was an increase in underground or esoteric secret societies. Infiltrators of the social establishment may have become even more certain that they had to wait for a real New Age. Bernard of Clairvaux knew the Cathars were good people and so should everyone alive today. The few who escaped

Diverse Druids

the genocidal insanity of the Catholics went to join the Bogomils of the Balkans or the Huguenots who came to America. The persecution continued but we hope the time has come to generate a real ecumenicism and bury the hatchet of old prejudices. Mani attempted to do this during the time of Augustine who had been a Manichean before he sold out to the power-mongers. We can see the roots of all religions have common ground and good things to say. Why not speak about these truly good things rather than 'My religion' or 'My gender' or 'My race'?

The Druids were most like the Yamabushi firewalkers of Buddhist Shintoism or the Kahuna of Hawaii, where many of their kind had spent millennia of time to understand reality. There is little written evidence of what they did for scholars to use. The truth is they knew intellect was secondary, or at least offered ego and greed to rear its ugly head. They had a law against exposing powerful knowledge or that which might engender racist ideas. They knew we are all 'connected' as 'brothers and sisters'. Because they believed in reincarnation, they could not possibly persecute women. But they saw no reason to do this anyway. They were not into owning land or creating nations and armies but they also feared no man

The 'Logos', Tower of Babel and String Theory:

The 'chhi' or 'shakti' is not bent on 'siddhis' or the pursuit of power. In modern String Theory, which is derived from ancient Chaos Science we read about the basic building blocks of all energy including matter. This 'one dimensional harmonic force' is very much like 'in the beginning was the word'. The ancient vowelless languages of places like Byblos on the Persian Gulf that we think is Dilmun of the Sumerian records and not the Byblus in Lebanon expressed much of this knowledge with 'BBL'.

The academics who study one ethnic history or era may think the reason the Bible was named after the parchment or papyrus that came from Byblus or Byblos; but there are more levels and layers of meaning than that simple interpretation. 'BL' is the start of it all in the Keltic hierarchy of forces. Bel is the Keltic god we find in Mesopotamia and as Ba'al of the Canaanites or Phoenicians. At Mystery Hill, New Hampshire there is a temple that honors both; clearly the Phoenicians were welcome to join with their Keltic 'brothers'. This shrine has Ogham dating to 800 BC. Many other artifacts in the region support this truth of a history few fully comprehend.

All white people can be traced to the Caucasus by genetic markers including the Haplogroup X marker that is not found in Asians (1) but is found in some North American Indian tribes. They worked on the all- important metal hunt near Lake Superior for millennia including the time when most men did not know how to smelt ores. There is only one other area of the world that they would have been able to use such ores from and that is Cyprus. There is a great deal of proof we will start you on the path to discovering about these things in this book. The more thorough analysis is in *The Prehistoric Worldwide Import of the GREAT LAKES*.

This Caucasus region later saw the Sarmoung Brotherhood that can be traced to 2600 BC and Gurdjieff found interesting in the early 20th Century. These Sarman or Sarmoung seem a lot like what the Greeks called 'gymnosophists' and may have something to do with the name of Yogananda's guru who had the Sarman name in his personal name. But Marija Gimbutas and her work that we highlighted in *The Kelts: Children of the Don* provides much more of the grist our mill needs to tell this story. Thanks is due to Herodotus and Posidonius and many others who had the courage to give us a little insight in what the Greeks called 'Keltoi' or 'ancient ones'(ogygia). The story thus begins 35,000 years ago in the genetic research of the Caucasians who made Casiberia into what is called Atlantis and Mu.

The Mungo Man of Australia also needs consideration as the teachers of the De Danaan or 'Aes Dana'. These pygmies were fully modern way according to the research that shows they were already in Australia long before Homo sapiens

sapiens flowered around 45,000 years ago. Could we really cover all these things in one book? There have been over 25,000 books published on Atlantis alone. The Egyptian records that place a higher value on a pygmy than a whole ship from a Punt expedition make interesting reading. Is it true these advanced hominids were unable to genetically reproduce with humans? Did this make them more interesting sexual partners? The research by geneticists states they are unconnected in the human DNA make-up but could they have developed genetics that would allow them to take a part in the development of humanity? There are many skeletons of these pygmies in America and Professor Barraclough Fell believed they joined the Phoenicians from visits they made to S.E. Asia. Col. Churchward certainly could say these Mungo Man people are the cultural teachers he refers to in his Mu legends.

Apparently the art of the dance was a special attribute or cultural heritage of these people which Balinese dancers retain some of the insights to or from. The Sarman, Dervish and Yogis with mutras or mudras and the work of Georges Gurdjieff are possibly connected as well. When the human body integrates its energy or 'chhi' there is a powerful enlightment potential as Kundalini devotees can tell you. The mutras allow this integration of the brain lobes to actualize and assist supposedly schizophrenic people to remain centered enough to function in equilibrium. True schizophrenia is not nearly as common as the medical profession likes to diagnose it requires a smaller brain size due to nutritional uptake difficulties. This can be detected through MRI's or the more dangerous radioactive cat-scans. There is only 0.6% of Schizophrenia that shows up without a smaller brain. Drs. Breggin and Cohen are great reporters on the problems our society faces in psychiatry and they call the neuroleptic drugs 'pharmacological lobotomies'.

Enlightenment or 'direct cognition' as MacDari termed it, might well have allowed very early humans to use the quantum reality without any need for all the accoutrements of Industrialization or massive technocracy. There are many people in the West who have been impacted by the arts termed 'Eastern' but we will give history some pause to consider the 'Tuatha De Danaan' as the originators of these spiritual arts.

The Mungo Man issue and impact on humanity's cultural development is far from provable with artifacts or records and so we must relegate them to the vestiges of history even as we respect whatever contribution they made. Dance often goes hand in glove with chanting and a spiritual music that probably involved hallucinogens. I do believe the origin of language and speech has a debt to pay these magical arts. The archaeological tools that allow us to know Neanderthal had advanced drugs 90,000 years ago give us part of this connection, for some hominids, at least.

There are many reasons why Empire Builders began to keep secrets and appear all knowing or divine to their colonies or conquered peoples.

In relatively recent history the Incas more powerful magic enabled them to control the conquered territory with temples rather than garrisons of troops. They also educated the children of the leading families from those territories. South America deserves a great deal of attention and some day we will probably have to write a whole book on Puma Puncu (or Punku) and the Andes canals that are so like Pohnpei's of the Caroline Islands area of the S.W. Pacific. That book will require a lot about Yonaguni that is still unreported in America but definitely worth more than just an article in *Ancient American* magazine. Peru is the key supplier of cocaine to the ancient world as Balabanova's forensics tested by numerous other labs has shown. The Egyptians were 'hooked on' cocaine, but I suggest there were other medicinal ingredients in the potions of the Phoenician traders, as well. The Anatolian Blue Lotus and many other herbs may have been part of the reason for the Sardinian 'nuraghi' fortifications.

Ligurians, Etruscans, The Battle of Alalia, and the Pythagorean Bruttii:

In other books about the Phoenicians, we have explored the importance of the Battle of Alalia and enough of history that can be pieced together; outside of the fictions of Quintus Fabius Pictor or other Praetors and Consuls of Rome that made for the Romulus and Remus fairy tale. It was not one battle and lasted in apparently unknown places for many years. Indeed, we could go so far as to say it was a worldwide war of the stature of the Trojan War; that would have been left on the dung heap of myth except for the facts whose discovery is attributed to Schliemann at Troy. This battle also has recent archaeological proof to substantiate some of the legends but no author I have read or heard about has shown the full extent of the connections and alliances. In fact none have brought the Genoese and Cisalpine Gaulic Kelts into the picture which we feel deserves a lot more attention than we can give it here. The two sides line up as a further fight between corporate Empires who had developed separate ethical constructs though were originally part of the Phoenician Brotherhood.

Michael Grant writes about the Phocaeans winning a naval battle that saw them beat a far larger force but lost most of their own fleet. He mentions the affluence and sleaziness of the Sybarites and questions whether some of the reports of their ability to hire huge mercenary armies could be correct. Of course, he skirts the issue of the drug trade with America or the gold and other assets these people had been accustomed to having a near monopolistic position in. He tells us the Sybarites were trading partners of the Etruscans. They shared some of the indolent attitudes of profligate wealth including sexual over-indulgence. He mentions they had trading relations with some of the Greek city-states as well. Perhaps most importantly he documents how recent digs discovered the site of Sybaris that had been inundated and covered over by the Pythagoreans of Croton when they re-routed a river.

Robert Baird

Grant's *Rise of the Greeks* is a valuable compendium of records and reports from various sources of these times. He shows how Naucratis in Egypt's delta was an international trading zone and the people who were allied in that place are the people I think were against the Carthaginian and Etruscan/Sybarites at the battle of Alalia. They include the Lelegians and Ligurians as well as the Milesian complex that Phocaea was part of. It would appear Sardinia and its 'medieval' fortresses that Jacquetta Hawkes notes are almost two millennia out of place (There are over 6500 towers that might well have prevented any invading force from getting off the beaches of the island. There are also the 'tombes de giganti' which we think has something to do with the very tall Red Heads or Kelts, such as are found near the Great Wall of China or in places like Hawaii and the Mississippian/Adena.) was a large part of the reason that the Phocaeans escaped the Persian onslaught in Anatolia and went to found Massalia (Marseilles) with their Iberian/Tartessus allies. These are the Veneti, Iberian, and Kelts who had kept much of the egalitarian ethic despite the growth in Empire and macho-domination the Mediterranean had witnessed.

The war continued after a lull when the Bruttii were relegated to near slave status in the north of Italy and fled to a place near the Crotonites in southern Italy; where Grant shows Phocaeans settling near their former foes the Etruscans. The Brutti are the founders of Britain and the 'Sons of Aeneas' from the Trojan War. They did not like the label 'runaway' for their Italian cousins perhaps because they felt sensitive about what happened in the Trojan War. In any event, you will find Britannica even acknowledges there likely was an event wherein this led to the founding of Rome. It amazes me that academics like Donald Strong can argue against the cell diffusion and large movements of elites who founded Etruria. Perhaps they look for waybills and shipping ledgers or maybe a docent to tell the story. If one follows the money and the trade with the Americas, one gets a better perspective. This internecine war between corporate entities should not be so surprising. The Society of the Phoenician Pirates played an increased role in all these matters after the Trojan War.

The Hyksos to Trojan Period:
The foregoing is a miniscule summary of critical events that led to the founding of the classical cultures we like to refer to as the beginning of civilization. Nothing is further from the truth. The technology was greater and the ethics and education for all the people was better and freely available to all no matter what sex or race - during the ascendance of freedom and Brotherhood. Let us look a little closer at the History of Genoa from the website, to see what they have to add to the issue of Phoenicians and Kelts:

"The Phoenicians and the Celts Founded Genoa in Italy the ancient name of Genoa comes from the word 'knee'(Genua) or the gate to the sea or 'jaw', the mouth to the sea. It was founded around 2,000 B.C. by the Phoenicians who sailed in from Tyre in Phoenicia. (Sardinia's nuraghi nearby are dated starting around 1800 B.C. and the expansion or last effort of the Hyksos ('foreigners') such as the Hittites and Hurrians of Scythia to re-institute the former Brotherhood and free trade ethics, was everywhere apparent. However, academics only write about small ethnic groups and do not want to look for a free and egalitarian state of Hyperboreans including Amazons. The archaeologic record in Scythia now avails proof of the Amazons over 1100 miles of steppes. The Tyrean and far more ancient Ba'albek Brotherhood residents were still working on the egalitarian side, even as Dido the Tyrean princess founded Carthage, in 814 BC.) They came through from their settlement in Corsica and settled in Genoa with the Pagu or Tribe of Ambrones, one of the earliest ancestors of the Celts from Iberia. There is archaeological evidence in Chiavari of chariot-grave—the "inverted bell cup" culture - that proves this lineage. They had dominion over the Province of Padany and the area between the Eridanu ('Danu' again!)River (now Po River) and Etrury. The

Robert Baird

Romans called them Ligures from the Latin verb 'to settle behind.' The community of Phoenicians and Ambrones inhabitants of Genoa became the pirates of the Mediterranean and were called Thyrrenoi by the Greeks. The Ligures were divided in three social classes, the Druids or Priests, the Military equipped with chariots, bows spears, shields and mystical necklaces, (The Keltic 'torque'). and the Working class. A king ruled them all." (2)

The king was not primo genitur or hereditary although the Keltic dirfine was being re-interpreted and noble families were asserting themselves in degrees from century to century. Aristotle's *Politics* reports he found Carthage an exceedingly democratic state. The 'king' was a matter of common consent until Carthaginians of the likes of Hanno began to take control of the army just before the ascendance of Rome.

Scholars who think divination is not a science often call the Druids priests. If this author was to say the spiritual scientists of the Bardic tradition or perhaps make reference to the Cabiri and other metallurgists or alchemists who were part of this order we might forgive him. The 'vascerri' were the myth-making priests and the Sibylls or Oracles were the Dryads. Unfortunately, the masses and average people of the Mediterranean had more interest in the phantasm rather than the sublime.

The degradation of discipline that led to Roman barbarianism and focus on power is much regrettable. This author makes a report on what might be the Ogham of the Druid's oak groves in this next quote:

"There are reports of their megalithic monuments that date back to 1,500 BC and illegible inscription, now preserved at the Bocconi private collection. The first report of their readable phrases goes back to 800 B.C. with vertical Indo-European wedge characters preserved at the Archaeological Museum of Genoa. Of the legible text the word 'Mezunemusu' or central sanctuary is identified. The word comes from Nemusu or the sacred wood, the sanctuary of the Celtic tribes. In the 8th century B.C., Phoenicio-Celts of Genoa co-founded Massalia or Marseilles with more Phoenicians." (3)

On the Matter of Good and Evil - Abraxas to Zotz:
Zotz is the Mayan god of the underworld and a vampire found throughout the world. Count Dracul is a proud member of the Christian Mystery schools, such as the Sarkany Rend Rosicrucians like DeVere and Gardner, whose books are making many people, take note. It isn't just the Tarot readers or palmists who know that dualistic attitudes of good versus evil have much convoluted rationale associated with them. Mani or Augustine and all the stuff about 'evil' have occupied thousands of books if not millions. No less a human observer than Cicero noted, "Ignorance of good and evil is the most upsetting fact of human life." (*De Finibus in 44 BC*) He knew the Druids before the bounty was put on their heads and many of them retired to more peaceful climes amongst loving people like Hawaii and North America offered.

It is possible that Cicero and his friend Posidonius on Rhodes were well aware of the need to harmonize the cosmic energy and purpose of God/Goddess that the Druids and Taoists or other truly observant ethical people come to realize. Posidonius was a great lover of Kelts and he is quoted in the works of many other scholars. Is it pure happenstance that almost all Druidic works or reports thereon are no longer extant? No. The Druids did not want their knowledge put on paper or Papyrus.

Today's New Agers call it the 'Harmonic Convergence' and they quote physicists as much or more than I do. The Druids were the physicists more than the priesthoods. Their knowledge was even more integrative and all-inclusive. They studied navigation to necromancy and could DO things few scientists can imagine except in fancy formulizations.

I doubt most readers of *Genesis of the Grail Kings* or other books by Gardner and HRH Nicholas DeVere are able to imagine the full extent of what is contemplated therein. I can assure you it is not fiction. My personal psychic battles include 'action at a distance' events of murderous intent. On at least three occasions I had these battles with what is known as 'witches' or Wiccans. At one point I joined a Wiccan Temple for six months after intensive interrogations by myself of a person who was also part of the Dragons. I think it is the same Dragons Gardner and deVere belongs to. She wondered why I joined as she said "Why are you joining us, you already know so much?" Later she engaged spies against me and I heard she thought 'I was a Machiavellian Prince sent to overturn her Temple." The most relevant aspect of this experience to this current book has to do with her world travels to places like Hawaii. She said the only true Druids remaining on earth were in Hawaii.

The Egyptian theory of Abraxas is a good explanation of the good versus evil continuum of energy. It proposes that good and evil are necessary parts of the whole reality that we live in. Good will triumph when it is combined with understanding in the absence of fear. The Keltic Creed is big on the 'No Fear' aspect of this; because they knew the soul was immortal. Thus when their warriors would be confronted by the magic of other people they were able to achieve 'protection' through their knowledge that came from having seen the Druidic mind-fogging or having learned to do some of these things themselves. It takes a very special kind of energy from the spiritual world to have a momentary physical impact on a person in battle. In fact, if the intended victim is 'protected' and unafraid, little is achieved by the sorcery. I cannot say for sure that spiritual force will cause a significant physical impact in a moment at all, other than in concert will forces of nature like weather. I have seen this happen too, and thus I accept what I have read about others including the Druids or St. Columba, as I have said.

In today's spy networks and psy-ops venues, they have developed thought cloning (see the work of Laurence Persinger or Jose Delgado on 'Psychocivilizing Society') and other ELF or EMF technologies. These are the kind of things Druids did through ultrasound or psychic and electrical means. There were many forms of energy beyond

Diverse Druids

just the kind of electrical energy Numa (a Roman) harnessed; two of his machines survive in the British Museum.

What academic has written about the Huns being Druids? My father told me Genghis Khan was a Red Head like me, while I was being ridiculed as a 'freckle face'. There are no books on him that explain important things; including what the full knowledge of his 'smith' family heritage, is all about. His Pax Tartaris was the most Just, recent Empire and one chronicler says a woman with a gold tray on her head could walk all across his Empire. Why did a Taoist sage spend almost a year with him near the end of his life? I think they discussed the Red Heads we have now found near his Altaic homeland. These mummies and their adept people came from the Altaic region and Lao Tzu went to meet his Ancient Masters there near the end of his life. Lao Tzu wrote the book on Taoism in case you don't see the connection. He also used a word or name to describe this place that includes 'MU'. In *Neolithic Libraries,* we show there are many mystery writers and historians who enjoy the Atlantis and lost continent theories. We think these civilizations were in many places but this place near the Great Lop-nor Sea is a place where Mu and Atlantis definitely joined in Brotherhood.

With the acceptance of at least three and a half million years and possibly six million years of human (non-Australopithecine) existence in 2001 there should be some changes in thinking. The probability of man having developed advanced culture, even to the point we are at today, and such legends or myths as included in the Hindu *Puranas*, becomes a lot more real. *The Hidden History of the Human Race* by Cremo and Thompson is full of good evidence that supports very ancient modern humans. Of course, if these things are true and there were many hominids developing genetically on Gondwanaland the supercontinent, before it split - then the Druids and their travels to legendary civilizations is only the tip of the iceberg. Nevertheless, it seems unlikely that Antarctica was the site of Atlantis even if it did have the same genetic material as its Gondwanaland partners; India, Madagascar, Africa, South America and Australia.

These are exciting times for interested people of the post-Modernist era. The experts and conventional academics have egg on their face. The idea that anything is absolute, black and white, or even nearly, known has suffered the setback all egotistic certainty suffers. Thus, we must comment on the many pretenders to Druidic knowledge who use names like Bairds, Ovates and Druids. Many of these 'Dragons' and pagans are pleasure driven, naïve, and misled - even though they have decent motivations compared to Churchians and other ecclesiasts. This, is the nature of good and evil, they might say, as they justify using power for their own interpretation of spiritual necessity.

Anu and D'anu:
In Ireland and Scotland today we find the god/goddess entity or more appropriately, if you accept the Druids were scientists observing nature's universal forces, representational deity - 'An' and 'Anu'. In Gardner's and Sitchen's Bible Narrative of the Christian mystery schools we find the Anunnaki. Some of these stories are great fiction. The Scientologists have Zenu, and authors like Norm Paulsen have bought into the Builders or Biblical Elohim. There might well be a grain of truth in extraterrestrial origins of human life, but I do not accept the reptoid theory of Sumer's ascendance. Sumer was a colony or crossroads between Findias and Ilvarta (Harappa). It was a melting pot of Uighur misogyny and Keltic egalitarianism at a time when certain noble Phoenicians were thinking they might have power over God and all people. From the Irish and other Keltic legends of the followers of Danu (pre-Dionysius and Dianistic) or the Tuatha De Danaan, I find no reason to assume these people were inclined to belittle their 'brothers'. Truly wise people don't need to put others down and they are often engaged in enabling education or uplifting enterprises. The 'Shining Ones' of Ba'albek or the

Diverse Druids

Heliopolitan centers of latter 'Brotherhoods' strove to know the same things the De Danaan knew. They were Druids or they were the teachers and megalith builders of the Druidic Order - I cannot say for sure. It is likely that over thousands of years their role changed.

> Let there listen the gods who are in Heaven,
> And those who are upon the dark-hued Earth!
> Let there listen, the mighty olden gods.
> Formerly, in the olden days, Alalu was king in Heaven;
> He, Alalu, was seated on the throne.
> Mighty Anu, the first among the gods, stood before him,
> Bowed at his feet, set the drinking cup in his hand.
> For nine counted periods, Alalu was king in Heaven.
> In the ninth period, Anu gave battle against Alalu.
> Alalu was defeated, he fled before Anu—
> Down to the dark-hued Earth he went;
> On the throne sat Anu.
>
> - *Kingship in Heaven*, a Hittite epic tale

The Hittites and Hurrians are Kelts just as those who returned to Gordian as the Galatians are Kelts. Agatha Christie's husband was an archaeologist who worked the Hurrian digs dated to 2,000 BC. At this time they still allowed women to own property. Although that may not have been as good as things once were, it is a far cry better than many other burgeoning Empires would allow. One can see a little of Allah in Alalu and the real story might have played out in a battle for territory between ancient Allans of the Caucasus and their Scythian neighbours.

I respect archaeomythology and I do not go far along the path of accepting the myths themselves. That is what the Rosicrucian ritualists or 'Dragons' like Gardner have done. Of course, I may be wrong, and each person has to decide for him or herself.

As a linguist, Ignatius Donnelly of *Atlantis* authorship and potential running mate of Abraham Lincoln (a possible Melungeon), could see the Turanic or Turkish races were of

Robert Baird

Atlantis. He said Phoenician was the language of Atlantis. The Hittites and Hurrians as well as the Armenians and Medes or Persians all came from the Danube/Don region at a time when there was no Black Sea. The rise of 400 feet in water levels around 5500 BC that caused the Black Sea to form in a two-week period or less; made these people have to move in with their relatives. That was probably one of the origins of growing conflict in the region. Displaced people from fertile and preferred territory with lots of education who lost a great deal might well have been less than hospitably received.

Carl Jung called the Bible Narratives 'The Ur-stories' and it is true the *Targum Onklos* and even today's Bible is talking about Chaldeans or the people of Ur and Egypt. However, the root of many of these stories is more ancient and comes from other places. The Immaculate Conception was already old when Plato was supposedly conceived in this manner. Sargon the Great of 2350 BC had the head start over Moses in his nativity story of the bulrushes. Indeed I've often heard the rushing of the bull (not Mithras that brought us Xmas Day) as I listen to proselytizers on their pulpits.

What Provenance or Credibility Do I Have?

When I met Ogham scholars in 1990 I was already quite well versed in esoteric philosophy. They felt I was the person who could embellish and up-date Connor MacDari's book *Irish Wisdom.* Looking back on this experience and what I have learned since then, brings me to the point of saying this was the beginning of a new life and purpose for me. Having already been a self-made millionaire by the age of 30 and a special non-degreed entrant into Canada's top business Master's Program as well as being selected by my fellow students to sit on the Master's Program Committee is just one of many blessings or accolades I had received. In the mid-eighties I was co-developer of an alternative ISDN technology that would have given everyone free hook-ups to the worldwide web. Greed and reluctance by the Big Boys to allow such a thing to happen caused this product to be shelved. You could liken it to Tesla's wireless energy transmission that would have made General Electric into a small player. J.P.Morgan was the Rockefeller/Rothschild agent who shelved that eminently worthwhile technology. Philip O'Faillon (anglicized Whelan) and his sister are the only people I have heard about who could speak all five dialects (to speak even one is unheard of) of Ogham. He knew more about my last name than I did. It seems like the hand of fate was at work, as I look back on my life. The Bairds were poets like the Bard of Avon and I sensed they were great esotericists related to the Druids. I had no idea the Keltic international council was headed by King-Bairds. It would be a good thing to have six people of both genders act as trusted consultants to the people today. The Kelts did not have hereditary rights to kingship in most of there colonies and almost never in the lands they were the primary citizens.

Thus my King family ancestors like Rufus King who signed the Declaration of Independence (one version) and ran for President of the U.S. were joined in genetic history or something even more, like Atlantis and the builders of the Pyramid. I already was certain Churchward and many others had been right about Egypt being a colony. Even the writing of the man whose King's List pandered to Ptolemy and was the basis of Egyptology and the Bible Narrative said Isis founded Egypt as a colony of a greater civilization. But historians have always been willing to write what their masters wanted them to write, in recent times. The Bairds or Bards were different. They satirized the authorities and kept them grounded and in touch with the people. I liked that idea. Now I'm doing what they did so long ago, and you can judge whether or not I have the facts put together in a way that will allow us to break the chains of propaganda.

Definitive scholarship of Druidic beliefs would be difficult even if they didn't have a law against writing this kind of knowledge. The many millennia and different cultures they were involved with would have made it even more confusing. The fact that we know their ethics and can see the results in the Brehon Laws and attitudes of egalitarian people is more than a good start. Plato observed that knowledge suffered with the introduction of writing in Greece by the Phoenicians. When people take the path of easy answers found in books they can become mere Sophistic self-centered simpletons; in comparison to the disciplined memory that once was necessary. But even more important than facts or the things of writing and memory is the art and self-awareness of soul and developed intuition and attunement that the absence of TV and all the busy-ness afforded. In the Eastern traditions they call this Maya or samsara. Illusional hard facts that cause avoidance of the true self do not necessarily add to an individual's potential. We have a hard time knowing the extent to which the Western world is deluded by materialism.

Einstein is Kin of the Druids!

"Schematically, the universe is presented as a trio of concentric circles with Abred, the source of life, as the innermost. All living things pass through it, during their sojourn, experience every form of existence and suffer every sort of hardship, before ascending to the next circle, that of Gwynfyd (=Purity), which the evolving soul enters when once it has qualified for membership of the human race. The last circle is that of Ceugant or Infinity inhabited by God alone, but apparently somewhat similar to the Buddhist Nirvana and the Hindu Brahma in that the soul that attains it merges with the divine. Some of the details in the *Barddas* accord with what we know of Druidism. Three, (The Triune Nature of Man or Tao + Spirit) the number of the concentric circles, was sacred to the Druids, (And showed in the Triads of the Bards.) while the dualistic character of the *Barddas* system might help to explain why Pliny brackets Druidism with Persian Magianism, which was also dualistic. However, these cannot be taken as evidence for the authenticity of the *Barddas*. Anyone attempting to reconstruct Druidic doctrines would obviously incorporate what was known of them and, as a whole, the work is regarded with suspicion. Anachronistic Christian figures and events appear and many of its ideas can be traced to the fashionable Neo-Platonism of the author's time. What is more, there is a complete absence of any confirmatory hint in the mythology."(4)

When Neils Bohr came up with his model of the atom it was pretty symbolic but people accepted the electron rings and nucleus as true reflections of the atomic structure because little was known about it. Today we have quarks and Plancks as well as the ability to split muons that are eerily connected. This happened in Sudbury, Ontario in the deep nickel mines once worked by INCO. When one half of the muon was energized the other half responded though it was separated by a relatively long distance. Researchers are not able to define consciousness and who knows if we will ever understand the soul and its structure or make-up. Actually many of these realities or possibilities have been fairly well contemplated by the ancients and I see this author draws the proper connections to Buddhism and Hindu philosophy; which we will deal with some more as this book progresses. However, we have left the meatier aspects of harmonics and lattices of energy to other books.

Neils Bohr said something about truth that makes a lot of sense; "A great truth has an opposite that is also true. A trivial truth's opposite is simply false." (I may have a couple of words wrong.)This Abred or 'source of life' may well be the 'chhi' or 'pranha' and vital energy that instills meaning and purpose to harmonize all energy. But beyond the concept of energy (and electricity is only now largely understood, as a result of Bearden's work on the Morley-Michelson theory and Tesla) we have the most sublime and ethereal (Newton's ether being a small part of what history in science has used.) aspects of consciousness and the soul. The quote above makes a lot of sense to me. It incorporates Karma and reflects the fact that the Druids and Kelts knew each soulful entity would have to experience all there is before moving into the oneness of Nirvana.

This is why they would not abuse their women because the woman they abused might be their father or grandfather.

Robert Baird

They lived according to this philosophy to the extent that they loaned money to be repaid from the afterlife.

Most people will have a hard time swallowing the statement that Einstein is the kin of the Druids and I guess it is a little bit of a stretch.

When you know the Hebrews are named after their language you will hopefully agree that linguistic roots will provide the evidence of who the Hebrews were. In the last five or six years I have seen what Philip told me about Hebrew having come from Phoenician become accepted knowledge. I saw it on JEOPARDY! MacDari said the same thing, of course. He had a whole chapter devoted to Hebrew as the sacerdotal code to protect the knowledge of the designer/builders of the Great Pyramid.

The Bardic Institute on the worldwide web has a home page that highlights a quote from Einstein. It captures the essence of the difference between the spiritual world of the Druids and the materialistic world of the present:

"The intuitive mind is a sacred gift and the rational mind is a faithful servant. We have created a society that honors the servant and has forgotten the gift."(5)

The Druids fully understood this 'sacred gift' and knew no one person in this incarnation could know it all. They sought to increase the harmonization of energy in this realm through utilization of as many human souls as possible in that cause. The pyramids connected the human, cosmic and earth energies.

There are many other reasons why the Bardic Institute highlights Einstein along with W.B.Yeats. Yeats headed the Hermetic Order of the Golden Dawn (HOGD) at the time Winston Churchill (an Iroquois of the Brant nation) was initiated into a revisionist Druidic Order at Blenheim Palace. Yeats and many other bards or well-known people like Florence Farr (the mistress of G.B.Shaw) were part of the HOGD before and after Aleister Crowley ruined its humanistic idealistic focus. Dublin, Ireland is the home of the Dublin Institute of Advanced Study where many 'atom-mysticists' like Eugene Wigner spent a lot of time. My

Diverse Druids

Ogham scholar/mentor told me Einstein went there to learn the Boulean math that Druids had known since the time they designed the Sphinx as part of the Gaza monumental symbol.

The Chaos Science from 13,000 years ago became part of the Ha Qabala or Table of Destiny. It was re-copied in part by an Egyptian scribe around 1650 BC in what is called the Rhind Papyrus. The binary digitized 'bits' are 'I' (closed neural path) and 'O' (open, but later a dot was added to form the Aten symbol - this dot is the wavicle infinitely small aperture through which light can pass) of the I O Torus. Dualistic or left-right brained neurological functions were part of the symbolic or mathematical formulations of many adepthoods throughout the world.

Einstein later participated in the founding of Princeton's Institute of Advanced Studies along with Wigner's Budapest boyhood classmate John Eric von Neumann. There is a great deal of powerful knowledge associated with Princeton (true of Yale and the Order known as Skull & Bones, too) that surrounds Merovingians like the Rothschilds. The Rothschilds did not even exist as a family name until Meyer Amschel Rothschild chose this name from the hotel sign of his father. It means 'red shield'. This Rothschild was closely associated with St. Germain(e) from his financial role with the Hesse family. St. Germain(e) had been tutored and adopted by the De Medici who had held the Templar monopoly in finance since their deconstruction and break up into many other segments including assets going to the Maltese Knights who held them until Napoleon acted as a Merovingian agent after marrying into them through Josephine. It is a long story we deal with in greater detail elsewhere.

However, Vienna (also Venice and the Keltic Veneti wherever they were since their Diaspora from places like Hallstatt in 2,000 BC) is the important site of many Qabalistic students including Silberer who did good work on alchemic symbolism before Jung. They were both students of Freud as well as Wilhelm Reich. Reich's 'Orgone' energy and devices expanded on the Newtonian 'ether' and became part of many black ops projects run by von Neumann. It is near to certain that Einstein and all other Jewish and Hibernian Qabalists (verbal tradition) learned from generation to generation the esoteric secrets of their ancestors. They are not mere programmed plebians of whatever current educational propaganda set by politicians. It is interesting to note that Buddhist scholars know that the origin of Buddhist iconography was for public consumption. The real knowledge of the eastern sciences was not big on icons and ecclesiastical structures or representational deities.

There appears to be a great effort undertaken in the 6th century BC to develop regional variations of the core sciences of Druidism from places like the Tarim Basin where the Red Headed mummies have brought us such excellent images and artifacts. Lao Tzu is not the only one who learned from these Ancient Masters. Zoroaster and Buddha, Confucius and probably many more could have been influenced through missionaries or visits to these people. After the monks or 'Tulkus' of Tibet had worked with and contributed to this knowledge for a number of decades or centuries it was necessary to provide others with degrees of initiatory steps to achieving the knowledge with a safety or disciplinary ingredient added. For simple lay folk unable or unwilling to give the necessary commitment to learning the iconography and dogma of priesthoods was developed and unfortunately devolved from there.

Mt. Meru (Or Maru, or Shangri-la and Agarthe, etc.) may have its origins there and it is nearby enough. There are many who think that is the place that Hinduism and other theologies come from. We may never know for certain. He who has a dog-ma has a canine for a female parent. Our species has nursed on the teat of dog-ma way too long.

Viennese Vagaries and Vagabonds:
It isn't just a case of generational family or clan education through rabbis and elders that was at work. There were cabals of esoteric groups ever since Tuthmosis and

Diverse Druids

probably before. Pythagoreans were largely continued through Masonry and led to the Kelley/Cagliostro/Crowley entity or other opportunists later thought too far out for the mainstream of Masonry. There are infiltrators of the Catholic and other ecclesiasties and vice versa as well as some out and out 'black magicians' such as Hitler's '99' Lodge. Nostradamus, St. Germaine, Da Vinci and Fulcanelli played varying roles in the expansion of these schools of esoteric thought leading to Theosophy and other good potentials. Vienna was a central meeting place and Prague had been a key medieval center for these sciences. The development of Tantrism and yogic thought had outstripped the growth of the Western participants in this knowledge as a disciplinary pedagogy since the monastic orders of Iona and others had been diminished in medieval purges and profit hungry power seekers.

Hitler spent many years in Vienna and left in the same year Jung split from Freud (1917). He was a Jew even if you don't count his father being an illegitimate son of a Rothschild in the Viennese hotel of Salomon Rothschild. This is well developed in *The Mind of Adolf Hitler: The Secret Wartime Report.* This book completely evades and doesn't even mention what Hitler was doing in Vienna as his father did before him. Hitler mentions how important these Viennese esoteric studies were in *Mein Kampf* so we can be sure they had access to it.

When he was in Berlin if not sooner he almost was adopted by the famous family of maestro Wagner whose work participated in the propaganda. Nietzsche lost his mind in some way by being part of this, as was his sister Elizabeth. In a book in search of her I read about Nueva Germania in Paraguay where she and her husband had gone near the turn of the century. This book made it clear the Kelts and the Druidic Ogham was all around the area since the 6th Century AD. Can you say Ostrogoths? They took Italy and left after about 60 years and no historian has an answer that fits the facts.

Robert Baird

If one looks into the roots of Nazi thinking it includes some great academics and that is truly a reflection of all academics; but those who paid the higher price by this association often were just defending the freedoms we all should have, to think outside the box. Campbell and Carlyle are part of that group. Canada's Prime Minister and many other politicians were supportive of Hitler. His country had succeeded very well during the post depression era. Hitler knew about the Rhinemaidens and other Wagnerian themes of the Teutonic Kelts long before he went to Vienna where his father had also gone for years of esoteric studies. It could be said that Hitler made a pact with the Devil (if you believe in Satan as Catholics created him) when he was in Vienna.

The rather poor Decree reminiscent of a Druidic 'glam' that I quote shortly was not in the OSS report as one can imagine in a world that didn't allow Nazis to explain the occult influence used on them at Nuremburg. My father was there with the Judge Advocate General Corps after the war for six months. It is OK for Prince Bernhard of the Netherlands to belong to the Thulean Society in the Gestapo and "have a lot of fun" and then go on to found the Bilderbergs though. The hypocrisy and murderous treatment of the Waffen S.S.; or the actions of De-Nazification is the equal of the horror of the Holocaust. But if you even dare to mention this you run the risk of being branded an anti-Semite. As a Jew, Hitler knew the vagaries of public perception and prejudice firsthand. It can be confusing when you know the facts. He mentions runes and they are the derivative of Ogham the very ancient 64 tract with five dialects - healing, divination, music and history - alphabets.

> "I often go on bitter nights
> To Wotan's oak in the quiet glade.
> With dark powers to weave a union -
> The runic letter the moon makes with its magic spell
> And all who are full of impudence during the day
> Are made small by the magic formula."

CHAPTER TWO:
Hail Atlantis! And The Brotherhood of Man

Winny, Vedi, Vici
   Churchill joined a named Druidic Society at Blenheim Palace and Hitler joined the FOGC (Freemasonic Order of the Golden Centurion) which I believe had Aleister Crowley as a member in England. It is part of the bad blood between Hitler and Crowley. As I often note, Thomas Paine who was a member of the founding steering committee of the Enlightenment Experiment called the U.S.A. wrote that Masonry is derived from Druidism. This steering committee is the Rosicrucian Council of Three and Paine spent little time in the U.S. So in the world of 'seems to be' or what we are taught in history; it is evident there were foreign intrigues involved who were British and French or some of the U.S.'s supposed enemies. It continued long after Paine and Franklin sat on this steering committee that I suspect reported to the Dragons who were headed in America by the Adams family. Not the "creepy and spooky" ones from TV but a far more insidious and powerful organization that included Dracula when another Crusade was on the front burner of our Catholic/Anglican or Romano-British Empire people that Joseph Campbell called "culture-crushers". The recent Rwanda International Commission blamed these parties in proper order for the genocide there.
   They are also implicated in Hitler's funding and through other secret organizations we will relate to the Druids, who are not Druids as they once were, before Rome put a bounty on their heads under decrees like the one Claudius authored in 54 A.D. Hitler was a 20th Century Druid 'Fakir' (!); even though his organization may have maintained some knowledge from the 'Lost Chord'. A book on or by Franz Bardon who battled Hitler's FOGC makes me say this, when I read about the *TEPAPHONE*.
   Many scholars refer to Plato's *Timaeus* and other writings as if they were the origin of the Atlantis legend. The lost

continent thing may even relate to a different Mediterranean than these people have presumed. I do not find favor in the lost continent theory and the legend is full of miss-interpretations but closer to truth than the Ussher time-line of a Bible Narrative. Archaeomythology and the interpretations of linguistic variations and coded esoteric meaning is a maze that amazes me. Plato was right when he noted that alphabets for writing (given their former colonies by Phoenicians) actually reduced the disciplined knowledge and memory capabilities for sharing. I have been open to lost continents in the past and find no geologic rationale for this reasoning. I do find reason to believe there have been major climatic changes and glacial effects that inundated areas or made them into deserts. This is how the legends got their start and over time and translations became interpreted other ways.

We are dealing with the Phoenicians when we are talking about Atlantis and we may also be dealing with them when we talk about Mu. There is exciting new information that makes me say Mu was very much associated with Atlantis and not superior to it as Churchward said by calling it the 'Motherland'. On the other hand Churchward has something going for his theory with the Mungo Man being more ancient yet modern and even having been found near his location for Mu. Many linguists see Phoenician and Luwian Crete (one of their key administrative centers where Hybrid grains are found 5000 years before Sumer or the Fertile Crescent) in the Azores and off Cuba or the Paraiba stones of South America and other places. South-west Africa has the 'White Lady of the Brandberg' dressed in Minoan style. The I Ching has its counterpart in Keltic ancient practices too. In fact there is so much evidence of a worldwide civilization now; I almost wonder if I need to make the point. But, my nose has been buried in these things for a long time and I do read academics who are still preaching Clovis and other Flat Earth infected propaganda. It is propaganda and not errors or interpretations, make no mistake about that.

Genetics is taking the lead role in a lot of the proof today and forensics is a great addition as well. The geologic core samples and the various methods of dating biological material are so vastly improved in the last decade or so that all the old arguments questioning the validity of the data are withered and gone by the wayside. Now the 'history journalists' or propagandists have to be better liars or debunkers to say the least. Casiberia and Mayax or Yoniguni may one day be a lot more pre-eminent in the history books or knowledge of mankind again.

It is no small task to undertake the exposure of the combined forces of repression and academic 'me-too' think. They encourage an adherence to the laws and structure of our society. But if it is a pack of lies, so are our laws and ethical constructs. That is what you will decide for yourself or read about just before the eventual outcome affects you so much that you can't stop it. There are too many terrorists and not enough love. That personal insight will re-occur in different manners or methods of expression but most of this book is heavy on the past events that form the basis of all religions.

If a person passes judgment based on flawed scholarship or the approval of people paid to lead others there are lots of ways to believe in Sumerian or Bible origins. The authors of the past are usually beating the same drum. Today we have so much information that even the National Geographic has had to ask who colonized Egypt. They have had to be aware of the prevailing paradigm in the past but the preponderance of evidence makes it imperative that a re-working (at least) of that largely Bible Narrative ideology be changed. After all, they are a publication covering costs of exploration and the Egypt Exploration Fund had specifically denied funding to projects that would prove the Bible Narrative is fraudulent. Gardner covers that fact from their Articles and Memoranda of Incorporation and there is lots of reason to believe that aspect of his otherwise questionable though well-researched Narrative that purports to suggest we are ruled by alien reptoid offspring called Anunnaki or Elohim (from the Bible).

Robert Baird

Needless to say I prefer the human origin explanations such as the genre of cell diffusion history and what has been called Atlantis or Mu. I prefer these things because they provide the greatest insight and have been proven more correct than the normal history for many decades I have been an avid researcher (since the age of five). My Grade Eleven history teacher was told by another student that I thought she didn't know or understand her subject and was not a good teacher. I was wrong. She let me take over the class for the last half of the year; she quit teaching and had a baby. I was wrong because she showed honesty and integrity and these are the things most important and missing in teaching and history.

The quest for a scientific approach to mythology was hampered until the end of the last century by the magnitude of the field and the scattered character of the evidence. The conflict of authorities, theories, and opinions that raged in the course, particularly, of the nineteenth century, when the ranges of knowledge were expanding in every field of research (classical and Oriental scholarship, comparative philogy, folklore, Egyptology, Bible criticism, anthropology, etc.) resembled the mad tumult of the old Buddhist parable of 'The Blind Men and the Elephant'. The blind men feeling the animal's head declared, 'An elephant is like a water pot'; but those at his ears, 'He is like a winnowing basket'; those at his tusks. 'No, indeed, he is like a plowshare'; and those at his trunk. 'He is like a plow pole'. There were a number feeling his belly. 'Why,' they cried, 'he is like a storage bin!' Those feeling his legs argued 'that he was like pillars', those at his rectum, that he was like a mortar; those at his member that he was like a pestle; while the remainder at his tail, were shouting , 'An elephant is like a fan.' And they fought furiously among themselves with their fists, shouting and crying, 'This is what an elephant is like; that is not what an elephant is like'; 'This is not what an elephant is like; that is what an elephant is like.'

'And precisely so,' then runs the moral of the Buddha, 'the company of heretics, monks, Brahmans, and wandering

Diverse Druids

ascetics, patient of heresy, delighting in heresy, relying upon the reliance of heretical views, are blind, without eyes: knowing not good, knowing not evil, knowing not right, knowing not wrong, they quarrel and brawl and wrangle and strike one another with the daggers of their tongues, saying, 'This is right, that is not right'; 'This is not right, that is right.' (1)

The two learned disciplines from which the lineaments of a sound comparative science might first have emerged were those of the classics and the Bible. However, a fundamental tenet of the Christian tradition made it appear to be an acts of blasphemy to compare the two on the same plane of thought; for, while the myths of the Greeks were recognized to be of the natural order, those of the Bible were supposed to be supernatural. Hence, while the prodigies of the classical heroes (Heracles, Theseus, Perseus, etc.) were studied as literature, those of the Hebrews, (Noah, Moses, Joshua, Jesus, Peter, etc.), had to be argued as objective history; whereas, actually, the fabulous elements common to the two precisely contemporary, Eastern Mediterranean traditions were derived equally from the preceding, bronze-age civilization of Mesopotamia - as no one before the development of the modern science of archaeology could have guessed. (2)

True, but, there are ample reasons to have 'guessed'. The pre-Sumerian history is talked about in the non-Western or Euro-centric Puranas of the Hindus. They deal with human existence in millions of years and cycles or astrological ages. The Keltic legends were re-drafted by Bible deviates at the point of the dagger (like King James who had eight scribes killed while doing the present predominant Bible) but you can find the origin. When Lao-Tzu writes about going west to see the Ancient Masters we could have known about the Red Heads by looking at the frescoes and art of the region near the present Great Wall of China. In fact Conan Doyle and many others did 'guess' these things. The point of the separate teaching of Bible as history and others as literature is the vital and KEY element of this quote! Conan Doyle knew Cornish language was derived from Phoenician and there is a reason to think it goes both ways as we will see.

Linguistic Lineages and Loud Aryan Noises:
The whole field of knowledge in all disciplines is involved because the ancients did have much more knowledge than they have been given credit for. Psychology owes as much to the alchemists as science or chemistry. At the Eranos Conferences put on with the help of Bollingen (Mellon Money) there were some awesome integrations of science and philosophy. The archetypes of Jung from Silberer and Freud were meeting with the archaeological transcendentalists like Joseph Campbell while all other sciences played their proper role. Today the Human Genome Project offers further room for considering what Eranos and these giants of psychology and history (true history, not propaganda) were working on. The Human genome is 1.8 metres long and the amount to make a human is a small percentage of that, at 2.5 centimetres. The difference between us and a worm is so small as to boggle your mind. Unfortunately that is true about our acts though worms really aren't bad at all. The Director of this Project is Dr. Collins and he says there is a 'History Book' in our genes along with a parts and operations manual. That will make the akashic or Thodul states written about in Jung's favorite *Tibetan Book of the Dead* seem prescient, to say the least.

A third, and ultimately the most disturbing, discipline contributing to the tumult of the scene was the rapidly developing science of Aryan, Indo-Germanic, or Indo-European Philology. As early as 1767 a French Jesuit in India, Father Couerdoux, had observed that Sanskrit and Latin were remarkably alike. (3) Sir William Jones 1746-1794 - The West's first considerable Sanskritist, judge of the supreme court of judicature at Calcutta, and founder of the Bengal Asiatic Society - was the next to observe the relationship, and from a comparative study of the grammatical structures of Latin, Greek, and Sanskrit concluded that all three had 'sprung,' as he phrased it, 'from some common source, which perhaps no longer exists.' (4) (My Ogham scholars echoed this man who is the model for 'Indiana Jones' of the Spielberg trilogy. He added that Ogham is that source and he may be right though I find sign language and chanting before, that was a form of communication enhancing the extra ESP of Neanderthal just as likely, and I am sure the Mungo Man did a lot more than chant or hum 'OM'.) Franz Bopp (1791-1867), published in 1816 a comparative study of the Sanskrit, Greek, Latin, Persian, and Germanic systems of conjugation. (5) And finally, by the middle of the century it was perfectly clear that a prodigious distribution of closely related tongues could be identified over the greater part of the civilized world. Thus a continuation from Ireland to India had been revealed. And not only the languages, but also the civilizations and religions, mythologies, literary forms, and modes of thought of the people involved. No wonder the leading scholars and philosophers of the century were impressed!

It was a fateful, potentially very dangerous discovery; for, even though in the terminology of tranquil scholarship, it coincided with a certain emotional tendency of the time. In the light of the numerous discoveries then being made in every quarter of the broadly opening fields of the physical, biological, and geographical sciences, the mythological Creation story in the Old Testament could no longer be accepted as literally true." (6)

Just as Akkadian became the language of trade and politics in the Mediterranean from the time of Sargon to the time of Christ and Acadia continues to be an area of interest to my research, there are many intriguing stories to tell. The elite have made their stories of family legend into a worldwide religion still followed by many as if it were Holy Scripture. When I first met the Ogham scholars I was a well read esotericist with some sense of archaeo-mythological history and a definite belief in a World civilizing cadre such as the De Danaan or Atlantean Red-Headed League.

Robert Baird

I told Philip I thought the Phoenicians built the Great Pyramid and thus began the watershed event that since 1990 has consumed my life. Today I find myself engaged in a Grail search on Oak Island, this group includes an Essene of the present day who is also a Zionist Knight Templar and not part of the Masonic 'octopus' (he thinks). Where I am sure Roosevelt and his Oak Island Salvage & Wrecking Company or Rosicrucian Council of Three paladins (Baruch and Frank Lloyd Wright, who carried out the reconstruction plans for Europe in league with Pierre Plantard de Saint Claire who later headed the Priory of Sion.) to the Rockefeller/Rothschild corporate continuation of the Phoenicians, have done damage control. Can I prove Roosevelt was part of this elite steering committee that founded the US in the days of Ben Franklin and Thomas Paine who are acknowledged members of it? No. Can I prove Lincoln is a Melungeon or white pre-Columbian and even pre-Christian? Genetics shows they and others like the Sioux are white, and were here before they even arrived in Europe perhaps. But I do see the name of the DNN of Homer in the daughter of Sargon En Hedu'anna and I know she was a vital priestess and her lineage interests me greatly.

Philip had a book that I eventually re-wrote. In it the potential vice-presidential running mate of Lincoln turns out to have thought many of the same things about the Atlanteans who spoke Phoenician. So many little tidbits and intuitive kernels or acorns of knowledge started to come together for me. I remember telling my ex-wife who was visiting as we met Philip, that this was a 'blessing' or curse as we talked about the import of what was going to happen even before I saw this book or met Philip's associate who later worked with me on this project, to a limited extent. In fact she thought I was close to 'nuts' for being willing to give my life to simply do whatever it took to make mankind see how he once lived and flourished within the bounds of egalitarian ethics. I have given my life in ever increasing proportion since that fateful day in San Diego.

Diverse Druids

I've mentioned Connor MacDari and the Ogham scholars before. His book from 1923 is able to show the Irish connection and origin of vowelless Hebrew just as Sanskrit was a vowelless sacerdotal code. Hammurabi and his ancestor Sargon the Great from five centuries before are Phoenicians but by the time of Hammurabi the Hittites and Hurrians of their Brotherhood were major players and there is certainly lots of strife between them. It wasn't just the changes that saw Hammurabi encode women as chattel to keep peace in his area that once had been their Sumerian colony out of Byblos (Dilmun). The northern peoples were still letting women own land and have rights as Hittite and Hurrian records show. It is likely that the farther north we go the more this is true although the Uighurs are patristic and came from the east we can safely say they weren't outright women haters. There is a great deal yet to learn about these times to say the least.

The Amazons are a known fact now. Eleven hundred miles of tumuli and burials attest to their influence but I think they were just the shock troops of the larger Keltic clandoms. Women are lighter and have more body fat when in top shape. In addition to these endurance factors which would have been very important when weapons of war weren't able to carry the fighting 'men'. Women are the stronger sex. They don't faint when they lose a little blood like men do. These are biological realities.

That might be just one reason why the farther north one goes into Hyperborean Scythian territory we find evidence of women having greater equality. The spiritual soulfulness and psychic abilities of women (e.g. The Dryads or Sibylls who were great Druidic oracles) made for real influence. The Keltic men admired this and weren't prone to fear. The Keltic Creed can be simply stated as 'No Fear' and Fear (the word) is Irish for 'man'. Another word for 'Northerner' is Thule but I think it was further north than Scythia which is named after Scota like Scotland. Herodotus had been almost demeaned to being a fiction writer because he wrote about Amazons and other Kelts. Soon (I hope) the tables will turn.

45

Robert Baird

History is the FICTION! That includes the Aryan origin of the RgVeda in 1500 BC. It was twice as far back in time as India's Ilvarta scholars know. 'Rg' is Irish for 'King' but their kings reported to the people and were never hereditary.

In our continuing additions to the number of philosophies and cultures which exhibit near identical emphasis on the freedom so well portrayed in *Braveheart* and the Keltic Creed; I offer Josephus talking about certain Jewish people Jesus may well have been involved with at different times in his life. (It comes from *Jewish Antiquities* 18.23-25.) "As for the fourth of the philosophies, Judas the Galilean set himself up as the leader of it. This school agrees in all other respects with the opinions of the Pharisees, except that they have a passion for liberty that is almost inconquerable, since they are convinced that God alone is their leader and master. They think little of submitting to death in unusual forms, and permitting vengeance to fall on kinsmen and friends if only they may avoid calling man master."

The Armenians and their Antiochian school of Christology join the Ukrainians, Irish and Jews on the table of the enemy who persecutes them throughout time. The 19th Century saw success for these enemies of ancient egalitarian Keltic modes. In Easter Island and the Chatham Islands a complete genocide was achieved. In Canada an even more ancient segment of these 'giants' growing up to 7' tall were eradicated with a bounty on their heads. That was the Beothuk with their unique watercraft and ochre painted red skin that led to the term 'redskins'. The epithet Pict meant 'red shanks' when hurled over Roman parapets by those who love to deride what they cannot understand. This 5000 year 'nightmare' as James Joyce calls it, must be stopped. If not we will see Nietzsche's 'radical aristocrats' rise in another Reich.

"The Renaissance had, opposed to the Judeo-Christian ideal of obedience to a supposed revelation of God's law, the humanism of the Greeks. And with the discovery, now, of this impressive ethnic continuity, uniting that humanism, on the one hand, with the profound, non-theological religiosity

Diverse Druids

of the Indian Upanishads and Buddhist Sutras, on the other hand, with the primitive vitality of the Pagan Germans, who had shattered Christianized Rome only to be subdued and Christianized themselves in turn, the cause of the pagan against the Judeo-Christian portion of the European cultural inheritance seemed to be greatly enhanced. Moreover, since the evidence seemed to point to Europe itself as the homeland from which this profoundly inspired and vigourously creative spiritual tradition sprang - and, specifically, the area of the Germanies (Note: - For a modern review of this evidence, see Paul Thieme, 'The Indo-European Language', 'Scientific American', Vol. 199, No. 4 (October 1958), pp. 63-74, and Peter Giles' article, 'Indo-Europeans,' *Encyclopaedia Britannica*, 14th edition (1929), Vol.12, pp. 262-63). The homeland of the nuclear folk is placed by Thieme in an area between the Vistula and the Elbe, in the late fourth millenium B.C., and by Giles roughly in the same area of the Austro-Hungarian Empire. A. Miellet and Marcel Cohen, on the other hand, in their work on *Les Langues du monde* (Paris: H. Champion, 1952), p.6, place the area 'in the plains of southern Russia and perhaps earlier in Central Asia. - a shock of romantic European elation quivered through the scientific world. The Grimm brothers, Jacob and Wilhelm (1785-1863 and 1786-1859), gathered the fairy tales of their collection with the belief that there might be discovered in them the unbroken remains of a nuclear Indo-European mythology. Schopenauer greeted the Sanskrit Upanishads as 'the most rewarding and elevating reading possible in the world.' (7) And Wagner found in the old Germanic mythologies of Wotan, Loki, Siegfried, and the Rhinemaidens the proper vehicle of his German genius.

Thus it was when a couple of dilettantes with creative imagination brought this sensational product of philological research out of the studies of scholars, where thought leads to further thought, into the field of political life, where thought leads to action and one thought is enough, a potentially very dangerous situation was created. The first step in this direction was taken in 1839, when a French aristocrat, Courtet de L'isle, proposed a theory of politics an the basis of what he conceived to be the new science, in a work entitled *La Science politique fondee sur la science de l'homme; ou, Etude des races humaines* (Pais,'39), and Count Vacher de Lapouge's *L'Aryen et son rôle social* (1899). The tendency was developed in Count Arthur de Gobineau's four-volume *Essai sur l'inegalite des races humaines* (1853-1855), and required, finally, only the celebrated work of Wagner's English son-in-law, Houston Stewart Chamberlain, *The Foundations of the Nineteenth Century* (1890-1891), to supply the background for Alfred Rosenberg's *Der Mythus des 20, Jahrhunderts* (1930) and break the planet into flames." (8)

This is a good analysis of the way propaganda works and the horrors it created. The reality is close to what was discovered and the Don and Danube of Gimbutas as well as the genetic Haplogroup X data adds a great deal to the time line. It is not a reason to hate Jews though. In reality Hitler was a Jew and the secret wartime report prepared for the OSS says his grandmother was impregnated by a Rothschild in Vienna. Beyond that the very Aryan high priests were the Hebrews (a language derived from Phoenician as all scholars now know.). So is all this war between the Benjaminites, who were thrown out of their homeland 3,000 years ago, and the rest of the tribes of Israel what we must endure? Campbell knew the war didn't need to happen!

Churchill Joins the Druids!

On 15 August, 1908 the venerable Winston Churchill son of Lord Randolph joined the Ancient Order of Druids who met at Blenheim Palace but he did not study this knowledge as intensively as Adolf who spent over five years in Vienna making himself powerful. The Druid societies of today are not real Druids or at best pale imitations of what once existed. It is interesting to note that many of these people are entirely capable of keeping a secret and that Churchill may have learned more than I surmise from his acts and written words. He certainly knew about the medieval use of the

Diverse Druids

Plague as a bio-weapon of terror employed by the agents of change. He says it in his book *The Island Race*. You can see William of Rubruck's reports to his Catholic masters to set the stage for this totally incredible claim if you care to challenge my research and the words of Churchill. The only acknowledged use of these plagues was in Ft. Pitt many years later.

Because Thomas Paine says Masonry is derived from Druidism does not mean the Druids would approve. Whatever I say about what they might approve is also a speculative guess. Even if I demonstrate a specific act or concept existed and we can draw a conclusion the same proviso applies because they changed over the millennia, I guess this is true about anything. So when we see this Masonic 'octopus' or I say something about the Druids knowing it that is just an opinion of the specific time and it may (usually is) be that I don't think the real Druids would approve. Perhaps I should try to define Druids in categories of time such as 5500 BC when their Black Sea homeland was flooded and post Pyramids of 3000 BC onwards. The post Christian period and the like are no clearer because of the destruction and prohibition by Rome. There will be times when I can and will do that. Although I may mention the possibilities of Mungo Man being the very valuable item mentioned in the records of Hatchepsut and earlier 'giants' larger than the often seven foot tall Kelts I hope you can forgive these more fantastic forays that also might be true. They are in all the legends.

Churchill was part Brant Iroquois as I understand it and that might be through Jenny Jerome or by some other means. Of course you can say we are all related and that would be good if we acted like it. The more interesting connection with the Bush family and many other great public figures is well documented to include the British Royalty. The Iroquois are white according to genetics just like their related Sioux 'brothers'. I have gathered the proof to show the Canadian Encyclopedia is conservative in saying they can be traced to 4000 BC. That is in other books in great detail including the work of people the Smithsonian call "authoritative". Poverty Point is one of the keys in that search and the new find off the coast of Cuba is related as well, I think. It would have been near the mouth of the Mississippi when it was the route glacial waters flowed from the Great Lakes a lot further back than 4000 BC which is why it may relate to the Carolinas Bay meteors that explain some of the Bermuda Triangle occurrences. That was around the time when the North American horse disappeared and

Some think Atlantis as well. Aztlan is one name for the Upper Mississippi Copper Culture of Phoenicians in this period around 8300 BC and before.

The Mohawk tonsure or hairdo is much like the Druids. The Druids had the hair from ear to ear whereas the Mohawk had it from front to back. The turning of the hair is a sign or code of fealty and loyalty in the token system of Phoenicians and their Green Languages.

The word Mohawk means 'Guardians of the East' and Seneca means 'Guardians of the West' or vice versa. They weren't just guarding their nation as one goes back in time to the Megwi and earlier to the Old Copper Culture. The fact that Churchill became part of the Rhodes Round Table intrigues and spent his last years on the Merovingian yacht of Onassis as well as his father's name Randolph has not escaped my inspection in other places. The people who kept the secret of drugs and the sea routes or potions are still with us and leading us with a questionable ethic. If Churchill can justify the use of the Bubonic Plague against Europeans and North American Indians (in *The Island Race*) maybe the Australians are right to say he sold them down (or up) the river. Certainly the Boer War and even the Second World War could have been stopped. It was part of a plan; and if it wasn't a conspiracy - then we need a plan or conspiracy of Love, as Teilhard de Chardin called for humanity to join.

Diverse Druids

Archaeomythology is a Science!

Campbell's earlier quotes were written before he did the foreword to Marija Gimbutas' *Language of the Goddess* and her great fieldwork in the Crimea or Old Europe. He said he would have done a lot of his earlier work differently if he had known what she proved.

He goes on to say some important things that linguists and forensic analysts of knowledge also can agree with, yet many academics have sneered at the proof they have delivered. The linguists are not sneered at when they confirm the existing paradigm.

Clearly, mythology is no toy for children. Nor is it a matter of archaic, merely scholarly concern, of no moment to modern men of action. For its symbols (whether in the tangible form of images or in the abstract form of ideas) touch and releases the deepest centers of motivation, moving literate and illiterate alike, moving mobs, moving civilizations. There is a real danger, therefore, in the incongruity of focus that has brought the latest findings of technological research into the incongruity of focus that has brought the latest findings of technological research into the foreground of modern life, joining the world in a single community, while leaving the anthropological and psychological discoveries from which a commensurable moral system might have been developed in the learned publications where they first appeared. For surely it is folly to preach to children who will be riding rockets to the moon (Now Alpha Centauri and terraforming Mars) a morality and cosmology based on the concepts of the Good Society and of man's place in nature that were coined before the harnessing of the horse! And the world is now far too small, and men's stake in sanity too great, for any more of those old games of Chosen Folk (whether of Jehovah, Allah, Wotan, Manu, or the Devil) by which tribesmen were sustained against their enemies in the days when the serpent still could talk.

The ghostly, anachronistic sounds of Aryan battle cries faded rapidly from the nineteenth-century theatres of learning as a broader realization of the community of man developed—due primarily to a mass of completely unforeseen information from the pioneers of archaeology and anthropology. For example, it soon appeared not only that the earliest Indo-European tribes must already have been mixed of a number of races. (The Kelts main goal in fostering this might have been to expand their numbers due to them being small in number once they were created or mutated. They kept doing the egalitarian thing a very long time and there are other good reasons to have done so, in trade and in the area of sharing and learning. A one point shortly before Rome became ascendant and even after among the wealthy, they sent their kids to far off cousins after a certain age in order to keep the cultures in touch and to share the wealth. It was a paid training at good institutions of learning and Rome sent many of her early saints and prelates like Columbanus to learn in places like Bangor.)

A sense of the import of these new discoveries for the nineteenth-century image of man can be gained from a summary schedule of a number of representative moments; for example:

1821 Jean Francois Champollion derived from the Rosetta Stone the key to Egyptian hieroglyphics, thus unveiling a civilized religious literature earlier than the Greek and Hebrew by about two thousand years.

1833 William Ellis, *Polynesian Researches* (4 vols.), opened to view the myths and customs of the South Sea Islands. (Now we know of a far earlier modern man from Australia who probably came from somewhere else and is not part of the African genetic stream.)

1839 Henry Rowe Schoolcraft, *Algic Researches* (2 vols.), offered the first considerable collection of North American Indian myths.

Diverse Druids

1845 Sir Austen Henry Layard excavated ancient Ninevah and Babylon, opening the 50 treasures of the Mesopotamian civilization.

1847 Jacques Boucher de Crevecouer de Perthes book, *Antiquities celtiques et antediluviennes* (3 vols.), established the existence of man in Europe in the Pleistocene Period (that is to say, more than a hundred thousand years ago) and, on the basis of his classification of flint tools, identified three Old Stone Age periods, which he termed: (1) 'the Cave Bear Age', (2) 'The Mammoth and Woolly Rhinoceros Age', and (3) 'the Reindeer Age'.

1856 Johann Karl Fuhlrott discovered in a cave in eastern Germany the bones of Neanderthal Man (Homo neanderthalensis), mighty hunter of the Cave Bear and Mammoth Ages. (The original hunchback was an incorrect assembly of the bones.)

1859 Charles Darwin's great work, *On The Origin of Species*, appeared.

1860 Edouard Lartet, in southern France, unearthed the remains of Cro-Magnon Man, by whom Neanderthal had been displaced in Europe during the Reindeer Age, at the end of the Pleistocene.

1861 The *Popul Vuh,* an ancient Central American mythological text, was introduced to the learned world by the Abbe Brasseur de Bourbourg. From this momentou decade of the sixties onward, the universality of the basic themes and motifs of mythology was generally conceded, the usual assumption being that some sort of psychological explanation would presently be found; and so it was that from tw remote quarters of the learned world the following comparative studies appeare

Robert Baird

1868 simultaneously: in Philadelphia, Daniel G Brinton's *The Myths of the New World*, comparing the primitive and high-culture mythologies of the Old World and the New; and in Berlin, Adolf Bastian's *Das Beständige in den Menschenrassen und Die Spielweite ihrer Veränderlichkeit,* applying the point of view of comparative Psychology and biology to the problems, first, of the 'constants' and then of the 'variables' in the mythologies of mankind.

1871 Edward B. Tylor, in his *Primitive Culture: Researches into the Development of Mythology, Philosophy, Religion, Language, Art, and Custom,* directed a psychological explanation of the concept of 'animism' to a whole range of primitive thought in a systematic manner.

1872 Heinrich Schliemann, excavating Troy (Hissarlik) and Mycenae, probed the pre-Homeric, pre-classical levels of Greek civilization.

1879 Don Marcelino de Sautuola discovered on his property in northern Spain (Altamira) the magnificent cave-painting art of the Mammoth and Reindeer Ages.

1890 Sir James George Frazer published the culminating work of this whole period of anthropological research, *The Golden Bough.*

1891 In Central Java, on the Solo River, near Trinil, Eugène Dubois unearthed the bones -92and teeth of 'the Missing Link', Pithecanthropus erectus ('the Ape-man who walks erect') - with a brain capacity halfway between that of the largest-brained gorilla (about 600 cc.) and that of the average modern man (about 1400 cc.).

1893 Sir Arthur Evans commenced his Cretan excavations.

1898 Leo Frobenius announced a new approach to the study of primitive cultures (the *Kulturkreislehre,* 'culture area theory'), wherein he identified a primitive cultural continuum, extending from equatorial West Africa eastward, through India and Indonesia, Melanesia and Polynesia, across the Pacific to equatorial America and Northwest coast. (9) This was a radical challenge to the older 'parallel development' or 'psychological' schools of interpretation, such as Brinton, Bastian, Tylor, and Frazer had represented, inasmuch as it brought the broad and bold theory of a primitive trans-oceanic 'diffusion' to bear upon the question of the distribution of so-called 'universal' themes."(10)

And that is still a major difference or conflict to this day. Cell Diffusion is the opposite of the fallout of the Flat Earth theory. I am not a believer in any part of the Flat Earth theory and frankly can see little reason for any intelligent person to buy into the slightest part of it. I do see it was part of a need to keep a monopoly and trade advantage and then I see it as necessary to keep serfs from leaving Europe for the Americas.

This is the continuing state of DENIAL despite the work of Heyerdahl, Severin, Humboldt, and many others of the Western schools. Of course, the Indian or most of the rest of the world never bought into this DENIAL. To call these schools psychological is a reflection on the control or therapy in social engineering. If Churchill can justify using the Plague to shock and make society change - then anything is possible and we must also remember he said we can fight while the prospect of winning still exists. Otherwise we are destined to be part of a Matrix. His use of these words in WWII era history is a part of his broader authorship and understanding of history and many inner sanctum secrets. We have been fed like mushrooms that thrive in the dark.

Twenty-First Century Archaeomythology:
The myth researchers and cell diffusionists have a lot to crow about. We have been vindicated by all disciplines of

science and helped immensely by satellite 'remote viewing'. Side-scan sonar is turning up many of the old legendary cities and some that we may never even know the names they went by in the time before the glaciers melted. It is difficult to say which is the most important or fantastic! Let me just take the template provided by Campbell and make some comments on things he did not live to see though intuited, as much as any scholar of the last few centuries.

1821 - Now we have a Saharan culture with wooden henges and a usable alphabet for common people a thousand years before hieroglyphics. This was the opinion of Sir Flinders Petrie (see *Formation of the Alphabet*) in the early 20th Century but he could not prove it to the conditioned and motivated academics or Egyptologists. The same area shows there was an advanced culture that used agricultural methods that disappeared and then the hunters and gatherers reclaimed the land. This culture was a meeting of Timbuktu people and the white Berbers in a Brotherhood that maintained relations in places like Olmec Central America. The Basque figure into this group when the Iberian/Tartessus Strabo said had a 7,000 year written history was a key part of a Druidic pan-Tribal internationalism. They may not have been called by that name or it may have been the King/Bairds going back to Isis and Osiris who sat in a council of six men and women to give advice to Elders and act as arbiters in disputes.

1833 - Heyerdahl showed the 'experts' it could be done and that the natives knew more than they had been given credit for. A woman took a small craft without navigational equipment from Hawaii to Easter Island in the year 2000. The genetics of the Easter Island white people and the Chatham Island Moriori Kelts is the same; but 'experts' say this proves the Phoenicians weren't the Easter Islanders. Barabudur and the Tarim Basin are central parts of the spread of new religions like Buddhism by Druidic trained people around the years 600 BC through the time of Christ and until the Taklamakand Desert finally swallowed up the Tarim Basin and they moved to places like Wisconsin and became known as the Sauk Indians (500 AD).

1839 - The Mayan code was broken and although the Franciscans were very diligent in their destruction of the Mayan libraries we now can begin to put a few things in order. The Mayans developed the mathematical zero just a century before the Indians of the sub-continent and academics have not seen this as a reason to believe in 8th Century ocean travel but rather a co-incidence. The Purple dye of the Phoenicians and cotton has similar technological co-incidences to be sure. In fact the co-incidences are endless as the Canadian Museum of Civilization lied about pre-existing Ecuadorian pottery technology and there have been numerous cover-ups such as Kennewick Man and Manitoulin Island.

1845 - Kehoe's pottery from the Ertebolle Scandinavian culture and the sweat house technology therefrom is all over pre-Columbian American continents in the very places the Phoenician Kelts or Brotherhood was said to have been. Genetics shows Berber blood in Pima (SW U.S.) Indians as well as many Keltic Caucasoids like the Sioux, Yakima and Yuchi clan. The linguistic evidence is just as related and Ogham is found to be the root of many Indian scripts while the inscriptions on dolmen and rocks is something the Catholic horde didn't fully understand enough to destroy.

1850 - Kidmet Enrob and pre-Harappan Ilvarta and other sub-continent discoveries and research continue to arrive in the media on a monthly basis. There are sites being kept under wraps by some very shady characters who might have some concern about the rights of sovereign states based on colonizing and enslaving Empire to keep the countries and governments they run. Yonaguni, Azores, Acambaro, 'giant skeletons', Alaskan mummies, and a host of questionable practices or crucifixions for qualified 'experts' who dare do what the U.S. Government made clear was unacceptable in events like the Palmer Raids. These official pogroms of the early 20th Century around the time of the Rhoda/Tucson finds, can be compared to the acts of the House Un-American Activities Committee and black-balling of thinkers who spoke out in the 50's and 60's.

1847-65 - Neanderthal cross breed babies from after their supposed demise join the list of interesting debates with scholars almost evenly divided. The Black Skull overturned the australopithecine lineup and threw the evolutionary development of humanity a major curve in 1997. Since then there have been many significant finds to make the idea of our development from apes almost without proof. Maybe the apes developed from humans and we came from alien or Time Travelers. The point I'd like to emphasize is simply this - the 'experts' and their absolute certainties are often totally wrong. The man who discovered Lucy says he no longer does Evolutionary Trees.

1856 - Neanderthal was not a hunchback with no culture or technology. The original assembly of his bones was flawed and we now have proof they developed music and advanced refined drugs. They had a 10% larger brain and yet little speech lobe capacity. Did they rely on ESP? The Neanderthal seems less inclined to organize for war and was larger and perhaps wiser than other hominids. Cro-Magnon is still of uncertain derivation and the alien origin theorists use that fact with wild abandon.

1859 - Darwin also had a theory of Love and the qualitative quantum leaps of Intelligent Design are serious theories shared in many scientific disciplines.

1860 - Today behaviorists and psychologists join with biologists and zoologists to prove Locke and his TABULA RASA was utterly false! The Scale of Nature took science by storm in all the Western egoistic prejudice that goes with it. This tripe was still in vogue in some academic circles until the 20th Century. How could anyone seriously think animals can't communicate or that they don't have both a soul and the conscious capacity for compassion and more? Kanzai the chimp is more erudite than these supposed great philosophers. The porpoise may be superior to humanity in many areas. They have five separate communication channels. Clearly the 'heathen' Pagans had a different world view than Christians in this regard. Do you see any propaganda at work? Some Kelts worshipped their horses and dogs and their burials are proving this all over the world of mounds and tumuli in their style of burial.

1861 - The voyages of St. Brendan have been replicated by Tim Severin and scholars like the Abbe Brasseur de Bourbourg or Humboldt who dared go against the Columbus 'fiction' of discovery are being vindicated rather than vilified.

1868 - Modern quantum physics and the Hubbell photos are proving the ancient Chaos Scientists were right about most things. Nobel Laureates and the top people are writing about how the Mandukya Upanishads and Tao Te Ching show the same mathematical or physics comprehension needed to win their prizes. The Rhind Papyrus from 1650 BC had been copied from earlier documents and it shows an understanding of the basis of computeronics in binary math. We have yet to grasp their concepts relating to the Earth Energy Grid and Harmonics as encapsulated in the 'Lost Chord' or even Pythagoras and his 'Singing of the Spheres'.

1871 - One thing Joseph Campbell fully appreciated (as shown in his address to the Sarah Lawrence students at the entry of the US into WWII, called Permanent Human Values) is the nature of war and men who need power rather than transcendent enlightenment. Who are the real Terrorists? A cursory reading of Chomsky might change any flag waver's opinion that has an open mind. The war against

Robert Baird

the soul is a more perverse matter than he might even have imagined as he warned about the loss of values to come as a result of the war propaganda machine, in this prophetic speech.

1872 - It is hard to say which of the new 'finds' is most important because there is little information available even when Cuba is trying to give us all the pertinent information and the US is not in Bimini and the Azores. Certainly Yonaguni is quite impressive and the facts are incontrovertible yet there are those who have not looked at the facts who say otherwise. It is an all too frequent re-occurring theme, in the Ivory Towers of academia, politics, education and the other media.

1879 - After the warming of relations occurred between Russia and the U.S. we got to see the Tarim Basin Red Headed Mummies near the Great Wall of China. We will show how this one region may be the original Mediterranean from pre-Glacial time. It may be a key cultural center of Atlantis and Mu; all in one place! I truly would have loved it if Joseph Campbell could have lived a year or two longer, so that he could have garnered the result he really intuited so well. Yes, there has been at least the 462,000 years of advanced human culture that he wrote about.

1890 - Joseph Campbell wrote many books including the Hero with a Thousand Faces series. Andre Malraux showed art from all over the world was stylistically different but spiritually the same. Humanity can start thinking about man getting back to egalitarian roots and the New Age has rediscovered the past. Margaret Meade and her influence on Jean Houston are the kind of thing I hope continues.

1891 - Ms. Moore, an archaeologist working in Angkor Wat found a couple of very interesting things last year. The writing on the temples is easily translated and gives detailed cosmological reasons for the reservoirs and moats but

Diverse Druids

archaeologists or others have generally assumed the natives lie or something. After all spirituality and the earth energy grid aren't THAT important. Ms. Moore used remote satellite and plane modern technology to show the reservoirs never had water leave them to the rice paddies. Of course the fact that a major nearby river could always have supplied the water seems to have been overlooked. She also found another complete Temple complex with the triune cosmological design a few miles away. It was from a thousand years earlier! The human brain wavelength frequencies are:

Beta waves (14 to 30 Hz)
    Normal waking state 40 Hz in a few healers
Alpha waves (8 to 13 Hz)
    Earth Energy at 7.5 and environs
Theta waves (4 to 7 Hz), and
Delta waves (1 to 3 Hz).

1893 - Today we know Evans bought many faked artifacts and sold them to many 'experts' in museums throughout the world. His methods were shabby but his heart was in the right place.

1898 - The Neolithic or Stone Age people appear to have a completely advanced science that didn't need the methods or machinery of today to avail themselves of the energy we call electricity or Dark Energy or 'shakti'. We are finally employing acupuncture and other ancient science in more situations rather than calling chiropractors quacks. Yet the medical community and health plans still abuse what works in favor of modern supposed science.

In 1964 Gwyn Jones wrote a book called *The Norse Atlantic Saga*. It still says things that no major school will teach even though the L'Anse aux Meadows site has been definitively accepted by the 'Gods of Archaeology'. One can see that early secrets about trade routes were very important to greedy people:

Robert Baird

"Who first saw Iceland, and whether god-impelled, mirage-led, wind-whipt and storm belted, or on a tin-and-amber course laid north to roll back trade horizons, we do not know. But he was a brave man, or an unlucky, and it was a long time ago.

The dragon prow of a Norse adventurer made the first recorded circumnavigation of the island about 860; the curraghs of Irish anchorites had reached its south-eastern shore in the last years of the eighth century; but it is probable that Iceland's story starts in a remoter past than this. We have learned in the last seventy years that man's early knowledge of the sea and willingness to venture out upon it resulted in voyages undreamt of by nineteenth-century historians; and that this is true of the northern as well as the southern hemisphere, of the Atlantic as the Pacific. By 2500 BC, and maybe much earlier, the sea was man's highway, and already the funerary ritual of the megalith builders of Spain, Portugal, and France was being spread by sea throughout the islands and peninsulas of the west, and from these northwards through the Irish Sea and Pentland Firth. The western sea-routes have been frequented ways ever since, for though profit and policy have often led peoples to stow knowledge under hatches, as did the Phoenicians in respect of Africa and the Cassiterides, or the merchants of Bristol in respect of their illegal fifteenth-century trade with Greenland, such mind-cargo is rarely lost to human memory. Someone knows, or confusedly recalls, that far out on the ocean's bosom lies a Land of Promise, Eternal Youth, silent refuge, stockfish profit. There is therefore nothing improbable in the notion that the Greek astronomer, mathematician, and geographer Pytheas of Massalia acquired in the purlieus of Britain as much news of Thule as he is thought to have bequeathed to it.

Unfortunately Pytheas's account of his voyage of exploration to Britain and further north in 330-300 BC has not survived. We have to rely instead on pieces of not always consistent information, at times derived from careless

Diverse Druids

intermediaries, imbedded in the writings of later and often derisory Greek geographers." (11)

The decade just past has brought archaeological proofs galore but there always was enough written (even though Roman liars derided them) to make a good case for the facts we have now found. Bucky Fuller knew the ancient navigators would have learned trigonometry from the observation of positions of stars as they traveled the oceans. Now we know Flores Island was visited by humans 800,000 years ago. The potential vice presidential running mate of Honest Abe Lincoln wrote a book on Atlantis where he correctly identified Phoenician was the language the Atlanteans spoke. That was the 19th Century and much proof has come to his aid since then. The Father of Biblical Archaeology who said the Bible was a Phoenician literary legacy in the 1960s is just one of many reasons I wonder why there is any argument about the matter.

The 'Quickening'!

When the Scottish Rite Templar Prince Henry Sinclair (Jarl of Orkney became 'Glooscap' in the Indian tongue.) came to Nova Scotia about a century before Columbus he was welcomed by the Indians who already had a lot of contact with his people. The very name MicMac has a Scots/Irish ring to it, but that is not great proof or even evidence. What is interesting is the practice of sexuality and learning that the Indians employed which was the same as the Kelts and their 'Brotherhood'. Their young women were encouraged to experience pre-marital sex. Is this 'barbaric'? The hypocrites who later became Puritans and the like were to say (still do) that more than five strokes is perversion because it didn't seem necessary to the procreative purpose of God.

Frederick Pohl was a serious historian of good standing when he wrote the story of Prince Henry Sinclair long before the acceptance of the Norse in America centuries before Columbus. In Michael Bradley's books he carries the story further with geologic core samples and other evidence. The

Robert Baird

timbers in the Money Pit used to fund Stuart Wars in Europe for a millennium or more are carbon dated to 800 AD. FDR was involved in a 'wrecking company '(?) that dealt with Oak Island as was Frank Lloyd Wright his appointee to the reconstruction of Europe. It is not a co-incidence that Wright named his estate after Taliesin who was a Druid and wrote the story in the *Hanes Taliesin* that documents the main Merovingians from the time of Abraham to his 6th Century time.

The following quotation of an article on the World Wide Web dovetails with the gift of Eastern Europe to Stalin and Truman's shady deals that lead to the Cold War. It made for continued armaments spending in a 'play both ends against the middle' tactic few would want to know all the details of:

"It seems clear that if we had accepted the offer a whole lot of lives on both sides would have been saved. But what was the offer? This is what was offered to the Americans.

1. A full surrender by all Japanese forces.
2. Surrender of the Japanese army, navy and munitions.
3. There would be an occupation of the Japanese homelands and islands by allied troops that would be under American direction.
4. The Japanese would withdraw from Manchuria, Korea, Formosa and all territories seized during the war.
5. There would be a secession of the production of the implements of war.
6. Japan would turn over all of those who the United States designated as war criminals.
7. The release of all American prisoners of war held by Japan.

As you can see terms that were offered differed little from the final terms. So what was the problem? First, it can be assumed that Roosevelt sought to buy out the Soviets. I think it is also safe to say that the United States had intentions of using the atomic bomb as a warning to the Russians. While this seems to be a contradiction at second

Diverse Druids

glance it is not.

But one other question remains. Should the press have reported the overtures? I believe that they should. It is not the job of the press to follow policy. It is their job to report the news. While many will disagree with this statement I think history has shown that the people can make decisions for themselves.
- Walter Trohan, Chicago Tribune"

For the youth of today who watch the movies and TV series based on the Highlander or Raven there are facts they may find interesting in this book that relate to the 'quickening'. I like the words of Sean Connery as he plays Ramirez of Iberia at the end of the second movie. He said, "You are generations being born, and generations learning. So don't lose your head."

Duncan MacLeod said something even more relevant just before the end of the movie to his lady, "I can know the thoughts of every person in the world just by concentrating." The Animus Mundi of the 19th Century French salons is the World Mind that is building and creating our reality. Bucky Fuller wrote about the same thing as he talked about 'creative realization'.

When a Wiccan High Priestess who I interviewed for two weeks heard I wished to study with her, she said: "Why? You already know so much?" My hope was that I could learn some more - I hope you are willing to listen to the past that I know goes back to a time before the Wiccans who claim a heritage of 25,000 years through their Druid brothers who kept this history in books now destroyed like the *Psaltair na Tara,* which was kept by the Bairds (Gaelic for Bards). I cannot promise a 'quickening' but I can tell you about the 'quicken sticks' of Ogham made of Rowan wood. These sticks are similar to the I Ching and the Australian aboriginal 'message sticks' that Alexander Marshack who proved the 30,000 year old accurate lunar calendar was not scratches or 'notation' writes about. He quotes his fellow

Robert Baird

anthro-archaeological experts and you will find many great scholars are the people I quote as well.

Maybe there will be a point when you will reach the same or similar difficulty I have. Why did mankind turn against women and egalitarian modes of living and governance?

CHAPTER THREE:
STRABO AND THE OAK!

In the Bronze Age, tin was extremely important and commanded great barter value. The only real tin beyond pure local use was in the Cassiterides or Cornwall and near Glastonbury where Phoenicians like Joseph of Arimathaea plied their trade with the assistance and involvement of their Phocaean and Tartessus Iberian co-venturers of the Phoenician Brotherhood. Before that they were the controllers of copper in places like Lake Superior which was the only real source in the whole world that produced usable tools in the pre-smelting era. That pre-smelting era is a matter of some doubt. The secret of alloying and smelting was closely guarded and some Armenians are known to have had it in Pontus around 7000BC if not before. Others didn't get it until 5000 years later.

Crete was an important administrative center for at least 10,000 years in this Phoenician Brotherhood and the next quote shows a correlation with New Grange that makes a lot of sense when you believe man traveled the whole world since before the glaciers melted or retreated. The land around the Great Lakes rebounded about 2/3rds of a MILE over the last 9,000 years or so. It is still readjusting isostatically. The oceans level rose 400 feet in quick time. Imagine the terrifying alterations and inundations that went on in prehistory as they call it. We will try to pierce that 'pre' or we will never learn what could be, in human egalitarian governance. Certainly we have not developed appropriate Brotherhood ethics. At the same time we must consider how the egalitarian models were destroyed in favor of globalized greed or what Dr. Janice Boddy calls "the global re-ifying thrust of Materialism'. It is very difficult to pierce all the 'spin-doctoring' the last three thousand years has wrought.

"We may take the Irish royal burial mound of New Grange as a typical monument of the period and a sign or marker, furthermore, of the northwestward diffusion. This tomb is the largest of a number in a broad area on the river

Robert Baird

Boyne, about five miles above Drogheda, known as 'Brugh na Boinne ('Palace of the Boyne')' and traditionally associated with a mysterious personage called variously 'Oengus an Brogha' ('Oengus of the Palace') or 'Oengus mac in Dagda' ('Oengus, Son of the Good God'). The height of the burial mound of New Grange, which originally must have been greater, is now some forty-two feet, while the diameter is nearly three hundred. Originally the whole hemispherical surface was covered with a layer of quartz fragments, so that, sparkling in the sun, the monument would have been seen for miles around. Moreover, a curb of slabs, about a hundred in number, some four feet in breadth and six to ten feet long, forms an unbroken ring around the structure and on certain of these formidable rocks engraved designs appear of zigzags, lozenges, circles and herring bones, spirals and linked spirals. A rough and narrow passage, roofed and walled by great slabs, some as long as fifteen feet, penetrates the southeast quarter of the mound, from behind an extremely handsome engraved curbing stone; and at the end of this tunnel is a cross-shaped burial chamber, where the remains of the kings were placed, probably in urns.

The relics, however, and everything else portable, were removed in the year 861 A.D., when the grave was plundered by Scandinavian pirates, so that today nothing remains but the eerie passage, 62 feet long, and the chamber, 21 feet from side to side and 18 feet in depth, (1) with its curious labrynthine spirals on the walls and ceiling, an interesting floor stone with two worn sockets, where a man might have been made to kneel, and the still more interesting circumstance that precisely at sunrise, one day in eight years (or, at least, so the local story goes), the morning star may be seen to rise and cast its beam precisely to the place of the stone with the two worn sockets. The tale may be true or not, but the coincidence of eight years with the period assigned by Frazer to the reigning term of the kings of Crete gave me a shock when I heard it; and here it is, therefore, for the reader to take or leave as he likes - or to go to Ireland, perhaps, to prove.

These grave tumuli in Ireland are associated with the fairy folk, who of old were the mighty Tuatha de Danaan, 'the tribes of the fold of the goddess Danu.'(2) Defeated in a great battle by the Milesians (the legendary ancestors of the Irish people, who are supposed to have arrived by sea from the Near East, via Spain, about a thousand years before the birth of Christ.), the people of the goddess withdrew from the surface of the land to the 'sid'(pronounced shee), the fairy hills, where they dwell to this day in Elysian bliss, and without the touch of age, as the fairy folk. Danu, their mother, is again our goddess of many names. She is Anu, a goddess of plenty, after whom two hills in Kerry are called 'the Paps of Anu'"(3)

There are two complete books required to explain this one quote. I may never get around to doing them because I do go into enough detail on the lozenges and mandala type traps. Here we see the root of the Biblical Anunnaki that Gardner and Sitchin have created such a recent storm about. The aliens or Elohim of the Bible are the Anunnaki (reptoids for Gardner and original sea people for Sitchin). Campbell did the foreword to Gimbutas' *Language of the Goddess* many years after writing this. At that time he said he would have written things differently because of what she discovered in the original homeland of Danu and Don (DN in the vowelless original scripts). After Marija died came the genetics that dovetails with her findings. It has been exciting for me to witness the De Danaan come alive out of the myths and legends that priesthoods and interpreters have created for their own purposes. D. J. Conway says something like Campbell and adds a little when she says that Finn and the Fianna are the Irish/Keltic king and his warrior fairies. She goes on to show this is where the name Phoenician came from.

The very important correlation of timing of rituals with the transit of Venus or the morning star he refers to is vital to an understanding of the Mayan calendar and Captain Cook's original voyage was largely justified by this observational quest. The point in time that Campbell wrote this, he might have gone some distance with the prevailing academic opinion that all things originated in Sumer or the Fertile Crescent. The Milesians and the Phocaeans lived next to each other and are part of the Phoenician Brotherhood with others of the Trojan War. Phocacans established Massalia or Marseilles with the help of Tartessus (Iberians just as the Milesians where paramount in Cas-Iberia after the Trojan War), there was a Druidic University of long standing near Massalia and we also find the unusual pentagram of mountains where Nostradamus was born near Rennes le Chateau. There are many books written on each of those places or people and I have dealt with them in detail elsewhere. In very ancient times Massalia (there are underwater mines we've found there) was the entrance to the route to the Atlantic and through which people traveled on their way to Lyoness.

    The Sons of Mil(e) are the central 'Bees' in the Merovingian intrigue and why the robe of Napoleon had artifacts from Childeric's grave to wear on his robe when the Pope was to let him take the crown and put it on his own head. The Royal House of Mallia on Crete is one of their ancestral conquests and there the famous 'bee' was found as Jacquetta Hawkes and other archaeologists know. The Stuart/Stewart historians know the import of these Milesians who held the meetings of Perpetual Sailors that I think have their continuance in the Bilderbergs. The bee may have begun as a butterfly according to Gimbutas who also sees a connection with the Bull (As in Mithras and from whence comes the date we use to celebrate Xmas via Constantine.). The Phocaeans have it on their coinage. Michael Bradley covers the import of Napoleon marrying into the Merovingians (if he wasn't already one through his real father General Marbouef) and wearing the 'Bees' of Childeric in a Chapter titled that way in his *Holy Grail Across the Atlantic*. The bee is also the emblem of one of the main cults in pre-Tuthmoside Egypt.

Diverse Druids

Venus and The Mayax Root Considered:
The science of astrology was (and is) very real to people up until very recent times (ask Nancy Reagan, Ronald's wife). Venus and the planets that shine brightly in the sky has been the object of observation by life on Earth for longer than humans and apes have existed. Observation sometimes occurs in unconscious ways and the energy of the cosmos washes over all our senses continuously from before birth. Venus is the key factor in the accurate and prophetic Mayan calendar which begins in the 35th Century BC if not before. They also work a Long Count relating to the Pleiades, and the 26,000 year sidereal movement that reflects the Polar Wander Path of the tilting axis of the Earth.

The origin and extent of such mathematical knowledge will still be hotly debated when historians start to admit what archaeology proves. There are lenses found in Olmec land at La Venta, Mexico. The fissures of the earth that allow magma quartz to ooze slowly to the surface have benefited the people of this region for a very long time. In Hueyatlaco a credible geologist proved Hueyatlaco had humans 250,000 years ago. Today you can buy crystal balls at any tourist stand 'for cheap'. The scrying skulls that abound in Mexico which you have seen in Spielberg's Indiana Jones trilogy are part of what people did with this oozing magma that could be formed in ironwood enclosures or sand crucibles.

In Acambaro, Mexico another interesting piece of archaeological mythology exists. The archaeologists who say Mexicans didn't have ceramics in 5000 BC are not considering the natural effect of the magma or of cenotes by the ocean. In these cenotes a bellows effect is created which in conjunction with the ironwood (named for its weight and density, which makes a fierce heat when burned) would easily generate the required heat. Julsrud found thousands of ceramics and the content or images these ceramics contain are why archaeology needs to destroy them or his research.

When I was in Chichen Itza, I met the manager of the Villas Archaeologique. He was an inner sanctum

Robert Baird

Rosicrucian and our meeting was 'freaky' to say the least. He had been with the Club Med people for some time and had been in the South Sea Islands as well. We talked about Churchward and Mu, they are connected to the Mayans and the Mayans I met in a later year of living with them accept this fact. He had seen many of the remains of Mu on the Polynesian Islands and was an amateur archaeologist who did personal excavations and the like. Since then we have had two important discoveries. The last one, off Cuba, may be Churchward's Mayax and Yonaguni is certainly part of his lost civilization. I do not believe in a lost continent and I think people writing about or talking about their ancestral homes having be inundated could easily have made them into larger land masses than they were.

Churchward says that the Polynesians are the origins of white men in Europe. I think it may be the other way around but he would still be largely right. If genetics is right about white men starting in the Old Europe of Gimbutas and they came to the Americas in the 30,000 year ago period they may well have established themselves in Mayax or Aztlan's Old Copper Culture before going to Europe. That does seem to make sense of the present facts. Thus the Emerald Isles of the Caribbean may have preceded the Emerald Isles created around 5300 BC by ocean level increases associated with the glacial subsurface lakes release. This is when the North Sea was created. Churchward was not fluent or a believer in geology and that is to his detriment. He may have been right about early geology but it is by far the better source of knowledge compared to his legends.

On the other hand the Mayan and other legends of the composite deity Kukulcan - Quetzalcoatl - Veracocha - Xolotl etc. seems to point to a civilizing knowledge and astronomical input from Druids and certainly from white men. But I think this was long after the Mayans had their calendar. The Toltecs are Druids who left Europe when Rome put bounties and other things on their heads. The Roman statue found on the shores of Mexico that is a 99% archaeologic certainty probably comes from the Roman

Diverse Druids

attempt to pursue them and even to try to take American lands from them. The Prince of Palenque is such a white man and there are many sites with drawings of the white men. It has been negated or covered up by Catholic intrigue for far too long. The genocidal elimination of the Easter Islanders is part of this horrific history that the Pope called two millennia of "heinous acts". He has not apologized or offered anything about the many other things they have wrought. His apology is damage control for what is already proven. I like this Pope but I honor the Mayans his people burned and tortured - a lot more.

    This Prince of Palenque whose tomb held the equal of King Tut's treasure had a jade brooch of 'Zotz' hung large around his neck. This 'Zotz' is a god of the underworld and a vampire. The Rosicrucians like deVere are proud of their other great vampire - Vlad the Impaler who as Prince of Wallachia was a Catholic hero and Crusading Knight of the esteemed Order of the Dragon. (4) Which direction the knowledge flowed at different times is only of minor interest I suppose. The kind of knowledge is very important as is the fact that there was no civilizing race that had a right to colonize or subject heathens to their RULE and sword or other Plagues:

    "Although the first language on Earth is considered to be Sumerian, this enigmatic alphabet was irrefutably dated to at least 2,000 years older. A startling revelation that indicates that rather than ancient civilizations migrating from east to west, from Mesopotamia as previously believed, these peacefully co-existing societies migrated from old Europe to the Middle East. This also explained why the Mother Goddess worshipped by all ancient civilizations, including the Hopi who still revere her as the Snake Mother who came to earth to create mankind, is still recognized as AN or ANNA in Ireland and Scotland, whereas in the Middle East, the early northern semites had altered the female name of AN or ANU to that of a male 'god'. At the same time, Sumerologists have acknowledged a fact that has been largely suppressed, a distinctly female language existed in

Sumer. This language was used exclusively for sacred purposes.

Although numerous scholars have known about this sacred script, a phonetic language that contains approximately 17 letters of the English 'alphabet' (including the vowels - A, E, I, O, U), since it was first discovered in Transylvania it has virtually been ignored by traditional scholarship." (5)

This author is not what I call the best source for this knowledge but I like what she says. Richard Rudgely has covered her argument well in his book *Lost Civilizations of the Stone Age*. It is also possible she is talking about another script such as the one recently found in Turkmenistan. I think vowels were not part of most alphabets at first and that this is an offshoot of Gimbutas' language or Linear A. Thus you can see I think language and alphabets were around before the Ice Age as the lunar calendar work of Marshack does appreciate the possibility of - there is a great deal of change sifting through academia today. As to the 'snake', I think we can look to the Milky Way and see the Cosmic Serpent that Incans allowed to rule their lives. Analogies in myths that reflect symbols of star-gazers were around before the Queen of Sheba and her star-gazers with their green crystals I think are Green Vitreole. The serpent leading to the tomb of the Prince of Palenque and the one that appears on a certain day at Chichen Itza as the light moves it up the Pyramid are all part of an advanced science we yet do not fully understand.

RG is Irish for King and the RgVeda is from 4500 BC not 1500 per Westerners:

The Keltic kings were common consent appointees and the use of the word king as we know it today connotes something far different. The pre-Harappan culture of Ilvarta is now coming into a clearer view because of linguistic evidences but where it makes the most intriguing entry into this particular work on the Druids is through Rongorongo. This Easter Island script is the subject of debate where white

Diverse Druids

people were genocidally eliminated with the help of disease (a tried and true method we have examined from William of Rubruck to Churchill regarding the use of the Bubonic Plague) and slavery by Catholics from Peru once they were found by Roggeveen and before Cook arrived. Some say it isn't even an alphabet while others see a Phoenician connection to the Harappan script. Now there are Indian scholars who can translate the pre-Harappan. This is making the old Western academic justification for Aryan colonization and Empire a questionable factor that they are quite enraged about.

The Kelts did not have Primo Geniture or hereditary kings. They had a democratic equitable and egalitarian approach even into the Roman times as Aristotle's work on *Politics* does show. He was somewhat surprised to see the kings in Carthage were not kings as others thought of them and that Athens had no more democracy than Carthage.

We see the transit of Venus making Crete and New Grange kissing cousins or good reason. The Kelts kept in touch across long distances by various cultural means. They sent their children to be educated in a distant land in order to have a more aware and worldly society. There are scholars who say this spread the wealth but we always must remember there was thousands of years and many different approaches were taken in different places at different times. It was part of a Brotherhood thing that they may have had to intermingle because they were the smaller number of people wherever they went (certainly at first). They were taller and some of them stayed fairly gene pure judging from the mummies in the Tarim Basin and elsewhere. There are also mummies that show they intermingled that have the same techniques as other places. The Guanche of the Azores and the Peruvian people or the Tarim and Aleutian who are part of the Old Copper Route going back at least 9000 years. I have laid these facts together in another book which makes a compelling case for these assertions even without the genetic Haplogroup X evidence.

Robert Baird

In the Americas it is possible to see the last of this Phoenician Brotherhood with the influence of many millennia. There are some regions and reasons why certain peoples were locked into very ancient practices and beliefs so we get to see the progression of governance and ethics as the circumstances changed and the once highly prized copper was replaced by gold, then emeralds then a place to hide from Romans. Whole biolabs of culture are available to witness but there are often none of them left to tell us their story. The Beothuk were the origin of the epithet 'redskin' and the bounty on their tall heads (again up to 7' tall) with unique watercraft reminding us of NW Europe, and their last lady lived to almost see the 20th Century.

You can imagine the controversy in Canada about bounties on heads, and Farley Mowat is now being ridiculed for championing the Scottish people who came to Canada in the 8th Century AD. You would think the 'media spin doctors' and governments that once called him communist and wouldn't let him in to the US would have more respect for him after he won the day with the Norse data in his book *Westviking.* Another Canadian icon is Pierre Berton and he says it was a government backed program too. The mouthpieces of government even have to admit (by and large) that it was a travesty. Yet the story has not been fully told. They were ancient Copper Route maintenance staff going back to even before the St. Lawrence Route opened up. They were still happy with their Neolithic pay of ochre (thus the redskin) when beaver or gold was the European prize. Thule has much to offer the searcher after the horror of mankind and history.

There is one interesting burial of a 'giganti' in the Beothuk archaeological record. The bones of one tall person were disinterred and ochre was put on them. I suspect this was a man who led the people (Tuatha) and may even have been born in NW Europe. The ochre on his bones reminds me that the Mungo Man also had ochre on his bones from a period 60,000 years ago. I assure you the Druidic 'peryllats' (alchemists) knew the mercurious nature of cinnabar and

Diverse Druids

ochre. Do the archaeologists know about cinnabar which looks like ochre or some hematite? I see nowhere that they consider the alchemic importance of cinnabar but I will leave that interesting tidbit of 'possibility thinking' for another time. It would be nice to have genetic tracking tests done on this man who like most Keltic Gods and goddesses earned his Divinity as a mortal first. Even Hercules or Herakles is such a man that I think are the legendary De Danaan like Lugh and the Dagda.

Barry Fell is a great researcher who studied the pygmy skeletons in America and ties them in with SE Asian pygmies. Could the Mungo Man be the ancestor of these pygmies and will we ever get genetic testing on these thoroughly modern pre African strains of Homo sapiens sapiens? He also found Tiffinaugh or Ogham on Peterborough's petroglyphs but the government hanky panky recently allowed Norse ships and the like to be ground off the rocks. Fortunately they are well photographed and my nieces were surprised to hear their ancestral forefathers records are treated this way by 'politically correct' Indians and governments.

Churchward wrote about white men coming from Polynesia through Mayax to Europe and even though we now have genetics to give a lot more clarity Churchward may still have been on to something. I think the site off Cuba was administered by Crete when it was the key glacial period Keltic administrative center. But if it is also part of the Aztlan Copper Culture and what Churchward called Mayax it might even have been the most important of the four legendary Keltic centres including Findias that I think had been where the Black Sea is now. At these times the nobility was organized through six King/Bairds of the Druidic schooling just as was true with Isis and Osiris. But let us avoid the legends that many scholars can pooh-pooh with good reason. I learn a lot from them but I must admit they are not proof. Are maps of the whole world from 12,500 years ago proof of something or just a hoax?

Robert Baird

Mapping Philosophers Beyond Posidonius or Polybius (Columbus had their maps):

There is a map traced by Hadji Ahmed that he also inserted Ptolemy's map of the Mediterranean. This map shows the secrets outside the Mediterranean that the Phoenicians had known for 12,000 years (at least) before he traced this map that has been in academics hands for the last five centuries. The Bering Strait or land bridge is shown as it was in the 12,500 year ago period that modern geology and mapping didn't know until 1958. (6) The lines and dots of the Mayans and others were used as a code on a secret signature of Columbus as well. When Polybius (like Caesar) was taken from his Greek/Phoenician parents to be raised in high Roman families and write their version of the history to come he had access to the best available documentation and previous scholarship.

He also was a sea-farer who I believe went to South America. When the Romans or Greeks used the word Libya they meant all of Africa according to modern historians but I think a good case can be made for what the records actually say in the case of Solomon and Hiram of Tyre's (Phoenicians) expeditions. They say "the KNOWN world" (past Libya or Africa) and many records and scholars make it clear the world was known to be a sphere. The Flat Earth became a major part of Roman Catholicism and Cosmas Indicopleustas was rewarded with a Nestorian priesthood for his creative fiction. The Nestorians were in China as recent Byzantine coins found in the Chinese archaeological digs confirm. Seven centuries before Marco Polo China was within the sphere of influence of the Catholic masters, in Rome, Austro-Hungary or Constantinople/ Byzantium. It may be a stretch to say this but the Roman statue found in Mexico and many other things led me to believe the Romans were concerned about the Carthaginian/Phoenician American trade conglomerate.

Pseudo-Aristotle or a student from his school has left a written record saying the common people of Carthage were forbidden to go to the Americas in the 4th Century BC. So I

Diverse Druids

propose when we know Polybius was raised or lived with the family of Scipio Africanus that the Africa known as Libya also was the whole world in someone's knowledge bank. This *bank* of knowledge was a monopolistic hegemony we may never fully comprehend but I see a lot of corollaries with the Globalized corporate New World Order of the present. Unfortunately they are gifted circumventers and creators of Plausible Deniability so you are allowed to call me a conspiracy theorist. Thus I ask you to become part of a conspiracy - for if there is not a plan or conspiracy there should be one. We need transparency and access to information such as has been in the catacombs of the Vatican and is classified by alphabet soup people. Their multitudinous contingency plans have an ethic we should examine as the movie Three Days of the Condor does demonstrate. We need what Teilhard de Chardin has called for in order to make templates of a really New World Order - *a conspiracy of love*!

I hope that enough doubt exists in the readers mind at this juncture to question the accepted history that highlights supposed classical 'civilizations' over the 'barbarians' or 'Berberoi'. The Greeks certainly regarded the Romans as uninspired militarists who only copied and followed their own leadership. I deplore the scholars who regard Roman propaganda as the starting point for discussing the Celts or Druids. They are lazy imitators who cannot study the real culture and religious reality of a people who lived the words they worshipped. The Ussher time-line has infected us with prejudicial attitudes all too evident in the Hume to Gibbon letter and scholarship of their ilk. Even though it and the Bible Narrative(s) are passé, we still bear the brunt of this ethic entirely counter to the Keltic egalitarian modes that saw the great female leaders like Isis, Dido, Ariadne and Boadicaea or Boudicae from whom we now have the word bodacious. It isn't so easy to do what Dennis Miller (the comedian) recommends in his frequent phrase - 'eschew obfuscation'!

Robert Baird

Now we are going to delve into the work of Peter Berresford Ellis who wrote *The Druids* in 1994. He should have titled it A Study in the Roots of History and Historians as well. This quote deals with the origin of the Greek perception of an immortal soul that was central to their Druidic teachers and the Danaus or DNN and DN they were the descendants of (see Homer's Iliad).

Diogenes Laertius also cites the anonymous writer of the second century BC., whose work *Magicus* was wrongly ascribed to Aristotle. Kendrick has pointed out that such works, written long before the Romans conquered Gaul, showed that the Druids had a great reputation as philosophers outside the Celtic world and that this must have been a long established reputation.

The Pythagoreans link with the Druids has been romanticized by the claim that a Druid named Abaris traveled to Athens and discoursed with Pythagoras. An examination of the first reference to this in Strabo's work has been translated as:

"He came not clad in skins like a Scythian, but with a bow in his hand, a quiver hanging on his shoulders, a plaid wrapped about his body, a gilded belt encircling his loins, and trousers reaching down from the waist to the soles of his feet. He was easy in his address; agreeable in his conversation; active in his dispatch and secret in his

management of great affairs; quick in judging of present accuracies, and ready to take his part in any sudden emergency; provident withal in guarding against futility;

diligent in the quest of wisdom; fond of friendship; trusting very little to fortune, yet having the entire confidence of others, and trusted with everything for his prudence. He spoke Greek with a fluency that you would have thought that he had been bred up in the Lyceum, and conversed all his life with the academy of Athens."

Now Abaris is described as a Hyperborean. A Hyperborean, 'a dweller beyond the north wind', was a member of a fabulous people believed by the Greeks to exist in the inaccessible north. It was John Wood in 1747 who

Diverse Druids

stated 'the Britons and Hyperboreans were one and the same people...' His authority was, apparently Hecateus of Miletus who identified the Hyperboreans as dwelling in the British Isles." (7)

Hecateus is a credible contemporary source of this story. He goes to the point of saying Abaris was the man in charge of the training of Pythagoras who also had a Phoenician parent. The Druids called 'kapnobatai' in Thrace were an important part of the training Pythagoras received along with Sarmoung/Zoroaster and Therapeutae of Egyptian Pyramidal knowledge. I can surely understand how anyone would question the Abaris dean of education idea if they don't believe the other schools mentioned are Druidic based as well. The Orpheus Bardic schools of Hesiod and Homer are part of this same outpouring of certain specialties that came from the Keltic Druids but you will (hopefully) require more proof of that statement. In the case of Hesiod it was a very watered down and almost solely theatrical understanding and his women hating was evident. In the situation with Pythagoras some like to attribute these contemporary ideals to him but he had many female members of his group in Croton and did believe they deserve an education. I have reason to respect Plutarch as well and he had a map he did showing Iceland as Ogygia which is the name given to Kelts meaning 'ancient ones'.

Roman Repression

Professor Jean Markle, in his *La Femme Celte* (1972) makes the following argument as to why the Romans attempted to suppress the Druids

"When Rome spread its empire over the whole Mediterranean and into part of Western Europe, care was taken to eliminate anything that might harm its socio-political organization. This is very evident in Celtic countries: the Romans pursued the Druids until they disappeared into Gaul and later into Britain. The Druids represented an absolute threat to the Roman State, because their science and philosophy dangerously contradicted

Roman orthodoxy. The Romans were materialistic, (and we are their progeny as the present is described - "Global Reifying Thrust of Materialism" (8)) the Druids spiritual. For the Romans the State was a monolithic structure spread over territories deliberately organized into a hierarchy. With the Druids it was a freely consented moral order with an entirely mythical central idea. The Romans based their law on private ownership of land, with property rights entirely vested in the head of the family, whereas the Druids always considered ownership collective. The Romans looked upon women as bearers of children and objects of pleasure, while the Druids included women in their political and religious life. We can thus understand how seriously the subversive thought of the Celts threatened the Roman order, even though it was never openly expressed. The talent of the Romans in ridding themselves of the Gallic and British elites is always considered astonishing, but this leaves out of account the fact that it was a matter of life or death to Roman society."

Pliny the Elder (AD 23/24-79) seems to be the first to raise questions about the reasons for the decline of the Druids and certainly has no hesitation in attributing it to Roman repression. Yet one cannot really take seriously the claim that this was done because of Roman outrage against a religion they associated with human sacrifice (Just as Nero called the Christians cannibals, for reasons I have dealt with elsewhere.) when Rome itself was so used to mass sacrifices. Eminent men from the nations that Rome conquered were dragged through the streets, chained to the chariots of her victorious generals (in imitation of Ajax in the Trojan Epic), and ritually strangled in the Tullianum at the foot of the Capitol to propitiate Mars, the Roman god of war. Vercingetorix, the famous leader of Celtic resistance to Caesar in Gaul, met his end here. (After he and his family were tortured in a dungeon for six years in order to get others in his position to come calling or heed the Roman 'better way'.) It can hardly be believed that the Romans, especially during the reigns of such emperors as Caligula

Diverse Druids

and Nero, could be shocked by human sacrifice. It is only the Romans, of course, who would have us believe in their sensitivity to human sacrifice. The curious fact is that no Insular Celtic Literature, nor traditions, provides evidence for the practice of human sacrifice as a religious rite.

When Augustus excluded the Druids from Roman citizenship by forbidding Roman citizens to practice Druidical rites, when Tiberius banned the Druids by a decree of the Roman Senate and when Claudius attempted to 'wholly abolish' them in 54 AD, it was not, I believe, in disapproval of 'inhuman rites' practiced by the Druids, but to wipe out an intellectual class who could, and did, organize national revolt against Rome. (Even from within as we see Rome was colonized by the Bruttii in the study of the Battle of Alalia and the Sibylls their leaders consulted were Dryads or Druid women which show up in the Bible as well.)

Further, my argument is that the Druids were not entirely suppressed in the Celtic lands under Roman rule as is commonly thought. Nor would I accept Nora Chadwick's contention that they perished by slow strangulation from the superimposition 'of a higher culture on a lower'. (Such propaganda is the same garbage behind Manifest Destiny.) Mrs. Chadwick, for example claims that when the inhabitants of the chief town of Aedui in Gaul, that is Bibracte (Mont-Beuvray), were transferred to the new Roman town of Augustodunum (Autun), and their oral Druidical school was replaced by a Romanized university, the Druids were driven into the backwoods where they eventually perished. On the contrary, I believe that the Druids remained and adapted to the new culture.

The great Gaulish intellectual Decimus Magnus Ausonius (c.AD 310 - c. 393) provides us with some fascinating evidence in this respect. He was the son of a physician of Burdigala (Bordeaux) where he taught for thirty years before being appointed as tutor to Gratian, son of Emperor Valentinian I. When Gratian succeeded as emperor, Ausonius became prefect of Gaul and finally consul in Ad 379. He was nominally Christian, but without any deeply committed feeling. He wrote one discourse on the properties of the number 'three', so closely associated with Druidic teachings... Ausonius came from an educated Celtic family which would have been of the Druidic caste before Roman proscription.

Ausonius himself admits that his contemporary Delphinius, famous for his eloquence, and a likely teacher of his, also descended from a Druidic family. Delphinius' father was Attius Patera, a famous rhetorician, whose own father, Phoebicius, had been an 'aedituus' or 'temple guardian' of the Celtic god Belinus at Bordeaux until he had been persuaded to become a teacher in the local Latin university." (9)

There is so much to cover from this one excellent piece of research. I hesitate to disagree because as it stands there is much to recommend about it. However, I disagree with the use of the word 'caste' which Ellis buys into in the Aryan derivation of things. This is as I have pointed out, part of the academic ego appeal to Euro-Centrism. He goes on to equate the Druids with Brahmins but I hope we can see the Brahmin lack of egalitarian ethic is counter to Druidism. It is true that Druids were connected to all religions and political forms of societal development but we will see Mt. Maru and Tarim Basin origins for the Eastern religions that are honest enough not to claim they were the originators of these things too. The Triune nature of man and the number three of the Triads are definitely important enough to devote at least one book to them. You will have to see the truth of the Trinity in them for yourself however, because there is more important business to prove or elucidate. Christian dogma is not original at all; and the point has been well covered by many scholars. We, of course, have to deal with many of these things because of the pre-eminent role Rome has continued to play in our lives.

His use of the phrase 'freely consented moral order and 'collective' are the essence of egalitarianism or ecumenicism. Some scholars devote their time to saying Druids are a priesthood but they led through science and

Diverse Druids

understanding or actually demonstrating the things we call magic today. It was up to lesser folk in later times to get into the myths of priesthoods or religion. The 'vascerri' were one title I have found for that area of work. I am not saying that Druids weren't aware of the uses and potentials of theocracy but I think they eschewed it as a dangerous medium for developing good behavior among their own peoples. It would be surprising if they didn't actively take part in the rituals of their culture as relate to priesthoods but the best way of demonstrating the difference can be seen when Minoan culture around the time of Ariadne on Crete started putting these rituals inside buildings. It co-incided with a boom in the building of fortresses as well.

The Mediterranean is the area where they had colonized before the glaciers of the last Ice Age but they were not able to keep the misogyny and base human urges of men in check. This is evident from the way priestly proselytes made YHWH into an all male deity or the prostitution that was made mandatory by priesthoods for all women in Mesopotamia. I think the establishment of certain areas such as the Etruscans and Sybarites made in their Italian home were elite cadres of Keltic people after the Worldwide War that took place over corporate empires like drugs and with the male issue-oriented backdrop figuring heavily in it as well. The Genoese and other Kelts had settled the area a millennia before that if not even sooner. But academics like to say there is no certainty about this cell diffusion theory. The facts may not be as good as they would like but it appears this is the only explanation that fits what facts are known. One of the facts that must be integrated are the over 5500 'nuraghi' on Sardinia. Jacquetta Hawkes describes them as medieval yet they were built in 1800 BC and added to at key dates in the increasingly warlike world. What are medieval castles doing off the coast of Rome and on the Phocaean way to Marseilles (Massalia)? Surely this wasn't a prison colony to send children who misbehaved like we do today. Can you say pharmaceuticals? Genetics? What was so

85

all fired important? Could it have been the collective bank of the Phoenician Brotherhood or all of these things?

Ellis says Ausonius was only a nominal Christian which makes sense until one considers he may have been a true Christian - not a Romanized or Pauline one. The Source of the learning that Jesus and his family were always into, since the time of Solomon or Miriam before that, is what one would have to understand in order to see Ausonius as a true Christian. And this is where my search got more obsessive and interesting. It was through MacDari's initiation to the linguistic roots of Irish Masonry that I learned about Iesa. Iesa was a concept including the Brotherhood of Man that the Great Pyramid was built to honor. Iesa became Zeus in one language and Jesus in another; Yeshua ben Joseph may never have accepted the Messianic role and the moniker Jesus despite how the Gospels portray him. One must study to see how Rome wrote these documents to blame Jews for 'Killing our Saviour'! Maccoby and Silver have written good books on the matter but Bloom in the Gospel of Thomas goes to the real Jesus and Source, I think. This Gaedhilic Gnosticism or Samaritanism was not as much magic as science.

Rome was excellently structured in its ability to win without even shedding their own blood. As their Empire grew it was ever easier to convince the potential new colony or its elite that they would be better off within the Empire. The Parthians remained apart from this by managing a significant union of their own. The Pharisees were well respected throughout both of these empires and they supported the rights of the indigent and underprivileged despite what people today say on their pulpits while asking us to part with money for their cause (or wallet). I believe the Pharisees including those we now know were at Qumran with the brother of Jesus as their 'Righteous' leader James, are Keltic/Phoenician traders and merchants like the Benjaminite Joseph of Arimathaea. Their rabbinical leaders are much like the 'vascerri' of lesser Druidic learning and some may even say they are almost of the Druidic level of learning. But there is another element of Judaism that more spiritual energy is ensconced within - the Hassidim and Sephardic Jews who's Kabbalah is part and parcel of the ancient Verbal Tradition. If you put the Pharisees and the Hassidim together you get the knowledge of a Druid. The Verbal Tradition is the Bardic Tradition. It goes by other names in many places as the 'speakers' and musicians or dancers weave their way along shamanic paths so ancient as to make one think it started long before Homo Sapiens.

Jesus was a person of wealth and stature as we know he came from a royal heritage. He must have traveled to nearby Egypt and some suggest he had the benefit of the same teacher who taught Cleopatra. She is an alchemist with extant treatises in her name. One of these treatises deals with cosmetics and was probably a re-writing of an earlier Keltic book she found in the Great Library at Alexandria. It is most unlikely to imagine Jesus did not visit this library that the Gnostics maintained. These Gaedhilic remnants of the people who built the Pyramid and who did not leave with Moses/Akhenaton include Simon Magus and a school many Kelts sent their children to throughout many millennia. This line of reasoning was obvious to the Romans and they needed to diminish Jesus and his family in order to increase the power and image of their administrative allies. Herod, Paul (a Roman claiming Pharisaic background that is false) and his Sadducee bosses were the benefactors of the Roman Gospels that show Jesus and Joseph as carpenters or shepherds. The Septuagint written in Alexandria and in Greek, paints the truer story when it identifies them as 'archtectons' from which we get the word architect.

Arch is the word or prefix that goes along with being the 'high' Druid just as St. Columba was at the Synod of Drumceatt when he saved bards from further degradation. Ellis is on the right track when he says the Druids were assimilated into the culture Rome created. Unfortunately he may be far closer to the truth than any earlier Druid could imagine. The details of this hegemony are becoming clearer to me and other researchers into the things Rome and

Catholics have done. But are those who sold their soul to this One World Order what we can call Druids. Clearly St. Columba and others had Druidic training as we see him using the natural forces of wind and rain in a battle with a Druid in Scotland. But that is not enough for me to say the Druids made their bargain and became this New World Order of Empire and Globalization. I think the court is still out on whether those who went to America and other places are the real Druids or these myth-makers who stayed behind.

In the present day we have former Papal advisers like Malachi Martin to thank for some truly incredible insights to what is and has been going on inside the world's most powerful global entity of the last two millennia. His book *Windswept House* contains things a friend of mine confirms that his fellow schoolmate and adviser to the Pope has told him. The Pope is not a Catholic and I can suggest the Jesuit Alumbrados never were. They brought Aquinas and alchemy to the world. But what does a professor at the Vatican's Pontifical Biblical Institute or the Father of Biblical Archaeology (W. F. Albright) know that the faithful flocks are not privy to? Certainly the Cathars would have been a better choice to institute the humanistic hermetic or alchemic goals. They were believers in honest education and the 'living love' of Jesus. They had female priests or 'parfaits' and 'perfecti' that people saw were better than their own corrupt priests who sold them for ransom in the sanctuary they thought the church was supposed to be as told in the writings of Gregory of Tours. The more things change the more they stay the same.

The Kelts resisted these changes that saw their mothers and sisters become chattel and those that stayed in places like Poland or the Baltic states didn't fall totally under the Teutonic sword of the Crusading Catholics but made a deal that saw them keep a lot of the old ways. Those who opted for real freedom went to Easter Island after South America and other places throughout the world including Santa Catalina off the coast near Los Angeles. I think Jesus would 'roll over in his grave' if he knew what has been done in his

Diverse Druids

name. In a book called *The Kelts: Children of the Don* I dealt more specifically with the details of the Polish Queen who got together with a Lithuanian King who had beaten the Teutonic Knights. These Knights are one of the many Christian military orders like the Templars and Dracula's Dragons who figure heavily in other books and articles I have written about the Masonic 'octopus'.

The Slavs or Balts and other people who stayed in touch with the Old Europe of the Danube and Don returned to lands they had lived before the last Ice Age caused them to move. People are adventuresome and well traveled to say the least and to imagine otherwise is quite naïve. The archaeologists bring us 23,000 year old settlements near Moscow that show straightened mammoth tusks for homes and spears. The archaeologists can't say how they straightened the tusks and I guess they never cooked carp. This culture may have already become Patristic or male dominated and I think they are the Uighurs but they could also be Kelts who intermingled and were ostracized for being patristic. Ostracism was the primary social jurisprudence punishment of the Druids.

Perkunas is the name given to the main Romuva or Baltic/Keltic god. It is the same deity as Cernunnos or other similar gods and names that represent certain natural forces in other lands and colonies. Perkunas studies and communes with the oak trees. Mr. Ellis goes outside of normal Druidic scholarship and questions whether the Druids had an affinity with the oak. Perhaps he does this to fit his theory about Indian Brahmin origin. It may well be that the rowan was its equal but in the present day most Druidic (albeit a mere shadow of real Druids) people are convinced the oak is their primary tree. The Battle of the Trees led to a healing alphabet within Ogham's 64 or more tracts. The debate is not worth making a big issue about and we all are challenged to find what real Druids did or believed. I think one must read a great deal and have some experience or they can easily come to false conclusions and I am still changing my opinions as new facts become available. The Tarim Basin and genetics has taken me away from the Emerald Isles as the seat of pre-eminence and now I find Gimbutas even more valid. Here is some of what Pliny says about the Druids:

"The Druids—for so they call their 'magi'—hold nothing more sacred than the mistletoe and the tree on which it grows provided that it is an oak. They choose the oak to form groves, and they do not perform any religious rites without its foliage, so that it can be seen that the 'Druides' are so called from the Greek word (The Phoenicians or Kelts gave the Greeks their alphabet and the Greeks called them 'ogygia' which means 'ancient ones').

Anything growing on those trees they regard as sent from heaven and a sign that this tree has been chosen by the gods themselves. Mistletoe is, however, very rarely found, and when found, it is gathered with great ceremony and especially on the sixth day of the moon. They prepare a ritual sacrifice and feast under the tree, and lead up two white bulls whose horns are bound for the first time on this occasion. A priest attired in a white vestment ascends the tree and with a golden pruning hook cuts the mistletoe which is caught in the white cloth. Then they sacrifice the victims praying that the gods will make their gifts propitious to those to whom they have given it. They believe that if given in drink the mistletoe will give fecundity to any barren animal, and that it is predominant against all poisons."

Today we look askance at such worship of trees or the idea that they have wisdom. However, science has just found two most interesting things about trees. Hardwood trees that have their leaves burst out with color in the fall have been thought to do so as the frost kills them but it is not the case. Recent research points to annual insect arrivals and the trees are saying something to the insects. 'Don't come here, we are strong vibrant and able to defend ourselves', is one way of putting it. There is a pine tree that eats insects through its sap or tar and the roots; this too has just been proven. Shamans or Druids have been able to communicate with trees for as long as man has eaten plants (6 or 9 Million years of hominids). That in itself is beyond the conception of

Diverse Druids

most wooden-headed intellectuals since 'sins and demons' became the Dark Ages central ideology. I have been involved in affecting the wind and rain so I do not doubt the St. Columba story but I can understand how incredible these things of nature can be to those who will never witness or see such things.

The discipline of the Christian Monastic Orders like Iona in early Christian times was far more in keeping with Druidism than what happened in the couple of centuries after the Synod of Whitby in the 7th century after England or Britain decided to go along with the Roman plan and seize the assets of the Celtic Church. Many early Christian saints are closer to Druids than most who call themselves Druids today. Ellis doesn't go far enough in explaining how influential Ausonius and others like him were in the early Christian church before Churchianity became a hellish and terrifying thing for most people. Even the Venerable Bede admits Celtic Christianity had the higher moral discipline.

One great act of compassion they achieved was unfortunately not made universal. If the Celtic Church had succeeded I believe there would be a far better world a long time before now; and yet I still think these people who chose to work from within sold out to Rome. The Monastic Order of Iona had their own island named after them or the place in Ireland they came from. This island is near Greece and they were still there after the Moslems took Jerusalem. In 697 AD, Adomnán the Abbott of the Iona in the Emerald Isles brought forward the LAW OF THE INNOCENTS to protect women, children and the elderly in times of war. The only places that paid any attention to it were in Ireland and Scotland. I must be a Cynic like Jesus as described in Crossan's *The Historical Jesus*.

There is much about the martyrs who often fought against the very church who later chose to honor them or put words in their mouths, which I like. Francis of Assisi is one such man and here is a little of his story. "It is really only with the emergence of the Mendicant (literally 'begging') orders in the thirteenth/seventh century, therefore, that we encounter

Robert Baird

Christians undertaking missions to Muslims, using 'mission' in the sense in which the word was used in the early Christian centuries and has become generally understood in more recent centuries. (Biblio: B. Z. Kedar, 'Crusade and Mission: European Approaches toward the Muslims; Princeton University Press, 1984).

The key figure in the transition to this new approach was Francis of Assisi (1182/578 - 1226/623). The son of a wealthy textile merchant, during a pilgrimage to Rome in 1205/601 he had a vision in which he was commissioned to rebuild a church near Assisi. In order to do this he sold his own goods and also some of his father's, for which he was disowned by his father, but Francis persisted in his task, and in 1209/605 he established the Franciscan Order, vowed to poverty, preaching and caring for the poor. Francis was not only concerned for his homeland, however; he was also concerned for the Muslim world, but his approach was to be very different from that of his crusading contemporaries. Attempts to get to Syria in 1212/609 and Morocco in 1214/611 were frustrated by the weather and by illness respectively, but the third attempt, in 1219/616, succeeded. Francis and some twelve companions sailed to Acre and then on to Damietta in Egypt, which was at that time being besieged by the army of the Fifth Crusade.

Francis' encounter with the realities of a crusading army, however seems to have been something of a shock: instead of heroes imbued with Christian virtue and dedicated to the service of God under the sign of the cross, he found adventurers and fugitives, whose whole approach was a rather mercenary one." (10)

Another monastic who held great honor in even earlier times was Pelagius. He might have made this group of Churchians (they are not followers of the teaching of Christ) become something akin to the Druids: if he and his fellow wise men had been able to stem the tide-force of Greed. He was taken to trial by Augustine on three separate occasions and Augustine is a major deviate (11). Fortunately Pelagius won

and we do have his writings on Free Will to remember him through. Here is what Mr. Ellis writes about this matter:
"Pelagius went to Rome in about AD 380. He was distressed by the laxity of moral standards which he found among the Christians there and blamed it squarely on the doctrine expounded in the writings of Augustine of Hippo, which maintained that everything was pre-ordained and that Man was polluted and sinful because he took on the original sin of Adam. Further, God had already ordained this therefore Man had no free will in the matter. Pelagius believed that both men and women could take the initial and fundamental step towards their salvation, using their own efforts and not accepting things as preordained. Pelagius believed that Augustine's theories imperiled the entire moral law. If men and women were not responsible for their own good and evil deeds, there was nothing to restrain them from an indulgence in sin on the basis that it was preordained anyway. In Pelagius' earliest known writing, about 405 AD, one philosophy became clear: 'If I ought, I can.'"(12)

It is easy to see the appeal of such a religion. It appeals to everyone who wants to do what they want to do. It didn't appeal that much to those who were what Augustine called "the harbingers of the original sin" - WOMEN! But that just made it better for the men who thought they could more easily dominate women and believed this somehow was good for them. The church was wise in the ways of marketing and was not interested in sharing the wealth and power with the ordinary people of Italy or those they had bargained with and made into Roman citizens. Yes, the Church leaders like Constantine were not Christians they usurped it! They were the Roman Caesars and the like who saw a way to grow larger and keep more of the proceeds.

Gibbon says the Roman Empire ended in 1483 with the fall of Byzantium or Constantinople but I don't think it ever ended. It just made new arrangements with people like the British nobles who had been Roman citizens as Joy Chant explains in *The High Kings*. The fall of the intrigue that was Byzantine actually served to increase the power of those who are truly in high places and the Borgia/De Medici or Alumbrados are part of this incestuous and ever-growing 'octopus'. The Treaty of Tordesillas that was dictated by Rodrigo Borgia (Pope Alex VI) after Columbus returned from his mission with his secret reports and journals should be required reading for all school kids. He split the whole world into two camps or vassal states that he had control over. In the case of Isabella and Ferdinand he had the Papal Bull that exposed the fact that they were incestuously related that had been in his possession from before he became Pope in the year Columbus went on the Vatican arranged mission. This nefarious Treaty states their goal of spreading the Inquisition throughout the world:

"In practical terms all this meant Clovis's (Clovis was a Merovingian King of the Franks.) domains had lost such discipline and unity as he imposed. The Church, generally on a subtler level than others, joined in the prevalent ethic of murder, robbery and sexual excesses. Gregory of Tours, a conscientious chronicler of the period, painted a sorry picture of the strife and unity that were spread wide. (12) In his pages, cathedrals and churches lose their value as sanctuary when churchmen connive, for money, at the slaughter of fugitives within. Bishops side with kings and princes in their squabbles, change sides, change back, and grow fat on the commission. A year after Columbanus arrived the bishopric of Paris was bought openly by a Syrian merchant, Eusebius, who looked upon the cloth as a step up from commerce." (14)

Today the issue of celibacy is debated and the church says the reason it was instituted in the 11th Century is because priests were able to own property and pass it on to their children. Interesting! What happened to the emphasis on spiritual commitment and avoiding the temptations of the flesh? Now they say it was just another money grab and in this they are probably right. Celibacy in the Celtic Church was a real spiritual giving or 'sacrifice' of the Mass. 'Mass' is Irish for 'buttocks' and there are many who sit upon their massive butts in pews and pedestals who have all the spirituality of another kind of ass - Jack! Pardon the purple humor or vain attempt at it, please.

CHAPTER FOUR:
Ogham and the origins of communication:

The majority of Linguists today believe there is *one* major root for *all* languages. This certainly supports the idea of world travel from the earliest of times in my humble opinion. Surely some would have crossed the desert sands to bring new women into their world whether it was the Sahara, Gobi or Taklamakand Desert. If we were to believe man only grew cultured enough to be interested in sexual variations in the last four thousand years we would be guilty of stupidity in the highest degree. But if one thinks long and hard that is what people are taught when we hear Columbus discovered America or Marco Polo opened a route to China. The facts are found throughout the world and archaeology is more reliable than Bishop Ussher or Cosmas Indicopleustas as far as I am concerned. If it wasn't sex or drugs it would have been adventure and inquisitiveness that drove any hominid over the mountain range beyond the present valley. Just how Kennewick Man got to America is of much interest because the Bering land bridge was not there 9400 years ago. The destruction of the underpinning of the Flat Earth Theory is central to my premise that a worldwide diffusion of religious ideologies took place through the 'Messengers' from places like the Tarim Basin in the 6th Century BC:

"The public was outraged and drew cartoons of Darwin with an orangutan's body. People were angry that Darwin had opposed the old idea that God had created humans with a pre-set special capacity to receive and invent language. Darwin's theory implied, instead, that human capacity for language had evolved when humans had." (1)

Locke's Tabula Rasa would almost have suggested Ussher's Time Line was correct and it all fed into the Scale of Nature that prejudicially allowed Europeans to dispossess the 'lesser' and sometimes even unsoulful hominids. People of certain religions in the West are inculcated with their superiority through Machiavellian appeals "to base human urges" in a Neo-Platonic and Hegelian managed manner. They love to think they are some kind of ascended being on some tree or chain that allows them to look down on others. Now that we know man was not an australopod 3.5 million or 6 million years ago and that evolution has no Tree - the field is open. The real 'experts' including the discoverer of Lucy don't make 'trees' anymore. The possibility of great civilizations that were technologically advanced gains evidence and proof beyond the Puranas every day. This time around we may not survive!

Paget was an English scientist who theorized that the earliest humans used their hands and mouth to communicate silently. Then they added sounds to go along with the hand movements. I say they didn't just move their hands and mouth because of my many years in sales and through reading books about body language. The communication between parent and chills is similarly rife with all kinds of clues, intuitions, eyes and smiles, Paget's theory became known as the 'ta-ta theory' and that is probably because people knew children communicated in this way. Intuition may actually have been more effective as a means of sharing then. For me it is hard to imagine it wasn't and Plato observed a similar loss of clarity in communication occurred when writing took the predominant role in our communications and thus availed sloppier and less disciplined communication.

Today Steven Covey talks about empathic listening and that is the essence of great communication. The Druids were averse to writing things for these reasons and because weak minded people might succumb to temptation and misuse knowledge written but not properly taught by someone who knew when the ethics of the receiver or their understanding warranted the reception of the knowledge. Knowledge is power, and I must admit certain people like to keep it to themselves but I see little evidence of this ethic in the Keltic/Druidic educational system. Freedom comes best when people know what they are free to do, feel and share.

Diverse Druids

Freedom and the lack of Fear among their people was the paramount desire of Druidic teaching.

Locke's 'tabula rasa' honed in even more on the five physical senses and made thought the key ingredient in what separates us from animals. He was a smart man in the general scheme of post 'Dark Ages' Western denial of common sense. But didn't he have a dog or observe a friend having to avoid saying 'walk' in front of his dog. Other 'experts' like Herder were catering to the convention that showed its ugly face in the Scale of Nature or the Great Chain of Being idea. These prejudicial and racist ego driven ideologies still have emotional and intellectual proponents in academia of the 21st century. One can easily see Bishop Ussher and his 4004 BC (down to the specific minute of a day in October) origin of man in much of the mush that passes for scholarship when current authors quote earlier authors writing about Ogham:

"People often like to hang on to their old, comfortable beliefs. The sports fan believes his team is best long after the winning streak has passed. Those who believe life exists only on planet earth scoff at UFO reports. It is not surprising that many people ignored or resisted new scientific findings in the early 1900s when the findings challenged old, common beliefs.

Several discoveries affected the way new scholars studied the mystery. First, geologists had discovered that the earth was much older than anyone had previously thought. Second, Charles Darwin found evidence that all species, including humans, had changed and developed slowly over billions of years. Third archaeologists found fossils and were able to establish stages of human development. Fourth, a linguist and a doctor studied the human voice mechanism and spelled out how it makes phonetic sounds. Fifth, many scientists did research on the way the brain works, showing how it makes thought and speech possible." (2)

With the recent MRI mapping and SPECT data that Harvard and others have done we now can prove the Yogis and other Eastern meditators do achieve a 'oneness'. They

Robert Baird

have been explaining these things for thousands of years but the smart people in power didn't want you to know about it and often were studying the techniques of Tantra for their own pleasure. If Mr. Ellis had compared the Druids to the 'gymnosophist' yogis I would have to agree, but the question of which came first is clearly in favor of Druids when one acknowledges this reality. I am not saying Ellis is one of the academic Aryans we have developed earlier, but I do think he panders to that demographic. It should be clear that the linguist above is a far fairer source with few major biases to overcome. The 'oneness' 'collective unconscious' and other spiritual realities of the Druids is the most compelling reason for why we should know what their technology such as the Lost Chord was comprised of.

When we consider the world of academia in relation to the Druids we must allow for the bias of the anti-parapsychology 'police' as well as the 'Clovis cops'. The whole reductivist or Kuhnsian gradualistic paradigm is counter to what the Druids knew. Perhaps the same battle lines were drawn between intellect and ego in their time too. It is easy to imagine how Steve Fuller prefers anarchy over Kuhn's reliable model that forgets how often science is dead wrong while risk takers push the envelope. Those who win the Nobel Prize always seem most interesting and I love the article from August 1980 in Psychology Today called *Rediscovering the Mind* by a Yale microbiology Professor Harold J. Morowitz. It details how the ancients knew much more than most people imagine.

Clarice Swisher talks about Neanderthal as a human from 100,000 years ago that disappeared about 40,000 years ago with the arrival of Cro-Magnon. The discovery of the Portuguese cross bred baby Neanderthal from 24,000 years ago and other recent finds make the debate hot and heated between those who want us to be different and better and those who observe the reality, as I see it. It wouldn't surprise me if Neanderthals still walk the face of remote regions of this planet. In some way the pejorative use of the word Neanderthal applies to all academics who seek to prove

Diverse Druids

theories rather than observe facts. Clarice is not one of them when she notes "cave man as a grunting brute who mistrusted females" was how flawed academics (based on little evidence and a skeletal assembly that hunched and skewed reality) was accepted as true. But when she made the comment 'experiments to teach chimpanzees to talk in words have largely failed" I wonder why she needs to have others talk as we do. Kansai in the Yerkes Primate Center research can equal a seven year old human and understands grammar and words up to the use of 2000 different words (Koko, elephants, and porpoises). Do we speak porpoise? What is the purpose of their extra four channels of communication? In this quote we see the origin of the vowelless sacerdotal alphabet. Ogham and its derivatives like Sanskrit and Hebrew were all vowelless according to my linguistic mentors and research.

Origins of Ogham:

"According to Diamond, the first speech sounds were consonants and the 'a' vowel, the sounds easiest to make. Vowels are harder to form than consonants, except for the 'a' which can be made without moving the tongue or mouth. Generally, there are three categories of consonants: 'nasals, n, m, and ng,' which are made in the nasal passage; 'plosives, p, b, t, d, k, g ('c' and 'g' are often interchangeable in alphabets derived from Ogham)' which are made with a burst of air out of the mouth; and 'fricatives, f, v, th, s, z, sh, zh,' which require more control in the throat. There are a few additional consonants, the 'l, r, j, and w,' which are made low in the throat." (3)

We all know about 'l' and 'r' with Asiatic peoples who eat lice (not 'r'-ice) and there is Spanish with the Hey-soos thing for 'j' and the aspirant 'h'. In the detailed three lines of one of the Ogham tracts included herein we see the fingers were part of the origin and that in itself suggests to me that it was a very early language. The knuckles are also part of some of the original Ogham and in this matter I think there is a connection with the 'quipas' in Peru. When I see it being said that the early people of the area could keep poems on these ropes most scholars think are tally systems I am almost certain of it. In short, Diamond is pretty correct about the likely origins of language and it probably happened before art. We can use our hands and mouth to sign languages before we take to pictographs and other methods of counting and notation. Yet most historians are pretty fixed on rather eccentric cuneiform and the like. Again we see a physiological or biological and other discipline from outside history has made some sensible contribution to the development of man's culture that makes one wonder about history writers.

The 'futhark' is derived from the pregnant female body. Marija Gimbutas did the groundwork for much of the things that rest at the root of what you will read in this book. The genetic Haplogroup X marker research is the easy way of seeing where the white people come from in her pre Black Sea region of the Don and Danube near the Caucasus Mountains and what later became Casiberia or one of the Iberias that roved and traded throughout the world. Her book 'Language of the Goddess' was a godsend for me, in terms of understanding how alphabets develop. It is even possible she would see the figurine found at Berekhat Ram is another goddess figure. This early sculpture may be as much as 400,000 years old and is at least 200,000 years old. Joseph Campbell who did the foreword to her book would love to have seen all the things that have happened since the both died. Sometimes the symbol is called a 'fupark' and it rivals the Swastika as a symbol of Aryan stupidity and cupidity.

I see a connection of 'th' symbols in many early alphabets with what is called the Mark of Qayin which is the coded origin and meaning behind the Bible's Cain character. To what extent one can meditate and connect to other realms through symbols and the geometric lattices of harmonic energy is an area of research that man is just recently making some great strides in, but the ancients knew a great deal we have yet to understand. I believe the Qabalistic mystery schools started with this symbol and the butterfly, bull, bee

Diverse Druids

connection demonstrated by Gimbutas. Druids and shamans from 30,000 years ago already had a wealth of homeopathic and spiritual knowledge.

It is unlikely we will ever find archaeological proof or books to prove that Druids or what they derived from were around when Isis founded Egypt in the 36,000 year ago era, that Manetho writes about as he panders to Ptolemy. Other legends do support these theories but history has a bias against these early dates in the Western world. The Hindu Puranas and historians are quite the opposite as they speak of millions of years. I say man has been culturally advanced for a million years and use the archaeologic record from data such as Flores Island supplies but it would not surprise me if it was far older than that. It becomes exceedingly difficult for many artifacts to survive this long. However, anyone who has read *The Hidden History of the Human Race* by Cremo and Thompson will probably have an open mind about humans being around for a great deal longer than we think. There are so many possibilities that I cannot cover them all in one book, as I often say. I would love to know more about the Table of Destiny or Ha Qabala and be able to understand mathematics enough to see how true it is that much of Chaos Science or other esoteric doctrine resides in this early document that was verbally handed down from who knows how long ago.

In 1991 the Mayan language being proven as a pictographic PLUS phonetic language (as even Bishop Landa had written that the Mayans told him) adds much to our speculations about this culture and what kind of knowledge they had. Their calendar begins in the 35th Century BC if not before. Many people including archaeologists I met when I lived in Belize and Mexico agree the Mayans came from Asia and may have been in Peru first but were already in Central America around 5000 years before the date of the recording in this calendar that also prophesizes the future. The archaeologists tell us they had the wheel before anyone else but only used it on toys. The Mayans had many nature-provided technological

Robert Baird

advantages as well as science of their own but I think they were part of the Phoenician Brotherhood and much of the knowledge was due to sharing with others. There is no definitive proof I can provide and you will have to make up your own mind. In other books I have dealt in greater detail with all the evidence for cross oceanic pollination and in that I am certain the proof is all that is necessary. But to prove the extent of knowledge that Druids like Kukulcan/Quetzalcoatl/Veracocha/Xolotl amalgam personas brought to the Americas is probably only going to be considered speculation by most readers at this point.

    I assure you it is not my intent to minimize the native Central Americans or say it is white man who did all the teaching. When we get to Buddhist belief systems integrating into Mayan culture from Barabudur and probably occurring around the same time the mathematical concept of zero went from Mayans to those on the sub-continent things become very interesting. The academics credit the Mayans with this all important concept leading to the decimals and algebra. But it may have originated in any number of research centers that we will explore in the remainder of this book. Certainly the lenses of the Olmecs at La Venta are easy to make and/or find near the wondrous pure quartz lava flows of the area. Almost all people know the Olmecs include black people from Africa and it is obvious from the huge heads that the Spaniards were unable to destroy just as they couldn't destroy the large Pyramids. Paper of greater quality than papyrus comes easily from a tree. Rubber originated here and they even had childproof drug containers. How anyone who knows their civic centers and the fact they are built in a grid system connected to the earth energy can think the Mayans were not very advanced people is beyond me.

    The Basque speaking people found in a Central American enclave and the grammatical syntax connecting the Maya, Vietnamese, Basque and Denhe (NW American Indians) that most linguists accept are joined by the Russian linguists Heyerdahl addresses in a connection to Rongorongo of the

Diverse Druids

Easter Island and the pre-Harappan of the Indus. In this month's (April 2002) Archaeology Magazine there is an underwater Indus site dating to the 8th Century BC that is laid out a lot like Yonaguni that is near Japan and at least as old as that. Man has been traveling the whole earth for a very long time but either man made catastrophes or natural events have caused cycles of chaotic regression that equal the Dark Ages imposed on Europe by the Catholic deviates. So much technology has been lost and then found again. How many times I do not know and I haven't seen any great evidence that we can effectively date stone of the vitrified rocks that might have been caused by atomic blasts and are widely separated. It is possible the ancients had something akin to Greek Fire that would equal napalm of the Vietnam era. Heck, it is even possible the recent find off Cuba is the Mayax Churchward said white man developed and then wrested Europe away from the less advanced hominids. We must keep a very open mind rather than find ways of making everything fit a neat theory by throwing out the facts that don't fit and saying they are fraudulent. This kind of Fraud perpetrated to justify European colonization and Manifest Destiny is still the basis of history in schools today.

    Clearly the sign language root and chanting roots of language traveled with man wherever he went. Ogham has both these elements and I think one of them (chanting) came from the Mungo Man. That is another whole book though. The Pima Indians of the SW United States are recently found to have Berber blood. What are these 'Sea People' doing in the American SW where Rhoda was found and expertly dated to the 8th Century AD and the Egyptian/Buddhist looking temple of the Grand Canyon (which is less provable but covered in more than one issue of Ancient American) that is confirmed in far earlier Chinese dynastic records? The uncertainties are evident in this excerpt from the highly qualified authors of *Carthage*:

    "Such a language group seems to be just what scholars have for many years called Hamito-Semitic (or often just Hamitic), named after Noah's son Ham in the Bible, who was believed to be the ancestor of the African people (Incredible!). This language group, now more often discussed under the designation Afro-Asiatic, spread from an unknown center (a number of scholars have suggested the Caucasus, but this is quickly passing out of vogue) at an unknown date before the fourth millenium, developed into languages such as Akkadian (The language of business and diplomacy for much of Classical Civilization history.), Egyptian and Hebrew, and ultimately branched in to such diverse languages as Coptic and the Cushite dialects of Ethiopia. But this whole approach to classifying the Berber language has become widely challenged because of the amazing diversity of Berber dialects and the difficulty of separating out contaminating elements that result from Berber contacts with other peoples in historical times." (4)

However one imagines the peregrinations of the Berbers, Basque and ancient Iberians one gets a lot of possible answers. Here we see the Berber language is what one would expect of all the inputs from every race and human ethnic group. The same is true with their crania. The fact that some are still born with blue eyes and blond hair and that Stewart historians say they can trace themselves to Berbers 20,000 years ago seems to make a good fit with my theory of a Worldwide Brotherhood of Phoenician Kelts from the genetic group starting near the Caucasus 30-35,000 years ago. The Berbers may have been the mixed race people that were persecuted at certain times but they were still coming to the aid of Carthage and its Phoenicians when Rome finally conquered that great city that stood guard over the access to the Americas from the Mediterranean or in the opposite direction. We have records from the school of Aristotle that say the Carthaginians forbade their people from coming to the Americas around this time. Why?

When my Ogham scholars first discussed Ogham with me they told me it was the origin of all other languages and in some ways I still think it is. However, there are as many roots to Ogham as there are common languages it seems.

Diverse Druids

What is Ogham?

Thomas Jefferson was a multi-dimensional scholar with a great insight and interest in the Indian languages of those beautiful people he grew up around. He developed a large volume of information on 50 languages of Indians that he traced to pre-Cyrillic Russian which is one of the many Western languages that came from Phoenician roots. No wonder (!), the Scythians are the Phoenicians and they and their brothers are a large part of the Russian people. The Phoenicians and they relations built the mounds all over America and all the other things we have only touched upon in this book. If you have a hard time with that assertion or the Hyperborean and Amazon stories of Herodotus you are in good academic company but the facts are rolling in to support Herodotus and others who actually knew the Keltoi or 'ogygia'.

There are other things I have discovered in reference to Thomas Jefferson and one particular speculation I would like to share deals with the idea of miscegenation and melding of the races that Phoenicians believed in. However, by Jefferson's time the prevailing ethic and power aspects were totally different. Jefferson grew up buying into the prevailing paradigm of his day. The Scale of Nature and its related prejudicial ladders of ascended being all had the European at the top of these horrific models of human cultural evolution. By now the rumours are settled in reference to his being the father of his wife's black half-sister's children from the time she was thirteen in France. His modern family has allowed the black descendants of Sally Hemmings to attend the family reunions. The prevailing scientific garbage had the black people coming from a gross event by a stupid white person (presumably Polish or some other denigrated people like 'Wops') and an orangutan. It is hard to imagine this but some people in the 20th Century school systems were still teaching the Scale of Nature when I was in public school.

The fact that Jefferson married a Randolph and that the Randolph's recruited his father to their estate due to genetic factors (I suggest) leads to the birth of Frederick Douglass the half black leader of the early civil rights movement. Both of them grew up on Tuckahoe Creek and even if Jefferson wasn't his father that is probably more than a co-incidence. No one knows (except Frederick's mother who kept it a secret) who the father of Douglass was. Jefferson had retired to the estate he grew up on and was there for the appropriate time, His history of miscegenation or enjoying black women is a factor but maybe even more important is the common courage and basic Brotherhood ideals they both shared. Now let us go to South America and Neuva Germania to see what further Oghamic roots exist in places academics will seldom acknowledge. In *Forgotten Fatherland: The Search for Elizabeth Nietzsche* we have:

Jim Woodman, "was very earnest. 'The Celts were here ages ago, way back in the fourth, fifth century, and the Vikings and the Africans. They were all here.' His pamphlet said: 'I'm also convinced the trail crossed America years ago. It, perhaps, was one taken by the bearded white gods South America's shadowy legends say brought knowledge and culture to Andean tribes.' The walls of Jim's house were covered with photographs of fertility symbols and inscriptions he had found in caves around Paraguay, some not far from Neuva Germania. Most were in Celtic Ogham, which supposedly has an alphabet something like this.

To me they looked more like the sort of notches bored prisoners make to count off the days." (5)

His illustration can be described simply if you visualize a line being the plane of the palm or from where the wrist allows the hand and fingers to move. I will include a drawing and other Ogham tracts but for the written portion of this book the description is what really counts. B, L, F, S, N are the fingers/thumb pointed down from the plane of the palm. H, D, T, C, Q are the fingers or digits upward from the plane and A, O, U, E, I would be up then down if signing but a line drawn through the base line equal distant on either side if scratched or etched on stone. This in itself tells us how old this kind of alphabet probably is. Clearly sign language predates written word unless we are taught by aliens and

Diverse Druids

some like Sitchen or Gardner in the Christian Mystery School traditions would have you believe that bunk. Finally M, G, Ng, Z, and R are angled to the right through the base line and I think these plosives or variations came later in most Ogham tracts. C became a G, M is an extra wave on the symbol of N that is seen in Gimbutas' Old European symbols she takes back 25,000 years. We still have Asians who pronounce R like L, and Z is perhaps most recent of all but there were other variations in certain locales that are well documented by the likes of Barraclough Fell who is anathema or a nemesis to academia.

Jim Woodman is an epigraphist or linguist who was living near the Wagnerian/Nazi anti-Semites who came to Paraguay near the turn of the century. What would these Aryans say if they knew Hebrew was a sacerdotal code created by the designers of Ogham and the Pyramid? This is the language that led to their (the Aryans) adept group being called something more than 'arch-tectons', as the Septuagint or early Greek Bible calls the family of Jesus. The Hebrews that Moses led in the Exodus were not all of the 'Eire-yanns' or Hyksos (foreigners) who were in Egypt. If the Gnostic Gaedhils of Simon Magus are a clue and the Elephantine or Temples like that of Onais from the archaeologic record are to be considered one could say the elite fighting forces of Pharaohs were these same Israelites in the ensuing millennia. 'Yann' means 'people of' and Eire was the site of one of the most sacred Keltic places in the Emerald or 'Blessed Isles'. Tara and New Grange where we saw the coronation of a non-hereditary king took place just as in Crete in the words of Joseph Campbell. Eire is Ireland and Erin is too, as we chant for hopes of freedom in 'Erin go Bragh':

"A study of the individual words and syntax has led scholars to the belief that there really was much more to Phoenician thought and writing than evidence would indicate. Some scholars now feel that the early Hebrew Bible shows an enormous amount of influence from Canaanite and Phoenician sources; W.F. Albright has gone so far as to say: 'There can be no doubt that the Bible has preserved some of the best in Phoenician literature. Without the powerful influence of the Canaanite literary tradition we should lack much of the perennial appeal exerted by Hebrew poetic style and prosody, poetic imagery and the vivid description of natural phenomena. Through the Bible the entire civilized world has fallen heir to Phoenician literary art." (6)

In 1990 I was approached by Ogham scholars to re-write a 1923 book called *Irish Wisdom* by an old style Masonic linguist named Connor MacDari. They needed my esoteric understanding and certainly I was ignorant of Ogham other than a little reading of Barry Fell who called it Ogam. At first I thought Philip Whelan was talking about 'OM' the universal sound. MacDari's book had many perspectives that I could agree with and good sources but was out of date and very passionately anti-British because of what the British had done to the Irish in the Black and Tan or Potato famine. I could understand his rage but felt there was great deal more than rage which I needed to substantiate and make his points clearer. I admit his insights form the basis of a great deal of my research but little that he actually said is used in my writing today. Other more authoritative authors confirm his thought. There is a growing body of alternative history and I sincerely hope we can finally reject all the attitudes born or fostered by Dark Ages or early Enlightenment limitations.

The astronomical aspects and mathematical co-efficients like 'PI' and 'PHI' were extremely important in the Pyramid complex at Giza that MacDari asserts were built by ancient Celtic adepts of a Magian Order that would be similar to the Heliopolitan syncretic cults of Ba'albek or Heliopolis. The Bardic Tradition that fostered these different cultural communities including Pharisees and Magi in various regions and time frames in the Middle East were all in contact and shared their knowledge at some point. We may never know all the reasons for the growth of the independent or power motives but the more I see of it, the more I think drugs and women or their control was at the root of many disagreements. Corporate secrets were definitely a factor as well but it seems likely that most of the Keltic family emporiae known as Phoenician were able to travel the whole world and kept on decent diplomatic footing until the Hyksos Period and by the time of the Trojan War the different factions and families had allied themselves in groups that continued to fight or limit others from greater access. The knowledge of metal working is often thought to have been important to those who succeeded in carving a bigger piece of the pie at these points in time but the possibility of more advanced technologies in even earlier times is worth serious consideration.

Conflicting Conventionalism

The Gnostics and later offshoot of the Cathars still tried to bring Brotherhood ideals to the fore long after the rise of Empires and noble lineages. Today the same arguments seem prevalent. Should we really try to be tolerant and help our fellow man; or will we band together to make our group (race, nation, religion) more powerful? The Gnostics knew the Original Sin that separated us from GOD and truth is Ignorance and there have been times I have marveled at my own ignorance. The dynasties of Egypt are largely concocted to fit the Bible Narrative and many now know this as Rick Gore of National Geographic has made clear and Velikovsky proved decades ago. The Hyksos or 'Sea Peoples' are the Berbers or remnants of the great cultural civilization's colonizing efforts and worldwide trading Brotherhood. No mere 'bedouin' or 'berberoi' and 'barbaroi' are these seafarers who along with the Basque traversed the world with the Red Heads and pygmies who might be remnants of the Mungo Man from the dim reaches of hominid development:

"Essentially the Sea Peoples theory was a convenient and plausible invention of the 19th century, designed (largely by historian Gasten Maspero) to fit very limited facts." (7)

Competent humanists like Jacquetta Hawkes, Marija Gimbutas and Joseph Campbell provide a light to guide our way. If we used the situational ethics derived from considering actual precedents and knowing the rich are more 'blessed' and thus more responsible; ethics that are apparent from what little remains of the *Senchus Mor* - I think it would be better. These old Irish Canae or Laws are thought to have existed for 25,000 years and that most likely means in places other than Ireland which we will see almost certainly includes the mummies from near the present day Great Wall of China. But the deterministic or anti-free will element that Pelagius and others fought against as the early Christian Church became more of a Roman Empire has homogenized rather than collectivized our soul. This was largely based on the Salvation dogma that allows people to behave without discipline and 'confess' or pat the church to gain absolution. Absolution from what? From the very 'Sins' and Satan that this Church created and seems more interested in serving.

Hawkes' scholarship was unassailable and her academic brethren were afraid of her. She didn't fully sell out to conventionalism or the paradigm as she noted 'precociously advanced' cultures in Anatolia from 10,000 years ago and the medieval towers from Sardinia that date to as far back as 1800 BC. Archaeology fought against linguists for much of the time but linguists have been vindicated by the subsequent discoveries made through satellite imaging and modern forensic analysis. There are many anthropologists who put words in the mouths of those they study and other cases where the natives told them what they wanted to hear for many decades while it was all fiction yet reported as fact. On the whole though, anthropologists are more open-minded and willing to consider value in people not just the Western idea of value and/or systems thereof. The debate rages about possessions or spiritual means of gaining knowledge but neurophysiology has proven much about the ancient sciences. In the last little while Harvard showed the physiology of interior meditative states in mystics and MRI has shown acupuncture is based on solid reality when once it was considered pure quackery. Soon the same will be said about much of the ancient sciences including some (like Harmonics and energy grids of fields) that we are almost ignorant when compared to what was commonplace in Neolithic time.

The Druids and their shamanistic forbears were the masters of the reality that creativity and purposeful soulful attunements can achieve. They were willing to share it rather than keep power to themselves and they did it so that it wouldn't fall into the hands of those who would not have the appropriate ethics. Many suggest the Kelts were illiterate but Strabo notes there was a 7,000 year written history in Celtiberia Tartessus. Of course the dirty deeds of the Romans like Patrick led to the destruction of much pre-Christian literature. However, it is certain the Druids did not allow certain things to be written and kept it as a verbal educational tradition. This reflects or originates the third law of the Magi that says "Scrire, Potere, Audere, Tacere" or 'Know, Will, Dare, Keep Silent'. The divinatory runes are from Ogham and many scholars are able to see that while others like to make Ogham come after Runes in order to further the 'barbarian' illiterate lie.

The lifelong education and joy of learning that was fostered amongst those who attended the Bardic schools was shared by the population at large who treated them with a respect equivalent to the kings who were paid the same for their services. The kings were not as we envisage kings today, or in the medieval sense. We don't do our future citizen-leaders any favors by enforcing regurgitative rather than functional skills. The Bards taught the kids language and rhetoric to use as they developed their musical skills through minstrel to jester stages. Performing in front of people goes a long way to defeating insecurities and fears but these are also the best time to learn such things as we now know from neurophysiology and other sciences dealing with stages of personal development. The whole society was soulfully aware and magic (majik) was a part of their common bond. In the healing arts and homeopathy they were well equipped and had the first public hospitals and medicare type programs for poorer people. These same ethics were revived by the Cathar Troubadours in Southern France a millennium after the Druids had been eradicated from European society. Now we have to look at the matter of academic cover-ups that still are affecting the history that gives us the 'barbarian' Druids largely built upon Caesar's journals written by Hirtius for propaganda purposes:

"Ogham is a form of alphabetic writing used for inscriptions belonging in the main to the fifth to eighth century and found only in the British Isles. of which the best known is 'Ogam Craohh', 'Tree Ogham'. A connection with runic writing has been suggested, but it is highly speculative." (8)

Britannica is a great place to find the 'prevailing paradigm'. Their near innuendo and 'speculative' projection upon alternatives is something you could see for yourself in this brief quote. To suggest 400 AD as the origin of Ogham and that it is only found in the British Isles is important to the Flat Earth/Columbus/Polo history that allows colonization to have become modern sovereign states through such wicked work as Manifest Destiny. My work may never get published for just this one reason. Regardless of whether I am a good writer or ever become one this one thing is very threatening because common people and the courts might well demand compensation from all those who ripped off the real and truly harmonious people of places like North America where there is more Ogham inscription in just New England than in Ireland and Wales. Recent finds on wood in Denmark also suggest it was not just put on stone as Anne Ross has written. She (at least) takes it back to 800 BC, but she says it was for ceremonial purposes only; and none have seen a connection with the Quipas of Peru that could also keep poetry and are not purely abacus type tally systems.

How anyone can say Ogham only started in 400 AD is beyond me. There is common agreement that it was used by the Druids. Druids were still able to exist in Ireland at this time because Rome never got control (outwardly at least) of Ireland. But in almost all of Europe the Druids had been decimated and were only found in hiding places with little

Diverse Druids

chance of passing on their knowledge from generation to generation. I see a connection with Alexander Marshack's acknowledged 15,000 BC lunar calendar that was once called mere notation and was found in Iberia of Spain among artifacts showing a culture dated to 30,000 years ago. Even Mr. Ellis who we have quoted seems to go along with this plot to maintain the Ussher time line ideas in human cultural development. Perhaps he had to do this in order to be published and you can be certain I will NOT! He also says many things that indicate he does not buy into this picture just as Professor Mac Manus seems to have veiled many messages in his early 20th century book *The Story of the Irish Race*. Ellis says Barry Fell claimed Ogham existed in 500 BC but I know Fell thought 850 BC is provable in New England in his early writings and through Libyan (Berber languages) was able to translate Harappan and almost all languages of the world.

Fell will probably be proven right in the long run if my Ogham scholar is correct. His work on the Peterborough petroglyphs near my family home and on the way to our cottage is a clear message for those who would dare to re-write history and tell some truth. Here the government has stopped people from taking photographs and the Indians were allowed (or encouraged) to grind the Norse ships with the Phoenician prow off the rocks that include Tiffinaugh which is an Oghamic tract or early Keltic relative of Ogham. My nieces were amazed to hear this when I told them the fact in the last year. They have been to Newport Tower and their mother is Norse derived and a member of the Norumbega Society that had a mass wedding there at the millennium. A key part of the reason for this cover up is the soulful science that the Druids taught and enabled people throughout their leadership of egalitarian ethics and society. Professor Emeritus Kelley who is Canada's top linguist and participated in breaking the Mayan code is able to confirm the Tiffinaugh and he worked with Fell and Ivan Sanderson and many other researchers trying to break the shackles we still suffer under.

Robert Baird

Soulful Sheathing!

Clearly if the Druids and Kelts were to be minimized as 'barbarians' or marginalized as heathen sacrificers and murderous scum it was absolutely necessary to eradicate their language and culture as well as such a long history of human Brotherhood. Fortunately America is the repository of much more than the crosses 'Christian' missionaries destroyed upon their arrival in America.

The psychic power of the female intuition that the Greeks called *unlimited* and *out of control* according to noted scholar Michael Grant; is a reality connected to the Sphinx and the Yin of the Tao. The Sphinx was a beacon of enlightenment in the desert of man's physical pursuits. It was part of a complete and complex symbological representation and library of the ancient scientists. I had sensed such things before I met my Ogham scholar who had learned with his sister as they grew up in Ireland amongst the rocks or dolmen that have it scratched all over them. MacDari contributed this greater complexity from his Masonic background as he berated and bemoaned how Masonry had been taken over by the British "ale-house denizens".

This monumental complex was designed long before the Great Pyramid appears to have been built but the capstone on it might have been used for the first few millennia. There is a great deal of controversy about when the Sphinx was built as part of this complex located at the center of all the earth's land masses. The fact that is so accurately placed is testimony to the fact they had mapped the whole world and a great deal more than that. The Sphinx as a stand alone monument represents the feminine aspect of mankind and the dualistic universe. The whole complex renders through symbolism the complete cosmological relationship of man and nature in the ethic and insight *of as above, so below*. This is the second law of the Magi and one attributed to Hermes Trismegistus who is about as mythical and legendary as Thoth. I think he likely did walk the face of the

Diverse Druids

planet and was a Babylonian who became leader of Egypt in the time they still gave leaders their position based on merit and ability. The Thoth/Hermes or Imhotep/Asklepios syncretic cults that were the norm among intelligent and educated people (of the Mediterranean) in the 2nd millennium BC until the fall of Alexandria's Library are largely compiled in his *Corpus Hermeticum* which includes Gnostic input.

Much of this 'Heliopolitan' sun or 'son' worship is derived from Druidry as Thomas Paine says in his pamphlet on Masonry which I often quote. It is science in the name of alchemy and integrated metallurgy and healing. Gardner says Tuthmosis reorganized earlier esoteric schools and perhaps amalgamated many of them. I think it was more a matter of distancing themselves and making themselves more important but it matters little in the long run. There can be no question they lost the willingness to operate with good intent for the benefit of all mankind around this time that male gods like Jehovah were created to marginalize women.

The Sphinx originally had a female face and the powerful lion's body. In the legend of Theseus the Sphinx also has wings of the Dragon and plays the role of enforcer of certain positive ethics and intellectual disciplines. I think Amun or the one god concept is also incorporated in the Sphinx long before Aten and the supposed Moses/Akhenaton monotheism. I can't get my mind around this monotheism that destroyed all graven images but somehow led to more idolatrous imagery and deities or semi-deities that any other known religion. How can it be monotheistic if the Pope is Infallible and the Holy Trinity makes so many mistakes? Fifteen hundred angels and saints with more due every year or so. When they created Satan or the Devil did they not create another pantheon of gods? In Judaism they diminished the female deities called Shekkinah and then eventually removed females from the Pantheon until reinstalling them in the medieval Zohar with the Matronit after many centuries of horrific persecution.

Robert Baird

In the face of the Sphinx and the powerful dynamism of the lion we can see the dual gender forces and attributes of man. I think it is ideal to balance both attributes of passive and dynamic and indeed many esoteric cults find androgynous people becoming gay perhaps for this reason. It is also true they would have had a hard time finding a woman they could talk to or share with, when all the Mediterranean Empires had made it impossible for women to get an education. The Sphinx was built during the wet phases of the last Ice Age according to geology and early French Egyptology using the Inventory Stele. But the Bible Narrative didn't fit with that kind of antiquity so we find Chefren and a male god/king replacing the feminine, once again. The myth-makers or priests in the Druidic system were called 'vascerri' at one point in time but it is hard to know if the Kelts had them throughout their early civilization and the many millennia it spanned.

The following quote includes the Shekkinah in an orthodox Jewish ritual of the present and it also makes clear the awesome beauty that one can receive through symbols that open the pathways of the neural net which has buzzing thalami and quieting superior parietal lobes to enable what MacDari called 'direct cognition'. You can decide where that cognition comes from even though this ritual makes overuse of the word God. The Sphinx was the psycho-spiritual symbol of our soul which woman is closer to understanding and nurturing:

"Unsheathing the soul prepare to meet your God. Prepare to devote your heart. Purify your body and select a special place where no one in the world can hear your voice. Be totally alone. Sit in one spot in the room or the loft, and so not reveal your secret to anyone. If you can, do this by day, even for a little while, but the best way is to do it at night. As you prepare to speak with your Creator, to seek the revelation of his power, be careful to empty your mind of all mundane vanities. Wrap yourself in your 'tallit' and put 'tefillin' on your head so that you will be filled with the awe of Shekhinah, who is with you at this moment. Wear clean garments, all white if you can. All this helps immensely in focusing your awe and love. If it is night, light many candles until your eyes shine brightly.

Then take hold of ink, pen and tablet. Realize that you are about to serve your God in joy. Begin to combine letters, a few or many, permuting and revolving them rapidly until your mind warms up. Delight in how they move and in what you generate by revolving them. When you feel within that your mind is very, very warm from combining the letters, and that through the combination you understand new things that you have not attained by human tradition nor discovered on your own through mental reflection, then you are ready to receive the abundant flow, and the abundance flows upon you, arousing you again and again.

Now turn your thoughts to visualizing the Name and its supernal angels, imagining them as if they were human beings standing or sitting around you, with you in the middle like a messenger about to be sent on a royal mission, waiting to hear about it from their lips, either from the king himself or from one of his ministers. Having imagined this vividly, prepare your mind and heart to understand the many things about to be conveyed to you by the letters being contemplated within you. Meditate on them as a whole and in all their detail, like one to whom a parable, a riddle, or a dream is being told, or like one perusing a book of wisdom, pondering a passage beyond his grasp. Interpret what you hear in an uplifting manner, approximating it as best you can. (Chant?) Based on what you understand of it, evaluate yourself and others. All this will happen after you fling the tablet from your hands and the pen from your fingers, or after they fall by themselves due to the intensity of your thoughts.

Realize that the stronger the mental flow, the weaker become your limbs and organs. Your entire body will begin to tremble violently. You will think that you are about to die because your soul, overjoyed at what she has attained, will depart from your body. Consciously choose death over life, knowing that such death affects only the body and that thereby the soul lives eternally. Then you will know that you are capable of receiving the flow. If you then wish to honor the glorious Name by serving it with the life of body and soul, hide your face, fear to gaze at God, and come no closer, like Moses at the burning bush. Return to the physical dimension, rise, eat and drink a little, inhale a fragrant aroma. Return your spirit to its sheath until another time. Rejoice in what you have, and know that God loves you." (10)

    The power spot in any room or place you might choose to worship and meditate in this manner was often found near oak and rowan trees for the Kelts and their Druids. Cenotes are truly wondrous caves that get one feeling the root of nature and the need to be secret about the place or the practice has to do with ego and peer response seeking. Many are they who proclaim their religiosity while having no real connection to what this soulful attunement contemplates and activates. Just how the vectors of force are contained in such symbols or the letters activate templates in our mind is not fully understood by modern science and maybe it was pure trial and error that first led humans to know these things. However, it is possible that the direct cognition of any number of means shamans or dream dancers used was able to provide the symbols which became the alphabet. We know Hebrew comes from Phoenician and that the Phoenicians are the Keltic Brotherhood that gave Greece its alphabet which includes Tau just as Hebrew does and so I will take just that one symbol for a brief moment in order to convey how great the knowledge and meaning of these things can be.

    In Gimbutas' book *The Language of the Goddess* there is a figure of a human with arms crossed and elbows out that looks like the Hebrew letter TAU, it is from Sardinia in the 5th millennium BC. This TAU cross has a lot to do with Constantine's cross and is adapted to the cross of St. Anthony. A study of crosses in the pre-Christian era would convince even the most unwilling scholar that people once believed in a wide variety of forces that they used crosses for protection from and integration or use thereof. Crosses are mandalas with four entry points for the primary forces and are often used for personal talismans as Catholics and others often do even though they may not know what a talisman is able to do. If one gains insight beyond semantical language and gets the synchronicity of ideas and conscious forces there is a far greater beauty and literacy possible. I think this one meditation is a great insight and has many levels of potential to appreciate. The intersection of the lines connecting the sephirah on the Tree of Life often makes the novitiate feel in a maze or even amazed; Gimbutas gives us a little idea of an obvious symbol and the cryptic shorthand it contains in the quote below. The Tree is found in Mayan lands and through Churchward and an article by an attendee at the archaeological conference held in Copan recently we show how it dovetails with Kundalini and the mutras (or mudras). In fact this presentation in my book *Neolithic Libraries* is just one of many things religious left to the 'Libraries' theme. It would not surprise me if a publisher thought the two books should be combined and that will be true for all my Keltic books too:

"Graphically, a pubic triangle is most directly rendered as a V. This expression and its recognition are universal and immediate. It is, nevertheless, amazing how this early bit of 'shorthand' crystallized to become for countless ages the designating mark of the Bird Goddess. (BRD = Baird, Bard but also maybe this is the root of the wishbone fable). for example, waterbird figurines from Mal'ta in Siberia are marked with rows of incised V's, and faceless anthropomorphic waterbirds carved of mammoth ivory" (11)

Paul Brunton provides a little of the saying attributed to Jesus which I think should be one of the few Magian Laws. That saying might even replace the one which no longer deserves to have its Keep Silent part included. It is 'Be Still and Know, that I AM (YHVH)'. Here are his all important words dealing with the ego:

"Be still and know! This is to be done by practicing the art of meditation deeply, and then - for it cannot properly be done - tracing the ego to its hidden lair. Here it must be faced. Being still involves the achievement of mental silence, without which the ego remains cunningly active and keeps us within its sphere of influence. Knowing involves penetrating to the ego's secret source where, in its lulled and weakened condition, it can be confronted and killed.

The ego knows that if profoundly concentrated attention is directed toward ascertaining its true nature the result will be suicidal, for its own illusory nature would be revealed. This is why it opposes such a meditation and why it allows all other kinds." (12)

Further Thoughts on Ogham and Divinatory Deities

The Languages of the Birds is one of the names for Ogham. Then there is the matter of the adepts and legendary culture-bearers called 'messengers' and anthropomorphic Gods throughout the world. It would appear these Red Heads are not derived from the Mungo Man or pygmies they are known to have traveled with as they mined copper in North America. However, these ancient pygmies may have taught the De Danann or Megalith Builders quite a lot (especially about harmonics). The records of the court of Hatchepsut indicate the pygmies were extremely valuable in her time and we must think they died off some short time after that. Velikovsky and Flinders Petrie are two good sources for insight into Egypt as a colony that had earlier cultural impacts. The possibility of Churchward being right about Mu is not totally lost on me but I think it was this connection between the Mungo Man and De Danann that he found some clues to and there is a lot more available almost every year than he had to work with.

"A subject of much difficulty in the earlier accounts of the objects was the marking of 'Greek letter' on the back of many of the tiles, Sir Flinders Petrie wrote. (13) According to an explanation offered by him, 'Greek letter had a pre-existence in Egypt.' (14) This presupposes that the Egyptians who had used hieroglyphics, also had an alphabetic system which they used only on rare occasions to cut on jars or tiles and bricks. This script was known in Egypt (and recent finds in the Sahara confirm)for a thousand or thousands of years; it was never used to write down an Egyptian text." (15)

The alphabetic rather than pictographic alphabet seems to relate to the colonizers of Egypt who had a continuing trading and other relationship with Egypt as the archaeology at Elephantine shows post Moses Gaedhilic Israelites were a major military force in Egypt after the Hyksos and Moses took many of the people to a new land. Research at the Temple of Onais shows a complex use of sacrifices by followers of Moses. In time the ones who remained became Good Samaritans like Simon Magus.

Velikovsky goes on to show the archaeologists trying to deny and explain away these artifacts that throw much of Egyptian history into doubt. Many of the top scholars had to agree that any of the history was pure guesswork and near specious speculation but Velikovsky saw it was part of the Bible Narrative and what he describes as The Three Pillars of Ignorance. Griffith in Naville's *Mound of the Jew* says "Light will be thrown on the question someday." The recent discoveries led National Geographic and many scholars to say all Egyptian history is "fiction. And the real question should be who colonized Egypt. This is a huge step towards what I think is the Phoenician or Atlantean history that has been expunged by misogynistic Empire. Man began to like being worshipped and sometimes took names of prior heroes like Ptah and Thoth which leads to so many of the legends being with little more than an amalgam of history and totally unverifiable. Nonetheless there are many who believe in Thoth or these semi-deities with great conviction.

Such ego led to concern and vanity related to image rather than results and mush of the discipline and science held close to certain schools and enterprises was lost. I have heard there are bagpipes drawn on the Great Pyramid whereas Cheops has a cartouche as the only remnant of him. This cartouche is located with later reconstruction gang graffiti. No indigenous bagpipes are in the area of Egypt to my knowledge but they are important to Kelts. There are so

Robert Baird

many reasons to know the Kelts and their Brotherhood made these monuments that it can easily be seen as the biggest part of the overall fraud that usurped prior civilization.

I have dealt with the BEE symbology in books like *The Bards and the Bees* and it is one of the zoomorphic allies that are coltishly followed in Egypt before the Sons of Mil became the royal family on Crete as the House of Mallia in 2200 BC. This 'bee' that Napoleon took from the grave of the Merovingian king Childeric to wear on his investiture robes is of utmost import to this very day. The Mormons and Sarmoung have it prominent in their iconographic heritage that indicates sources of knowledge and lineage from far more ancient times amongst the Kelts of Old Europe or the Danube:

"This connection between insects, the bull, and emergent life occurs in Roman times in the writings of Ovid, Vergil, and Porphyry (Ransom 1937: 107-14). The latter unknowingly echoes religious ideas as old as the Neolithic in his comment:

'The moon (Artemis), whose province it was to bring to the birth, they (the ancients) called Melissa (bee) (The ML or Milesians is here this long ago.), because the moon being a bull and its ascension the bull, bees are begotten of bulls. And souls that pass to the earth are bull-begotten. (Porphyry, De ant. Nym.:18)'

The epiphany of the Goddess as a bee is engraved on a bull's head carved of bone from the Cucuteni site of Bilcze Zlote, c. 3500 B.C. The Goddess's body is an hourglass whose upraised arms are bifurcated and whose head is a dot. But the tradition of her epiphany as bee or butterfly was already thousands of years old by this time. A butterfly sign next to a bull's head is flanked by whirls on a wall painting of Catal Hüyük's Shrine A VI, 6, c. 6500 B.C. The butterfly sign in combination with whirls is also incised on Linear Pottery dishes of Central Europe from c. 5000 B.C." (16)

Gimbutas is confident this culture goes back 25,000 years from the archaeological record and there was a great deal discovered after her work in the Ukraine. The genetic

Diverse Druids

Haplogroup X marker dating the white people to 30 - 35,000 years ago and the Amazon Scythian graves are still making great new information that supports her work. Marshack's calendar and the Tarim Basin or Urümchi finds are truly fantastic. The 5000 BC Khvalynsk finds on the Volga and the manner of Genghis Khan's heritage in a tradition of shamanistic 'smiths' must really deserve the utmost attention in history. Unfortunately he is still painted as a barbarian nomad even though he developed the largest and safest Empire of modern history that no Catholic scholars were willing to debate in the court of his descendant, the great Kublai Khan.

The Rowan 'quickening sticks' of the Kelts, the message sticks of Marshack's aboriginal Australian work and the I Ching sticks are possibly all derived from the same source if the Mungo Man was an early missionary. Certainly the Kelts were in all these places at later pre-Christian times but the veils of history might forever remain closed to us in much of what has transpired. Personally I think there were written records of great reliability which certain disgusting people destroyed. It isn't just the words of Strabo that convince me of this when he writes about the 7000 year written history of Tartessus and the Celtiberians of the Iberian corporate trading complex.

In keeping with the worldwise and wide impact of these ancient missionaries who were dedicated to sharing and learning we take a brief glimpse at Hawaii. I was told that the last five true Druids can be found in Hawaii by a High Priestess of Wicca who had traveled the world for much of her life. I know the Kahuna are adept firewalkers and I believe the knowledge they have is shared with Druids but again it is hard to be sure which begat which. It is also interesting that a single woman took a craft with no navigational equipment from Hawaii to Easter Island in 2000.

Max Freedom Long "was inspired to look within the Hawaiian language for a code that would reveal the psycho-religious system used by the Kahuna of Hawaii. The meaning of the words and combination of words gave forth definitions of what it meant to be a human being and the tenfold concept of an individual person. the spoken word that had never had a written version.

Hawaiian sounds each have a unique vibration pattern that can change the quality of your speech, your throat, your sinus passages and your brain. Working with tiny speech muscles, some new vibratory patterns can be utilized to create changes in your experiences of life. I suggest that as you come across the various Hawaiian words you try chanting them in order to gain greater insight into the meaning of each individual word.

The internal structure of the Polynesian language indicates its high antiquity. The laws of euphony which regulates the changes of consonants are fixed and uniform in the New Zealand, Samoan and Hawaiian languages (New Zealand being considered the most primitive in its form.). There is no distinction between B and P, T and D, G and K, L and R and V and W." (17)

New Zealand is the site of the Moriori who were genocidally eliminated by the Maori with the assistance or direction of the 19th Century British as they escaped to the Chatham Islands. Genetics indicates they are connected with the while people of the Easter Islands and the Rongorongo script of the Easter Islanders is related to Central America and the Harappan of the Indus near another recent underwater site dated to 8000 BC. The fact that the mathematical concept of zero passed between Central America and India in the 8th Century AD (if not before) has a long history of knowledge diffusion. I personally believe it traveled with the assistance of ships rather than astral or spiritual means but academics just avoid the matter with words like co-incidence. In the alphabet chart herein you can see 'tel-ta' of Cara-Maya is the same as the Greek Delta. This correspondence and translational fact of Cara-Maya and Greek led me to Chichen Itza and a stele that confirms the work of Col. James Churchward to a certain extent. In the matter of another cell of culturally advanced people known

Diverse Druids

as Etruscans you can see 'G' and 'K' as noted in Hawaiian if you revolve the letter symbol. The 64 tract of Ogham that are known indicate a living adaptive language that probably learned to change in various colonies or through their ancient trading partners going back to Ilvarta and Ba'albek of the late Ice Age if not even more distant in antiquity to Timbuktu and Zimbabwe/Peru.

The concept relating to the Mutras of India that Deepak Chopra talks about in one of his tapes does the same thing to the mind that Huna does and the Mudras statue in Greece. This statue shows body positions that affect the brain lobe centres and fMRI technology allows us to map in present science. A wise man knows there is much more to learn every time he opens another door or finds some new insight. What is language when it doesn't share these kinds of knowledge or stultifies the rhythms of life like Latin did? Knowledge in the hands of a few is POWER - we need to recapture the symbolic power that accesses our souls which was a vital part of the Druids use of Ogham which is found all over the world. 'P' & 'Q' Celtic are two later forms of Keltic language that have post Christian scholars noting the derivation of Green Languages employed to cryptically mislead those who would seek to ferret out Druids and other Hibernians but these esoteric thoughts are best left to a later time.

In order to conduct their trade and other missions throughout the world the Bards had to develop language skills and alphabets for many cultures and I think they used the existing basis of the people they met. There were times that a seven year post graduate program was in existence for these adept scholars. This is after having focused on language, rhetoric and all other things nearer to home during their early educational years.

Robert Baird

CHAPTER FIVE:
Greenbacks to 'wetbacks'

Zoomorphic or Animistic Languages and Forces

Vicente Fox is the current President of Mexico who brought the first real change to Mexico since the Spanish families who invaded with Cortez. In April 2002 his Senate cancelled his plan to travel to the U.S. and Canada. This is the first time such a thing has happened since Mexico became a sovereign entity. I am concerned for his life as much as I have always been concerned for the Mayan people. A worldwide analysis of government determined Mexico was the number five most corrupt place in the world in the mid 90s before Fox became President and from my experiences there I sure can see why Afghan Taliban government could be no worse. If there are more corrupt regimes and a near total control of life (just 50 families in Mexico own over 90% of the country's assets) in other areas of the world - so what?

How we can allow our trading partners to revile and destroy human existence to the extent this police or feudal Empire does is beyond my moral grasp. I have to admit Ross Perot was right about the polluting effects NAFTA would engender even though Perot is no intellectual brother of mine. People really should read Chomsky but that won't happen as long as truth is hidden by oppressive forces. Mexico has been a despotic sinkhole of human tyranny ever since the Franciscans burned the librarians of the Mayan/Aztec people and this chapter will only gloss over my experiences there. I don't remember if I knew about the Pelota at Chichen Itza being used to settle disputes in the pan-tribal Druidic style over all the Caribbean when I first went there in 1993. In fact I don't remember when I learned a lot of things about this part of the world because it has always been of interest to me. I am pretty sure I knew most of the government literature was pure hogwash before I arrived that first time after finishing the re-write of Mac Dari

Diverse Druids

for my Ogham mentor. It was my first visit to a non-earthen pyramid and I took a copy of my manuscript *The Pyramids: Libraries In Stone - Their Builder's Legacy Of Truth*. Mac Dari's Masonic writing has a lot of morality to it and he would have us believe the British are the ones who watered it down from Phre (Fire or Sun and thus Druidic per Paine) - Masonry. I am not convinced.

The Chanes and the Olmecs or other Phoenician Brothers had been frequenting Central America for thousands of years. The discovery of Luwian/Cretan script at 2200' feet below the Gulf of Mexico last year off Cuba is an important part of my book on the Old Copper Culture sometimes called Aztlan. These Chanes and the subsequent Mayan nobility boarded their heads to look like serpents or the name 'Chane'. I see the hand of the Dragons in this matter especially when the white man whose great tomb equaling King Tut's fortune is found with a prominent jade brooch or pendant honoring Zotz. Zotz is a vampire just as Dracula was in his membership with the Catholic crusaders known as Dragons who were around at the time of the Knights Templar and Teuton. I do not accept the alien reptoid theory of the Anunnaki and Elohim that many Christian esoteric mystery schools propose. I should also note they are called 'schools' while those who worship women or just nature and science are called 'cults'. This is the pot conversing with the kettle as far as I am concerned.

If MacDari had been talking about the Hibernian Mysteries members in other more secret esoteric cults I might agree. There can be no doubt that during the Middle or Dark Ages many people kept secrets very seriously or they met their demise in some horrific ways but it is also true that some people before that had financial reasons to keep certain trading information just as secret. The drug trade had always been surmised by authors like Rudgley but with the forensics of Balabanova we can be certain the Peruvian cocaine joined the blue lotus of Anatolia in a world of potions that might have been manufactured in fortified places like Sardinia. There has to be some reason(s) for nearly 7000 castles on an island that was technologically far ahead of other constructions. The cryptic Green Languages and token systems of the Phoenician Pirates or traders also made a major impact on the symbology and science contained in early languages.

One interesting aspect of this has to do with dowsing water in the Chilean Desert or altiplano where the Nazca Lines are being shown to correlate with deep rivers in fissures under the surface. Another has to do with an astrolabe found in Wisconsin that Ancient American magazine has reported as well as the Aztlan constructions on earth energy points in geometric designs thereof. This highly esoteric area of research by solid state chemist Dr. Don Robins on Ley Lines and other open-minded scholars will continue to add to what we know or once knew. The elemental zoomorphic representations and effigies are connected to earth and cosmic energy. Ms. Moore has proven the cosmology of Angkor Watt as described in a well known language was right. There were no uses made of the reservoirs for irrigation. She used satellite and other remote sensing equipment to show the anthropologists were projecting their own limitations on ancients (again). She also found a thousand year older site laid out in a similar manner some few miles away. Thus the astrological symbols which are also zoomorphic and the 22 letters of the Hebrew code set or Tarot's Major Arcanum all connect with languages and the early symbols or archetypes of Intelligent Design. Any one of these points would require a whole book to explain and I hope it isn't bothersome to know that no one knows all there is to know about these things.

The 'Language of the Birds' that David Ovason writes about in *The Secrets of Nostradamus* as he connects this with ancient Keltic languages barely scratches the surface of what few scholars wish to address. The 'birds' were once 'BRD' in early language and this is the very Bards of the Society of Bairds, Ovates and Druids such as the name of a latter day Druidic Society in London of the present. Just because my name is Baird or Gaelic for bard does not mean I am fully aware or more aware of all these things that I have researched most of my life. Ovason quotes the legends as he talks about 'gods' having to take the form of 'birds' to adjust to this earth plane of physical or material constructs. He describes the Green Languages as being derived from this 'Language of the Birds' and appropriately also comments:

"There are other Green Language techniques which are not mentioned below: their omission is due to the complexity of the occult methodology, with which we need not trouble the general reader, even though we do make passing reference to one or two in the following text. In essence, these are numerologically based, and are linked with Hebraic Gematria, Notaricon and Temurah." (1)

I would include the Enneagrams and much of the whole Qabalistic system as being connected by to Chaos Science and the lozenges or pentagon-dodecahedron if I were to do a book on pure cryptic or esoteric Codes and symbols. Jung's archetypes and Eliade and others who write about mere symbols have often missed the mathematics and S-Matrix that quantum physicist's note in all these things. The best selling book by Redfield called the *Celestine Prophecy* is the best introduction to what the Enneagrams and attunement arts of these ancient sciences can offer the initiate.

In fact the bulk of orthodox Hebrew study of the Kabbalah is 'twisted' according to noted occultist Dion Fortune who was a member of the WWII Allied anti-Hitler psychic squad that included Crowley and Ian Fleming. What 'twisted' means, may be different by degrees from what I have written and will continue to develop in some small way. I think the Kaballah or Caballah (and all so many variant spelling) is not the Qabala because cabals of medieval Sephardic Jews altered the original 'Verbal Tradition' substantially. However it is quite likely this differentiation had been on-going since the time of Moses and the Exodus that separated many Gaedhils or Kelts. Yes, there are many Jews who are Keltic and directly connected to the builders of the Pyramid who colonized Egypt from many of the far flung colonies of this worldwide Phoenician

Robert Baird

Atlantean enterprise. The very existence of so many pyramids and megaliths throughout the world as well as the similarity of names, are good clues for the open-minded.

The Qabala at the time of Jesus and the Pharisees or Magi of Zoroaster was certainly closer to the Bardic 'Verbal Tradition' but the priests were developing their separate identity at this time and from the time of Moses. It is clearer in the Orphic and other Greek Traditions and any place where the Kelts were still in close land proximity. The Trojan War is a very important point in time when the Kelts re-formed and new power structures and empires in far off places changed. It was not just Troy but 19 separate theatres of operation as we find Jericho and Miletus were decimated in the same year - 1200 BC. Obviously many other books are required to tell the whole story that propaganda has kept from us while giving us 'his'-story. The Gnostics kept close to the Bardic thought and are involved in protecting the Great Library at Alexandria as well as being part of the Cathar experiment that would re-energize mankind if it was to be allowed to happen. It is also true that the knowledge can put people in touch with things that create fear or can be misused so perhaps the Kaballah is safer by being 'twisted'

The Green Languages of the Emerald Isles:

"The Green language creation in this quatrain is 'ognion', in the last line. 'Ogmion', sometimes 'Ognion', sometimes 'Ogmius', seems to have come from the Celtic mythological figure 'Ogma', who is supposed to have invented the 'Ogham' alphabet (which some scholars say may not even be Celtic in origin), which was at times called the 'Ogam', 'ogum', and (in Gaelic) 'oghum'. When first translated to Roman Gaul, he was known as Ogmios, but this may have been due to the misunderstanding of the poet Lucian, who believed that he was a Gaulish deity, the Nordic equivalent of Mercury, and tutelary over language. The Ogmios figure probably grew physically by association with later variant names on the Italian debased - Latin, 'orco', meaning demon, which eventually flowered as the French word 'ogre'

Diverse Druids

some considerable time before Perrault used the word in his fairy stories, at the end of the seventeenth century. The later French encyclopaedists tried to fix him as 'Ogmius', and made him one of the Gallic gods, a version of Hercules." (2)
If you make a complete study of rhyme and assonance it is almost certain you will agree with Constantine Nigra and Hyde who are two continental scholars who attribute the Irish (who maintained Ogham dialects the longest) with the origin of Latin in support of Mac Dari and others who say it is a very early alphabet. My Ogham mentor was certain Sanskrit is derived from Ogham and when he said Hebrew was similarly derived it was not the accepted norm (it is now) in academia. Perhaps some day even Britannica will offer alternatives to their trashing of Ogham and the resultant denigration of Keltic culture. Ridicule and epithets are more hurtful in cultural contexts than and sticks or stones. To label Eire as 'lost' ('Ir' in Latin means 'lost') is the height of it.

Why do most people (even the Irish born) use the Roman 'Celt' rather than what the Greeks who knew them as the ancient ones ('ogygia') called them - 'Keltoi'. I suggest with due deference to my Euro-centric Empire followers that it has to do with pride and plagiarism which served to build all that our laws are now based upon. If people had known these truths they would not have accepted Romanism so entirely and even today we would be questioning our leaders who thrive on cultish behavior like Nationalism and prejudices borne of belief in some ascendant religion called monotheistic rather than 'barbarian' paganism which was always egalitarian and valued soul over assets. It can be characterized as a War on Women (like the Cathar 'parfaits') and an abortion of man's soul. Yes, I do believe these things that allowed special dispensations, confessionals and Salvation are at the heart of our ethical turmoil today.

Why haven't the Amazons been properly portrayed? It wasn't real when academics sought to marginalize them to the point of being mere legend. Sure the program worked to all intents and purposes but some people knew better. Herodotus and others of great respect are not pure fiction writers, even less than Homer. It is only in the last decade or so that archaeology can show the 1100 miles of graves that bear witness to their import. Yet it still seems most academics minimize and castigate these proud warriors who fought the rising tide of misogyny as best they could. It wasn't healthy to a man's career to honor the Amazons (or many others that people like Jacquetta Hawkes made waves about) in academic circles intent on macho morays and manipulation. The buzzword or label used rather than Aryan today is Proto-Indo-European which avoids detailing the Euro-centric program which minimizes the completely different and far more ancient cultural evolution of mankind that is evident in the Rg Veda or Puranas. It is not pure happenstance that the Irish word for king is 'Rg'. An even more secretive symbiosis is connected to Ovason's observation on Napoleon that follows. I have tackled this and do not choose to say something like: ". its significance is beyond the remit of this present work." However, you would have to read three other books I've written to get a decent idea of what 'significance' Ovason does not 'remit':

"Napoleon made a serious attempt to reintroduce the arcane bee into the French national symbolism. (Michael Bradley suggests Napoleon gave Jefferson the work ups for the 'Great Seal of the United States'.) A fine example is the flag made for the last public ceremony attended by Napoleon, and now in Les Invalides, Paris. It is almost Masonic in its symbolism. Even the arrangement of four groups of eight bees is designed to reflect the Seal of Solomon, and to evoke the Greek word 'Nike' (Victory) sigil which is, of course, echoed in the capital N in the wreath. The arcane bee is found on the sculpture of Diana (From Dana, dealt with earlier) of Ephesus, and frequently appears in alchemical imagery: its significance is beyond the remit of this present work." (3)

The Seals of Solomon are most important to people like David Koresh of the Seventh Day Adventist splinter group called the Branch Davidians. The House of David to Rothschild Benjaminite relationship is something I am continuing to research and may never know all the details necessary to prove what I suspect. My stele behind the Pelota has 'Seals' that I thought might be those of Solomon but was not able to find their equivalent in books on them. That does not mean they are not connected to Solomon and the Masons or other Phoenicians who almost worship him. A Seal is a powerful Mandalic symbol which has much power built into it. For those who study palmistry they might find it important that I have a Ring of Solomon but I wish I had rather been blessed with a Girdle of Venus in the Dianistic vein of talent. My stele also has the old Masonic T-square attributed to Ptah but evident (according to Churchward) in the Americas as far back as 12,000 BC and elsewhere up to 50,000 years ago. It was a great story that I love to tell as I met the Rosicrucian inner sanctum member who managed the Villas Archaeologiques who watched over this stele with all its esoteric and historical meaning. He was the recipient of my manuscript that I took with me:

"The efforts of Valerie Hewitt in *Nostradamus. His Key to the Centuries,* 1994, to show numerological factors at work in Nostradamus, and reveal the great sage's concern with, for example, Margaret Thatcher and John Major, are nothing more than sub-cultural fun; however, it misses completely the point of sixteenth-century arcane techniques. The whole purpose of the Green Language is to obscure the intentions of the writer from the general reader, in favor of a specialist reader. In addition to achieving this aim, one proficient in the Green Languages can make use of terms which lend a second, or even a third, level of meanings to words and phrases. This, as we saw on pages 31 and 158, can even lead to a single verse giving rise to two (or even more) convincing readings. Curiously, then, the Green Language is expressly used both to delude, elucidate and condense. Nostradamus practices this art with such consummate skill that Ward is right to observe, 'Nostradamus can hint in a phrase of three words what would require a long paragraph to make explicit in an

ordinary way. This is truly the language of prophecy.'
(Biblio: Charles Ward, *Oracles of Nostradamus, 1891)*

Such word-puzzles will delude those who are not familiar with the art of the Green Language, yet elucidate for those who are familiar with such rules. This means, of course, that only an alchemist would be able to understand the Green Language used by alchemists, and only one learned in astrology would be able to understand the Green Language of astrology. The matter is further complicated in the case of Nostradamus, who was writing about the future in languages which, even were they not (in any case) intentionally obscured by Green Language, would have been obscured to some extent by the passage of time. We have already observed that Rabelais, who also used the Green Language, has actually been translated from his sixteenth-century French into modern French. This is an interesting reflection upon Nostradamus, for the interesting thing is that Nostradamus wrote in a French - not to mention a style - which was far more obscure than that used by Rabelais. Among the letters from astrological clients which have surfaced in the recent discovery of the Nostradamus correspondence are several complaining that they do not understand what Nostradamus is saying, even in regard to personal horoscopy. Poor Hans Rosenberger, who seems to have had much trouble persuading Nostradamus to cast horoscopes, wrote to the savant asking him to remove the ambiguities from his recent chart-reading. 'To tell the truth', he writes in 1561, 'I am not versed in the obscure language of the enigmatic Arabians.' (Biblio: Jean Dupèbe, *Nostradamus Lettres Inédites, 1983.* Hans Rosenberger's observation is from Letter XXII, dated 8, April, 1561 (OS). Rosenberger was not alone: see, for example, letters XVIII and XX from Tubbe to Nostradamus.) . The fact that we can examine the techniques of Nostradamus in the light of analytical tools of English literature should not disguise the fact that Nostradamus often made up his own linguistic rules. This, of course, means that in some cases his methods are beyond simple classification.

Diverse Druids

Anagram the word 'Rapis' stands for Paris, to produce a secondary meaning (raptor, rapist or raped).

ANASTROPHE. Reversing of a word. the anastrophe of *Hiram* to *Maria* (He also connects Maria correctly to Miriam of the Bible and Moses' sister, then he makes the Masons and their Hiram Abiff ritual make more hidden or occult sense. I think his Sons of the Widow are also able to see deeper into antiquity to find Isis as the original Widow.) . virtually every line of the *Prophéties* must be considered anastrophic.

ANTONOMASIA The substitution of an epithet to stand for a proper name, or the use of a proper name to represent a general idea. 'La Dame' is Catherine de' Medici.(By such words used by enemies who might call themselves such epithets as Picts or Irish the elite would know the level of success their propaganda had instilled.)

APHESIS Omission of a letter or syllable at the beginning of a word.

APOCOPE The omission of a letter or syllable from the ending of a word.

ARCANE ASSOCIATION This literary technique lies at the very basis of the Green Language: it is the use of specialist words in such a way that they may be interpreted as giving rise to further words with meanings evident only to those familiar with the specialism.

ARCHAIZING The use of old terms to denote things and places.

EPENTHESIS The adding of a letter or syllable to the middle of the word.

HOMONYMS Words having the same sound and/or spelling as another, but with a different meaning or origin.

HYPALLAGE When, in a figure of speech, the epithet is transferred from the appropriate noun to modify another, to which it does not properly belong.

HYPHAERESIS The omission of a letter to form a word.

ICONOMATIC This usage occurs when a word is intended to be read as a rebus, as though relating to a figure. One iconomatic has survived (like 'coq') into modern

Robert Baird

symbolism, for 'l'ours' (the bear) is sometimes used of Russia.

INVENTION The invention of a new word only peripherally connected with an existing word in a familiar language. In Nostradamus, the familiar language is usually Greek or Latin, but he occasionally invents from Hebrew, and such European languages as English, German, Italian and Provençal. The phrase 'Mars en Nonnay' is invention, for there is no such planetary position: almost certainly the 'Nonnay' is Virgo (Virgos such as my rising sign, are often thought virginal and thus there is humor in them being 'No' and/or 'Nays'.), from the French 'nonne', or 'nonnain', as in quatrain X.67. Another example is the 'sedifragues' of quatrain VI.94, which is from the Latin 'sedem frangere', 'to break a siege'. The phrase, 'Le Port Phocen', for Marseilles, seems to be a more complex invention, for the Greek 'Phocis' was in ancient times a country of central Greece. The seaport town of 'Massalia', founded as a colony from Phocaea was eventually known as Marseilles. Perhaps Nostradamus used the ancient Greek reference because the Phocens were warlike, being allied at times with the Spartans. (Perhaps a great deal more! He was probably of Tartessus stock himself and the Phocaeans were invited by their Iberian corporate partners of ancient times to Massalia just before the all important Battle of Alalia. I think they and their Milesian partners of Naucratis and elsewhere were part of the drug trade and processing on Sardinia. Marseilles is still a vital part of the drug trade.) The bellicose planet Mars, which begins the modern name 'Marseilles' is connoted in the French word 'Phocus' (with its undertones of homonymous 'focus') is not merely Marseilles, but a warlike Marseilles in a state of martial endeavor, or even a revolution. (Marseilles and Rennes le Chateau are part of the Cathar Southern France that was Druidic and had a university for Druids that was well known to ancients. The French national anthem is also of note.)

METATHESIS The interchanging of consonant sounds to produce different (though relevant) words. For example,

Diverse Druids

'brune' is metathesed by Nostradamus in 'brume'. In quatrain III.53, which deals with the Second World War, Nostradamus subjects the German place name Augsburg to metathesis by rendering it 'Augspurg'. The new word is relevant because the quatrain seems to relate to the expulsion of the Jews, (literally, an 'aus purgans', to remain with the Germans) under the Nuremburg Laws.

METONYM A word used as a valid transference, in which an attribute of a thing or person is used to denote that thing or person.

PARAGOGE The adding of a letter or syllable to the end of a word.

PROTOTHESIS The adding of a letter or syllable to the beginning of a word.

REBUS A riddle by which pictures, letters or sentences are read in terms of sound values. Rebus in its arcane sense, seems to be from alchemy, and is linked with 'Rebis', which means in ablative Latin, 'the thing twice'. The thing twice is the thing seen from two aspects, once in a material sense, a second time in a spiritual sense. In some alchemical documents the 'rebis' is said to be an egg, (Cosmic eggs, Druids Eggs and all that Easter eggs were derived from are very important.) or the contents of an egg, consisting of red and white, (I think relates to the red cinnabar from which mercury is taken and also the white light attunement state necessary to make the Stone for a real alchemist working with the right ethic.) 'in the same proportion as in a bird's egg'. There are seven levels to every alchemical symbol, but this red and white is the blood and tissue of the human being who, as the Buddha said, lives in an eggshell, even though the shell of the philosophic alchemist is a far from auric thing, sheathing bodies quite invisible to ordinary vision. The Red (rouge) and the White (blanc) to which Nostradamus frequently refers in his quatrains are at once alchemical, political and ecclesiastical symbols, according to the spiritual legacy of the reader. See also ICONOMATIC.

SYNCOPE A Greek word meaning 'cutting short' - in literature, an abbreviation.

Robert Baird

SYNECDOCHE A literary technique of 'part for the whole', by which a less comprehensive term (such as the name of a town) is used to represent a more comprehensive term..." (4)

Nostradamus was more than just an alchemist as he had the Philosophers Stone just as Da Vinci did. It is no coincidence that the De Medici/Borgias were a major part of their lives. Leonardo was also the head or 'Nautonnier' of The Priory of Sion which is the founder or co-founded by the same people who made the Templars. The connection to Solomon is no accident but I still do not know if there have been two warring parties all through recent history in these inner sanctums. Johannites of Da Vinci may be counter to Merovingians and thus the world we know is a contest of *their* wills. But that is beyond the scope of this book as Ovason notes when he refers to the 'bees' and Napoleon. I am sorry to leave such an important connection lying fallow. If one follows the *Hanes Taliesin* information back to Melchizedek who is honored in the name of the secret steering committee of the Mormons one can see the possibilities of alchemical games that are at the root of much we suffer under. I am a hermetic philosopher and those who claim I am disparaging them are wrong. I am trying to atone for the acts of those who took power too far, in the spirit of Socrates.

The *Most* Important 'Thing' In My Life!

The stele at Chichen Itza is a cornucopia (or cauldron of Kerridwen) of symbols and astrological mathematical knowledge. I should dearly have loved to have been able to bring it under some research auspices to interpret them all. Unfortunately my efforts to that end were stonewalled and I was threatened with life in a Mexican prison while no recourse was legally going to come to my aid. I was made to sign a document that made it clear if I were ever found in a Mexican archaeologic site again that I would be subject to imprisonment and having foregone any rights of American and Canadian citizenship by this document, I did not

Diverse Druids

continue my quest so actively. There are bigger fish to fry connected with it that I am trying to elucidate in my books. Subsequent to my first visit to Chichen Itza in 1993, I found the photographs taken of the side of the stele that had what I believe is the Cara-Maya alphabet did not turn out in the photographs we had taken of the pristine pink granite with its symbols (etched or formed?). Col. Churchward notes this alphabet is the medium to translate the Greek alphabet as the story of the end of Mu. I knew these things were important as soon as I saw the stele and now I wonder if the Rosicrucian guardian had something to do with the photos not turning out. I really didn't even think about this until this moment because Bernard and I had such an open conversation. Maybe someone he reports to had someone else watch over my acts upon my return to Las Vegas. Pure Paranoia you might say - but I am reaching the point where I see that all sovereign nations on earth are founded by the people who abuse their citizens and keep the fiction alive which courts might otherwise change. It is probable that most people only get a little of the picture and I am only able to present a limited number of facts and not a complete story of it either. Perhaps I should not even mention it. If 60 Minutes can't get the US Army Corps of Engineers to tell them who authorized the cover up and destruction of the Kennewick Man site you can imagine I will have a hard time pursuing my suspicions.

    This stele may hold the key to Time Travel according to a Masters Degreed person in Archaeology who I showed the pictures to. Whoa NELLY! That was my reaction too. But now that NEC Labs at Princeton have produced 300X the supposed absolute speed of light I am buffeted in things I have studied for a very long time. That too, must remain for another book that I have done. Time travel at a subatomic level is already a proven thing and the 'time viewing' aspects of the Philosopher's Stone and Great Pyramid are well worth serious consideration.

    In 1997 I returned to get the information from this missing panel after having sent letters and copies of the photos to some 15 U.S. Universities who work with the Mexican government on things archaeological. The stele had been painted over twice. The final coat was drab Army green and the Army was guarding it from a distance but I didn't think that could be so, despite what my lady said. The former beauty was now made into a phallic symbol just as all the Mexican men seem so oriented. They took the camera and ripped out the film and the charcoal rubbing on the newspaper we had placed over the stele as we were starting to rub was confiscated as well. I was taken behind fences and had to wait for 'the boss' in a small cubby hole of an office as all the men were acting as if something serious had been done. It was a surreal event for me until the thought of a Mexican prison came to my mind as I heard the 'boss' call someone in Mexico City. I do not know who it was but after reading the story of Julsrud's ceramics in Acambaro; I am pretty sure it was the same people who seek to discredit all that might give insight into the great antiquity of human culture.

The National Museum and government in Canada is also proven guilty in the matter of the Jomon/Ecuadorean pottery. The National Museum of Canada is now the Canadian Museum of Civilization (!?) and what they did to Dr. Lee and the Director who supported his Manitoulin artifacts is a crime against humanity. I am not naïve but sometimes I can be pretty stupid or thick-headed. I still learn about the great depths of intrigue and control of society every day it seems. At this point in time I was still deluded into thinking someone might want to know about the rich heritage mankind truly has. I still don't know who the good guys are, if there are any. When I learned the Russell's including Bertrand have a Merovingian lineage that includes setting up Skull & Bones and the creation of the Opium Wars I was more than surprised. Having great respect for Bertrand Russell I began to wonder if he was part of the Hegelian dialectic that plays both ends against the middle. There is still value in the words his grandmother wrote in his Bible: "Thou shalt not follow a Multitude, to DO evil!"

Diverse Druids

As to the Chichimecs having the key to Time as my archaeologist told me (she was also a Hereditary witch) I have my doubts. The work on dimensional chaos and quantum physics has much more to learn about the nature of Time and what the mystics seem to be right about if current research is correct. Carlos Castaneda's mentor Don Juan (the self proclaimed last Toltec) was definitely part of the stele and my awareness of these dimensions. It had always been somewhat intriguing for me when I heard about the team who won a match at the Pelota got to choose who would die. Clearly it would seem a very easy decision. The stele is right behind the Pelota and it has a place on top where a person could sit and transcend this reality. Then I saw what the British Museum has when I read Gordon Brotherston's book *Painted Books of Mesoamerica*. There is a map/picture showing the Toltecs meeting the Chichimecs as they came from what I think was Cahokia. The Toltecs are wearing civilized cotton tailored garb and acting like the white men from Europe that I know they are in the 11th Century.

I think the Roman proscription and bounty on Druids caused many to come to Mesoamerica around the early Christian times and the Adena to Cahokia people are Phoenicians from a long time before. This meeting of distant relations seems most like the Brotherhood which kept in contact through many millennia. The Toltecs as Druids seem more likely the ones who put this stele there as they built Chichen Itza or designed it. The Prince of Palenque and all the written words of Kukulcan's speeches and other reports of the white men and their influence in all the America's are extensive. Kukulcan is also Quetzalcoatl, Veracocha, Xolotl and others. Through many centuries and millennia these Brotherhood people were deified into one character in the various legends of the Inca, Mayan, Aztec, and Chichimecs.

Debunking *My* Myth!

I am always willing to change my mind and consider the possible relevance and integration of new facts. One valuable resource is the academics who debunk the alternative history that I accept is true. By ridicule and the very nature of their questions one sees the agenda more clearly even though it is the perverse or obverse perspective that has merit. The fact that the founders of the US are able to acknowledge they owe their beliefs to Druids as Thomas Paine does in his Pamphlet on Masonry should be kept in mind as we consider the Merovingian question and some thoughts from a great scholar and promoter of the 'prevailing paradigm' named Jerome Bruner. This author does not seem to know the Carolingians are just a Merovingian continuation after one of their bastards named Charles Martel founded a new dynastic line. But you hardly expect to see anything negative written about Merovingians who still control our global society because you are supposed to believe global travel is a recent thing. Bruner is a Professor of a Graduate Faculty on Social Research at New York University and that title alone is enough to make one think of the enigmatic 'social engineers' who are the running dogs or paladins of the financial and armaments oligarchs in Merovingia. Merovingia (?) or Matrix, I am not sure if Earth is the right name for where we live - it certainly isn't appropriate to call it Gaia anymore.

    Yes, there are many layers of 'spin-doctors' including Archaeology Magazine and Professor Wiseman of Boston University (a contributing editor) who would consider me a mere Post Modern dilettante even though I have devoted more energy, time and effort in my research than he ever will. Bruner's book *Actual Minds, Possible Worlds* is published by Harvard University Press and I doubt I will ever be so fortunate. He makes it seem open-minded and scholarly a great deal more than the others I have mentioned with disparagement. It is a book worth serious consideration, as is Fukayama's *The End of History and the Last Man*. If we do not understand the guile of Neo-Platonic authors who seem (or are indoctrinated into their mindset) so authoritative, we might well continuing to follow a path that has led us to war and prejudice. I hope my interruptions can be forgiven as I quote him. There is a connection to what the

Bards did with the Green Language which is the real reason I selected this from numerous other debunking doctrines like Shermer and Randi. You might even find a connection to Hugo's writing as he talked about the "waves of the marvelous" which Shakespeare moved him to analogize eloquently with due appreciation:

"Return to Pope Leo III crowning Charlemagne as Holy Roman Emperor at the Vatican on Christmas Day in the year 800, and to Louis Halphen's reconstruction of the 'causes' and background of that unique event. If we are to understand it, it will not be by means of a positivist archaeology in which everything particular about it and everything leading up to it are finally dug up, labeled, and collated. However much we dig and delve, there is still an interpretive task. (Who gets to be the interpreter? The 'EXPERTS'! But all post-modern people are equally able to make up their own minds if they really look into the facts and let their heart guide them. We are all the children of God; is certainly part of the message Jesus brought to bear on society. That message was never more relevant than it is today long after most people have forgotten Dec. 25th was the date of celebrating Mithras the Bull that Constantine continued to worship and incorporated into the dogma as the Bible editor.) It is a task promoted by rich hypothesis generation, some of the hypothesis obviously being subject to falsifiability. Was Leo the brother of Charlemagne, a nepotism theorist may ask? Well, plainly not. That can be falsified. Was Leo trying to strengthen his alliances to protect the church against the advance of Arab power? Well, possibly, for that power was still on the rise. And more universally, is it not the case that heads of state always seek to form alliances against impending encroachment? (The great emperor in all his HOLINESS paid Alcuin a huge ransom for the scroll of Jasher when it was found. The Arabs were more inclined to accept learning was possible for people and didn't go as far along the path of Dark Ages oppression. I dare to suggest the Catholic fear of impending encroachment was the Manichean and Bogomil type of ecumenicism of Gnostic origins that was threatening to make people act responsibly and avoid interpreters who would sell 'sins and demons'. I don't think Bruner really considered these things and he surely didn't address them in what I read of his book. So rather than arguing about politics and journalists who write history for politicians it is important to avoid IGNORANCE which the Gnostics describe correctly as the Original Sin that separates us from God.) The historian can surely look for congruent evidence in the archives. But we, as seekers of Carolingian history, will look for alternative hypotheses - even if we already believe in the alliance theory.

For the object of understanding human events is to sense the alternativeness of human possibility. (This sounds reasonable to say the least. However, he ridiculed James Joyce and was not as truly open as this sounds.) And so there will be no end of interpretations of Charlemagne's ascendance (or Jeanne d'Arc's fall, or Cromwell's rise and fall) - and not only by historians, but by novelists, poets, playwrights, and even philosophers.

So in the end, what shall we say about the relation of the sciences and the humanities? What shall we say about Lucretius's 'De rerum natura'? An evocative poem but bad physics? If hypothesis 'making' is part of physics, well, Lucretius's poem is full of interesting, original, and eventually falsifiable hypotheses. Its evocativeness as a poem comes precisely from the rich bed of metaphor from which it grows, so that it is readable to us today as a metaphoric perspective on the world of nature.

Aristotle in the *Poetics (11.9)* puts the conclusion well: "The poet's function is to describe, not the thing that has happened, but a kind of thing that might happen, i.e., what is possible as being probable, or necessary. And if he should come to take a subject from actual history, he is none the less a poet for that; since some historic occurrences may very well be in the probably once possible order of things: and it is in that aspect of them that he is their poet." (5)Yes, the bard or poet is an interpretive thinker of possibilities who often cuts to the chase of the real moral dilemma. So what are historians? I posit the historians are no more correct and frequently they are motivated by appeal to convention and the current victor or paradigm which has a very suspicious continuity. One must therefore look to broader issues and timeframes or the ethos of the whole period and era during which the human drama is played out. These motivations are often simpler to see rather than debate Charlemagne and his recorded acts. Do we hero worship Charlemagne as Holy Roman Emperor and another red head who came from the Merovingian lineage because he was a great and ethical person? No. We do this because we are presented with perspectives that honor their greatness; made great by those who wish us to model ourselves after these false heroes. The words put in the mouths of others (especially once they are dead) are often changed as the paradigm shifts. Cleopatra and Jesus are prime examples that I started this book by mentioning.

Mandalas and their Forces
　　The shamans go by many names in this whole wide world. Sometimes their intricate designs on the sub-continent seem almost too busy and they are not symmetrical with the four entry points that simple crosses or the swastika easily demonstrate. These kinds of designs are able to capture spirits and lock their energy in the tapestry of lattices or mazes that are purposefully designed into them. Solomon's Seals and the labyrinth with its Minotaur are similar constructs to deal with these forces. My stele also had a design with 88 intersecting points made by semi-circles; this was located over astro-mathematical formula on one of its panels that I spent many hours contemplating and lots of time researching. I am not able to say all that is entailed but I would like to include a piece on the mandalas so that people might grasp a little more of crystalline and geometric force along which our cosmic soup real world operates. The plaids and lozenges or swirling designs of early Keltic art and architecture are especially relevant and

were part of what took Elizabeth Wayland Barber to the Tarim Basin to study the red headed mummies near the present Great Wall of China. This will play an important role in bringing a lot of things together once you see some of what she discovered.

The music and rhyme of the lyric bards aroused passions in the libido and soul through something called the Lost Chord which I think is Harmonics and a very different science we are just on the verge of knowing in the science of today. The Dervish or other Dream Dancers as well as crystal therapy and aromatherapy all go to create contacts between people and the spiritual world. The title of this book will provide a little insight into how the author sees some of the connections between the brain and the rest of our existence. It is originally written in Italian in 1961 and the name of the book is: *The Theory and Practice of the Mandala, With Special Reference to the Modern Psychology of the Unconscious*:

"Cognition (by virtue of which consciousness becomes cognizant of itself and of things) is not an hypothesis. It is the embryo of the supreme sound identical with the very essence of consciousness. And it is cognizant of all the union of 'śaktis', of the powers of God which bring about the universe in all its extensions. The principal powers of God are three, the supreme power ('anuttara'), will ('icchā') and expansion ('unmesa'). This triple aspect of cognition is symbolized by the three vowels A - I - U. From this triad proceeds the diffusion of all the powers. Beatitude ('ānanda') is the point of rest in the supreme state; creative capacity ('isāna') is the point of rest in the will; and the wave ('ūrmi') is the point of rest in expansion. (Which Hubbell photos prove our universe is doing at variable increasing speed according to astrophysics.) This wave is the principle of the power of the act." (6)

This 'rest' or stillness that unifies one with each of the different aspects in triads (of great Keltic import) such as above requires a balance of the duality of our brain that values both 'yin and yang' or male and female, or left and

Diverse Druids

right hemispheres of the brain etc... A oneness can be achieved and lived in while still incorporate in human form and we have mentioned the fMRI research that goes to prove the mystics have always been more aware than Western science gave them credit for being. This knowing or 'tapping in' as I called it in the early 70s or Hippie culture days is akin to the saying attributed to Jesus - 'Be Still, and KNOW, that I AM (YHWH).'. Jung's collective unconscious and the harmonic convergence DO converge in this description of the Eastern philosophic impulses of the things we will see originate in Druidry and its shamanic roots that may well all be drawn to the Tarim Basin mummies with their 'witches hats' or pyramid headgear that enhances the Pineal Gland or Third Eye performance:

"First and foremost, a 'mandala' delineates a consecrated superficies and protects it from invasion by disintegrating forces (Integration is vital to Harmony and balance.) symbolized in demoniacal cycles. But a 'mandala' is much more than a consecrated area that must be kept pure for ritual and liturgical ends. It is, above all, a map of the cosmos. It is the whole universe in its essential plan, in its process of emanation and reabsorption. The universe not only in its inert spatial expanse, but as temporal revolution and both as a vital process which develops from an essential Principle and rotates round a central axis, Mount Sumeru, the axis of the world on which the sky rests and which sinks its roots into the mysterious substratum, This is a conception common to all Asia and to which clarity and precision have been lent by the cosmographical ideas expressed in the Mesopotamian 'zikkurats' (ziggurats, built to reach the god Mardak or whatever) and reflected in the plan of the Iranian rulers' imperial city, and thence in the ideal image of the palace of the 'cakravartin', the 'Universal Monarch' of Indian tradition. Such correspondences and theories, of Mesopotamian origin, accord well with primitive intuitions (Aka 'shamanic') according to which the priest or magician marked out on the ground a sacred area. This, by the line of defence which circumscribes it, represents protection from the mysterious forces that menace the sacral purity of the spot or which threaten the psychical integrity of him who performs the ceremony; it also implies, by magical transposition, the world itself, so that when the magician or mystic stands in the center he identifies himself with the forces that govern the universe and collects their thaumaturgical power within himself." (7)

There are so many reasons to talk about the Angkor Wat cosmological constructs and Wiccan or other consecrations but I hope the reader can see all the things herein that we touch upon in all the esoteric things discussed. The 'temporality of existence is becoming very questionable through the 11 dimensions of String Theory and these Mandalic interfaces of protection (talismanic) or consecrated attunement are very important to the centering process of the individual. And in case you are Asian or 'open' enough to put your mind around these entirely spiritual concepts let me point out that Lao Tzu of the *Tao Te Ching* went west from China to meet the Ancient Masters he was indebted to when his appointed time to ascend from this realm was upon him.

"Some Chinese mirrors are known, because of certain designs with which they are ornamented and which suggest the capital letters T. L. V., as 'T. L.V. mirrors'. These have been considered as sundials, which they are not. They are 'mandala' schemes of the universe - round heaven, the pole star or 'axis mundi' in the middle; square earth; the four gates of the Chung-kao of China or of the royal palace correlated with the 'axis mundi'. The graphic representation of schemes of the universe which are made in this manner serve, none the less, a magic end, that of Return, of Unification with the central point from which, as soon as it has been attained, is derived the omnipotence of him who achieved this. The 'Tao' - first principle and Prime Mover of all things (see Karlgren: Early Chinese Mirror Inscriptions, p. 31, in the *Bulletin of the Museum of Far Eastern Antiquities,* No. 6(Stockholm, 1934)) - is identical with the center and unity: 'May your eight sons and nine grandsons,' reads the inscription on one of these mirrors, 'govern the center'; that is, may they unite themselves with the Supreme Mover, source of immortality and of thaumaturgical power. The grandsons are nine because nine is the perfect number: specifically, four females, even number, 'Yin' the female principle, the moon; and five males, odd number, 'Yang', the male principle, the sun (cf. Karlgren, p. 43)." (8)

He also says: - "I AM it (the real) and in it (that is) in myself all is reflected." In all religions there are the same mystical premises and I am not the first to draw the speculative premise that the travels of ancient people have a lot to do with that. The archaeology of today is far more evidence than is needed to draw the conclusion that it did happen. If one was to accept some coincidence is at work in all these things it would test the credulity or speak to a God that instructed all in some direct manner. Without disregarding that possibility I choose to think man is responsible rather than aliens but I do agree the collective attunement of Animus Mundi or the World Mind could be a factor. We must accept our ignorance if we are to keep an open mind.

When I returned from Central America I was towed in by the Coast Guard and treated like a 'wetback'. I lost all the resources I had and may never recoup them. It will matter very little to me, if I can affect greater respect for the people who are abused by leaders who look down upon natives, all over this beautiful planet.

Robert Baird

CHAPTER SIX:
Sumer, Shamans and Silliness

Dilmun Deliberations

The tablets found in Sumer number in the hundreds of thousands and are very clear on the fact that some of them (the leaders or teachers) came by ship or watercrafts that are illustrated on these tablets. The idea of the Fertile Crescent or Sumer being the birthplace of or 'cradle of civilization' certainly appealed to Bible Narrative promoters. How anyone could seriously consider this in modern times is beyond my imagination - yet most books still repeat this highly prejudicial and false ideology that appeals to so many white people. This appeal serves to inflate the ego of some highly volatile people in the misogynistic area that has historically brought so much war to our planet. It is not likely that some people in high places have not had access to the books that were gathered by Alexander the Great or Ptolemy and told a far different history. In fact the Hindu Puranas make it clear that man has been evolved culturally for at least the 462,000 years that Joseph Campbell wrote about. Civilization is a word bandied about by elitists who desire to impose their will and rip off other people. This is not a case of over inflating the reality or making incendiary remarks and should easily be accepted as the War on Terra (Bush does sound like he is saying that.) continues unabated.

I think the Egypt Exploration Fund's articles and memoranda of incorporation are a powerful example of how this hegemony has wound its ethics and goals into a history James Joyce correctly called a 5000 year 'nightmare'. Jung called the whole mess 'Ur-stories'; but why listen to a man who had 'visions' even if he is the Father of Modern Psychoanalysis? The Fund's articles state they would not fund any excavation that didn't dovetail with the Bible Narrative and Memphis was the key site of the original colonizers. It has been built over to such an extent that now (when funding and religious issues are less uncertain) we

Diverse Druids

may never find most of this Keltic administrative center. But enough is being found and National Geographic correctly says we should be asking who the colonizers were rather than talking about the place or what it now is inhabited by. The fact that the head of antiquities in Egypt is associated with the Cayce Foundation and that Edgar Cayce and his father were both Masons is something a few researchers such as myself, are following up on (*Stargate Conspiracy* is worth reading). Zahi Hawass is this top government official and I find his explanations of artifacts and the Giza Plateau beyond simply disingenuous. When they allow alternatives to be talked about on TV shows they usually include alien possibilities rather than other serious possibilities. Christopher Dunn and Dr. Davidovits have great technical expertise on how the Pyramid was built. Some suggestions like one covered in Archaeology Magazine when they intimate it was a mere imitation of nature is farcical.

The Sumerian records are being interpreted by Sitchin and the Rosicrucians like Sir Laurence Gardner and his forwarder HRH Nicholas deVere with a complex Anunnaki alien reptoid theory well supported by Biblical scholarship. I touched upon this earlier while mentioning the D'anu and Anu the Keltic goddess that brings the Tuatha de Danann to the stage of a history more real but considered legend, by propagandists or historians (if there is much difference).

The Sumerians write about Dilmun, Makan and Meluhha. I believe the Phoenician port of Byblos in the Persian Gulf, which the World Book Encyclopedia says Egyptians were buying ships from in 2900 BC, is what might be called the present day Bahrain. There have been many climate changes and upheavals since then but there were far more in the period shortly before that and especially around 5500 BC when the Black Sea was created by a 400 foot wall of water. It came from the Mediterranean as it broke through the Dardanelles which are named after the Dandanai or Dardanai who are linguistically traceable to the De Danaan. The Greek people know they are related to the Danaus or the DNN and

Robert Baird

DN of Homer. Makan is 'Magan' and we saw how 'G' and 'K' are interchangeable in Huna of Hawaii.

Dilmun is a matter of dispute with some saying it is in Casiberia or Armenian northern Persia while others favor the Persian Gulf. I say it is both! The reason for this is both were Phoenician and the Casiberia or Iberian enterprises were located in many other places as well. I know Ilvarta of the Indus pre-Harappan culture plays a major part in this as well. It could be Meluhha is a name given to it by those who spoke other languages. Findias in pre-Black Sea times was a vital Keltic (one of four) center. I think it was inundated by the Black Sea and the people from there moved to relatives and colonies on higher ground such as Tiflis which was called Iberia until recently and is where Herodotus has the Amazons cavorting in his day. Tiflis was also a capital of a far larger region called Iberia, then there is Tartessus on the Iberian Peninsula as well as Ireland that Agricola called Ibherniu are others in this worldwide Iberian trading empire. In each millennium during glacial changes the people moved and the harbors filled with silt such as happened in Aa-Mu (Troy) on several occasions. The Basque are the most intriguing and omnipresent but unknown part of this whole mix for me still.

Berbers play an important part in North Africa and the Middle East and they are sometimes the Sea People or Hyksos according to various historians. As bedouin they would have a key role and I think they intermingled with the Basque. Berbers are still sometimes blue-eyed and blond and the Stuart ('Bees') historians trace their lineage to them in some manner. But the one telling thing about the Basque comes from linguists who note a similarity in syntax and grammar between SE Asia (Vietnamese), the Denhe of the Pacific Northwest (near Kennewick Man) and Central America where priest found a Basque speaking enclave in recent times. Genetics says the Pima Indians of the American Southwest have Berber blood and RH factors connect Iberia to them as well. Central America also had the purple dye of the Phoenicians. It is a technology that experts

Diverse Druids

have made strong connections with. There are so many things like these few examples and the Berber languages are so numerous along with their cranial types that one must think they traveled the whole world in the way the Megalith Builders did.

Recent satellite photos led to the discovery of the legendary Kidmet Enrob on the Persian Gulf Silk Route near Magan (per National Geographic). I think Dilmun was most likely Byblos in the language of the Ilvartan or Meluhha people who were another partner in the Phoenician Brotherhood that included a special science and research component with universities in Puma Puncu Peru, Malta, and the Tarim Basin that we are going to deal with in more detail. The Garden of Eden may also be part of this Byblos enclave that taught the Sumerians about languages as included in the Tower of Babel legend. Babel, the Bible and Byblos all are the same when put in vowelless alphabetic form that was the case amongst these people. BBL also comes from the Keltic God Bel and Phoenician Ba'al to bring us another Byblus later, in the region of Ba'albek where they had a prominent center for a very long time due to nearby resources on Cyprus (such as the copper) where the original Mt. Olympus was located. We saw how the Green Languages use techniques that fit with the doubling of consonants. I think it often indicated a people or location once removed or cousins of the original. This is seen in DN becoming DNN as the followers of Dana or D'anu become the Danann and then De Danann. Ba'albek is the site of huge stones (just as mountains in Peru) which we cannot move with modern technology and the Shining Ones or Heliopolitans who worshipped the Sun like the Druids (SN = Sun and Son) are traceable into the dim reaches of history. The clues or speculations are based on amalgams and integrations of hundreds of authors and I must give some more from them at this point. From Heyerdahl's 1981 book *The Tigris Expedition* we see:

"As we reached the first water channel, two tall marshmen in flowing Arab gowns were waiting for us, each with a long punt (Punt is a Phoenician location as is Pont, one is on the Black Sea.) pole of cane. One held back a long black canoe with his big bare foot as they welcomed us and signed to us to step on board. This was their usual 'mashuf', the slender, flat-bottomed longboat built to standard lines by all Marsh Arabs today. While formerly built of their own reeds, they are now pegged together with imported wood and covered, like their reed prototypes, with a smooth coating of black asphalt. Prow and stern soar in a high curve like the Viking ships, following the five thousand-year-old lines of their Sumerian forerunners." (1)

Reading this book will convince anyone that food is often available on these voyages. The ships themselves have crabs that eat the remains of the shark or Mahi Mahi that follow the boat. It was interesting to read about storms that brought all kinds of spiders and insects of land far away while he went to Africa and back. He is famous for Kon-Tiki and the biological and linguistic proofs that caused academia to do a re-think on their Polynesian program. Most of the legendary voyages using old technology have been re-enacted and shown highly doable. Tim Severin recently did the St. Brendan voyages and I would love to see a follower of Admiral Morison and his Columbus discovered America school of thought (?) debate Heyerdahl or Severin.

The Real 'Berberoi' or Barbarians Are In Rome!

The Greeks called the Romans barbarians and the Romans called the Kelts and others by such epithets derived from insecurity when people meet foreigners with different customs, and then seek to conquer them. Philistines and Sardinians or Pirates all have been castigated and denounced for doing what all variety of people did in Sybaritic fashion through what we call history. Most of these peoples have been shrouded in mystery or considered mere legend until such things as the site of Sybaris was found just where the Pythagoreans of Croton re-routed the river to inundate their opulent and decadent lifestyle at the time when Rome was founded after the Battle of Alalia near the end of the 6th

Diverse Druids

Century BC. Whoever can say what really happened in any brief ethnic era is writing fiction or some self-centered variation of the truth at a minimum. I hope this effort builds the possibility that man was not always so power oriented and that we can look for answers that are applicable in the repeating nature of our behavior. It wasn't just catastrophes like the Carolina Bays meteors that ended prior advanced cultures on earth. There are many earth sciences that tell us a lot more about the glacial and volcanic history which were fearsome and impressive during turbulent times. In fact all areas of science are participating in this grand rediscovery of man and his history. But no one is putting it together in the West which wants to proceed with 'status quo'.

Remember how much was made of Marco Polo? Some went so far as to suggest he discovered trade routes man wasn't always accustomed to using. A part of this fiction is related to the Columbus discovered America and the Flat Earth we supposedly believed in before that. I am not saying the Church didn't promote the Flat Earth and through their effort keep people staying on the feudal lord's land and fearing to escape to America. This started in the late Carthaginian period when kings began to take control of armies. But no navigator worth his salt could believe in a Flat Earth and there are lots of records still available that prove the ancients were not so stupid. The Polos made a lot of money selling slaves to Catholic dignitaries and the most valuable slaves were Tartar women.

The Kublai Khan offered to make all his Empire Christian if Catholic scholars could debate his scholars and demonstrate they knew what they were talking about. The Polos tried to get some scholars to return with them but the Pope had died and it took years to settle who would take his place. The infighting and buying of the Lord's only representative on earth was a sight to behold. The two or three who went with them, returned as soon as they found some sweet sexual slaves. The Templars guarded their return from a short distance and it was not likely they were afraid for their life because the Polos had a letter or documents from the Khan that made it clear they were to be treated with respect. Respect was a hard thing to find in Venice where rich men would rape virgins in church and only have to pay a prostitutes wage in compensation. The Catholics knew through their Nestorian priesthood how much knowledge there was in China. The Nestorians were well ensconced in Chinese politics when Genghis Khan or Temujin arrived there before the Polos. Archaeology provides Byzantine coins from the 5th Century AD being found recently in a Chinese Emperor's palace. When we get to the Tarim Basin that lies in between China and the Middle East you will understand why I think man has been in touch from East to West, for at least 25,000 years across three land routes as well as many sea routes.

Yes, there is little truth in history. It is a tool of social management just as the whole field of academics is - you tell me when this started to become the norm. William of Rubruck was a Catholic scholar who preceded Marco Polo to spend time in the Altaic Mountains. The author of a book on the history of technology thinks much of our technology originated in the Altaic/Tarim region which I think includes recent discoveries in Turkmenistan on the way from the Casiberian homeland of the Kelts. The University of Pennsylvania and others working in Turkmenistan may someday see it was on the way to Tarim or an outgrowth from it, but you will be able to decide for yourself whether the pre-glacial people were Kelts or not because it cannot be proven at present. Rubruck's writings are an important insight that led me to know the Catholics or their inner sanctums in association with others could have stopped the Plague. Later I found it was planned when I found a brief passage in Churchill's *The Island Race*. Clearly any group who would unleash the Black Death on their own people and encourage the Flagellants to blame the Jews is a very heinous cadre or cabal of disgusting people. Not just simple 'barbarians' but something far worse.

Rubruck writes about witnessing shamans affect the wind and rain. He and I share this perception but any reader who has not had the experience (and many who would have had it) will not easily accept that thought can manifest change to this degree. The psychiatrists or science that wanted to see acupuncture classed as quackery because it had a history of working for many millennia and they did not understand it are in control but maybe that will change soon. People are turning to alternative medicine in droves and elective treatment expenditures on alternatives equals the funds spent on conventional treatments according to a recent Time magazine cover story. Acupuncture includes the attunement with 'chhi' or 'shakti' that also relates to the exterior world around our bodies. We do have more than just our physical body but the science that only believes in what it sees ends up flushing the facts down the toilet. These Toilet Philosophers might say the solution to pollution is dilution and cloud our heads with facts they know about the bones and muscles or the drugs they use to control us - but we are soulful and spiritual *first* and foremost.

When St. Columba affects the wind and rain or Jesus manifests something, the church calls it a miracle because they do not want you to learn to heal yourself or exorcize the demons they wish to scare you with. Mircae Eliade clearly connects the 'smiths' and early metallurgists with the evolution of alchemy. Genghis Khan's family came from a long line of 'smiths' which I think are directly related to the residents if the Tarim Basin.

So he is just another alchemist who had to hide his interests somewhat. Actually he did not hide it as much as history would have us believe. It is more a question of historians wanting to paint him as an ignorant nomad with bloodlust even though his Empire was the largest and safest in modern history. When a Taoist sage spent most of a year with Genghis/Temujin I believe they discussed things historians would not be able to follow or understand, including what caused Lao Tzu to visit the Tarim Basin to meet the Ancient Masters of MU/Atlantis. Who (again) are the real barbarians?:

"Even Pope Dionysius (AD 259-268) is recorded as owning gladiators and attending the games. Ironically, it was not until the fifth century, when Rome was invaded by those they called 'barbarians', that those same 'barbarians' put an end to the bloody and violent spectacles." (2)

The Alchemy of Politics

The most barbaric thing of all is making people believe there is no soul or that only the Lord's representatives can know what all people should be encouraged to know. A good example is Sir Isaac Newton. He is roundly appreciated for early mechanics and science but about 25 years after his death the personal effects were researched and released that showed he was an alchemist. No matter what you think (Led by propaganda to the conclusion of hermits turning lead to gold.) it is quite oppressive to have to hide the truth of one's pursuits to the degree he did. Jung has recently been called an alchemist in a Time Life video. Hermeticists galore have been the most important people in science and the good Rosicrucians had to infiltrate certain social structures to make themselves safe from the grave (literally) results that occurred to their forbears. They are humanists and good people in the main. However, many pretenders to power have abused this knowledge and will have us believe they are humanists too. It is still a major issue despite what the common people think.

When Newton presented his magnum opus named *Principiaea Mathematica* he said it was much less than there was but much more than he should have laid before the people. The law that requires silence is a good law and the pentagon-dodecahedron knowledge made Greek sages like Pythagoras have to act with great circumspection. If this knowledge had fallen into the wrong hands it would have meant a possible end of life on earth. Newton and the Royal Society established by the Stuart patronage are the outgrowth of the Milesian (Sons of ML, Mil, Mile, Mallia, etc.). These 'Bees' have had their battles royal and are prominent in the truth of history till this very day. But that is

Diverse Druids

the proverbial 'other story' which I cover in other places already mentioned. I may never be able to prove Jefferson was a Newtonian to the satisfaction of those who wish to diminish the alchemists' lot in science and politics, but it is my opinion he was far more than his Rosicrucian fellow founders of the U.S. or Masonic 'Enlightenment Experiment'. You should ask how far off track did things in the New World Order move away from many good ideals established during this 'Experiment'.

The papal part in all of this reached the heights of true barbarism with the Borgia/De Medicis a millennium after the supposed 'barbarians' ended the 'violent spectacles' of Rome. It was a position of great power and quite literally up for sale. The De Medicis also took over the Templar monopoly on European finance at this juncture. These related facts also probably connect with the Alumbrados. They were the inner sanctum group who founded the Jesuit Order that has taught alchemy through St. Thomas Aquinas and the work of Aristotle ever since. They are great lobbyists and technocrats whose influence in all facets of society can be viewed as either good or bad by many. I am personally not averse to a New World Order but I don't think it is very new at all. Can any people today grasp how thoroughly wicked it is to have such a concept as the 'Divine Right of Kings'? Beneficent paternalism has a weak and tawdry political reality at best and an outright disgusting war-mongering greed at worst. You must decide for yourself, but how can you decide if you are always lied to? What kind of paternalism is it that seeks to minimize women, the soul, and each individual's potential to manifest great new ways of allowing life and GOD to harmonize? Who can limit GOD or Nature?

Enough pontificating or philosophizing, I must remember that everyone doesn't believe the Church is so horrific and move on to give further reason and argument to that end. When the International Independent investigators found the Catholic Church primarily responsible (with second going to their henchmen the Anglicans) for the genocide in Rwanda, did that cause an outcry? Did the Irish people clue in to what is happening in their Emerald Isles? Do they even care for anything more than their current political diatribe and guerilla warfare? Apparently few do. I posted an offer on an IRA website to give them a chance to engage their own roots and history. Sein Fein was started as a cultural educational and newspaper outreach but who cares when there are guns to fire and people to kill? The Keltic Creed or No Fear philosophy has a long heritage in Ireland but it is not properly applied when people do not know what they are really fighting or fighting for.

The Northern Irish have a financial agreement with the English and thus they say they are against Catholics. The English practice the same rituals in their Church of England (Anglican) as do the southern Irish. If it were really a religious difference wouldn't the North be against the Anglicans who really are not anything like their Protestant faith. I do Protest but not like the anti-Semite Martin Luther. I protest the crime against all life and the soul or spirit - I *protest* against the continued sheering of sheep and the lack of true history or heroes we are led to follow. It is barbaric and without compassion while empowering nations and corporations even more than *divine* kings who had to appear to care for their serfs. I am ashamed for the behavior of my fellow Scots who took Irish land given by England. I am ashamed of what has happened to Druids who bore my last name and the given name of Robert de Bruges that I bear. I am proud of the ethic for Freedom that William Wallace portrays in *Braveheart* but I wonder if one can be free while colonizing and bastardizing any real truth or potential for all mankind.

The Druids would be a far more preferable and trustworthy council to guide us. Genghis Khan had the best (albeit through use of force) government of his era and his Pax Tartaris treated everyone equally and with respect so long as they were doing the same thing for others. He was the one who opened the Silk Route when the Moslems or bandits tried to exact to high a toll. Everyone knew how to behave and they did - or else. This was also true among the Kelts who still took great pride in being fair when the English took control of Ireland. That kind of ethic was tops on the list for re-education amongst the English overseers, they had to change all the laws regarding land and marriage. One of the very fundamental things that Roman Christianity insisted upon is monogamy and the Celtic laws placed emphasis on care and rights for children and the extended family. There was no such thing as a 'bastard' until Rome had its way. That is clearly an over-simplification because other Mediterranean misogynists were doing foul things too. Carpini is another scholar who went to visit with the Mongol 'barbarian' often likened to Attila. This Catholic scholar waxed eloquent about how a woman could walk with a gold cistern on her head across the whole Empire with no fear of being raped or robbed. Does your image of Genghis Khan fit any of these facts?

The Druids called their alchemists (at one point in a long history) the 'peryllats'. The metallurgists like the Cabiri were a part of this knowledge enterprise as well. In the area of power and war their arts were very secret and most valuable. The people known as Armenians and some in India made early alloys before 7000 BC yet most others took until 5000 years later to get the knowledge. When you imagine secrets this is certainly one of the biggest but the trade routes and harmonics are even more ancient and more important. The Kelts/Phoenicians had shipbuilding technology that empowered them over any of their competition as well. There most surely was competition and there appears to be a time when Mu and Atlantis were working together. It is pure speculation to imagine when this started but it was certainly important 25,000 years ago.

Religion, Druid Alchemists, and Ecumenicism

The similarity of concepts in all religions often causes serious researchers with an open mind to lose their attachment to a particular belief system or ecclesiastical structure. At the same time once one sees the universality of these concepts it becomes far harder to maintain an atheistical view of our reality. People like Thomas Merton who went through the East before returning to Catholicism are offered a home for their ecumenical knowledge and this is good. But what we need is a lot less structure or money changers in our Temples as Jesus knew. We need Brotherhood and acceptance of the core issues that need no ritual or interpreters. Teachers who learn while teaching and keep their sense of awe rather than dogmatized deviates can see a great beauty in the collective soul of humanity. The next quote is from a Doctor and surgeon who was a Christian preacher when he went to India:

"I am the resurrection, and the life: he that believeth in me, though he were dead, yet shall live: And whosoever liveth and believeth in me shall never die. (John 11:25-26) This is literally true of all disciplines of (for) any saint. To them there is absolute no death. The last enemy to be conquered is death. To every disciple of a living Master, death is an occasion of rejoicing, for the liberated spirit simply steps out of the body as one would put off an old garment." (3)

The shamans are the forerunners of many adepthoods for sure. I could have focused on some other shamanistic discipline other than the Druids to make the main point of tolerance and soulfulness science. But the Druids were the most organized system, and you can clearly understand my lifelong study given my name - I do not think I am biased and I certainly hope each reader can see all peoples were part of this egalitarian Brotherhood before Greed reared its ugly head.

It may have started in our evolution as animals when we learned to differentiate roots and berries or leaves that were hallucinogenic from those that are poisonous. Certainly the sub-continent and the Indus/Ilvarta civilizations were of primary importance in the discovery of many spiritual realities and Asoka had a well refined government that was one of the best of the egalitarian or fair forms of government. But the Tarim Basin or Mt. Meru (Sumeru of the 'axis mundi' we covered through the dropping of the first

Diverse Druids

syllable?) is the best place to see an origin for much of their thought too. Then there was the genetic Haplogroup X factor that dovetails with Gimbutas' linguistic and artifactual record and the Hyperborean or Scythian Kelts. In the end I think we will take the cultural innovations back to Mungo Man or other hominids who survived to teach us (Homo sapiens) much of what our lives are truly based upon.

There are many reasons to think that the akashic or 'direct cognition' from Mac Dari are valuable sources now and for the humans who first intuited new knowledge. How does a puppy or kitten know that grass settles the intestinal tract when first let out your patio doors? Did hallucinogenic plants give man contact millions of years ago with some Godlike knowledge? Can man really know or attune with birds to sense their awareness of the Earth Energy Grid that guides them (and insects) to their seasonal homes? You may never believe in spirit guides, allies, and familiars and especially shape-shifting astral integrations such as all shamans demonstrate. You might have to walk on a Yamabushi/Shinto healing fire like Joseph Campbell did before you accept your own potential and part in all that we can be. The Keltic Salmon of Knowledge was one way they knew about the Earth Energy Grid and through the Lhasa Record's Salmon or other South American legends of the great Salmon I see a place where Solomon got his name. It most directly relates to the all important Sun (sol) and moon but this is part of his wisdom too. Crazy stuff! Not the kind of evidence that makes for real linear logical argument to be certain.

I find a lot of crazy insights in all religions and wonder why people ever believed any of it. The Empire-mongering theologians that historians like Fukayama call 'absolute' and Thomas Merton called 'higher' are even less logical in my mind. The shamans actually did what the major religions today call miracles. Logic is far too easily seduced by ego and man has projected himself upon nature and its real science of multi-dimensional or quantum forces. Thus we made God in our own image and started headlong into a path

163

of denial that our souls are part of the great soup now called the 'quantum or cosmic soup'. It seems so real now that generations of genetics has somehow captured these belief systems that I wonder if anyone alive today can really be free. Fortunately there are many millions of years encapsulated in our genetic "History Book" that Dr. Collins of the Human Genome Project talks about.

Alexander the Great is a Kelt and before he went on his manic or megalomaniacal binge of Empire building he went to the Kelts at a meeting we have some records about. He made a pact with his 'brothers' to make sure they wouldn't scuttle his plans from behind the lines. Many Kelts were great warriors and history records them fighting as mercenaries on both sides of many battles. In this meeting he remarks on the rashness of Keltic people who had NO FEAR. This part of the Keltic Creed is the essence of belief in the immortal soul and the fact that mere mortals are not Divine. Alexander is said to be the first to proclaim himself Divine by some historians. Certainly this attitude was politically attractive and because of his success the ball really got rolling. Some of these nobles began to believe their own press. It shouldn't surprise us too much - given the noble penchant for interbreeding.

Yes, I am trying to add a little humor to what kind of deviates our leaders really have been. Alexander was gay (at least bi-sexual) and quite an esotericist. It is said he found the Emerald Tablet of Hermes Trismegistus and his tutor Aristotle wrote a treatise on alchemy called the *Secretum Secretorum* for him. It is entirely possible that the world would have been better if Alexander had united all people just as the previous Brotherhood had been able to do in the millennia before his. According to my Honors Classical History graduate and associate researcher Peter Lye, Alexander was attempting to mix the world in a giant loving cup. His Professor who wrote *The History of Technology* that I briefly mentioned earlier was ostracized for saying such things. Appian was a Roman scholar who records that Alexander arranged a mass marriage of ten thousand couples from the Orient and Greece to solidify this ideal. I think he needed to proclaim himself Divine for political reasons and I do not think he was as much a megalomaniac as history has tried to paint him. His efforts to make knowledge available through Alexandria are further proof of his humanistic egalitarian ethic that Keltic leaders would have supported.

So why do I call our leaders deviates if they have made valiant efforts to rebuild a one world order without all the attendant conflict borne of racism? Idealists like Alexander, Napoleon and maybe even Caesar and the Enlightenment Experiment called the United States are not necessarily bad at all. It is not a simple matter to say the least. Let me suggest the reality is one of greed and a lack of honesty. I do not think the leaders have been fully honest among themselves and they really only talk about the ideals. This was not true of all of them and it is not true that all academics are fooled by history. Generalities are often only partially true at best. Thus our heroes can be seen as very human people. I prefer to think we could do a lot better if we all knew what the plan really is, and I do not wish to be part of some 'manageable' flock. That is the nature of my bias and prejudice, so I might get a little cheesed off at the lies and superficialities from time to time. Remember this when you find me ranting about the 'deviates' - we are all responsible in some way. If we aren't really willing to work at being what it takes maybe Machiavelli and Lewis ('beast with red cheeks') are right to appeal to our 'base human urges'. It is necessary to be on the same page and have order in society.

The Druids did it through ecumenical ideals focused on Brotherhood and the truth of our immortal soul. However, an element of their society also understood they were not a larger population and had to be great warriors in order to continue to exist if others wished to upset their world order. Somehow they got it right and many millennia of relative Peace and Harmony seems to have been their proudest achievement. Trial and Error and a cadre of educated Bards, Ovates and Druids were the key element. Through trust and

Robert Baird

fair play with even handed treatment of all members of the extended family of man. This is still what we need. Their Council of Six men and women who had no authority but had the trust of the people was what we need most. I ask everyone to look in the mirror or ask their congressman to do the same. Do we really know what the secret agencies and elite have planned for us? Are the right questions encouraged or are they even being asked? What are we going to do about space colonization and gene-therapy, etc.? When will we be told who gets to own or develop Mars even though our resources funded the project (like the Cell phone, computer and other corporate empires)? I would rather be sent to the next realm by a Druid who knew the seat of the soul and the reality of the dimensional soup through millennia of practice than get dumped into a sentient computer like Stanford did in 1999 with the contents of a human brain.

    The common consent management of society through those given titles like king (Rg in Irish and the RgVeda) was not something remotely similar to what the nobility and elite have made it into. It took a long time for them to get the ball so totally under their control. You might prefer it too what they tell you is the alternative but you and I must make an effort to get them to tell us why all the wars keep happening while churches get to rape us - tax free; while fomenting prejudice and differentiation. Bureaucracy and organized effort is only good if it helps more people achieve their personal potential. Our schools do not enable independent thinking or questioning in the Socratic mode. The schools are a battlefield of ignorance with some perverse focus on regurgitating lies like the Betsy Ross flag or the Emancipation Proclamation that freed the slaves of the US (it didn't - what it did was create a fifth column inside the Confederacy for purely political reasons - Lincoln didn't free the slaves in the North with this document).

    There is a great deal more for us to learn due to the destruction and Hellenizing of earlier civilizations. The fact that our leaders sought to keep us in the Dark and burned all libraries or books is proof enough for me that there is

Diverse Druids

something they don't want us to know. It wasn't long ago that the trivial explanation given the name 'Sea People's' served to satisfy most historians that we knew enough about the Phoenicians or Hyksos. The Old European culture of Kelts and Amazons can no longer be swept under the rug. Michael Grant has something to say from the decade before the discovery of the Old European script that Richard Rudgely notes Gimbutas proved in his *Lost Civilizations of the Stone Age*.

Hyperborean Semites Like Solon (therefore Plato) and Sargon

"The Thracians spoke an Indo-European language. However, although stories were concocted to claim that their mythical king Tereus (alternatively described as the ruler of Daulis in Phocis (we saw relates to Phocaea and the Milesians)) had married Procne, daughter of Pandion the king of Athens, they were not Greeks. They had no script or literature of their own, so that they are known to us only through Greek writers. These descriptions are fragmentary, pejorative and restricted to matters of Greek interest. But they are now supplemented, to a limited extent, by excavations.

More than fifty tribes could later be identified in Thrace. Out of these, the *Iliad* (listing contingents that helped the Trojans) mentions three, (4) the 'Thracians' beside the Hellespont, the Cicones between the mouths of the Rivers Hebrus (Maritsa) and Nestus (Mesta), and the Paeones, an originally Illyrian (?) tribe, who were later partially integrated with the Thracians and lived on what came to be regarded as Macedonian soil (Alexander had red hair too), beside the middle reaches of the Strymon (Struma) and Axius (Vardar). Homer also refers to a people at Sestus in the Thracian Chersonese (Gallipoli peninsula).

Finds at Vulchitrun in northern Thrace (northern Bulgaria) confirm significant developments in the later Bronze Age. In the south-eastern part of the country, too, megalithic graves and dolmens ranging in date between the twelfth and sixth century BC reveal a materially advanced civilization. Moreover, Thracians preceded the Greeks in some of the most important islands of the northern, central, western and eastern Aegean (Thaxos, Samothrace, Imbros, Lemnos, Euboea; Naxos; Lesbos, Chios). (5)

The sixth century ushered in a new, flourishing epoch in which the Thracian tribes strengthened their organization, and a revival of the arts began to be apparent. (Revival is right but Michael Grant, great scholar that he is, is not putting the Greeks in their proper perspective. He is doing what all Western academics have sought to do. Who are the Greeks? They are the Danaus of the Kelts who were later given their literature by the Phoenicians who gave them the alphabet. He knows much of this but he presents things in the old way. For example Abaris the Druid is from Thrace or Scythia and the two were pretty much the same Keltic clandoms of pan-tribal Druidism. They fought in the Trojan War but few academics tell us who won or what were the 19 theatres of operation because it was a worldwide war. The date of the fall of the walls of Miletus near Troy and far away Jericho on 1200 BC is just one of the clues. The Thracians were closely associated with the great sage Pythagoras as Grant notes and he also is fair when he says he knows little about the esoteric things Pythagoras knew - yet he calls his well recorded bi-location 'weird'. He notes the many accounts of Abaris teaching Pythagoras but he does not mention the Greeks called the Keltoi by the name 'ancient ones' or 'ogygia'. I learn a lot from his material but I am disheartened by the lack of integration and resultant bias towards the Classical History of Empire. The reason it was a 'revival' is, there was at least four centuries of a Dark Age after the Trojan War.) Several south-western tribes (in what was subsequently Macedonia) issued their own coins, including the Edoni (NB.! Ea in Greek = De = O, of Irish and Gaul, the word Don and Danu are DN and these are 'of' or 'from' the Danaus or De Danaan.). Their king is described as Getas, a royal designation which was also the tribal name of the Getae, the northernmost of the groups of Thracian peoples in the hinterland of the Greek colonies of the western Black Sea coast.

Herodotus may have been exaggerating about the size of the Thracian population (for example Thucydides has their cavalry as less numerous than that of the Scythians. Nevertheless, his words contain much that is relevant, not only to the historian's own fifth century, but to earlier periods as well. The revenues of the princes of Thrace, including the gifts they received from ingratiating Greek states, were enormous. They ruled over a warrior race, and their armies were large and impressive; the southern coastal plains encouraged horse-breeding. But they did not ally themselves effectively with one another. The Thracians, it is true, shared a common race, religion and culture." (6) (But they were part of a free Brotherhood including the Amazons and other Kelts.)

The Uighurs may be associated and may be enemies during development of this Keltic clandom called Thulean, Hyperborean and other names, there is much intermingling and their race was not so clear as a result. In 23,000 BC near Moscow homes with straightened mammoth tusks that archaeologists can't figure out how they straightened are part of the record. The extent of the Scythian domain or association of tribes was most expensive and we are finding many things Grant did not know when he wrote his book. His portrayal fits convention and one must ask why this convention exists. Is common thinking evidence of a plan? With the knowledge that Pythagoras and Thales had a Phoenician parent plus his knowledge that they gave the Greeks their alphabet to write with and his sense that the language was far older or derived from older similar ones I think Michael Grant is catering to this plan. You might say there is inadequate evidence but there is so much evidence it would bore you (and me) to recount it all in one book. We have to cover a lot of ground and make some observations that will make things relevant rather than pure regurgitational history:

Robert Baird

"During the middle part of the second millenium BC the Canaanite cities were ruled by separate kings and fortified by massive ramparts. Later, much of their territory came under Philistine (What IS the difference?) and Israelite control. The Canaanite language, of which the older stage is only indirectly known, evolved into Hebrew, Moabitic and Phoenician. (These are part of the north-western family of Semitic languages, to which Ugaritic (possibly a dialect of Canaanite), Amorite and Aramaic also belong.) Three scripts were used in the Semitic languages: Cuneiform, North Semitic and South Semitic. The North Semitic script has two main branches, Canaanite and Aramaic. (Sargon the Great who had the bulrushes story told about him a millennia before Moses was part of the Phoenician enterprise when the whole show began to break into colonial unrest and misogyny. The Hittites, Hurrians and other neighbors or Keltic 'brothers' of his were still egalitarian enough to let women own land three centuries later but his descendant Hammurabi had to cater to the Chaldeans and allow women to become property of men in his famous Code about a century after that.) The Canaanites are the first people, as far as is known, to have employed an alphabet, which they evolved from c. 1800 BC onwards. The Phoenician and early Hebrew alphabets were among its offshoots. All these alphabets express only consonants." (7)

BBL can be the tower of Babel which is the symbol of those who brought language and culture including adept healing and esoteric knowledge to Sumer (the Logos). It probably would be akin to the top university where these people once lived and taught, and in later millennia was also where the leaders lived in ziggurats they built to copy it and seem like the 'gods' who taught them so much. Certainly we know it was copied and rebuilt. The lack of vowels allowed a lot of leeway in creating different directions for a storyteller such as the bards and their early lyricists, jesters or minstrels like Orpheus. Such a performer could deal with the location associated with the letters and that might have been many locations where the De Danann had spread their

Diverse Druids

knowledge with their associated Red Headed League of Megalith Builders. He might choose to deal with a story about Lugh Long Arm or Sargon and maybe even Lhasa depending on who his audience was. These stories always had morals to teach and people learned and enjoyed at the same time.

BBL can have one of the consonants dropped and be BL or the Keltic god BEL and Phoenician god Ba'al of the Heliopolitan sun worship we have touched upon. The North American continent shows us a late second millennium BC site where Bel, Ba'al and their Keltic/Phoenician worshippers came from all over to be together. It is Mystery Hill, New Hampshire where the region has a long history of Europeans including Newport Tower and Templar artifacts. There is a whole hillside with a gold production and sluicing operation as well as farms terraced on the hillside according to those who should know. The languages of the native people can be shown to have many Phoenician colony influences including Egyptian. Professor Barraclough Fell of Harvard was an early pioneer in the field. Professor Wiseman who we mentioned writes for Archaeology Magazine stoops to questioning Fell because he was self-taught in Ogham. It is a mere fraud. Fell took courses at Edinburgh dealing with what little was known about Ogham.

In any event we are all ultimately self-taught despite what Professor Wiseman thinks in all his great knowledge about things he has not studied. My Ogham scholar is the only person I've heard about who could speak the language and its five dialects. He taught in the California University system as a lecturer, because he didn't have a sheepskin. He agreed with Fell about many things and had me study his work.

Another example of the vowelless languages we have mentioned is MLL and such times they have exerted increasing power as they did in Crete as the Royal House of Mallia where archaeology has the bee pendant to provide our inspection. The 'Sons of Mil (ML)' didn't move to Spanish Iberia after the Trojan War as much as they returned to this

171

Robert Baird

central Tartessus Celtiberian homeland that was always important in the trade with the Americas. I loved seeing the Phocaeans in Grant's work. He is a top numismatist in the world and he mentions the Phocaean 'bee' on their coins while noting their involvement with Tartessus but he does not integrate the facts including Strabo who tells us that Tartessus had a 7000 year *written* history.

So much for the 1800 BC origins of alphabets he talks about while he admits there are some more ancient roots he provides no insight for or to. These 'Sons of Mil' who then became the Stuart kings of Scotland and Ireland (sometimes England) are also in league with the 'Sons of Aeneas' and I continue to explore the associations of the Romano British New World Order that became the norm after the Trojan War. Dates and events are less important than results and motivations in my researches; perhaps this is my accountancy training coming through. Follow the money trail of power to see what is going on in all events of the past and present and you will know why you are being misled or taken down a path to visit the English garden of WASP-ish delight. That is not to suggest they haven't got a good cadre of Catholic and other partners and infiltrators to support their Euro-centric ego which is pablum for the proletarian plebians.

Women in the Mediterranean were forced to prostitute themselves at the patriarchal Temples according to Sir James Frazer's most excellent overview called *The Golden Bough*. He details how Mesopotamian elitist daughters had to do this even if it took years for anyone to avail themselves of the opportunity. True they only had to do it once whereas other Mediterranean cultures made it necessary over long periods of the youth of all women. These women in Phoenician families were obviously concerned and didn't like the fact that red-headed children were being burned at the graves of Osiris and all those semi-deities who were modeled after him (every major god). No wonder there was a Trojan War and the result led many Phoenician Kelts to return to the pre-Glacial Hyperborean 'northern' lands that had been inundated by ice and then water as the North Sea was created in 5300 BC.

Mysterious Meanderings

In *Leap of Faith* by former astronaut Gordon Cooper, he talks about his work with NASA in undersea Mexican exploration. "The age of the ruins was confirmed: 3000 B.C. Compared with other advanced civilizations, relatively little was known about this one—called the Olmec. Engineers, farmers, artisans, and traders, the Olmecs had a remarkable civilization. But it is still not known where they originated. Among the findings that intrigued me most: celestial navigation symbols and formulas that, when translated, turned out to be mathematical formulas used to this day for navigation, and accurate drawings of constellations, some of which would not be 'officially' discovered until the age of modern telescopes."

La Venta, Mexico archaeology has given us lenses where the Olmecs lived. The Olmecs included black people and all races of man in the Phoenician style or cultural Brotherhood so it can be hard for historians trying to avoid the Phoenicians to explain the reality. Some go so far as to talk about aliens just as many would guess if they did not know the earth oozes magma of quartz to provide Central Americans and extrusion machine to make skulls (scryring and divining) or lenses for looking a the heavens. But a simple 'turista' can walk into any souvenir stand and see all variety of cheap crystal balls.

Zechariah Sitchin writes and talks about the Olmecs in his alien theorizing in order to relate them to Thoth or his 9th planet. I believe the Egyptian colonizers like Thoth were involved but NOT likely on the alien thing. If it is aliens from the Pleiades who helped mankind at some point in our genetic development; that is not related to the Olmec or Sumerian colonies of Atlantean/Keltic/Phoenician origin. When academia and media promote Sitchin, West and others who trot out these wild theories it makes it hard for anyone else to get airtime without ridicule for other real alternatives that explain the facts. In Belize and Mexico during long periods of time that I lived and visited there I found most people accept the origin of Mayan people coming from Mu or SE Asia and some of them were archaeologists who knew the Mexican government is engaged in a foul cover-up. The Mayans were in Central America at least 3000 years before the date Mr. Cooper provides for the Olmec in the above quote. Their calendar starts at in the 35th century BC and took time to develop. In Frank Parise's reference book on all the world's calendars you can find someone writing with no bias that will confirm this for you.

    The Druids have been relegated to the paranormal by the same lack of scholarship and underlying encouragement thereof. It results in a fantastic fiction (like Ogham originating in 400 AD (!)) which benefits the Empire builders who ripped this Brotherhood off and then sought to destroy all knowledge they could not keep solely to themselves. Yes, it is difficult for journalists or historians to unearth the spiritual sciences the Druids employed. That should not mean Michael Grant and others have a right to demean Pythagoras and his 'bi-location' that acknowledged scholars witnessed and reported. It does not mean history should be infected by the alien or Elohim garbage, does it? The Druids are the designers of the Pyramid on the Giza Plateau at the center of the earth's land mass. This one Great Pyramid is like no other although the battery alignment of pyramids in Brazil may prove even more interesting if that oppressive government ever allows them to be studied.

    Archaeology Magazine had an article in 2001 when I was writing the first draft of this book which suggested the Pyramids and Sphinx were only imitations of nature (as if that isn't a source of great knowledge). In the article they did not suggest nature provides intelligent design or make any suggestion that science benefits from observing reality (Nature). The unaware reader of such an article would be justified in assuming the 'experts' think all the facts of geology (water erosion studies by Schoch etc.) and other esoteric or mathematical fact; as well as the recorded fictional history all means nothing. The ancients were ignorant just as the Bishop Ussher time-line had so many believing, I guess I am over-stating this a little but there is some reason to say it. Yes, there are natural landforms in places like Rio de Janeiro that look a little like the Sphinx and Solomon's Phoenicians went there too but they did not create a complete Sphinx or maybe they did nothing at all. It is kind of like the clouds, almost, when people see things in them. The Sphinx has man made or cut rocks at the base, which are weathered and datable. It is not just eroded by the wind. Chefren altered the original female face to put himself into posterity. The passive and dynamic duality as known in the Tao or 'yin and yang' was the purpose of its edification by and for man.

The same issue of Archaeology magazine has no mention of Kelts when it refers to the photo of a red-haired mummy from near the Great Wall of China. It does tell us the vast expanse of the (PIE) 'Proto-Indo-European' culture extended all across Europe and most of Asia. They acknowledge the artifacts and origins are centered around the Danube but don't mention the earlier fresh water lake and civilization thereabouts. Why are we not extending cultural development when we are extending backwards by millions and millions of years the existence of hominids on earth? Classical civilizations are not the height of culture or civilized behavior despite what history wants us to believe.

This 'red head' has a tattoo on his face that looks like the sun (Heliopolitan)! It appears to have the four primary forces that we dealt with in the piece on mandalas in the usual compass fashion of more Western simplicity. It has smaller rays in between and I think there are four of them, which would make it the four secondary forces, and in line with the escutcheon of the Royal House of MU that Col. Churchward describes!

The March 2001 issue of the National Geographic has a wonderful photo essay dealing with the skeletons found inside the mud-brick pyramid at Dos Cabezas, Peru dated to 450-550 AD. These children are far taller than people living in the mountains should be. Are they as tall as the Tarim Basin mummies near the Great Wall of China when on lower elevations? These 'giants' or 'giganti' are the Kelts found in Sardinia or the Adena of Poverty Point who grew up to 7 feet tall with regularity just as the Tarim Basin mummies are 6'6" like my nephews who have red hair too. Most pyramids are pale imitations of the Great Pyramid and many became tombs for leaders in need of glory but there are earlier constructions of a like to suggest the base of pyramids that allowed sanitation and defensive potential for their inhabitants. It is of great interest to me every time I see someone writing that the Giza pyramids were tombs. There were no human or other sacrificial or indeed any evidences to support this theory, yet somehow it persists. I hear there are bagpipes drawn on its walls and two sidereal charts of the heavens which led to 60,000 years of advanced astronomical knowledge in my estimation, and that of Professor Hobart of Amherst College in the early 20th Century.

    The 'giants' of the legends in South America were not mentioned. The gold laminating work is suggestive of electrum plating methods linked to Ophir and/or his workmen from Ireland, or another part of the Keltic world where one finds O'Reilly's and O'Regans, who built the Temple for King David in the Bible. Would it be reasonable for this conservative publication to go against the 'No cultural impact' of Europods in the Americas? Why are they reticent to do it or even suggest these 'giant' children are Kelts? Do they know about the Keltic statuary nearby from the pre-ceramic or early Peruvian culture before the Moshe or Moche they are writing about? The fact that Moshe Rabbenue or Moses bore the same title these people are named after may be a stretch of my overly active imagination. With all the other evidence I am aware of, I think it is reasonable to say the Hebrews were Phoenicians who came looking for Peruvian cocaine in the time forensics (Balabanova) proves Egyptians were 'hooked' on it.

Diverse Druids

Shamans, Academics, and the Black Plague

Ultimately the academic need to appear authoritative and able to answer or fit the paradigm they work under is counter-intelligent despite (or because of) the thesis to anti-thesis structure of co-opting change. Recently I read an article by linguists in Scientific American who offhandedly mentioned a 1.5 million year old throwing spear. It makes sense they were around long before that when one considers chimpanzees use sticks for hunting grubs and otters use rocks to break open clams. Of course it takes a special environment for wood not to rot. Two chronologies I checked showed spears coming long after the straightened mammoth tusks from 23000 years ago that I mentioned earlier. The advent of ceramics is similarly fraught with cupidity or stupidity.

Man has innate inventiveness or initiative and hunters use their wits more than urban dwellers as I see it. I love hearing about the people who think milk comes from a bottle and the like. The shamans and smiths who traveled in pursuit of unique bounties of nature and the meteorites that were made into 'celts' (tools like hunting knives) are very much the nature of our Druids. At least 200,000 years ago they may have made an alloyed sword like Excalibur from these unearthly meteorites. I also love to hear the recent neurophysiological studies that 'prove' music affects the motivational lobes of the brain and how modern therapy is finding sound works with depression and the like. We saw Huna knew the effect of chants in very ancient times and the drum beats of hollow trees was more than just a cell phone for early man over 6 million years ago.

Judgment and detective work requires thinking about possibilities. One of the things I've been thinking for a long time relates to the use of the Plague and other biologics against the North American people. I knew about Fort Pitt years later; they used the bubonic fever bugs on blankets given to women in a cold winter to infect a whole Indian nation. It was clear to me if they would do that when the Indian threat was minimal they would have used it before that when they first invaded Paradise. De Soto's meanderings had always seemed calculated to infect as many Indians as possible. The mindset of social engineering and 'sins and demons' or the 'Flat Earth' fear-mongering about monsters being somewhere other than the Vatican shows the kind of control and greed. The Treaty of Tordesillas makes it clear they intended (in the dictated words of Rodrigo Borgia as Pope Alexander VI) to spread the Inquisition through the whole world.

Motive, opportunity and modus operandi or prior acts were all present but I couldn't prove anything without the smoking gun. I wrote how odd it was that Columbus had dogs at the front of his troops and brought them all the way across the ocean. Usually dogs are not great weapons unless (?) they are carriers of fleas from the rats on board ship. Other people I discussed this with still said the Catholics did not know what caused the Plague and their own people were indiscriminately felled by the same pathogen. Good argument, I thought - but still I knew different and thus I continued to research.

Froissart and others calculated the European total at over 75,000,000 people. A war on the citizens and population control to scare the totality of European people! The Flagellants were a Catholic sect who burned whole ghettoes (like concentration camps) of Jews who were blamed for this Plague. I knew Paracelsus cured the whole city of Stertzing, Austria in 1524 and that he was drawing on earlier alchemic and homeopathic knowledge. But by this time other epidemic diseases were working on the few remaining Indians of North America. So what, Columbus flew the Templar flag like Da Gama, a papal astronomer and a friar cosmographer arranged his trip, and the result was horrific. This is not proof. Now, I have the proof that they knew about the plague and how to stop it as well as the words of Churchill saying it was done with design and for a reason he thinks is good:

"The first Western reports of the Black Death actually came in 1347. It broke out among the troops of the Kipchak

Diverse Druids

Khan, ruler of one of the fragments of the disintegrating Mongol empire. His army was besieging the Black Sea port of Kaffa when it was ravaged by the plague. In one of the first recorded instances of biological warfare, the Khan ordered his siege artillery to fling infected corpses over the city walls. In the next six years the dreadful disease roared across Europe in what has been rated the worst calamity experienced by the Western world at that time. A generation after Genghis Khan, Rubruck reported that 'there are plenty of marmots there, which in those parts they call sogur and of which in winter twenty or thirty at a time collect in one hole and sleep for six months: of these they catch a great number.' He also recorded the fact that whenever a Mongol was very sick, a warning sign was put up over his tent advising that it contained an ill person and that no one should enter." (8)

He also described the moving away from camp sites when black rats were seen and the sterilizing of clothes and bathing of people. The rats get the Plague from the Marmots and it is a weaker strain at that point - but still able to kill. It is only recently that we are able to understand the Plague itself more thoroughly than the shamanic smiths of the Mongols. Clearly this is rising to the level of proof given the fact that Rubruck was a top Catholic scholar whose writing were in the hands of his superiors. It is hard to believe that military people didn't savour such a weapon or use it when needed and we know they did at Fort Pitt centuries later. The other major disease that was used against Americans is smallpox. Homeopaths knew how to cure it long before the English allowed noted historian Gibbon to take the scab and inoculate himself. I am certain that 8th century homeopaths like Maimonides understood these cures and I think long before that it was part of the medicine bag of healers throughout the world. So the only missing ingredient is intent and Churchill provides that in his book titled *The Island Race*:

"Philosophers might suggest that there was no need for the use of the destructive mechanism of plague to procure the changes deemed necessary among men." (9)

Sherlock. Silliness, & Speakers

One of the most intriguing aspects of Sir Winston Churchill for me is his membership in the Baker Street Boys. This group of Conan Doyle aficionados would have tried to explore all the things in this book, and no doubt that includes the Druids that Winston joined. Conan Doyle knew that the Cornish language was derived from Phoenician and the story of Joseph of Arimathaea and the Glastonbury Thorn. In fact his real passion was the 'lost civilization' books and research. His Red Headed League (of Megalith Builders) is no fiction. It is fair to say the Winston had wide ranging interests and access to information I will never be privy to. However, he and Conan Doyle lived in a time when archaeology did not have all the evidence that I do have access to. Clearly Conan Doyle's Sherlock Holmes demonstrates that Conan Doyle was a very adept thinker and logician. His ideas about Phoenicians were ridiculed and you will hear people talk about his drug addiction as if that means he was not able to see the facts.

Coca-Cola had cocaine in it in the early 20th Century and Freud (as well as much of society) was addicted too. Winston also spent the last years of his life on the yacht of Aristotle Socrates Onassis. This is important because the Onassis family is a prime Merovingian family from the region of Sargon the Great's Anatolia. In Smyrna near Miletus the family may have a history that includes the blue lotus hallucinogenic plant. Archaeology tells us Smyrna has been inhabited since the 9th Century BC and even before Cätäl Hüyük that Jacquetta Hawkes called precociously advanced in the 8th Century BC. It is my belief that potions and hallucinogens (and the modern medical reliance of drugs) has always been an arrow in the quiver of social engineers. That does not mean there is no validity to the science of Egyptian cults of the Dead which some scholars

Diverse Druids

would have us believe. Easy access to insight through drugs does tend to diminish the reality for those who take this course but not all of their scientists were addicted. Maybe I am grasping for straws and I would be very surprised to find an admission in anyone's writing that would say the doping of people has always been part of the power game of noble elites. However, I was totally shocked to find Churchill admitting the Plague was a necessary agent for societal management, so perhaps my continuing research will come up with something more.

Yesterday I watched the Discovery Channel and a program on astrophysics and the field of X-ray telescopy. It was probably done before the discovery of 300X light speed at the NEC labs in Princeton in 2001 because they admitted to a quandary or paradox regarding heavy energy space particles such as iron and oxygen that bombard earth. They said the particles travel at light speed for only short distances and yet come from all parts of the universe. It would not be so paradoxical if they considered they observe these particles when they have slowed down to light speed, perhaps. This may just be silliness on my part, but there is another explanation or two that tie in with shamanism; I would like to share with you. We quoted Tim Severin and his book (one of less than a handful of books about this great man) on Genghis Khan a short while ago. Tim lives in County Cork, Ireland where my Ogham scholar grew up amongst the dolmen with his sister, and somehow learned to speak Ogham in five dialects. That is no mean feat, because Ogham as a spoken language is dead, like Etruscan. He studied all languages and alphabets and there are many Keltic languages or tongues to draw from. Let us say he actually spoke Ogham as he said. How can that happen?

Shamans can attune themselves with the knowledge of the ages just as the Eastern mystics speak of the akashic record or similar concepts. He may have tapped in or directly channeled to this knowledge or a time when people spoke this language. Please, do not think this is totally silly. I know it isn't. Tim Severin has chosen County Cork just as Georges

Boule did and the Dublin Institute of Advanced study that preceded the Princeton group with the same name. Einstein went there briefly when he left Germany and learned a thing or two to aid in his formulations of the Theory of Relativity then he came to Princeton to work with von Neumann and this new Institute. Schrödinger spent much if not most of his career at the County Cork Institute. Georges Boule is the acknowledged founder of binary math which is the basis of all computers. The Boulean mathematicians at County Cork have incorporated some of the knowledge of the Druids. My Ogham scholar told me Einstein tried to give them credit but the media was intent on making him the star of their new science cult.

How is this possible (you should ask)? Tim Severin witnessed something that may relate to a parallel dimension such as the astrophysics of String Theory formulates in this brief quote: "When she was in her role as shamaness, she had reversed the process, ... Shamans lived partly in our world and partly in the other world. and everything back on the mortal realm became upside-down, inside-out, or back to front in a mirror of reality." (10)

Another possible explanation for these energy dense particles coming from far away and only existing or being observed for short distances is affinity and folding of space or the Stargate theory tied in with Worm Holes. These things of science are quite amenable to the things mystics have always observed or were able to do. In Wiccan rituals they employ a process called 'djezzil' that comes from the time of the Druids. By working counterclockwise or counter to normal or natural process one accesses this 'other world'.

Red Heads Galore

In reading Severin as he quotes the reports made by witnesses of the time Temujin spent with a Taoist sage I see that few of these witnesses got to attend the nightly and daily meetings near the end of Temujin's life. In almost a year of two great people getting to spend time together I am sure the matter of Temujin's 'red hair' and 'smith' knowledge base came up. This knowledge is directly connected to the Tarim Basin and where the father of Taoism went near the end of his life to meet the Ancient Masters of a place that has a MU-Atlantis context in its name. Severin is more open than the others but does not mention or speculate on the connection I see. In fact he may not know the Tarim Basin matter and the archaeology that shows these mummies came from Temujin's Altaic Mountain region nearby. Imagine the extent of this verbal tradition of knowledge that Temujin was privy to and how as a politician he had to do and be something quite different. We are often faced with decisions to do something bad for the Greater Good.

This 'Verbal Tradition' (Qabala, Bardic Tradition, and other ancient knowledge) is said by Georges Gurdjieff to be genetically maintained in 'speakers'. He claimed to be 1/16th 'speaker' and the last of the 'speakers'. I have a hard time with this 'last' and other similar claims. I do believe Temujin was a keeper of this knowledge and have always wondered about the legend of him being the only student of a shaman who graduated early. To do so, required being as powerful as the shaman and then killing that shaman in a battle of psychic and physical prowess.

I am part of forums that include many top archaeologists and linguists. Gene Savoy's top man Gary Buchanan and Clyde Winters are just two of many shining lights in these forums. Gene and Gary have played a major role in ecumenical efforts based on true history. They discovered things in Peru that are equivalent to what Schliemann did in Troy. Here is one discussion of many on the matter of red heads around the world. It is important to remember these forums are informal exchanges and the writing is not always absolutely perfect.

Doug wrote: "Well, I had asked for citations for the legends Ani mentioned, and I haven't had any. So far as I know there are no such legends As I understand it, Inge Schjellerup's Incas and Spaniards in the conquest of the Chachapoyas: archaeological and ethnohistorica research in the north-eastern Andes of Peru contains anthropological

Robert Baird

studies of the Chachapoya which show no non-Indian characteristics."

My reply: Your side-tracks about what is red hair and all the rest is bogus. So are the supposed "anthropological studies" of Schjellerup and her cadres, Muscutt (myopic, couldn't find Gran Saposoa, even though he was right there), Lerche (claimed to have found Gran Saposoa after we already had/discredited for looting, etc.), and Guillen (who has for decades - long before DNA analysis - rejected the mixture of fair caucasian types among the Chachapoyas. It is really not so very far that 'you know.' Using this 'scientific' team, along with Lee and others of that ilk, is like asking R.J. Reynolds for a report on clean air.

These folks go into Chacha ruins, look for mummies with dark hair, dark skin, Indian height and features, then announce 'no fair-haired, tall people.' Then they do cheapo documentaries for National Geographic (or anybody else with money), and find genetic relations to present day villagers, who are, of course, mestizo. When fair-haired, tall, caucasian types were found at Chachapoyas' Laguna de los Condores, they were pronounced 'Inca royalty,' because everyone knows they could not possibly be Chachapoyas.

Add Kauffmann Doig and Adriana von Hagen into that circle.... and there is a group that would well appreciate your type of thinking, Doug.

None of these folks work directly with or are particularly on top of Dr. Woodward's DNA studies at BYU. Shame.

Now, the idea that there were tall Amazonian warriors, blonde, red-haired, green and blue-eyed is not new. It is an oral tradition that is still truth to the vast majority of folks who live there. In fact, there are descendents of these people, with the proper genetic markers for all to see, living in and around the Seven Great Cities of the eastern cordillera. Some of the clearest examples are to be found at Rodriguez de Mendoza.

I, myself, have seen these people.... and some on our earlier teams actually came face-to-face with tall, blue-eyed, blonde warriors on the trail. They are there, but have been

Diverse Druids

moving further west and disappearing as civilization encroaches. Many of the fairer villagers will sit and tell you about their caucasian ancestors. I have also seen hundreds of mummies all up and down the cordillera, and many are unquestionably tall, warriors, some royalty, and with fair hair the norm, red hair often, blonde upon occasion, The 'federation' had these racial types, no question. Bernardo's finds simply add confirmation, e.g., to the racial types and the epigraphy. One does not really need a reference in a book.

However, so you can have some, off the top of my head, the major legend is of tall, blonde, warrior-king aymlap and queen Ceterni and their retinue that arrived on the coast (south of Valdivia) and moved inland, i.e., to the eastern cordillera in early times. The 'lap' is typically Chachapoyan. It is used as a suffix on many structures in the Chacha realm, e.g., Kuelap, Tylap, etc. The legend has gone around for centuries, was reported to and recorded by the Spanish friars. A good version of the legend may be found *in The Peoples and Cultures of Ancient Peru*, Luis G. Lumbrera and Betty J. Meggars, Smithsonian, 1974 - and perhaps other of Meggar's books, e.g., with Evans. (Similar references: Tello, Julio C.: Origen y desarollo de las civilizaciones prehistoricas andinas, Lima, 1942. Valacarcel, Luis E.: Historia de la cultura antigua del Peru, Lima, 1959.)

There is also a well-known tradition of another group that arrived on the coast at a different time - also Nordic types, "giants," who, because they were so big and could not mate with the locals, resorted to homosexuality and became extinct. Many songs about this in the interior. I think that's in one of Meggar's books, also.

The actual name of the people, "Chachapoyas," is Sacha-puyos, i.e., sacha = tall/mountain jungle and puyos = fog, white/misty. In other words, they were tall, white mountain folk.... as described by the Incas, e.g., Tupac Yupanqui in his 1480 war in Chachapoyas. This is chronicled in numerous books, e.g., Hemming's and other histories of the Inca conquest. Linguists agree with this determination, which also links the language of the Chachas to the Canaris, Caribs, Arawaks, Tairona and others - mostly white-mixed racial types.

"Vigorous warriors with white skin" was the general description given by numerous chroniclers of the Spanish, e.g., Cieza, 1554, bk 1, ch. 78; Garcilaso, 1723, pt. 1, bk. 8, chs. 1-3; Calancha, 1638, bk. 2, ch. 8. These and so many other texts, e.g., the lost references of Blas Valera, tell us that the Chachapoyas were quite tall, often fair-skinned, sometimes blue-eyed and/or blonde, that the women - caucasian - were so beautiful that they were sought after by Inca and Spaniard alike. Indeed, Atahuallpa's mother was a Chachapoya, which is where he got his caucasian looks.... as can be seen is his portraits and as described in hundreds of texts. Pedro Cieza de Leon wrote, "the natural Chachapoyas Indians are the whitest, most attractive of all the ones I have seen in the Indies."

Amazing that Schjellerup, Guillen, von Hagen, Lerche, Musckutt, Doig and company cannot seem to locate even ONE Caucasian mummy! Must have been a case of spontaneous human combustion at death. That would be a lot more believable than some of the reports issued by these investigators. It's enough to turn my auburn hair gray.

Oh, then there's the reports of Pizzaro's men who met up with some Chacha warriors north of Cajamarca whilst holding Atahuallpa captive. (That would have been in the forests of Gran Vilaya.) The conquistadors met the tall, blonde warriors - women and men, naked, sporting deers' antlers and pretty much trouncing the Spaniards, which is why they later selected Chief Guamna of the Chachapoyas to help them fight against the Incas. The description given in the chronicles is of "Celtic-type" warriors.

And, while Viracocha, tall, white, bearded - with relief portraitures and busts - was said to be a Chachapoya, there are also the Santo Tomas/Didimo (the twin) legends that say that great religious figure was there, in Chachapoyas. There is even a tomb at Pueblo de los Muertos, with early Christian

Diverse Druids

cross, attributed to him, a church where his footprints are on display, etc.

This tradition was discussed and written about by the Archbishop of Lima, Santo Toribio - biographer Carlos Garcia. That biography, "Archives of the Indies," was semi-published in Seville. It purports to document the "twin Christ" and his mission in the Amazon.... "teaching the true gospel.... of the sun." Numerous chroniclers have touched upon this subject in Peru, e.g., Melendez, Antonio Calancha, Father Juan Vasquez, E.Torres Saldamando.

Irigoyen (another writer) gives specific reference ("On Santo Toribio," pp. 69-149) to Torribio's visit to, and experiences in, Chachapoyas and Moyabamba. On page 252 there is reference to existing parishes in those two towns - their size, amount and type of clergy, property, etc. - during Mogrovejo's tenure as archbishop. In other words, someone was there, before the Spanish clergy, setting up Christian churches. Interestingly, Moyabamba today is a well-known Christian retreat and mission. I hesitate to mention, but south of Chachapoyas, near Levanto, a village has been identified as primarily Jewish.... won't get into that here.

Then, Doug, you can actually sit down some day and read Savoy's books. There are plenty of references therein, none of which are given above. So, there are "citations" in regard to the racial make-up and culture of the Chachapoyas.

- Gary

In 1650 BC an Egyptian scribe copied a document called the Rhind Papyrus during the Hyksos (foreigner) rule of Egypt. This document includes the knowledge of binary math. I believe the IO Torus and the Ha Qabala as well as the Mark of Cain (Qayin) with its tiny dot in an 'O' is also part of a science well developed in ancient times. This science of Harmonics enabled accessing atomic power safely and apparently it also availed levitation. In my youth while listening to the Moody Blues sing 'In Search of The Lost Chord' I had already sensed the import of this Druidic knowledge. I continue my research in these areas and continue to find more reasons to think it is the case. Christopher Dunn's ultrasound drills are only a small part of this ancient science. The Universal Harmonic of light that mystics see in their experiences through the small portal and String Theorists with their 'one dimensional harmonic force' are coming together to make the Logos seem very true - 'In the beginning was the WORD!' I have dealt with the science of this more in *Neolithic Libraries* but I really would like to have time to do what I think needs to be done on Temujin. My first draft books already needing completion may take the rest of my earthly life to complete, so I will have to hope someone else will follow these leads to their logical conclusions. In that process someone should study Orgone and the machine a single man used to build the Coral Castle near Miami, and near where I lived when I read *Seth Speaks*.

Diverse Druids

CHAPTER SEVEN:
The americas are the last bastion of brotherhood:

A Sublime 'Octopus'

Masonry has many layers of mystery and we know Thomas Paine of the Rosicrucian Council of Three (higher than Masons) wrote Masonry is related to Druidism. I don't think the Brotherhood has been so very ethical but maybe they do know what they are doing. I do keep an open mind about it but I also must consider the facts that show a vicious result has been foisted on this planet and its people. By many sources I am sure Paine is right however, and there are many things these great thinkers write that I agree with. It is just as likely that 'spin-doctoring' and 'co-opting' of the Druids was institutionalized by Romano-British Masons; and though Mac Dari was a Mason he certainly railed against the British 'alehouse denizens'. I expect the upper echelon of the Christian Mystery Schools like the Rosicrucians and the inner sanctum of the Alumbrados/Priory could tell us a lot about how they get people doing apparently contradictory things to serve the goal they have in mind. The Iroquois and North American Indians on the other hand have a lot of Druidic acts and customs that include working with the Masons or Templars, in a time before the creation of the Grand Council or Anderson's Constitutions. The possibility is very real that despite the apparent differences between (for example) the various Rosicrucian sects and entities, they all serve a Grand purpose; must be considered.

Just because one high Mason thinks Hitler was never allowed entry to a Masonic Lodge does not mean he was not in a Lodge higher than the ones that particular Mason knows about. When Gelli created P2 and had top Masons from all over the world he didn't include all top Masons. In fact his P2 Lodge (they now disown, after it bankrupted Italy in League with the Vatican as seen in movies like Monsignor with Christopher Reeves) is very similar to the Freemasonic Order of the Golden Centurion (F.O.G.C.) that Hitler did belong to. Hitler was trained in Vienna where St. Germain(e) and other great occultists as well as the Qabalists, expanded the reach of these schools of thought. His father had been there before him and studied the same things. We saw the result in a Decree at the end of Chapter One.

The native ethics that include matri-linear society and land use or ownership that mirrors the Kelts is just the start of what caused the Iroquois Confederacy to have a Constitution much like the United States more than a century before the creation of the U.S. Many of their elders still know a lot about the tings the Druids and their shamans studied. The 'messengers' they spoke about were not angels or spirits; they were the Druidic teachers who spread the Good word of Brotherhood (Iesa) in ancient times. Grey Owl's description of one is often quoted to sound like Jesus himself, by various scholars. In this description he has 'copper colored hair'. This means that I think Jesus, the Arimathaeans, the Benjaminites, and the House of Judah are all Phoenician Red Heads.

This point has been covered in Robert Graves to some extent (*The White Goddess*), Michael Bradley and others such as Baigent and Leigh with Grail in the title. Michael Howard's *Occult Conspiracy* is a good book to read about the Masonic imagery in the occult paraphernalia of the state in the United States. You can see it on the back of your dollar bill and the declaration of a *new world order* is there for all to see.

If history has a lot of complex webs of deception or the apparency of unbridled despotism, there are few places more important than the Americas and the emeralds and cocaine so valued amongst the traders of pre-Christian times. The copper of Lake Superior was even more important in the pre-smelting period. Emeralds had only one source and it was not enough to supply all the emeralds that were around. The manufacture of green Vitriolic lenses by the likes of the Queen of Sheba's star-gazers might be an explanation but green Vitreole is part of the manufacture of the Philosophers Stone. Clearly it will not do for normal academics to deal with either of these possibilities. The same is true with copper and all its uses and many scholars say this is true for gold, although there are lots of other sources for gold. There were whole mining enterprises for each of these things and probably for unique agricultural products like cocaine. Two of the mining centers are named after Ophir who may be an amalgam of the Keltic metallurgical guilds.

I include a brief quote that comes from the 19th Century *American Journal of Science* and is authored by John Finch (7:149-161,) in 1824. It is the very 'duty' I feel which he refers to. "While the people of Europe boast their descent from the Goths, the Celts, and a hundred other barbarous tribes which the page of history has immortalized; the natives of America are considered as 'novi homines', because their existence can be traced only during two or three centuries of years. It is the duty of Americans to refute this groundless accusation, and at the same time fill up a chasm in the early history of their country; this may be effected by calling their attention to the rude stone monuments with which their country abounds, although they have hitherto escaped their notice, or been passed over as unworthy of regard.

Who is there within the limits of the wide world, that has not heard of the name and fame of the Druids, of their religious sacrifices, and of their instruments of gold, with which they severed the sacred mistletoe from the venerable father of the forest, the wide-spreading oak. The object of the present essay is to extend their empire a little farther than has hitherto been imagined, and to suggest that the Aborigines of America were of Celtic origin, that their monuments still exist in the land, and are the most ancient national memorials which America can show, and that if antiquity is to be a boast, this continent can produce monuments nearly as old as any in Europe, and derived from the same common ancestry."

The Mohawk hair do that so many kids (and Mr. T) wear is a Druidic token or tonsure. Much as we have seen the turning of the symbols in the Kaballah of the Hebrews leads

Robert Baird

to meaning and the Green Language manipulation of alphabet and language the same codes are here in this familiar icon or symbol. The Druid hair cut went from ear to ear (1) and the turn of 90 degrees to make it go from front to back signifies an allegiance to something far away but close to heart. The Nipissing Indian band had even more of the Druidic spiritual knowledge and they were highly revered by the Indians they lived amongst. This knowledge may have come more directly through the Tarim Basin and the Sauk Indians if Professor Joan Price is correct. She deals with a relatively late exodus from the Tarim Basin in her book dealing with the remnants of this all important cultural complex. Her idea of 500 AD being the origin masks a continuous and more ancient Copper Culture of the region, I believe. The Cree medicine bundles were more highly prized and valued than muskets after the advent of their arrival with the Dutch who gave many weapons to the Iroquois so they could almost genocidally eliminate their Huron and other neighbors before the Europeans arrived in force.

Montreal's importance at the confluence of trade routes to the copper makes sense of the Iroquois holding the Isle de Madelaine in such high regard. This is especially true once you consider the European need for the trade goods that came from processing centers such as Allumette Island in the 4th Century BC. A study of the Iroquois treaties and wars looks more like an extension of a European intrigue rather than a local concern. Why were the Iroquois so aggressive at this important juncture? It is certain they have white blood and are derived from the Mound Builders who go back to Poverty Point and even the Canadian Encyclopedia mentions they can be traced back to 4000 BC. Champlain may have been an agent (double or triple) in these arrangements:

"Champlain seems to have been playing a double game, and possibly, a potentially dangerous one. He had to map and explore Nova Scotia for the king and for plans of future colonization, but apparently his job was also, at the same time, to obscure parts of the province and to discourage anyone from bothering to go there. Champlain seems to have been infiltrated into the official colonization policy in order to deflect it from certain sensitive areas. Champlain seems to have been a secret agent for the Holy Bloodline. According to Champlain's maps (Bradley was a professor of navigation and mapping in Nova Scotia.) and narrative, Mahone Bay didn't exist, Minas Basin was a place of no worth, former Christian occupants had abandoned the area, and Norumbega was a fable.

Except for these places, Champlain's maps and descriptions are generally accurate, given the time he had and the great dangers he braved during his explorations.

It appears that in addition to being a great explorer and accomplished cartographer, he may also have been an agent of the Holy Bloodline of Godfroi de Bouillon (Founder of the Knights Templar with Papal Decree and passport through all Catholic territory.). Was his labour not to explore and map New France and Arcadia (Same as the name of the place in Greece that the Phoenicians took the Benjaminites when they were expelled from Israel.), but to buy a little time for Henry Sinclair's refugees?

It may be worth noting that *both* de Monts' and Champlain's fur monopolies were revoked because neither undertook any steps toward serious colonization, which was originally the whole idea of de Monts' proposal. Between them, they hindered effective colonization for 19 years, from 1603 to 1622. A royal edict in 1626 noted 'with some bitterness that the holders of the monopoly had taken out to New France during the past eleven years only eighteen colonists' and 'in 1628 Quebec could boast of not more than forty or fifty persons who might be described as ordinarily resident there' (2) . Champlain's descriptions might have fuelled this reluctance. The only people that did go to Canada were Protestant Huguenots, (They are linked with the Cathars and thus would be on the side of the Holy Bloodline and Templars according to other scholars.) while . A friend and faithful companion of de Monts, a Huguenot: Further, Champlain himself had formed a trading company in 1614 with a majority of Huguenot associates! How can we explain this inconsistency?" (3)

This is an illustration of the behind the scenes work that went on inside the Catholic institution itself. The questions are many and the answers are few. He goes on to explain how Champlain, and Lescarbot who used the words of Champlain, painted dire and devious pictures of North America to keep Europeans from coming to America. The involvement of the De Monts and Del Monte of Dole fame (in the present) in Italy, the Portuguese backers of Columbus and the Knights of Christ and much more leading to the Knights Malta being given serious consideration for taking over all of Canada are touched upon by Bradley who does excellent but dangerous work that might someday lead to an overthrow of national rights or laws therein. It is much more than just the protection of the Holy Bloodline of the family of Jesus (Merovingians) that was involved and his next book came closer to seeing that. In this particular book he missed the Cathar 'dove' symbol on the grave site of the Gunn knight near Boston. This 'dove' symbol of Peace and the 'living love' of Jesus means more on this one rock than any book you'll read (except perhaps this one, Ha!).

Potholes on the Pathways of History:

There is so much of world history that has been funded by the trade with America before it was 'discovered'. Bradley shows the 'Money Pit' on Oak Island was a bank of the Stuarts with carbon dated struts going back to 800 AD and it is possible they used the natural cave before that. This trade was the foundation of empires including Carthage and all the Milesian/Phocaean/Iberian enterprises that we hear little about due to their disappearance into the guises of other national identities of the Roman-British intrigue. A small factoid of some possible interest in the proving of this ancient trade relates to the 'mooring stones'.

Near my family's cottage on Lake Weslemkoon between Toronto and Ottawa there is what is known as the 'potholes'. The Royal Ontario Museum has identified numerous such geologic events as glacial effect from receding glaciers. This particular location has many of them close together and I think that is unusual. Be that as it may, the holes would have been used to moor ships or buildings by people along one of the many routes that existed while the earth rebounded 2/3rds of a mile in the six millennia or so after the glaciers retreated. That assertion would make no sense if there was not evidence of something definitely human that was used by pre-Columbian traders in the region encompassing the whole Great Lakes. Some stories have these 'potholes' being done by aliens and it probably was an Indian spiritual site. The actual 'mooring stones' have triangular chiseled holes about one inch in diameter that clearly are not caused by glacial effects. In a definite cover-up by Ontario's government the Peterborough Petroglyphs that were a major part of Barry Fell's *America B.C.* have had the Norse ships ground off the rocks. Let us look in on what Bradley says about Champlain again, in order to get a fuller picture of the potential Knights Malta or Templar intrigue involving the majority of the North American continent:

"Is it possible that Champlain left us the smallest hint of his role? Some little reference that, someday, might indicate his real impact on history?

Perhaps he did. In one of his journals, Champlain says:

'On June 17 (1613) we arrived at the rapids of St. Louis, where I found L'Ange, whohad come out to meet me in a canoe, to inform me that Sieur de Maisonneuve of St. Malo had brought a passport from Monseigneur the Prince (de Condé) for three ships. On landing, Maisonneuve came to see me with the passport from Monseigneur the Prince, and as soon as I examined it, I allowed him to take advantage of it with the rest of us.'" (4)

The rapids of St; Louis are the Lachine rapids. The site of this meeting between 'Sieur de Maisonneuve' and Champlain was, therefore the future site of Montreal, the refuge that would be founded 29 years later.

Champlain does not mention this Sieur de Maisonneuve 'of St. Malo' further. Who is he?

Robert Baird

The first leader of the Montreal colony was a 'Sieur de Maisonneuve'. It cannot be the same one, unless he was born at least 15 years earlier than all the biographers claim. But it could be the father. If so, this man had just had a son, born the previous year (1612) who would become Paul de Chomedy, Sieur de Maisonneuve, the first governor of Montreal. In the above passage, Champlain 'allows' him to set foot on Montreal.

Is Champlain telling us that he was high up in the great conspiracy? That he was the steward of the future haven of Montreal? That he knew the newly-born de Maisonneuve heir was to be groomed to be the first governor of the new refuge (or that he knew de Maisonneuve's real age which would be concealed from history?)?

And if he is trying to hint at all of this, or at any of it, then he is also sending a message down to future historians: Samuel Champlain was a paladin of the Holy Blood, and worthy to stand beside King Arthur, Jacques de Molay, Henry Sinclair and all other heroes.

At this point we may as well confront a question, and some readers may feel that it is long overdue. Has this entire reconstruction been a mare's nest of unrelated facts and unfounded speculations, or, does it have some claim to truth? Is it history, or is it imagination?

Since I'm responsible for much of this reconstruction, but by no means for all of it, I may as well answer honestly that I just don't know. On the other hand, I've studied history for some years and have lectured on it. I don't know what history is, either. Napoleon is supposed to have said that 'history is the lie commonly agreed upon'. Ben Johnson had equally caustic things to say about it. Scholars choose facts and ignore others when they create history to be read in books. Or, sometimes, they're just remarkably uncurious.

It seems a bit far-fetched to suppose that de Monts and Champlain were heirs of some Templar mission begun long before, but.

It is very difficult sometimes *to come to grips with the facts behind ordinary history, the kind offered in authorized*

Diverse Druids

texts. (Emph. Added) How much more difficult must it be, then, to come to grips with a history that has been purposefully suppressed by friend and foe alike? One is forced to become a suspicious detective, and to glean clues that others might miss, or dismiss. One cannot expect proof when seeking hidden history, one can only hope to find stray hints of a pattern that goes beyond the acceptable 'warp and woof'.

Champlain mentions a de Maisonneuve at the close of his accounts. At the very beginning, he mentions another mysterious figure. Champlain's first known voyage was to the West Indies between 1599 and 1601 and it was this experience that gave him the credibility to join the later French explorations which won him fame. Without going into all the details, Champlain owed his participation in the Spanish West Indies voyage to 'a nobleman named Don Francisco Coloma ('Dove' like 'Colon' which is the name used by Columbus and from which came 'colon'-ization), a knight of Malta', as Champlain describes him, who was leader of the expedition. Champlain needed permission to join this voyage and, '... we sought out General Coloma, to know if it would suit him that I should make the voyage. This he freely granted me, with evidence of being well pleased thereat, promising me his favor and assistance, which he has not since denied me upon occasion. (5) (Thus Champlain was brought by a 'we' to a member of the 'octopus' that controlled the whole world through the Treaty of Tordesillas while later a French (!) Governor.)

We do not really know when the since was in this passage because we do not know when Champlain composed his notes on this voyage for publication in France. It may have been 1601, 1604 or even as late as 1613. Champlain may have been a long-time protégé of this Don Francisco Coloma, a knight of Malta, who held so high a position in the Spanish navy, and whose name means 'Dove'.

I have spared the reader any history of the Knights of Malta until now because of fear of complication of an already too-involved story. But, briefly, the Knights of Malta were a sort of Templar back-up Order. They, too, were established in the Holy Land under the de Bouillons at about the same time as the Templars. Whereas the Templars were headquartered in Jerusalem at the Temple of Solomon, the Knights of Malta were originally headquartered in Acre. They 'relocated' to Rhodes, and then Malta, when the Moslems regained the Holy Land. (The Moslems protected the Jews against the Catholics, a little promoted fact in the present and continuing con or conflicts.) They retreated to a succession of island fortresses. (6)

Where the Templars were high-profile, the Knights of Malta were low-profile, but still attracted the flower of nobility. Like the Templars they were sworn to chastity (Sir Walter Scott paints a more real picture when he says they were 'drunkards and bullies'.) and poverty as individuals, but the Order itself became immensely wealthy. They, too, were answerable only to the Pope. And where the Templars specialized in finance and banking, the Knights of Malta took to hospital work. St. John's Ambulance is a descendant. They also engaged in sea commerce. (The Templar fleet equaled the combined fleet of all the nations of Europe and was garrisoned near where Champlain is said to have been born, La Rochelle.)

The Grail Dynasty throughout history has shown itself always to be one step ahead of everyone else through careful contingency planning. The Templars got into trouble fighting de Bouillon's enemies, the Knights of Malta remained neutral toward the Albigensians, and carefully orthodox.

So it came to pass that when Phillippe le Bel staged his dawn raids upon Templar priories and warehouses in 1307, such treasure as did get confiscated was awarded, by order of the Pope, *to the knights of malta*. Don Francisco Coloma, who started Champlain on his career, and who had assisted him 'since', was a Knight of Malta. (More important than the assets is the trail of power and the monopoly that went to the de Medicis/Borgia complex.)

Diverse Druids

It appears that Champlain's long-term friend and business associate, the Sieur de Monts, also had Templar and Knights of Malta connections. A notation in Anthiaume's *Cartes Navales* reads: "...In other words, it is said that de Monts was of Italian origin." This has been disputed, but if it is a fact, he may have been named after a relative, Pietro del Monte, Grand Master of the Knights of Malta from 1568 to 1572.

However that may be, it is an undisputed fact that the de Monts purchased the castle of Ardennes 'on the ancient estate of Godfroi de Bouillon' as a retirement home. This had been a Templar stronghold.

Philippe le Bel seized the Chateau of Ardennes along with other Templar property in France, but it passed on with much else to the Knights of Malta. The altar in the chapel is decorated with Maltese crosses. This is the castle that Sieur de Monts was able to buy, even though he was frequently bankrupt, and the place where he died, most probably in the year 1628.

Around the year 1635 during the last days of Champlain's term as governor. '...in Paris the Hundred Associates, under the guidance of Cardinal Richelieu, were meeting to choose a new governor. The reason is not clear - whether Champlain was regarded merely as too old, whether his policy had crossed that of the Cardinal, or whether some intrigue was at work. There was a plan afoot to turn Canada over to the Knights of Malta, but for all we know, Champlain may have approved the plan in advance.' (7)

I was both considerably surprised and heartened, therefore, to discover that an obscure but respectable French scholar had harbored similar suspicions about Champlain and published them in his obscure but respectable book. I had, as I thought, completed the text of this chapter and was checking bibliographic references to Champlain for the Notes and Bibliography sections of this book in the Toronto Reference Library when I noticed in the Canadian History card catalogue a book entitled *L'Incroyable Secret de Champlain* ('The Incredible Secret of Champlain'). (8) It had been publi9shed in Paris in 1959 and never translated into English so far as I could discover. The author was Florian de la Horbe who wrote it in collaboration with M. Meurgey de Tupigny, Conservator-in-Chief of France's National Archives. It did not appear from the stiffness of the book that anyone had cracked it open before us." (9)

Champlain apparently had a penchant for very young girls and that would mean younger than the eleven of twelve years old most got married at, in his day. I hope the bankruptcy to retirement castle plan is fully appreciated. There are many similar things done by old money in redevelopment of US cities. In real terms today I read there are 16,000 nobles who belong to the Knights Malta who have proven their bloodlines. My oldest brother and I were once recruited by the head of the Knights Malta in Canada. They have research on genealogies to match the Mormons who are founded by a 33rd Degree Mason. The outreaches of the esoteric schools are many and feeder groups abound. Most of them are quite educational and I once thought it was a great 'octopus' but I am not so sure anymore. I am not even sure if they were truly trying to help the Cathars and not double agents for the Pope. St. Bernard seems to have been more open as Inquisitor than the Templars who fought to protect some of the castles or some mysterious Grail object(s).

So, while Champlain (who may have been a different man who assumed another's identity) waffled and withheld the facts, from the king and court, other things occurred through the Iroquois. They (and the diseases brought by missionaries) were ale to spread a new form of society with a Masonic constitution similar to what the US eventually installed. The Holy Grail remnants whose 1100 members were near Kingston as Bradley demonstrates a geologic core sample proves the words of Donnacona (from Cartier's journals), went on to become important in Montreal. There were also many minglings with Indians and the half breeds became the Métis. The numbers of the Métis were enhanced with the Irish who came to fight on both sides of the Civil War. These numbers are far larger than would be expected if

Diverse Druids

they had not been expanding during a long period of time. There is also the matter of the Melungeon who some research may soon prove includes the likes of Abraham Lincoln. So, if these possibilities are true - Champlain is a hero of the old Brotherhood that tried to protect the ideals and ethics against the forces of colonization. During this time and earlier the Kelts of Norway and Ireland (Norumbega) had been trading and living in America. The Kensington Runestone has been thoroughly proven as of November 2000's meeting of the Midwest Archaeological Association despite what Professor Wiseman (who appeared not to know what transpired there) says in his article 'Camelot in Kentucky' from Archaeology Magazine.

The mooring stones relate to this well documented trip that really shouldn't be surprising anyone now that Lanse aux Meadows has been accepted as fact from the start of the second millenium AD. Perhaps it is the use of runes (Ogham) that disturbs those who wish to maintain such controversy. It tires me to have to constantly mention all the cover ups and intrigues. The original time when mooring stones were chiseled rather than using 'potholes' may never be learned:

"A mooring stone is a large rock with a small hole chiseled in it. These holes are not round, but triangular. The diameter of the hole is about one inch and the depth is 4 to 5 inches.

Mooring stones were used to anchor a ship in the following way: A rope was attached to one end of a ship, which was in the water near shore. The other end of the rope was tied to a ring bolt, which was inserted into the chiseled hole into the rock. An anchor would be used on the other end of the ship, to keep it perpendicular to and away from the shore. A crew could remain on the ship when it was anchored near unfamiliar land. If the ship was attacked, a crew member could jerk the rope, causing the ring bolt to pop out of the hole. Then the crew could immediately row away from danger.

In an attempt to find out if these two rocks on a hill west of Starbuck were actually mooring stones my brother contacted a historian at the Runestone Museum in Alexandria." (10)

These people are seriously interested in the reality of observable facts rather than the tired old theories that protect the status quo. The experts of the Alexandria Museum have over 300 catalogued 'mooring stones' from Canada to the southern Mississippi. The Hadji Ahmed map that details the Bering Strait or land bridge as it was 12,500 years ago (and many other things like the Manitoulin quartz mine between 35 and 120,000 years old) is significant. It wasn't until 1958 that modern science knew this yet this map was traced from earlier maps (adding Ptolemy's garbage of the Mediterranean) and has been under careful control for over 500 years.

Zoomorphic Effigies As Contacts with Reality

For the purposes of this book it is important to get a little further insight on the 'Dove' symbol that has appeared a lot in our ruminations. The next entry also has relevance to the Sphinx and the Slavs of Gimbutas' Old European and Danube origin of the Kelts that I deal with in great detail in *The Kelts: Children of the Don*:

"The Slavs believe that, at death, the soul turns into a dove. This bird partakes of the general symbolism of all winged animals, that is, of spirituality and the power of sublimation. It is also symbolic of souls, a motif which is common in Visigothic and Romanesque art. Christianity, inspired in the Scriptures, depicts the third person of the Trinity - the Holy Ghost - in the shape of a dove, although he is also represented by the image of a tongue of Pentecostal fire." (11)

In *Painted Books of MesoAmerica* by Gordon Brotherston and the British Museum Trustees from 1995 they have a map showing the Toltecs in civilized cotton or tailored clothes. They are meeting the Chichimecs as these people came to Mexico in the early 12 century. The book further notes their use of currency in the form of copper axes. These are the copper axes of Tutuepec from the Incas, and they are doubled axes like the Crete designs. Thor of the Norse is one of the Thunder Gods that most peoples have in their legends and some daring academics suggest the Crete to Norse connection as a result of these axes. When you consider this very similar widespread American use you can understand why botanists are noting cotton genes are instructive to the world of trade, in very ancient times. Heyerdahl caused a furor with the American sweet potato or yam, too.

I believe (speculate or opine) there is a good chance the Chichimecs were from Cahokia or the upper Mississippi Indian culture that had mined the copper of Lake Superior under the name Aztlan for many millennia. There are Masonic codes and treatises that say many of these things too, I hear. Cahokia disappeared around 1050 AD at a time when Quetzalcoatl returned to ask his white kin to return to their homeland to help in the words of Monteczuma. Is there a connection with the Norman Invasion of England? Cahokia was the largest city in what is now the US with 80,000 people and they did not live in tents. A Roman statue said to be a near 'archaeologic certainty' by David Kelley (Professor Emeritus and a linguist who worked on breaking the Mayan code) was found on the coast of Mexico. I have a long list that gets longer all the time. To talk about America as if it was 'discovered' is a farce. The white people of Europe may have come from America. Even though National Geographic and Scientific American ran cover stories in early 2001 that say Europeans were in America 24-30,000 years ago they still allow the 'no cultural impact' fiction to be promoted. This Columbus or Clovis Cops theory helps with legal or moral issues we have already shown might exist (especially the Plague). Because if Mayans had the kind of knowledge they did 3500 BC or before; including an alphabet that is both pictographic and phonetic then what was really going on was a corporate battle for power.

Robert Baird

It goes so far that one University of Illinois archaeologist or anthropologist offered that perhaps the Romans came to the Gulf of Mexico and not to America. The Gulf is part and parcel of North America and the Americas! The Greco-Roman statuary that is all over the Villas Archaeologique is even older than this statue; so I have great difficulty imagining how anyone can doubt the one statue that meets all archaeologic criteria. That statue was also missing for decades in a Mexican Government institutional 'safe place'. It isn't just Mexico that has this Dark Ages or feudal attitude towards keeping people like the Mayans down. The Kennewick Man debate could have started when earlier skeletons of the same age were found. Maybe it should have started with the Bat Creek Nine who were Jewish escapees from the Roman amphitheatre according to New York University's eminent linguist Cyrus Gordon:

"The Spaniards learned that Quetzalcoatl had been a supreme god or high priest, a teacher, a wise law-giver and merciful judge. He forbade human sacrifice, teaching that flowers, bread and incense were all that God demanded. He prohibited wars and forbade fighting, violence and robbery. Although the Aztec religion required sacrifice of humans, he was held in affectionate veneration. He was tall of stature, white or reddish in complexion, clothed in 'a long white robe strewn with red crosses (The Merovingian or the Templar, [maybe the Tau that is in St. Anthony's heraldry and comes from Orion and developed into the Dove, according to a friend of mine]), carrying a staff in his hand.' He brought with him builders, painters, astronomers and draughtsmen. He passed from place to place and disappeared."(12)

The staff is a scepter or wand, and does not signify shepherd as Catholicism later made it seem with Jesus. This is only one source of these legends of white men. There are lots of pre-Columbian drawings showing white men and there are statues still existing despite the destruction of all culture and melting of metal art by the heathen horde who said the Indians had no soul. The Pope finally decided they had a rudimentary soul in 1524. I am near to certain the

Diverse Druids

Toltecs were Druids and that Kukulcan/Quetzalcoatl/Veracocha/Xolotl where the main man in the various times that their legends cover. I do not know if Scota (13) did the same thing in Scythia or Scotland in a time 3000 and more years earlier; but there were times when women leaders were forced to have to attempt to mobilize all the Brotherhood, against the impending ethic we now call 'his'-story.

Industries such as pottery and metal craftsmanship are just part of the exchanges between all world cultures. The very fact that man has been painted as a relatively unadventurous, stupid sort by history is indicative of what THEY want to make us believe and BE! If we all knew how to access the soul we wouldn't need our priests so much and they priests might have to provide a good service rather than just con us out of our money. This is a well established fact that academics have to admit - the Mayans were advanced *beyond* the mathematics of Europe in their calendar and math. You have seen a former astronaut remark on their astronomical knowledge. There are many examples to give.

We have already touched on the use of Pelota to settle disputes throughout the whole Caribbean rather than going to war. Pelota also is related to the transit of Venus and recent Spanish Catholic rituals still had this element that somehow traveled the ocean in early Christian days (maybe even before Jesus). Parchesi was thought to be Persian but the Mayans had the same game. Lacrosse is like Hurling in Ireland, the mounds of the Mississippi and L'anse Amour, the Ertebolle or Jomon pottery, purple dyes in Mexico, cotton, and every manner of custom and belief are shared across the oceans along with the botanical and other artifactural evidences. Unfortunately for the historians - genetics is about to burst their bubble! There is enough evidence in genetics alone to disprove the no cultural contact theory. The Adena/Poverty Point people are an important part of the puzzle and I will try to summarize the situation starting with the 'head-shaping' to make nobles look like alien reptoids or 'Chanes':

Robert Baird

"Needless to say, these findings cast doubt on any exclusive Mexican (Head of a statue found near the Ohio River) head binding connection. That coupled with new studies suggesting the tough Adena skeletal type arriving not from Mexico, but from the southern margins of the Great Lakes, and the old pet theories were melting faster than the glaciers. New questions were being posed.

Since few or no other recognizable Mexican-type traits appeared among the Adena grave goods until the centuries-later Adena burials, why, after a many centuries lapse, did the traits indicating Central and South American influence appear in the Ohio Valley?

It was beginning to seem that everything distinguishing the Adena, with the possible exception of mounds for the dead, was already in the region for a very long time. It was no longer solid ground to theorize the direct ancestors of the first Adena moving out of Mexico and, after a time, up the Mississippi watershed just because there was skull shaping in ancient Mexico, and earthworks in the deep south.

Like a real mystery, there were more questions than answers. Investigators began asking whether a fresh, new scenario should be considered to explain the origins of the Adena.

Popular Theories

In about 800 years, and after Adena villages and towns became established throughout what is now Ohio, Indiana, Kentucky, West Virginia, and Pennsylvania, a new stock of people is, by inference, thought to have begun the process of transforming that culture very probably from within. (The Melungeons are likely part of this Phoenician complex that lasted until today, and might include Abraham Lincoln. This is the region where the Bat Creek Nine skeletons were found with Jewish script on a stone.) So in a sense, after the Adena seemed to supplant an older culture in the Ohio Valley, another culture succeeded them in a relatively linear fashion. Ultimately this new culture redefined the older Adena. This proposed phenomenon of transformation and replacement

Diverse Druids

characterized what is known as the 'Hopewell' era, which term, like Adena and Indian, had been assigned by the inheriting whites. Anthropologists as archaeologists therefore ask these questions. How did the Adena begin, and why did they end, and in the same vein, how and why are they so intimately related to the Hopewell? Why did this supposedly 'hybrid' Hopewell culture achieve such distinction and domination over their Adena predecessors, then, like small colonies of the Adena before them, seem to simply fade out from the Ohio Valley?

The main theory holding interest for many years has been simply that after these round-headed people arrived in the Ohio Valley, they gradually (though not at first) interbred with existing long-headed people, and over a few centuries slowly generated what we call the Hopewell culture. (This avoids the potential of European or Mediterranean influence which is part of the Columbus/Flat Earth fallout. The Adena may well have ended with the fight of the Skulls and Horns or white people coming to take over the Phoenician enterprises as part of the Trojan War. There is a huge battleground with up to 100,000 bodies near Poverty Point that may have started the Adena era and then the Roman/Carthaginian or Punic Wars may have led to the Hopewell takeover. This is just part of the work done in my book dealing with the Old Copper Culture of Lake Superior.) The Hopewell are believed, though not fully proven, to have evolved agriculture and art further than the Adena (The Burrows cave artifacts include many Phoenician Brotherhood artifacts.), and some of the accomplishments in the latter category amaze us yet today. What has kept our science most intensely interested about the Adena however, is that they constructed mounds for honoring the dead, and were selective about how they went about it.

It should be stated that until now, DNA testing has found no specific match between the Adena-Hopewell and any existing Native American group. There may be alternative explanations, however conjectural, for the Adena origin and exit. Based first upon the physical analysis, speculations and summations of Webb, Snow, Dragoo, and their colleagues and predecessors, the thoughtful entering of Native American legend into the analysis provides some clear fuel for that soon to be mentioned lamp shedding light on what has too long remained a dim pre-history.

As inferred, it is believed that the traits related as Hopewell began showing up around 200 B.C.E. or so. No Hopewell traits have been found in Adena tombs, and thus it has been suggested that Adena chronologically preceded and were culturally anterior to Hopewell. It required some time before the archaeological analysis discerned the Adena as separable from the Hopewell who themselves finally left the region about the middle of the first millenium of the Common Era. (Is there a connection with the 'Goths' like the disappearance of the Ostrogoths after taking over Italy?) It was determined that within just a few centuries after Hopewell began to appear, the purely Adena traits were virtually gone from the Ohio Valley. Yet artifact evidence of the Adena showed up in points to the south (the Copena Culture), and far to the east, such as the St. Lawrence and Delaware areas, before becoming extinct." (14)

Thus the Megwi are from Hopewell and became the Iroquois which I can track back to Poverty Point, and the Canadian Encyclopedia said the Iroquois can be traced to 4000 BC. The size of the Adena men and women is similar to all Kelts of the period who built the same mounds. The pygmy graves that Barry Fell worked on in Kentucky/Tennessee seem to confirm the Phoenicians were helped by what might even be the Mungo Man. It is exciting to see all of these things (in all parts of the world) that prove man was not the 'beast with red cheeks' or some violent cave man beating women over the head with clubs in the 10,000 year ago era. The Cherokee language is in the Iroquoian family and the stone with Hebrew or Semitic writing that Cyrus Gordon proved was not Cherokee is important. He said the 19th Century experts had the rock turned upside down. Does that mean one of our Green Language reversals was all that differentiated this alphabet when first employed in North America? The Cherokee had indoor plumbing and a system of laws and agriculture that was superior to Europe. The Trail Of Tears ranks with the Tuscegee Experiment in the annals of US terror.

I know that the questions and speculations raised in this chapter do not prove the Phoenicians were engaged in major (Bradley thinks over a million population in the Mound Builder era) American enterprises. This Phoenician Brotherhood is also connected to the on-going issue of brotherhood. If we take the acknowledged 'Enlightenment Experiment' that became what is the Global US influence of today it is not easy to characterize it as either brotherhood or its opposite. Each person needs to know more and the information is not easily available. Obviously it is a huge subject to deal with and I am dealing with it as I go through all the different books I am preparing. My thought is that someone might desire to question why we have bought into the supposed aggressive ignorance of humanity rather than the nurturing ethos of enablement some day, soon (hopefully).

Robert Baird

CHAPTER EIGHT:
Egalitarian doesn't mean weak!

'Streets Full of People!' (NOT 'All alone')

Koko is a gorilla with a web site who answers questions through Dr. Francine (Penny) Patterson. With a thousand word vocabulary and the ability to recognize two thousand words Koko can communicate as well as many humans. This is not just another language for Koko, like it would be for me in trying to learn French or Russian. Penny can't be sure that Koko knows the difficulty all gorillas face in getting food as man encroaches on their habitat. It does seem Koko gets emotional as this great gorilla thinks about the plight of his fellow gorillas and we may never know the degree of wisdom and insight they share or how they do it. This happens when people ask Koko what all gorillas need and Koko responds with candy requests because that is what Koko loves to eat. I suspect it is part personal and also a connection with the group that is actually happening but I cannot prove it.

An English boy fell into a gorilla pen in a zoo many years ago and the four hundred pound gorilla, who was the dominant male, tenderly stroked the unconscious child and protected it. Levan was the child's name and he believes he is connected with this gorilla by just a glance of a mere instant. He said he continues to feel this connection when he sees the gorilla as he grew up. Another gorilla had made dangerous advances and exhibited bad intentions. The TV show I saw this on had done a re-enactment with some actual footage of the event. I can understand why he might feel he owes the gorilla his life and wants to believe the connection is a two way thing. Of course this might just be projection on his part.

Another TV program that I saw recently showed the Scythian graves or kurgans where the people were buried with their horses. It did not even try to suggest there was a two way psychic or spiritual connection but it made it clear there was something more than just a need of self aggrandizement. I believe the Kelts were gifted communicators with nature and the animals in the style of Crocodile Dundee as he made the water buffalo change its path in the movie. I know people who train animals who agree this is what they use - soul or spiritual connection! The horses of a man who they loved so much and who loved them so much, would not want to have lived in his absence perhaps. Their souls are immortal too.

    The drawings of the hunt from the Saharan people dating to 7000 BC.; are also signs of the Keltic need for extreme challenges to test themselves against. In time they also made friends with the elephants and had elephant farms. The hunters who defended against threat or tracked animals best were given great honor and the North American Indians often saw the actual animals of their forest in their dreams. This dreaming was astral and real in my reading of the stories and experiences. Some of these people would have enjoyed the flattering attentions of others and it may have led to the nobility or aristocrats. In Keltic culture the nobles were not given great status to the extent anyone would really even call it more than a bureaucratic position. In time if their results warranted it they would become representative of the ideals and morals of the culture. That is why the bards who told their story might exaggerate and call them gods or demi-gods; I can't say for sure but it appears this was never done while a person was alive. I also like to think the behavior of the gorilla who saved Levan is the kind of thing the Kelts admired rather than killing helpless children. When spiritual people communicate with animals amazing things can be learned. Wasteful killing of animals or other lifeforms was regarded as a crime.

    These psycho-spiritual social evolutionary aspects of life and relationships matter as much or more than the wars and dates of some great man who drove his troops to kill other humans. My paternal grandmother was a Keough and her ancestor was Miles Keough according to family legend. Miles didn't marry the New York Governor's daughter who tended his grave until she died. It is a beautiful story but in order for us to be related to him there had to be a child. Politically it may have been necessary for her to keep this secret. It is also possible that Miles had a child with a Mandan woman of even the Sioux who genetics now proves are white people and that Ms. Martin whose name appears on the marriage certificate of my grandparents, raised another woman's child brought into this world by the man she loved. Captain Miles Keough of Custer's Last Stand was the owner of Comanche the Brave Horse who was the only survivor of this battle that may have been the last victory for the Phoenician Brotherhood. The Indians say the horse protected his owner and took many arrows and bullets. It is well documented that Keough was a great horseman, and the Indians actually liked Custer and Keough who respected the Indians.

    The story is not being addressed to talk about him. It is Comanche, that the Seventh Cavalry has immortalized, which makes this part of the book seem appropriate to discuss a little snippette of real history also called family legend. The author of *Shy Boy* and movies like 'The Horse Whisperer', or other gifted horse trainers are telling us about the kind of relationship that is possible amongst animals and people who often forget they are animals too. My sister-in-law has a cousin who married a Samoan and they live in California running an outdoor rafting and wilderness entertainment business.

    They have a daughter who is a gifted horse trainer and was a protégé of the trainer who created these renewed interests in horses and what we can learn from them. People are seeing that breaking the spirit of horses is foolish and a lot like how many children are raised. Mary Beth (the mother) and I talked a couple of summers ago. She was living in Samoa when the Westernization of values was eliminating the extended family and bringing a more professional or mechanistic model to that part of the world. She spoke with appropriate pride about her daughter and all relationships in her life. When the 'West was won', the 'civilizing' white man totally abused horses, and many other things. Sometimes this took a lot of time and led to broken bones. Mary Beth's daughter does it in a few minutes with kindness and psychic or other sign language.

Thomas Merton wrote about the Mayan cities and streets in this way: "The streets of those cities were not streets in which they watched somebody else going someplace else where all joy was hidden behind expansive walls. The streets were placed where everybody sang together, converging upon the central dance which was the life and identity of the city."

The elder councils and matriarchs or patriarchs valued all the children and abilities that can be achieved by humans, the most awesome ones are related to the soul and/or spirit. Brotherhood was not some idle hypocritical theology it was the collective that mattered most of all. The laws and ethics to support and encourage lifelong learning and sharing made every person a warrior for what is right about nature and humanity. Most would not achieve the 'Impeccable Warrior' state (I imagine) that the Toltec brujho Don Juan has taught Carlos Castaneda. Their saying that can be viewed in many different but always beautiful ways goes like this: 'Do not put yourself in front of your Self.'

It's Only Natural

The 'Christ' was the collective 'body' of what we might call the World Mind and was called Animus Mundi in the salons of 19th century France. The American residents knew these things better than the priests who came to teach after the diseases wiped out most of those who knew the old ways. It is interesting to note that the B'hai faith is mirrored in the Hopi and that crosses were all over America when the *invasion of paradise* took center stage. The mercenaries and their priestly commanders had a specific task to remove all remnants of the original Christian symbols and knowledge that had been shared through thousands of years in America.

Near the pyramid at Chichen Itza you can walk between columns that would remind you of the Greek designs such as the Parthenon. The statues in the Villas Archaeologique would have you feeling there is a connection with Greece or Etruria, even if you didn't know about the Roman statue declared a near *archaeologic certainty*. I believe the relatives or descendants of the Mungo Man from South East Asia found in Australia were here too. Simon Easteal told Reuters they 'Wouldn't stand out in a crowd today.' Other reports have them being a lot smaller, but so were the African relatives of many hominids developing there, at this period of time, over 30,000 years before Keltic white man arrived in the Caucasus to Don area (Casiberia). Although alien intervention such as von Daniken and many others write about may have some truth, I find most things have an earth origin explanation I greatly prefer. So if the Druids learned from aliens then I believe the aliens they learned from were previous hominid strains like the Mungo Man. They certainly learned a lot from all the creatures in nature and one saying goes 'If you want to know what the Druids know - ask a bee.' They knew strength and were large people so they valued the ability and strength that it takes to *love* and it was a crime to pick on a woman or child unnecessarily"

"Man relies on Nature for food and cannot help being influenced by Nature. He finds himself engaged in farming, hunting, fishing, etc., and each of these engagements contributes to his character, for Nature cannot be conceived as a merely passive substance upon which Man works. Nature is also power and energy; Nature reacts to human calls. When Man is agreeable and in conformity with Nature's way, it will co-operate with Man and reveal to him all its secrets and even help him to understand himself. Each of us as a farmer or hunter or carpenter gets from Nature what he looks for in it and assimilates it in his own field. To this extent, Nature re-moulds human character.

To treat Nature as something irrational and in opposition to human 'rationality' is a purely Western ides, and sometimes we feel the proposition ought to be reversed. It is irrational of Man to try to make Nature obey his will, because Nature has its own way of carrying on its work which is not always Man's way, and Man has no right to impose his way upon Nature." (1)

The Biblical 'sin' that supposedly reflects the animal Nature of Man is not correct and even if it was, why not develop a better thing to fear - like not learning or growing? To fear death is analogous to fearing a lack of growth when one observes nature. In nature if a tree stops growing it dies. There are many who live in fear of dying yet are already dead - from the neck up. Whereas those who change and have no attachment that prevents them from re-inventing themselves, live a full life in the Zen of each moment. We need not avoid our ego or personal needs by labels like 'sin' because someone seeks to make us manageable but we do need to give our best effort to help each other and not do the things that unethical immoral acts lead to.

Perhaps it is because of my masochistic need to give and express truth rather than seek personal gain that I empathize with 'Comanche, The Brave Horse' so much that as I wrote this during the first draft I 'teared up'. It is a corny story and I cry at all kinds of sappy things. Maybe it is because the fires of Keltic heroes and lovers of Nature still boil in my blood or soul. You can decide for yourself whether I am just a roMANtic fool, but I am proud to feel and know this 'fool' within. The intensity of feeling that comes as one digs deeper and deeper into the fullness of their soul allows all kinds of 'blessings' both here and in the hereafter. I look forward to meeting all the Red Heads like my father and Genghis Khan when I go to the 'happy hunting ground'.

Knowledge Filters

"We cannot yet identify the exact place of origin of the Chavín cult. It definitely was not on the central of south coast or in the upper Huallaga basin, because in each of these regions the Chavín style (or elements of it, on the south coast) appeared suddenly, without antecedents, as an intrusive (Pre Moshe Peru of 900 BC) complex that was soon blended with the older local styles. Numerous theories about Chavín origins have been proposed. Julio C. Tello felt that the cult originated in the 'montaña' and spread first to the highlands and then to the coast. (2) Rafael Larco Hoyle, on the other hand, proposed a north-central coastal origin in the Nepeña Valley. (3) More recently, a number of Mexican archaeologists have maintained that the Chavín cult was derived from early Olmec culture of southern Mexico. (4) Still another possible origin, never formally proposed but considered likely by many of today's Peruvianists, was in the north-central highlands." (5)

He is making it clear they do not know rather than assuming it away like the National Geographic report on the Moshe tomb of 'giants' we reported earlier in the book. Neither of them goes into considering or even mentioning the Diffusionist or Cell Theory. It is the kiss of death for those who want funding still, in this day and age. After all we really don't want to admit the Bible was stolen from earlier people or admit there was a time when man worked together in Brotherhood that saw Jomon, Japan bring ceramic technology and the Kelts bring many things we shall soon see to this region at this time and long before it as well. I think the Chavín were people who went from Peru to Mayan or Olmec lands a long time before and returned many centuries later.

The discovery made by rich amateur archaeologist Gene Savoy at the 8-9000 foot level of the Andes might be the Ostrogoths who built this massive European style fortification that the Incas had only just conquered (after 800 years of co-existence) shortly before Pizzaro and a new group of white men invaded. These are not the people who all the legends relate to, as I see it. The legends of bearded white men and their missions or trading and mining ventures of South America go back to before the time of Solomon and the Trojan War as we know from the work of Lanning even though he doesn't do more than present the Keltic figures and statuary that reminds one of Caesar's descriptions of the Kelts. The Diffusionist theory fits all the facts whereas the Bible or 'god guided ascendance' to some Euro-centric apex derived through the hard effort of our leaders to steer us

Diverse Druids

away from 'our' BAD nature has to leave the story of great pre-historic cultures out of their fiction. In this quote we see the Olmec again, and we remember astronaut Gordon Cooper assured us they were around in 3,000 BC.

Michael Bradley's *Iceman Inheritance* shows African Negroid people came to the Americas long before that. Zimbabwean motifs on the flag of Peru are testimony to that. These same motifs and construction methods in the Aran Islands near Ireland are in Keulap, Peru. The huge megalithic rocks said to be moved in Giza or Ba'albek are here too. How do you move 500 Ton rocks up mountains? The Spanish asked the Incas who were trying to act like they had built these things. A small rock rolled upon the Incans as they tried to do it:

"Five thousand ancient copper mines have been found on Michigan's Keweenaw Peninsula. There are at least as many more on Isle Royale, in the middle of Lake Superior, fifty miles north of Keweenaw. Ash carbon-dating tests conducted by the University of Michigan demonstrate the mines were worked from around 3,000 until 1200 BC. (Trojan War?), by unknown miners of great skill and incredible labor, excavating a minimum estimated 500,000 tons of copper.

Some investigators believe this half-a-million-ton estimate is too high by a factor of two or three, while others, like Michigan researcher, Fred Rydholm, suggest that the real figure may be at least twice as great. In any case, a minimum of several hundred thousand tons were mined and removed from North America in prehistory.

The vast majority of this copper was not used by regional Indians. Where then, did it go?

Eastern Mediterranean cultures used huge amounts of copper and its alloy, bronze (90% copper and 10% tin) for tools and armaments until the late 2nd Millenium B.C. Interestingly, most historians claim their local copper sources, such as Cyprus, had been exhausted by this time. (Geologists on Cyprus have shown [in National Geographic) how almost all the copper at any depth was gone from

Cyprus and how in far more ancient times there had been float ore of higher purity. There had been 18 full tree growths used to smelt the copper on Cyprus, and I think the Troodos Range there is the original Mt. Olympus where scary gods were created by those who sought to keep others away from these valuable ores for at least 5000 years during which no signs of habitation exist despite all around Cyprus having lots of people.) The Egyptians worked with large numbers of bronze saws, chisels and other tools for building statues, temples and tombs. Contemporary Mycenaean Greeks, Hittites, Phoenicians, Minoans, Babylonians, and other peoples required bronze weapons and armor for their armed forces. Bronze plows and other metal tools added to demands on the mineral, causing a worldwide search for additional sources.

By comparison, the world's largest copper mines, in Chile are getting an ore yield of only 6% to 8%. The ancient Michigan mines were unique in that their copper was mostly surface ore with an unheard of yield of 90%." (6)

We know the 'Ice Man' of Austria had axes and tools made of copper and that the Armenians could harden even copper in 70000 BC if not before and far earlier than most people in other cultures. All these secrets certainly were important and the Brotherhood of Phoenician traders continued to keep secrets and develop codes to keep this knowledge away from their potential enemies.

Here are a couple of quotes that illustrate the continuing secrecy and dangers of trying to expose those who have kept the secrets. The excellent books written by Michael Cremo and Richard Thompson called *Forbidden Archaeology* and *The hidden history of the human race!* are the causes of these reactions. "A stunning description of some of the evidence that was once known to science, but which has disappeared from view due to the 'knowledge filter' that protects the ruling paradigm." - Phillip E. Johnson, author of *Darwin on Trial,* School of Law, University of California, Berkeley.

"Your book is pure humbug and does not deserve to be taken seriously by anyone but a fool." - Richard Leakey of the 'establishment'." (7)

I think anyone so caught up in their own perceptions that they can not take serious alternatives seriously has a problem but I know this Leakey remembers what his ancestor Louis suffered at the hands of archaeology when he proclaimed 200,000 year old arrowheads near Barstow, California. Are men all this dense? Women certainly would be more amenable to negotiate and be diplomatic. There is a need for men to display their prowess I suppose, but in reality we are capable of much more that this continuing 'Cycle of Violence'.

"Plutarch tells us another story of a Celtic heroine of Galatia (South of the Black Sea includes the Gordian Knot.) who was clearly a Druidess, Camma, priestess of the goddess Brigit. Camma, an hereditary priestess, according to Plutarch, of the Celtic equivalent of Artemis. Camma was married to a chieftain named Sinatos who was murdered by a man named Sinorix who then forced Camma to marry him. But, as the ceremony involved drinking from a common cup, Camma contrived to put poison into it. She allayed Sinorix's suspicion by drinking first and so accepted death herself, as well as her would-be husband, Sinorix.

It is also from Plutarch's essay, *On the Virtue's of Women,* that we learn that Celtic women were often appointed ambassadors. They were involved in a treaty between the Carthaginian general Hannibal and the Celtic Volcae. Rome had already sent to the Volcae to demand their neutrality if Hannibal marched through their country. The Celts were obviously not enamoured of Rome's demands. Hannibal was being supported by other Celtic tribes (Of course, because the Phoenicians of Tyre and the Celts are one and the same in the Brotherhood at earlier times and were not into Rome's Empire-building plan.). Plutarch also says that women took part in the Celtic assemblies, frequently smoothing quarrels with their careful diplomacy.

Robert Baird

According to Irish sources, Macha Mong Ruadh (Macha of the Red Hair), daughter of Aed Ruadh, became ruler of all Ireland from 377-331 BC. Female rulers appear in the Irish and Welsh texts as well as the ideal queens of the Otherworld which, as Professor Markle, in *La Femme Celte*, has pointed out were 'symbols of an attitude of mind that patriarchy could not uproot from the ancient Celtic spirit' .The Christian writers have her (Tlachtga) raped by three sons of Simon Magus and she produces three sons at one birth, in the process of which she dies. She was buried at the Hill of Tlachtga, now the Hill of Ward ('Cnoc an Bhaird' - The Hill of the Bard) near Athboy, Co. Meath, which became associated with the Samhein Festival and sacred Druidic fires.

Tacitus comments in his *Annals,* in some apparent bemusement, that the Celts had no objection to being led by women and he repeats this point in his *Agricola.* 'In Britain', he says, 'there is no rule of distinction to exclude the female line from the throne, or the command of armies.' As Dr. Rankin points out: 'The city states of Greece and Rome had highly organised political structures which allowed no place for women in power. (Except for Lesbos) Greeks and Romans were all the more astonished at the relative freedom and individuality of Celtic women.' Certainly Pausanius makes a special mention of the notable courage of Celtic women.

The position of women, as it emerges in the Brehon law system of Ireland, at a time when women were treated as mere chattels in most European societies, was amazingly advanced. Women could be found in many professions, even as lawyers and judges, such as Brigh, a celebrated woman-Brehon. As Professor Markle has pointed out: 'The Romans looked upon women as bearers of children and objects of pleasure, while the Druids included women in their political and religious life. 'The Greek and Roman writers express little more than a prejudiced and impressionistic notion of the roles of women in the Celtic societies that they discuss.' Says Dr. Rankin. For example, Strabo makes the wild claim that the British Celts not only cohabit with the wives of others but with their own mothers and sisters and then, half-heartedly, admits that he has absolutely no evidence for such a statement. (But Kelts had about ten different kinds of relationships that all protected the rights and name for children so that it would become the kind of violent society born of large numbers of 'bastards' that Christianity evolved into under Roman guidance.) The phrase 'it is said.' could excuse many wild speculations. Caesar and Dio Cassius mention the practice of polyandry and communal marriage. What we are actually looking at is a more permissive and open society, not fully understood by the foreign observers.

This is not to say that the Celts had an ideal society at the beginning of the Christian era. Their society had already started to disintegrate into patriarchy. As we shall later discuss, changes from the initial 'mother goddess' concept had altered into a 'father of the gods' idea and slowly the male warrior society was replacing earlier perceptions. The introduction of Christianity, particularly the displacement of Celtic Christianity by Rome, gave the last kick to what had once been the equality of male and female in Celtic society. The uniqueness of ancient Celtic society lay in the fat that such concepts had lasted so long." (8)

The role of women in Phoenician society was perhaps the same and what with Dido founding Carthage we can be pretty sure that is the case in 814 BC at least. The Proto-Indo-European (PIE) ideology that Joseph Campbell showed led to the Nazism of Germany in our first chapter still thrives in the halls of academia. It is a scourge upon the soul of all mankind and not just that of women, because man is diminished through not knowing and sharing with an equal partner in many ways. Our souls teach more than our eyes will ever read and comprehend (especially when most of what is written is so utterly biased against the soul and true nature of man and the collective). Those who talk Aryan nonsense never point out that the North American Indians have many Ogham or Phoenician based languages or other customs. They do not want a return to egalitarian or matriarchal (Some say Iroquois society is matriarchal but it was not really fully that and just matrilineal.) government. Those who are focused on war and other criminal and immoral acts designed to make profit are not really convinced man is able to create or manifest good things but that is their problem and we need to help them learn it is not true.

SEX! - Now that I've got your attention. (Great Indian writer = Mark Twain)

John Ralston Saul correctly states that priests and politicians vie with prostitutes for the title of the 'world's oldest profession'. It is certain that it was practiced at the Temples of the proselytes in misogynistic Mediterranean cultures of the third millennium BC but the priests were the characters who benefited. There are a lot of words beginning with 'P' that fit these pubescent people who pimp and proselytize while pedophilia and pomposity plague plebian of the populace who never pressure them to produce results. The Druids were not a priesthood and though politically important they were not bureaucrats or politicians. The Algonkians whose women were encouraged to have sex before marriage with the likes of Prince Henry Sinclair clearly had little need of prostitutes long after Europe was a den of iniquity with all sorts of 'celibate' deviates and liars. You can decide if the Keltic women with all their rights had any use of prostitution. The story of Camma is not unique in the annals of Keltic lore and the Amazons would have emasculated any who tried to demean their sisters. These people knew what sex could be and how it could open the soul to the spirits. Yes, like today's Wiccans they had 'working partners' who were not their husband or significant other.

'Saint' (?) Constantine didn't make Christianity the formal religion of the Roman Empire when he became Holy (?!) Roman Emperor as most people think. It was his follower Theodosius who gave this edict shortly before the Council of Carthage in 397 AD. I can't prove the behind the scenes negotiations involved selling women down the river to the extent that occurred but I can look at the results and assume politics not Scripture (Divine or Devilish) was the factor. This Council and Nicaea of 325 should join the Treaty of Tordesillas in all schools or civics classes today that purport to study history or the truth about religion and politics. Carthage was clearly no longer egalitarian and Hypatia was torn limb from limb because she was smarter than the Bishop. This is when women were formally and forever excluded from the higher clerical offices of this Christian (?) church. Why don't we call them churchians, because they are not Christian in terms of following the ideals of Jesus; or the Chriost and Iesa concepts which preceded him?

The great 'Saints' like Paul and Augustine made the program acceptable to all the Catholics (but not Celtic Christianity and other orthodoxies) as they propagandized their foul creeds. St. Paul says (in the 'Epistles to Timothy'): 'Man is the head of women. who should not be HEARD in church.' There can be no greater example of scapegoating and projecting attributes onto someone other than the perp than we see in the 'Original Sin' of St. Augustine's creation. How can people today call these people Divinely Inspired as they claim 'woman is the harbinger of the 'Original Sin'? The Gnostics understood a truer 'Original Sin' that separates humans from God - It is *ignorance*! You could say this is the only sin as well as the 'original' one if you understand the hermetic law Right Thought =Right Action fully.

Constantine did almost stop the 'civilized' practice of Lions vs. Christians but I've never seen where the Druid 'bounty' of Claudius from 54 AD was lifted. In fact it could be said that the program against heretics is not yet over. In 1951 the British finally removed the Blasphemy Laws but a certain vocal minority still advocates a return to them. How about Affirmative Action for witches and nature-worshippers? Is it enough that the Indians were awarded a huge settlement for the Catholic destruction of their culture (with Intent)? This church is asking the Canadian

Government to share the cost of the Supreme Court award in the last report I saw. Let's hope the Canadian Government tells the Catholics It was their political influence that made the politicians do these things. It is interesting to note the hegemony is pointing fingers at each other a lot more these days, in court. Why aren't they really coming clean and stopping the negative institutionalized intolerance? Why is there still no Catholic woman priest, or a day care center in the Vatican? It has been noted that religions which worship or venerate women are called cults, such as the 'Cali' cult in India. Those that venerate men are real, absolute and higher religions. (Merton, Fukayama et al) It is truly quite revolting and hurtful.

No, please don't act with love to stop these things. After all, it is impolite and far too intense or 'rude' to discuss sex, religion and politics. The polite authors of alternatives are blending into the hegemony and being co-opted. Maybe change can occur from within and I wish them all the best, but someone must tell the truth about our leadership and the past - don't you think? Not with a view to blame, we must forgive! How can you forgive what is still on-going? The Pope asked for 'forgiveness and renewal' for two millennia of 'heinous' acts in 1999. Yes, I agree it isn't enough to simply inform yourself and speak out against abuse everywhere. I suspect most people who tell me this are hoping I will 'shut up'!

What has gone on (and continues) in Ireland is a crime against all human life and the civilization of Brotherhood that had a key spiritual center on the Emerald Isles. It is not just co-incidence. It is the same kind of secret 'behind the scenes destruction' of the Irish that has been employed to minimize other peoples by setting both ends against the middle (Hegel) and not even having to invade or expend great effort. The Rwandan genocide that the International Commission led by Stephen Lewis, blamed on the Catholic and Anglican Church is a good example; and the CIA or other agencies are doing similar things. The Organization of African Unity has asked for the forgiveness of all foreign debt. The Canadian Government has forgiven them the interest on this debt.

I join General Romeo D'Allaire of Canada who led the U.N. peacekeeping forces during this parade and charade of deceit. He decries the name of every person who allows such horror to be wrought upon this earth. Does this make us free of the karmic fallout? Dr. Janice Boddy of the University of Toronto has it right when she describes our reality as a 'Global Reifying Thrust of Materialism'. Romeo D'Allaire and I share some other acts of rage that people find outrageous, but we are not inclined to abuse our brother and sister. It sickens my soul. It also makes me doubt the power of the soul to harmonize in some collective, when I contemplate this kind of society that allows organizations to commit genocide through patsies and then suffer no censure or reprisals. It also makes me wonder what other kind of plan that people with such ethics might have in mind.

When the lifeforms on other planets or solar systems contemplate making a pact with us or allowing us into the 'Intergalactic Brotherhood' Kissinger spoke about to the Bilderbergs I think they find these inhumane acts of religious intolerance and divisiveness a deciding factor. Do you think it might be possible that our leaders plan to colonize the third planet in the Alpha Centauri system or terraform Mars without sharing the opportunity fairly? Earth is part of a relatively young solar system and NASA recently announced life is everywhere just as the mystics have always told us.

We are not so omnipotent or unique - ego is the cause of such rationale. If our solar system started some 5 Billion years or more after other solar systems too numerous to count how can we continue to act so inhumanely distant from our 'brother' lifeforms we share this earth with? We are just a blip in the development of life. History is an aberration of the human experience as long as it marginalizes morals and ethics. Let us hope we can access the history book that the Human Genome Director (Collins) says makes up our genes along with its part and operations manual. Maybe then, we will learn to recapture what our Mungo Man 'guides' who spoke to the viziers of Egypt and the Druids, were teaching.

We can dump the whole contents of a human brain onto a computer chip (Stanford 1999)
But that does not include the soul as I see it. In fact the soul in matter and the robot which might be more than elemental could create dysfunction of a degree we can hardly imagine. These sentient robots enabled by nanotechnology might be able to attune themselves with the cosmic soup or akashic better than we are doing and maybe even as well as the Druids and shamans once did. As the poem *Desiderata* quoted by Pierre Eliot Trudeau on many occasions said: "Whether or not it is clear to you, the Universe is unfolding as *it* should!"

Thomas Malthus was wrong about the *one pie* that we all must fight over. The 'Toilet Philosophy' that denies all that the five physical senses can not quantify is a problem of process and assumption that offers little opportunity to create in this quantum world. The dog that greets its master and wags its tail furiously when it sees the 'chewy' has more awareness than those who deny, ESP and the like. We would do well to emphasize the perception offered by the soul rather than empower ourselves over other souls. Yes, Canada is one of the best places on earth, but we are not a 'Just Society' and there are many hypocrites masquerading as something like sheep or shepherds when they are wolves, in fact. Nations do not have the right to operate by laws different than those they impose on citizens and corporations have so many ways to make their managers rich while investors and the other taxpayers suffer that one wonders how corporations were created and why. Chomsky bemoans how corporations and cronies get the research we pay for and then make billions exploiting these products at our expense.

In the Goth cult today I see a love of things Keltic that warms the cockles of my soul. The movie 'The Highlander' is one of their cult flicks and its sequel's title uses something

Diverse Druids

connected to the 'quickening sticks' made of rowan by Druids. The rowan is also known as the 'quicken' tree. It is about time for man to have a 'quickening' and enjoy the fruits of Brotherhood once again. The state of the medical model that achieved great success by getting people hooked on opiates like laudanum in the 19th century is a good comparison with homeopathy. The honest commentators of the time called it the 'killing trade' and then came the FDA and AMA politics which effectively reduced homeopathy and common sense to 'quackery'.

"Nevertheless, there was no system of medicine and health care in Greece that was, by law, available to all regardless of their position in society. It is now part of European cultural folklore that it was not until the Roman matron St. Fabiola (d.c. AD 399) set up a hospice for the sick and needy at Porto near Rome that the first hospital in Europe was founded.

Such institutions were, however, already established in India. The 'Charaka-Sambita' (Annals of Charake) tell us that Asoka (c. 273-232 BC), the emperor of India who, sickened by war and the struggle for power, turned to Buddhism and professed non-violence, established the first hospitals for the ailing poor.

The Irish sources refer to the establishment of the first hospital in Ireland by the semi-legendary queen of Ireland, Macha Mong Ruadh (d.c. 377 BC). She is said to have established a hospital called Bróin Bherg (the house of sorrow) at Emain Macha (Navan). Legend or not, we know that by the time of the Christian period, there were hospitals all over Ireland, some for sick people with general ailments and others serving specialist needs, such as leper hospitals. And when the law system came to be codified (I disagree with his interpretation of the origin of the *Senchus Mor*. I think he falls into the Christianizing trap rooted in the destruction of previous writings and his issues with Ogham are similar. Others suggest a 25,000 year history kept by the Bairds in this great book of law and the *Psaltair Na Tara*. It was certainly kept in the verbal tradition in any event.), it

227

showed the existence of an advanced and sophisticated medical system. The existence of such a system was in no small way a result of Druidic ideas which had been noted by Pliny." (9)

The Kelts cared for all members of their extended family and had communal land just as the Mayans do after the recent settlement in Chiapas. For a detailed analysis of the medical profession I recommend *Limits To Medicine* by the ex-communicated Jesuit educational expert and social activist, Ivan Illich. Zoltan Rona, M.D. presents some relatively fair insight in his medical encyclopedia. Any homeopathy book will make interesting reading and people can find Paracelsus and Hippocrates were alchemists whose knowledge made the growth of the industry into a real and helpful enterprise; despite the 'sins and demons' or other social and population control mechanisms of politicians and their cronies in the church (often the same people).

The Druidic 'peryllats' and healers like Diancecht are the models we find most amenable rather than the doctors who engage in professional patrimony and refuse to use what works to help people. This is changing slowly as people become informed consumers and the sciences outside medicine contribute new technologies. The Brehon Laws allow for food and health maintenance for everyone. This is the starting point for good health. In the Potato Famine, the English taxed the life out of the Irish farmers and drove a nation into near extinction. This author and I agree on the nature of the near utopian governance of Keltic law. Those (like Bacon) who study the Incan or Mayans can't help but see a more utopian ethic. But we can be sure this is also a co-incidence because Columbus 'discovered' America, right?!

Atlantis and Mu in the Tarim Basin

The area of the Taklamakand Desert today was once under the water in Paleolithic times and there are jasper arrowheads found around the shores of what once may have been the original Mediterranean Sea. It is on one of the routes that Caucasus white men of the Caspian Iberia would

Diverse Druids

have traveled to get to North America 30,000 years ago. They became the Sauk and the Sioux, which I have dealt with in great detail in my book on the Old Copper Culture of the Great Lakes. This region became totally uninhabitable around 500 AD but had been under increasingly adverse encroachments by nature for at least one millennia before that. The red-headed mummies found there are very much the nature of the Red Headed League of Megalith Builders and the De Danaan, in that they wear 'witches' hats' or pyramidal headgear to enhance the Third Eye energy amplification. They are tall just as the Adena and Sardinian 'giganti' are, and possibly the Peruvian kids we touched upon earlier grew to the same height, when at sea level.

I have mentioned this is where Lao Tzu, the father of Taoism, went to see the Ancient Masters in a place including the name Mu. If he had continued walking to the west he might have reached Aa-mu which was the name of Troy III. When we see 'A' in front and know 'A' in Greek reverses the meaning, it makes for interesting connections with the Trojan War. The matter of linguistic analysis is the most important aspect of the Tarim Basin residents because their language is unlike any of their neighbors. It is most like Irish and NW European tongues! I believe they were an adept colony working on research and formulating the Eastern religious experiences to come. Thus I take the same people to Barabudur and Central America. Although they are important to the book now being written, I have dealt with the source material in other books and so will only include a little of Ms. Barber's excellent research here:

"Beyond that, we had little context for most of what we saw. The labels read simply 85 Q Z, meaning they had come from the 1985 excavations near the town of Cherchen—written 'Qiemo' if you transliterate into Roman script the Chinese name of the place—at the little site called 'Zaghunluq'. (I never asked why they used Roman letters on the labels when Uyghur has now reverted to the Arabic script and Chinese uses its ancient system of word characters.) Those that I have described as coming from particular graves had the additional indicator M (for the Chinese word for grave)" (10)

This adds another possibility to who the Hyksos were and what corporate alliances they may have had within the Phoenician Brotherhood leading up to the Trojan War. Professor Mair of the University of Pennsylvania sees these mummies as making a major impact on all history. He is working in Turkmenistan to the west and they recently found a non-cuneiform alphabet there that dates to the same time as Sumer. The Greeks and the Trojans are both Phoenicians colonies and part of a large international or worldwide Brotherhood. The Hyksos came from Troy but it does not mean they were not part of Casiberia and associated with these Tarim Basin people who had such an affinity with the Emerald Isles and thus the Milesians who were there in 1500 BC by many accounts. This would indicate the 'Bees' are the plaid wearing ('lozenges' are like mandalas) Tarim Basin travelers who controlled trade in the Black Sea and had returned to the Hyperborean lands as the Milesians. In this view of corporate intrigue we also find the actual internecine accounts and double-dealing mentioned in Homer's Iliad that led to the defeat of the Trojans. However, they are shown to have escaped and the archaeologic and historic reality shows us many on each side continued to work together.

Shirley MacLaine and others prefer to call MU by the name Lemuria which in French would mean 'the Mu people'. Churchward tells us the Cara-Maya alphabet on my stele is the vehicle for translating Greek into the story of the destruction of MU. He dates its demise to the end of the last glacial period and it may have started in a far earlier glacial period if SE Asia and Indonesia are the underwater site of Mu near Barabudur and Angkor Wat. That is what I think happened and geologics is my source. I do not think it was a lost continent as he interpreted from the records and sources he used. Thus 'Amu' might mean 'not in the grave' or 'not dead'. The possibility of the Royal House of Mu in Peru having tightened the trade requirements for cocaine being able to make allegiances with certain families and the

Diverse Druids

resulting Trojan War is one I consider fits the facts we know. Buddhism of Barabudur did reach Mayan lands in periods after this and we know the mathematical concept of zero traveled this path. I cannot accept the co-incidence theory that denies all the cultural synchronicities and technologies. It is lunacy! The thing that drew Ms. Barber to the Tarim Basin in the first place was the plaids and technologies of the manufacture thereof. The 'lozenges' of Malta and the labrynthine mazes and designs are like corporate logos connecting Colombia, South America, Malta and Ireland with this one place that has the Phoenicians of Atlantis and the MU people living in harmony.

    The Tequesta Indians of South Florida are just another of the ancient cultures that had advanced technology who were said to be nomads by history until recently. There is no place in this world that I cannot give such details for. Why does our leadership keep saying our ancestry or human culture is so backward? The BBC web information says they had cities built on stilts to avoid the effects of hurricanes. The government of Florida paid $27 Million to buy and protect the site but in Yonaguni or the Azores we see they are not so open of forthcoming. Kennewick Man is covered over and wherever one finds Ogham or Phoenician (and Luwian, like Cuba) there is a program of destruction and denial. In my home city of Toronto I can find no one who will discuss the Phoenicians in any academic setting. A Keltic Dance Troupe official said occasionally someone comes through and knows some of these things. Why is there no Phoenician studies leading to doctoral degrees in any North American university? I hear there is one that has a Master's Program degree, but that is all.

Robert Baird

CHAPTER NINE:
Sex Magic, Sacrifices & Soulfulness:

New Agers Know the Past!

"Zen is a matter of character and not of the intellect, which means that Zen grows out of the will as the first principle of life. A brilliant intellect may fail to unravel all the mysteries of Zen, but a strong soul will drink deep of the inexhaustible fountain. I do not know if the intellect is superficial and touches only the fringe of one's personality, but the fact is that the will is the man himself, and Zen appeals to it. When one becomes penetratingly conscious of the working of this agency, there is the opening of satori and the understanding of Zen. As they say, the snake has now grown into the dragon; or, more graphically, a common cur—a most miserable creature wagging its tail for food and sympathy, and kicked about by the street boys so mercilessly—has now turned into a golden-haired lion whose roar frightens to death all the feeble-minded." (1)

It should be apparent to most people that sexual dysfunction and immoral mores of repression are caused by intellect responding to societal pressures or external agencies rather than any innate soulful need or introspective quest. The will in Zen seems less about ego yet includes a balanced and mature ego that can humbly know it is not important enough to stand in the way of 'What IS'. Will and aggression are inexorably entwined in sexual acts and the University of California Berkeley has said all sex is a matter of aggression and differences. I think the matter can be much more than that and that spiritual layers of intense beauty are there for humans to know. The mention of the 'serpent' in the above quote makes me think of many other disciplines and cults including Kundalini. The Dragon and the 'Chanes' we have mentioned, are all over the world. Sex magic was a key and vital if not most important part of all esoteric research and probably has been for millions of years.

It is in the archetypes of genetic or akashic memory and the alchemic serpents on the caduceus continue as representative symbols in science. Those who say we are descended from aliens such as the Sarkany Rend (Dragons) Rosicrucians like Sir Laurence Gardner must know the serpent is a phallic symbol. I am reminded of the joke about the Popsicle and the farmer's daughter. By making the phallus seem deserving of worship through the serpent connection with reptoid aliens some men otherwise unattractive, had a use for their manhood. No, it couldn't be that simple, could it?

An experience such as 'la petite mort', allows a spiritual and astral connection of the solar body with magical spiritual forces that few people ever tame. Those who do experience glimpses of it are 'blessed'; but the use of these soulful attunements gained through sexual union in one's everyday life, is another kettle of fish. Love is not just between the personalities or egos of the participants. That might well be what the UC Berkeley psychologists are studying. There are spiritual forces and connections that occur even beyond the perimeter of an individual's soul. The soul can allow 'collective' or simple spirits of other realms to co-habit the individual. This is often called 'possession'. Psychiatrists who know everything say there is no such thing and it is just hallucination. It is not!

Celibacy is a sacrifice of the Mass ('buttocks' in Irish) and it can achieve great insight as well. But to practice celibacy without knowledge is a fools quest that some have bought into, without much appreciation of the sacrifice they make. It can lead to a real growth and discipline that will produce results if the person is still compassionately involved with life around him (her). I guess you could say the energy formerly directed to sex becomes available for other spiritual usage. However, the love of an equal will surpass that energy and creative growth can occur.

'La petite mort' is described as an orgasmic experience where the individual passes into a state of unconsciousness and then comes back to consciousness while still having an orgasm. I can only imagine the fullness of mutual Bhakti or this spiritual ecstatic state. I believe it can manifest great things for all mankind if enough of us are able to be so connected. Such talk or words are trite anaphoristic, vernacular slang and there is no simple way to explore such beauty and empathy. It could be said that the brain is by-passed and the soul or physical consciousness of each chakra center that govern the physical components of the collective molecules in our body make contact with spirit guides or allies. This can be achieved without 'la petite mort'.

    The truth is, I have never read a treatise or heard a decent description of these things. But, 'a golden-haired lion whose roar frightens to death all the feeble-minded' come a long way towards the truth of the experience. Mr. Suzuki and his young lady Okamura probably explored these regions of the unseen illogical world or dimensional realities through this most pleasing intercourse. Needless to say 'a strong soul will drink deep of the inexhaustible fountain' relates to this kind of sex and other things as well. Zen can help with motorcycle maintenance too.

    There are many terms and jargon of the esoteric or erudite philosophers in the quote that begins this chapter. Specialist knowledge of concepts can make its superficial beauty seem almost of no value in comparison to the depth of the 'fountain' or the fullness of 'will'. Other words that are often used to convey the 'bubbling spring' of knowledge and the possibility of 'direct cognition' are often just as poetic. We must remember it is only recently that people with this knowledge were hounded and harassed into death at the stake ('autos da fe' - last one in Seville of the 19th Century, from the Inquisitors, but many since then under KKK) or by a form of ostracization called heresy. I personally have experienced some of the remnants of these attitudes in all levels of society. Obviously the 'born again' elements are the easiest to recognize. The funny thing is, they will be major obstacles to getting this kind of work into publication and thus the government or system that keeps them ignorant, through propaganda, is being protected by those they most abuse.

Esoteric Gurus

As an initiate, it is easy to think the concepts are understood when the process has only started. Explaining rudimentary terms or components (even in a scientific manner) is not where 'the rubber hits the road'. Now we can trace the neural functioning through MRI/SPECT technology and know the turning off or on of brain lobes and the like - so what? Yes, it is very good that scientists or the academics who denied these things because we couldn't 'see' them now have to accept they are somehow true. Regression, self-hypnosis, Erica, EST, Yoga and other techniques galore can bring forth insights to awesome things from the time/space/spirit/cosmic/ancestral continuum. That continuum is not within my grasp to fully elucidate or explain and I have only seen poetics do a decent job. Poetry or prose will never limit or circumscribe the real nature of our creative chaos. It is a chasm across which our feeble species has only begun to cross to the extent the Druids or the Chaos Scientists of ancient times were able to do according to Dr. Don Robins who I quote extensively in books like *Neolithic Libraries*.

The Druids weren't in the habit of explaining anything in writing about these most meaningful aspects. Alchemists like Socrates knew the Law - 'Know, Will, Dare, Keep Silent' which the immortal or enigmatic Fulcanelli preferred to state in his native French by 'Scrire, Potere, Audere, Tacere'. French makes Latin live with an energy it never had in Rome. Is there a connection between 'poetry' and 'Potere'? Is the power of the BRD and the Logos in poetry? Harmonics is a vital and fruitful field that I wish I had begun the study of while in school. Hermetics has its fakirs or power-seekers and those who might claim guru or teacher status. I can think of very few who rise to the level of ethics demonstrated by Socrates.

Robert Baird

The Toltecs have left us one great guru in Don Juan according to Carlos. Don Gennaro is on the speaking circuit and I have not had the pleasure of seeing why people pay to learn from him. I would love to make an assessment of him because I have so much respect for Don Juan/Carlos. Usually money and the pursuit of it goes not go well with true faith or knowledge but those whose books sell well and make money as a result of good work are numerous in the New Age environment of today. Don Juan's *Amber rays* go far beyond most sorcery and his 'way of the *nagual*' has much to offer. Because he is a Toltec or his knowledge comes from them - he is certainly one of the best ways to get to know what a Druid knew.

Dr. Wayne Dyer's book *You'll See It; When You Believe It!* Makes a stab at conveying the distancing aspect of Don Juan's IMPECCABLE WARRIOR. Gary Zukav's book *The Dancing Wu-Li Masters* takes an anthropological approach from the physicist point of view that is most worthwhile and I love the *Tao of Physics* and *Hyperspace*. Bucky Fuller always leaves me in awe and wishing I knew more mathematics or engineering. All Taoist and Yogic thought as well as some Sutras and Dharmas offer psychological coping skills that would be as beneficial as acupuncture of ayurveda if only we taught them in schools. The early research of Michael Faraday on Field Theory and its apprehension of whatever source Tesla came by it is a major area of interest that the quantum world is still working on, but unfortunately black ops often employ it against humanity. We are on the brink of what Dr. Jose Delgado (Yale) talked about in a book with these ominous titular words - "Psychocivilizing Society"! I must eschew giving this too much time in this particular book.

Most commentators on the Druids are unable to fathom the possibility of affecting the wind and rain or putting a whole army of enemies into a hypnotic trance. Healings such as the psychic surgeons of Brazil or the Philippines perform make most scientists quiver and quake. The harps of the Druids were able to focus the 'cosmic soup' through what

Diverse Druids

has been called 'The Lost Chord'. There is some possible connection to the King's Chamber of the Great Pyramid wherein Napoleon saw something he would never talk about (even to his trusted biographer on his death bed after the British filled him with arsenic). My temerity has extended itself to touch upon explanations for these things in other manuscripts. Now we move to a troublesome matter associated with St. Columba who learned and acted as a Druid but was part of the hegemony. He has his progeny in the likes of Sir Laurence Gardner who wrote the multi-national best-seller *Genesis of the Grail Kings*.

Laurence Gardner has gone some distance to usurp this knowledge and I do not know the full extent of their actual achievement of it. It is true some of their members like Sir Isaac Newton were adept in these matters but that does not mean a great deal when one considers how much Gardner claims their forbears knew. I do believe even more than he talks about was known. I do not want to appear unappreciative of his scholarship either. In the end it leaves me very cold and wary; I can see many people might believe their 'chest-beating' and power-trip. The Sarkany Rend 'Dragons' of the Christian Mystery Schools are not the only Rosicrucian Order. I do not know to what extent they work together. I think there are some major differences between them and it would seem they would speak out against each other if they did not in fact work together in some manner. I respect their willingness to lay their dirty linen out for all to see in the work of deVere who does the foreword to Gardner's aforementioned book. Dracula and his kin are the nature of this beast! Here are some of Gardner's titles and associations or credentials from the back flap of this all important book:

"Prior of the Celtic Church's Sacred Kindred of Saint Columba, the Jacobite Historiographer Royal, and an internationally known sovereign and chivalric genealogist distinguished as the Chevalier Labhrån de St. Germain, he is Presidential Attaché to the European Council of Princes. He is formally attached to the Noble Household Guard of the

Royal House of Stewart and is Chancellor of the Imperial and Royal Court of the Dragon Sovereignty which embodies the Knights Templars of St. Anthony."

Unlike many Masonic titles or pompous posing these titles all have much to offer us as we seek to know what the connection between them all might be. St. Germain and the Jacobites as well as Saints like Anthony and Columba are absolutely on point with our premises. The rest of it gives an idea of the political intrigues and noble heritages of the 'Sons of Mil (ML)' or Stewart/Stuarts. St. Anthony and the Hebrew Tau cross and its connection to astrological aspects including Orion as well as Rennes le Chateau are worthy of a book unto themselves. Crocodiles in Egypt are one of the forbears of the Dragons and their combined symbology has received a great deal of worldwide inspection and worship. The ibis and the Celtic crane are their symbolic consorts.

Secretum Secretorums and Outright Secrets of Secretions

I have dealt with the 'Star-Fire' ceremony and relationships with the 'Obscene Ritual' of Yale's Skull & Bones Society or The Order in other books. The Pineal Gland or Third Eye and other thalami research is briefly mentioned in a conventional type of book called *The Wonder Child* that makes good use of some of the knowledge. Because power in the hands of a few is more powerful and because the proclamation of the 'Novo Seculum Ordre' is easily found wherever a US dollar bill will travel; I suggest the New World Order is an important reality. It is more important than the UN though it may only include the IMF and FED, along with a few cronies. The Eastern Establishment along with Skull & Bones and Wolf's Head as well as the Beacon Hill Mob might have a few of these Dragons at play in their hallowed halls, methinks.

The melatonin needs of secret rituals and 'workers in the dark' (translation of melatonin) have a lot of similarity with other blood rituals including the communion or Eucharist and the protestant names for these same rituals (transsubstantiation). Dracula is a proud member of their austere heritage according to deVere (HRH and all that these few letters mean). Clearly we can have a lot of fun with him being a 'worker in the dark' and all the 'black ops' people who come out of Yale to work with the CIA and Bush. It really is no laughing matter unfortunately.

It probably would amaze most mundane (as averse to arcane) scholars to see words like 'flower' become 'flow'-er or 'she who flows' and the use of dried menstrual blood in the Star-Fire Ceremony that makes Scarlet Women important to more than just the Thelemics of Aleister Crowley who they worked with during WWII. We quoted Hitler as he 'worked in the dark' of wooded night at the end of chapter one and we can assure you Napoleon worked magic including maybe even the design of the Great Seal of the United States that he gave to Jefferson (per Michael Bradley). It is all connected and it hasn't disappeared just because it happens in the 'dark'. We have always had this kind of Dark Age, ever since the rise of misogyny and beneficent paternalistic or Platonist hierarchy. So when deVere offers his services as leader of the Free World or New World we should wonder and worry. Adam Weishaupt took Thelemic or tantric magic to his heart and 'Illuminized' Masonry. He is the man many scholars point to as the founding father of Russia, the U.S. and all this order stuff. His Bavarian homeland shared by Hitler and other Rothschilds are the most 'dark' of all 'workers', perhaps. On the other hand you could say they are Luciferians, as the Papal advisor Malachi Martin writes about being in control in books like *Windswept House*.

What do they know that makes them think we should let them run the whole world when they clearly have been a major part of it all along? What do they know that we don't? What is it that they think would interest us in being led by reptoid aliens that they claim to draw their lineage from in Sumer. Is it possible that they have their tentacles in every kind of organization from Scientology to the CIA? They certainly play both ends against the middle and benefit from all the wars they create. They are Cecil Rhodes backers and teachers or doctors who seem to have their pulse on every vein that carries any meaningful ounce of our blood:

"We saw that the serpent and the Tree of Knowledge were represented in the insignia of the American and British Medical Associations. However, various other medical relief institutions, worldwide, use two coiled serpents, spiraling around the winged caduceus of the messenger-god Mercury. In these instances, the central staff and serpents represent the spinal cord and the sensory nervous system, while the two uppermost wings signify the brain's lateral ventricular structures. Between these wings, above the spinal column, is shown the small central node of the pineal gland. (3) The combination of the central pineal and its lateral wings are referred to in some yogic circles as the 'Swan', and the Swan is emblematic of the fully enlightened being. This is the utmost realm of Grail consciousness achieved by the medieval Knights of the Swan, epitomized by such chivalric figures as Perceval and Lohengrin. (4)

In the hermetic lore of the ancient Egyptian mystery schools, this process of achieving enlightened consciousness was of express importance, with spiritual regeneration taking place by degrees through the thirty-three vertebrae of the spinal column (5) until reaching the pituitary gland which invokes the pineal body. The science of this regeneration is one of the 'Lost Keys' of Freemasonry, (Originally 'Phre' = 'Sun', masonry, 'sun' also is 'fire giving and that is the key agent in the birth and rebirth of matter in alchemy) and it is the reason why ancient Freemasonry was founded upon thirty-three degrees. (6)

In the days of ancient Sumer, the Anuists perfected and elaborated a ramifying medical science of living substances, with menstrual Star Fire being a vital source component. In the first instance, this was pure Anunnaki (Their alien origins) lunar essence called 'Gold of the Gods', but later, in Egypt and Mediterranea, menstrum was ritually collected from sacred priestesses (the Scarlet Women) and was dignified as being the 'rich food of the matrix'. The very word 'ritual' stems from this custom, and from the Sanskrit word 'ritu' - the 'red gold' (sometimes called 'black gold') (Due to blood going black when dried or fried.). Endocrinal supplements are used by today's organo-therapy establishment, but their inherent secretions (such as melatonin and scrotonin) are obtained from the desiccated glands of dead animals and they lack the truly important elements which exist only in live human glandular manufacture. (7) (This is why I believe the Skull & Bones people still eat human glands. They say they ended the drinking of blood and other things in a law, but here we see what powerful people value. With access to slaves and the increase in uncared for children ['bastards'] the Christian Mystery Schools continued their 'rituals' in high places.)

In the fire symbolism of alchemy, the color red is synonymous with the metal gold, and in the Indian 'tantras' red (or black) is the color of Kali (Celtic languages include 'nuil'=blood, and the old blood of the Nile makes black earth there that was a special initial ingredient of processes once started with meteoric material including iridium and rhodium that are also in the human brain though not naturally occurring in mineral deposits of the earth.), goddess of time, seasons, periods and cycles. (8) One does have to seek beyond the simplicity of the *Oxford English Dictionary* (under 'menstruum') to find the menstrual action described as being 'an alchemical parallel with the transmutation into gold'. The metals of the alchemists were, therefore, not common metals in the first instance, but living essences, and the ancient mysteries were of a physical, not metaphysical nature. The word 'secret' has its origin in the hidden knowledge of these glandular 'secretions'." (9)

It always makes me wonder what a person reading this 'stuff' for the first time must think?! WOW! HOOEY! Is it pure science fiction? Many words still come to my mind and it makes it hard for me to say I do not believe in evil even though I believe in evil Intent. I know there is some truth in what he says from various sources. I do not think his Rosicrucians are what they purport to be, or perhaps I should say I know there is an element of pompous propaganda and power-mongering that goes against the Laws of the Magi. His knowledge and sources are interesting and good. His assertions disturb me greatly and I do not think they (often at least) succeeded in making the Stone despite his claims. I think there is some protection built in to the cosmic attunements in these matters. However, I also think that machines and science today do not have these ethical constraints; and the fact that these 'noble' families are rich and powerful, should concern everyone on earth today.

Women in the Inner Sanctum?
In 1990 Mary Condren wrote *The Serpent and the Goddess: Women, Religion and Power in Celtic Ireland* which Peter Ellis quotes from in a major way. It is instructive to see how the Kelts of pre-Roman Empire were different and treated differently in their society that was heavily influenced by the Druids:

"'We can trace a gradual change of emphasis whereby what formerly was held sacred became profane and the new expression of sacredness took on an increasingly male character.'

Female church leaders were initially seen as equal with their male counterparts as they had been under the pre-Christian Celtic religion. This is apparent from the authority that the female Celtic saints had. Brigit, according to Cogitosus in the seventh century, presided over members of both sexes in her community as did the Irish trained Northumbrian St. Hilda. In the early Celtic Christian church the communities were often double-housed or 'conhospitae' in which men and women, and their children, lived as an extended family working in the name of the new god, perhaps carrying on the traditions of the Druid communities. Women were able, initially, in accordance with Celtic philosophy, to celebrate the 'divine sacrifice of Mass', as well as the male priests. This incensed the sensibilities of the Roman Church, whose long struggle for domination over the Celtic Church is well documented. Rome first seemed to notice the practice in Brittany and in about AD 515-520 three Roman bishops wrote a letter to two members of the Breton clergy named Lovocat and Catihern: 'you celebrate the divine sacrifice of the Mass with the assistance of women to whom you give the name of 'conhospitae'. We are deeply grieved to see an abominable heresy. Renounce these abuses.'

Mary Condren observes, 'One of the main problems that the Christian Church has with these religious women was that the god of the Christians was very different from their god. Just as the Israelite overthrew the gods of the Canaanites (Read Phoenicians who had queens like Dido and Ariadne as well as the wife of Solomon.) when they developed their patriarchal forms of social organization, so too the Christian priests would formulate a concept of god that would reinforce and encourage their new patriarchal consciousness. In its initial stages, the church may well have counteracted the power of the warriors, but in many respects its priestly practitioners were blessed with an equally virulent form of male reproductive consciousness.'" (10)

And the Epistles to Timothy probably were not the first to propose women should not be near sacred places in the church because they are unclean or mouthy, and the ritual continues to this very day. St. Paul says many vile things but none more foul than 'Man is the head of woman.who is not to be heard in church.' Both men and women suffer through the lack of equality allowed women. It leads to a cycle of violence in all relations that ultimately devolve into controlling rather than loving. I like the Yogic saying that is not meant to be taken literally: - 'If you meet someone wishing to be your guru or interpreter for God - 'Shoot him!'' There are many great people with wisdom and we can learn from each other but our soul is our best avenue of understanding if we could only get rid of all the inputs and propaganda. Walt Whitman is one of those wise people who I love to read, and he said, "The whole theory of the universe is directed to one single individual. Namely *you*."

Robert Baird

This does not mean each individual is more important than any other individual but it does mean we are all (each and every soul on earth) very important and responsible for all that happens. It is hard to accept that Jesus meant for each of us to act similarly as God when you have had so many inputs from priestly and political hegemonists who tell you Jesus was 'the only begotten' and you should not try to do as he did. In John 10:35 we see Jesus saying we are all God. In many places and by judging his acts there are ways to interpret good things about Jesus - it seems a debate of little use for me though. The fact I must face is this - the majority or prevailing paradigm has enslaved the soul of all people through religion. Marx said 'religion is the opium of the people'. He was married to British nobility and funded by Masonic interests, as he wrote his masterworks which many years later were used to establish a new 'Illuminized' country on earth - namely Russia! Yes, even Yeltsin is found talking about the enigmatic 'They' who did this to the Russian people rather than Africa, as the New World Order was taking more control of all things here on earth. It truly has been a 'War on Terra'.

The truth of the Druids has much to offer as an alternative because they were pan-tribal, enabled education and medicine for all, acted on the authority of wisdom rather than power or bureaucracy. They maintained extended family and laws of situational ethics rather than one law for the rich and another for the poor. That is what we have today. In their day the rich paid four times the penalty and couldn't scapegoat underlings. No one who broke the law as public trustee or official was allowed to continue in office. The underlying ethic in the Keltic Creed is the aspect most missing from our social governance today. They believed in an immortal soul and did not have psychiatrists to officially deny or drug those who would endeavor to enable the soul in every person who might actually demand compassion for all people.

Jefferson and Aristotle may be wrong about a lot of things but they are right (in my humble opinion) about

Diverse Druids

science and philosophy when they say its main object is the happiness and freedom of humanity. Freedom and happiness come with a price and require effort as well as good acts. François Fenelon (1651-1717) put the matter simply as follows:

"When you come to be sensibly touched, the scales will fall from your eyes; and by the penetrating eyes of love you will discern that which your other eyes will never see."

The Program of Sacrifices Continues

When you read Archaeology or National Geographic you will still find the emphasis on barbarous sacrifices by 'les autres' or the 'others' is afoot. As if the Romans weren't into sacrifices! By extension we are to infer our leaders are above the acts of indecency when we hear how horrified they are about Dr. Mengele. The truth is quite the opposite and human experimentation by doctors was rampant everywhere in the world. Germany was the only nation with procedural guidelines to follow. There are numerous examples of the pot calling the kettle black, to say the least. It is prejudice and racism as well as false!

When they implicate the Moshe or Aztec as well as the Kelts or their Carthaginian/Phoenician 'brothers' they are not telling the whole story. They suggest it was unusual and that classical Euro-centric culture was above such things. If the European influence on the Moshe isn't something you can accept then you could say they are truly overly into sacrifice but first it is important to know that the Devoted Ones mentioned in the Bible are sacrificial victims too (see Cahill's *Gifts of the Jews*).

The Keltic practice of cutting their enemies heads off is more humane than other forms of murder and warfare. To use the head in spiritual practices might well have been helpful to the soul of the departed and the Druidic practices respected their enemy or the soul of that enemy. I personally would prefer the ministrations of a Druid over the Roman Lions. The Druids felt that the head was the seat of the soul and consciousness. They were keen observers of healing and medicine and may even have been able to regrow limbs as the legends indicate and some Yogis are said to do today. Of course all these legends seem completely unbelievable or miraculous but when a chromic or Kirlian photograph is taken of a person who has lost a limb, that limb still shows up for a long period of time. There are many fantastic things that science and medicine can do and we are working on even more incredible things all the time. Our genes definitely include the information to make each limb and all that is needed is energy which they may have learned to focus and combine with the genetic knowledge. Now for some more Gardner and the Biblical murderers like Cain and Abel.

"The letter 'Q' - as in Qayin (Q'ayin) and Queen - is metaphysically assigned to the moon, and the 'khu' (Q) was perceived as the monthly (lunar) (What Crowley calls 'the blood of the moon'.) female essence of the goddess. The divine menstruum constituted the purest and most potent life-force, (11) and it was venerated as 'Star Fire'. Its representation was the all-seeing eye (the ayin), whose hermetic symbol was O (with the small dot to represent the light of the universal harmonic), (12) the 'kamakala' of the Indian mystics and the 'tribindu' of the oriental school. (13) The letter 'Q' derives from the Venus symbol (The symbol for the female sex or gender used in astrology.) - a symbol equally attributed to Isis, Nin-khursag, Lilith and Kali, all of whom were deemed 'black but beautiful' (Song of Solomon 1:5). Lilith and Kali were both titular names, with Kali appropriated from 'kala' (the periodic time of the female lunar cycle), while Nin0khursag was the ultimate Lady of Life. Hers was the 'genus' which constituted the true 'beginning' of the sacred bloodline - the Genesis of the Grail Kings. In the Rosicrucian tradition this 'genesis' has long been identified with the transcendent 'gene of Isis'.

'Genesis' (13) (origin, or beginning) stems from the Greek, and from the word 'genes' (meaning 'born of a kind'), whence also derive the words 'genetics', 'gender', 'genius', 'genii', 'genital', 'genre', 'generation',

Diverse Druids

'genealogy', etc. As an alternative, the eye of illumination was sometimes depicted with a triangle (With the small dot or wavicle of light) which represented the 'daleth', or doorway, to the Light. (The modern science of genetics was established by the Columbia University embryologist Thomas Hunt Morgan, who received the Nobel Prize in 1933. His work was founded, however, upon the records of Theodor Heinrich Boveri of Munich University who, in the 1880s, explained almost every detail of cell division and chromosomes long before the invention of the electron microscope. (14))

Qayin (Cain/Kain) has often been called 'the first Mr. Smith' because the term 'qayin' also means 'smith', as in metalsmith, or more precisely as in blade-smith, a required skill (or 'kenning'=knowing) of the early kings. In this regard, his name given in Genesis - like that of Hevel (Abel) and many others in the Bible - is a descriptive appellation rather than a real personal name. In the alchemical tradition he was indeed a 'qayin' - an artificer of metals of the highest order, as were his descendants, particularly Tubal-cain (Genesis 4:22) who is revered in scientific Freemasonry. Tubal-cain was the great Vulcan of the era, (15) the holder of Plutonic theory (knowledge of the actions of internal heat), and was, therefore, a prominent alchemist.

Qayin's heritage was that of Sumerian metallurgists - the Master Craftsmen whom we encountered at the court of El Elyon - and the supreme Master of the Craft was Qayin's father Enki, described as 'the manifestation of knowledge, and the craftsmen 'par excellence', who drives out the evil demons who attack mankind'. (16) The alchemical pursuits of this family were of the utmost significance to their history, and the expertise of their craftsmanship held the key to the Bible's mysterious 'bread of life' and 'hidden mana'.

So, if Qayin was not the man's real name, then who was he?" (17)

He goes on to spread the fable of the Bible out to include Ahura Mazda and the Magi like Zoroaster and we are to accept his assertions because he knows his Bible well. I do

Robert Baird

NOT! The idea that we are descendants of reptoid aliens is far too fantastic and yet this cult has wielded the greatest influence imaginable in this world. The BIG LIE is a technique they learned early and applied often throughout what we call history. His reconstruction of the Tower of Babel is more akin to the Pyramid at Chichen Itza or Palenque. The gods of Olympus including Zeus (derives from the same root word concept that Jesus does) were doing the same things for their master myth makers in the time before Christianity. Many of the legends are taken from other sources, including the bulrushes birth and the Immaculate Conception. What better way to get people to do what you want than this use

of myths? I guess I was biased against these lies to begin with but, I think I have kept a pretty open mind as I consider all the facts. Gardner and deVere are not alchemists in the tradition I associate myself with and his use of the word makes me cringe.

Land and Human Nature

Now I ask the reader to recall the movie 'Braveheart' and the Keltic penchant for freedom. While in grade school I read Thomas B. Costain's rendition of the story of Willie of Bannockburn. When I watched 'Braveheart' it was almost as if they were dealing with a different person in a different time and space. Costain diminished the cause and presented the hero 'Longshanks'. 'Prima Nocturne' (!) - god is in heaven, we need one on earth (Thank you Ingmar Bergman)! Divine Right Of Kings! (?) Where did that come from? (!)

The ability to alter the gene pool and cater to deviate sexual needs to get cohorts and nobles in the war of Edward I is not novel in the annals of priestly kings or Dark Ages management of society. Indeed the arrogance of these noble families was almost without bounds, as they traded land lordships through wars fought with evening tea and other intrigue shown in 'Braveheart'. It is such an abomination of the ethic of the Kelts and North American Indians that one can argue for their common ancestry on this point alone.

Diverse Druids

From a book called *Denendeh* (which is often shortened to Denhe and relates to North American Indians of the northwest) we have Chief Daniel Sonfrere saying something we know is in the Brehon Laws and its Keltic forbear the *Senchus Mor*. Land use and rights to own god or nature were early issues for the Empire builders to overcome in the destruction of extended family and Brotherhood:

"Before even the white people came or even since the white people came, when people were making their living hunting and trapping, although the boundaries are not drawn out on maps, the people from each community realize and respect other people's areas; although they are not written, although they are not drawn out on the maps, they have respect for each other's areas, but when it comes to helping each other it does not matter; they help each other." (18)

The Denhe were especially uninterested in farming or improving upon nature and some Plains Indians didn't do much in the way of agriculture either. There were many who did what the Iroquois and Cherokee did in places where it made sense to plant things like corn, tobacco and tubers. The earth didn't have to be ripped asunder or planted to maximize the use of a field till it was unable to bear fruit. They seldom built fences and left salt licks out for the deer that they honored as they ate them and used every part of their bodies with respect. Rather than pesticides there were flowers and herbs that helped deal with the insects.

In South America and its mountainous terrain they went to the degree or extent of irrigation that some compare with Etruscan methods. In almost every case there was a communal ethic and land was nature and nature IS god. Is there any god you know that is greater than all the reality, or What IS? This spiritual focus rather than our material focus does not mean the Incans and Cherokee or others were uninterested in technological advancement. That has been the way of presenting the 'primitives' through much of recent historical propaganda. The Incas were Bacon's model for his utopian authorship and the Cherokee adapted to the white man's way as if they had designed it. Thus the jealous white folk sent them on THE TRAIL OF TEARS in order to rip off their plantations and get their slaves. Potlatch, mentioned in the next quote is giving respect and assets to each other, and it was hard to tax so the Canadian Government outlawed it in the 1920s.

"Many gained influence and wealth through medicine-power (Biblio - De Smet, on the rise of Tehake of the Assiniboine, vol, iii, pg. 1108 & seq.); sometimes, indeed, the shaman had more authority than the chief. On the plains, men accumulated property for years in order to purchase a medicine-bundle, just as they hoarded skins and food on the Pacific coast to outdo their rivals in a potlatch. Women as well as men had their avenues of advancement. Many enjoyed high rank on the Pacific coast ('Ideas' is a radio program of the CBC that had a show on genetic dating of the Indians on Vancouver Island that had them tracked here for 35,000 to 70,000 years.) through the accident of descent; among the Iroquoians a few became matrons of maternal families. The great 'sun-dance festival' of the plains Indians brought together all the members of a tribe, from far and near; yet the Blackfoot and the Sarcee could not hold a sun-dance except in fulfillment of a woman's vow, (It involves sex and magic.) and the woman whose purity and self-sacrifice permitted its celebration enjoyed fame and honor throughout her days. Both sexes alike could qualify as shamans, although in this sphere women rarely obtained the same prestige as men. Indian society was, therefore, far from stagnant. If the fields for ambition were narrow this was no more than inevitable among peoples of lowly culture whose horizons were limited to their own vicinity (They traveled more than most urban dwellers of today, in mind and spirit. This is objectionable materially focused and supportive of the Columbus fiction, yet fairer than many.).

The principal check on ambition, a salutary check in the main, was the socialistic character of Indian life. Rank and wealth gave no title to arrogance. Except at ceremonies chiefs dressed in the same way. The fruits of the earth, the game on the land, and the fish in the water were for all

Diverse Druids

men's use, and while every individual was entitled to the products of his labour no one might claim an unfair share to the detriment of his fellowmen. So we read of the Hurons: 'No hospitals are needed among them, because there are neither mendicants nor paupers as long as there are any rich people among them. Their kindness, humanity, and courtesy not only make them liberal with what they have, but cause them to possess hardly anything except in common. A whole village must be without corn before any individual can be obliged to endure privation. They divide the produce of their fisheries equally with all who come.' (19) The most ambitious native never dreamed of creating tyranny or of subverting the established political constitution for his own advantage. So Indian tribes never knew those internal revolts that distracted the city states of ancient Greece and rendered our Saxon forefathers an easy prey to Danish and Norman invaders." (20)

Dr. Don Robins and Celtic scholar Anne Ross did the major work on the Lindow Man that Mr. Ellis comments upon in the next offering I choose from his book. Anne Ross once wrote that Ogham dates to 800 BC and that it was used only for ceremonial purposes so I have some issues with her. Dr. Robins is one of my favorite sources of insight and understanding. This Druid prince from shortly before the time of Christ may have been one of the victims of Roman bounty that we have covered earlier and it is not presented as anything but another Keltic sacrifice by most authors. The body and its clothing were remarkably well preserved.

"But what is the basis for such conjectures? The basis is that the 'human sacrifice' report of the Romans is accepted without question. The authors argue:

'Their (the Celts) penchant for human sacrifice shocked even the Romans, inured as they were to the horrors and carnage of the amphitheatre. Surrender to an enemy never figured largely in the Celtic order of battle. Prisoners of war, as we learn from Julius Caesar, were usually sacrificed to the gods. Caesar reports how captives were burnt in giant wicker cages.'

Caesar, with due respect to him, says nothing of the kind. On the subject of sacrifices he says that criminals were chosen first. References to Celts not taking prisoners of war, found in other Classical writings, could well have been simply a warning to Greek or Roman soldiers not to contemplate surrender and making them fight without quarter. But that's a maybe, And, as we have seen, the 'wicker man' report was not even an original one but a rehash of Poseidonius. 'In all cases the victim was chosen by means of the burnt piece of festival bannock.' (21)

Thus we have burnt bannock becoming Bannockburn, and William Wallace being shown in quarters to the realm of Longshanks. The changes of the millennia seemed to have the same themes and we can thank history for all the good role models. Needless to say, if I haven't already; I love 'Braveheart' and would die with Wallace even if I was the real 'Bruce'. I believe the colonial uprisings started before the Hyksos period but there is so little to work with and it probably doesn't matter if it was a thousand years or just a century anyway. It makes sense that the Kelts became increasingly more willing to die to protect their women and children as well as the all important culture they had developed but I also can't be certain they weren't always inclined to fight with the same ferocity. I agree with Ellis in respect of the Romans and Greeks telling their troops that the Kelts took no prisoners. Clearly slaves and prisoners were part of the booty of war.

Other scholars find no evidence that capital punishment was used in Ireland and the wicker man was not needed on islands where ostracism was the worst punishment. I think the wicker man was a way to send the former administrators to the spiritual realm at the end of their term at one point. It sure would be a deterrent to corruption if we re-instituted that policy today. Maybe some of the people who would apply for the 25 year term of office as king would think twice about what they hoped to gain by being king or President. They had a lot of ways to deal with criminals that I believe worked for all of their society. There are few systems in our current state of government that are more troublesome than the penal colony as far as I am concerned.

The issue of sacrifices as proof of 'barbarian' culture must be considered in broad context when you know they respected the soul and spirit of all things. Are abortion, euthanasia and capital punishment on the same continuum of moral consideration? Ellis is a little too defensive about the matter and he might not know the Biblical Devoted Ones were abused and then used as sacrifices. The Phoenicians definitely did sacrifice the leader's children in the times when the leader failed to appease the Gods that ruled their destiny. Some scholars think this served to build more concentrated fortunes in the rich families. Maybe this is what led to the kind of nobility mind set and deviate people like deVere and his kin. I think the Catholic sin of suicide has some of the most tenuous of moral arguments and that a lot of the reasons behind it were to keep serfs or concubines alive to enjoy another day's work from. I can certainly understand why Camma did what she did and why that kind of thing would cause the victorious king to be asking the priests to work their magic and get people into fearing death, as a 'Sin' or something with all the HELL type connotations. When it comes to barbarian or other epithets my favorite is power-monger as you may have noticed.

Robert Baird

CHAPTER TEN:
Before The Deluge of 5500 BC:

Scota - Princess and Progenitor of Scotland and Scythia
In *The Kelts: Children of the Don* I used a lot of quotes from *A Celtic Reader*. The story of Scota, a daughter of an Egyptian Pharaoh, whose name became the root of the word that Keltic people near the origin of the species in Old Europe became known by - Scythia. It is hard to know when these various Egyptian characters may have lived but it is my guess that Findias (Finias) was the place which disappeared when the Black Sea was created in 5500 BC. Subsequent to that there became a number of new entities and one can assume the Kelts lost much of their assets, people and wealth. Iberia continued in nearby places as well as throughout the world. Scythia probably was from around this time or a little later when the Pyramids were built by those who knew their culture was facing a likely demise now that they were weaker and their colonial trading partners felt an opportunity to become more important had presented itself. Then came the inundation of NW Europe; which created the North Sea and greatly reduced another of their four major administrative centers, with its spiritual site of Tara/New Grange. That was in 5300 BC according to the geologic record. A constant inundation of major centers around the world has been seen to have occurred and old legends are rising up from the deep now that we are looking for answers rather than facts to fit the Bible Narrative (Not to suggest that matter is fully put to bed.).

Some say that Narmer is Menes and who knows who Ramses III really was? At the end of the proverbial day and after years of study by many people National Geographic says we should be asking who colonized Egypt. The idea that it was a starting point (or Sumer) is pure Bible Narrative. The various confusing names are exacerbated by the fact that every Pharaoh had at least two names and there are so many languages those writers or researchers have used. But let us assume Scota was not just a magical name or at least assume she was an actual person who predates Narmer/Menes of 3000 BC.

The expansion of the Danube culture is well enough documented and Herodotus is supported by archaeological finds from the last century as we now know the Amazons were not mere legend. Before the Deluge of the Black Sea that saw a 400' wall of water come through the Dardanelles there were three other administrative centers according to the Ossianic legends and other sources. I do not know where they were for certain; but some of the candidates may be Crete (most certain through many millennia), Memphis (at least a major area for one millennia), Ilvarta (pre-Harappan Indus with recent underwater ruins discovered), Byblos (probably post deluge co-venture of Casiberia and Ilvarta), Tartessus or Iberia (near certainty but possibly part of Lyoness), Tarim/Urumchi (certainly a major research center after the deluge), Tara/New Grange/Lyoness (had to move during many glacial effects), Puma Puncu, Peru (where Lake Titicaca is being researched recently) and maybe even Yonaguni. Scota may be from the pre-Hyksos period and tie in with the Beaker People around 2600 BC. Here is an author telling us a little about her:

"The Scottish, and, to some extent, Irish king lists purport to claim a succession back to a female named Scota whose traditions separate into two different identities. In one tradition Scota is the daughter of an Egyptian Pharaoh named Cingris who became the wife of Niul, a wise teacher and obviously a Druid, who was invited to settle in Egypt where he befriended Aaron. Niul and Scota's son was named Goidel and was healed from the bite of a serpent by Moses himself (A son is often many generations removed in the legends.). Goidel was the progenitor of the Gaels and thus it was foretold that no serpent could live in the lands in which the children of Goidel lived (Obvious Bible Narratives wrapped around some facts. They also tie in Japhet and Noah.). This is clearly a story conjured by Christian scribes to explain the absence of venomous snakes in Ireland. The other Scota tradition was that she was the daughter of an Egyptian Pharaoh Nectanebus, who became wife of Mil and was killed fighting the Dé Danaan and was buried in Scotia's Glen, three miles from Tralee in Co. Kerry. From a combination of the two Scota figures descended Eber Scot who was the 'father of the Scots' as applied to modern Scotland. The name 'scotti', as recorded by the Romans, was thought to mean a 'raider'. Scota, however, at one time stood for the symbolism of sovranty of Scotland.

The name of Ireland itself, Eire, is the name of one of the triune goddesses; her sisters being Banba and Fotla. Each goddess asked the Milesians to remember her by naming Ireland after her. Banba and Fotla were often used as synonyms, particularly in poetry, for Ireland. But the Druid Amairgen, promised the goddess Ĕire that the children of the Gael would use her name as the principal name of the country." (1)

I think it is fairly obvious that there were many peregrinations and times amalgamated into one origin legend but that makes it all the more ancient. It isn't just the Trojan era Milesians and predates (as well as includes) the House of Mallia on Crete as the Royals: and it goes to Egypt. Since we know the artifacts including the bee pendant on Crete are from 2200 BC. we get to surmise or speculate that these pre-Hyksos enterprises headed by the sons of Mil are very far flung and important, as a minimum. There are many accounts and even maps from ancient times of the trip to Eire from the Mediterranean. In the tin trade or Bronze Age it was the most important trade route of all:

"No Celt has left us a record of his faith and practice, and the unwritten poems of the Druids died with them. Yet from these fragments we see the Celt as the seeker after God, linking himself by strong ties to the unseen, and eager to conquer the unknown by religious rite or magic art. For the things of the spirit have never appealed in vain to the Celtic soul, and long ago the Classical observers were struck with the religiosity of the Celts. They neither forgot nor transgressed the law of the gods, and they thought that no good befell men apart from their will. The submission of the Celts to the Druids shows how they welcomed authority in matters of religion, and all Celtic regions have been characterized by religious devotion, easily passing over to superstition, and by loyalty to ideals and lost causes. The Celts were born dreamers, as their exquisite Elysium belief will show, and much that is spiritual and romantic in more than one European literature is due to them." (2)

'Lost causes' and 'ideals' is a weak interpretation of ethics and Brotherhood. There are many weird things that might appear to be lost causes to those who did not or will not understand the psychic or quantum soup. The Kelts loaned money to others in the knowledge the debt would be repaid after death. Is it likely this practice would continue for centuries or millennia if there was no repayment or performance of the agreement? Most people during most of human culture have been able to commune with the dead. Scipio and Marcus Aurelius or Patton, the list of people from all walks of life is endless. Was Jesus such a 'dreamer'?

As to the recording of dates among the Druids or Bards it was not important. We value these things too much and thus we forget the ethical, spiritual and moral implications of all these ideals. They emphasized these aspects of each story or event. Does the inability to remember a date rank with the inability to know the meaning? The truest of meanings is what touches the soul and creates action or excites the imagination. The Ojibwa Indians of Ontario would say it something like this: 'I saw the event and therefore know'; 'I was informed by those who witnessed the event'; 'I was told stories of the past when no one now living was there to witness the event.'

These ethical or ethnical differences should not proscribe the possibility of learning from the past expressed by eminently truthful people who had no motivation to lie. The undue authority or sense of reality that comes by putting dates on lies is a matter that anyone who reads both sides of any story can come to grips with. The journalist can make

Robert Baird

the truth fade into a maze of facts and stats which Mark Twain wrote and spoke about as 'Lies, Damn Lies, and statistics'. I flatly state there is no truth in any religion that seeks to divide people and make them become enemies of their 'brothers' and especially 'sisters'. The Druids were very much averse to the misogyny that developed but it would appear they had to cave in or make arrangements with Rome at some point.

The Catholics are known to have used this divisiveness to create forceful changes that unfortunately aided the cause of whoever the Iroquois were working with as they obliterated the Hurons and depleted potential resistance in advance of European intrusions and invasions. They would not allow the Christian Hurons to fight alongside the non-Christian Hurons. What stupidity?! I am undoubtedly over-stating the case for idealism among all Keltic peoples at certain times but I do think the ethic of the Druids and their ideals are as I am saying. Their influence was different in different places in this world. The Druids are sometimes found stepping onto the battlefield between warring tribes to end the conflict. I hope that my idyllic or ideal presentation of them is appealing to people from a variety of current perspectives. I know that average people would find all the evidences of white men in America of utmost interest and I know someone is stopping these things from reaching those masses who might wonder why they get fed lies all the time. After each war we found people were right about the lies told during the war. Bertrand Russell is a good example from WWI and Kipling admitted he had been used by the propaganda machine. They don't just lie in times of war - it is their modus operandi, and besides there is always a war or plan for war to manage. It gets worse when we have standing armies and massive police machines that need to justify their existence.

Runestones And Keltic Culture

The Kensington Runestone has been called a fraud along with hundreds of other such Oghamic script in the Americas. This one is definitely proven to be a real document of a Norse visit to America before Columbus by the Midwest Archaeology Convention that brought all disciplines and science to bear on its' authenticity in November 2000. With all the things that I know about cultural worldwide impact from previous civilizations traveling this world (only a few in this book) I am thoroughly disgusted by the oppression of this information. It speaks to larger and more serious questions that I have mentioned and which some do categorize as 'conspiracy' in their ridicule and sarcasm. Those who say there is 'no cultural impact' as they work for government paychecks (Canadian Museum of Civilization, for one) are adhering to a culture that reminds us of the Palmer Raids in the U.S. and the House Un-American Activities Committee in the day of the tyrant blackmailer J. Edgar Hoover. When they were forced to admit the Norse were here some centuries before the Kensington crew, it seemed no apologies went to Farley Mowat or others who had said the paradigm was false. It seems almost as if the government had always been searching for the facts, if you only read the media.

To reconstruct history from the warrens of journalistic and other espionage or intrigue is not easy. On the other hand the paradigm has been proven wrong so often that some day we might hope for a real change. Facts must also have rational reasons for the secrets and societal or psychological and other changes that took place. It isn't enough to say it was just Greed, because there are lots of ways to get more power or money than going into these incessant wars. Those ways might take a little creativity and knowledge and be more risk prone to the elite however. Even Ellis who I am quoting a great deal is convinced or encouraged to buy into some very unreasonable positions.

He speaks of Ogham not existing before 500 AD and he ridicules Barry Fell:

"Others, like Dr. Barry Fell of Harvard, see Ogham inscriptions practically everywhere - both in Spain and even in America, and date such inscriptions to 500BC! We can be assured, however, that Ogham does not survive from before the fifth century AD." (3)

I found no reason why anyone would be assured of that and he did not give reasons. In fact, I almost wonder if some editor put this in on their own. He does argue for a Brahmin origin for the Druids and this may be why he needs to have such a late date. But, how can a patristic group like the Brahmins support an egalitarian society like the Kelts? They are the promoters of a caste system of horrific prejudice. The whole area of Celtic studies is confused and no one studies much pre-Christian work because the funding isn't there or might dry up.

Let us look at a little more from Mr. Ellis as he appears not to have seen the wooden heads with Ogham found in Denmark. I believe Anne Ross is justified because her writing is before its discovery whereas Mr. Ellis is just trying to minimize Ogham and saying things absolutely untrue. For example he said Fell thought Ogham is from 500 BC and he would almost lead you to believe there was a BC and AD mix up. Fell certainly is on record with Ogham many centuries before that. It reminds me of Professor Wiseman's attack on Fell when he said Fell was self taught on Ogham. If Ogham was only for ceremonial purposes as Ellis and Ross say and the Druids are the ritual performers of it, then they really would have to do time travel to teach or learn about it - based on their own scholarly assertions. Ogham as spoken and taught today was not available to Barry Fell in any school. My mentor and some others were after his study aided the whole field but Fell did take courses as available at places like Edinburgh. Why do they attack him and lie? There are very good reasons having to do with their tenure and supposed 'expertise'. Fell's influence grows more credible with recent discoveries and his scholarship was better as well as more open and insightful.

"Is it possible that instead of being committed to oral tradition, these texts were set down on the 'rods of the Fili (Bards and Ovates)' and kept in the various Tech Scretpa until burnt by enthusiastic Christian missionaries? The Ogham inscriptions which survive only do so because they were carved on stone. It is obvious that the wooden wands, if they had existed, would have been more easily burnt or, if they had survived the Christian zealots that they would have perished by decay over the years. And an interesting point is that the Ogham inscriptions which did survive are shown to be an archaic form of 'literary Irish'; archaic even at the time the inscriptions were made. (Doesn't fit with his 500 AD does it?) This correlates to the fact that the Irish law books, whose first codification, (First by the Christians who were re-doing everything under St. Patrick) according to the 'Annals of Ulster', was in the year 438 AD, was written in a similar archaic form known as the 'Bérla Féini'. This archaic form seems to be proof that the text was handed down for many centuries without alteration. As the language of the people changed, the ancient texts did not. They were, presumably, handed down in a strictly memorized oral tradition from ancient times until the point they were committed to writing. As Myles Dillon and Nora Chadwick have both observed:

"Ireland possessed a greater wealth of carefully preserved oral tradition from the earliest period of our era than any other people in Europe north of the Alps. For this reason the foundation of her early history from traditional materials is of general interest far beyond her geographical and political area, and second only to that of Rome and the ancient Greek world.

A tremendous literature and learning has been handed down to us from Ireland. But, even so, we can still lament the apparent destruction of the Druidical books by the zealot Christian missionaries which was clearly a crime against knowledge." (4)

Robert Baird

Is there any onus on tax paid institutions to explain how they have misled us when the new information they try to hide is finally acknowledged? They used to say we had been simple cave men or 'hunters and gatherers' with no advanced or adept people or groups thereof. They would even have wanted us to believe this was true long after the Ice Age.

The metal ages occurred over many millennia. Some didn't harden copper until at least 5000 years after the Armenians. Secret knowledge such as this had great power and potential. So naïve I am. The Berekhat Ram figurine dated to 400,000 years ago takes art back ten times as long as a decade ago. The Flores Island navigation of 800,000 years ago shows humans would have been able to understand geometry and rudimentary trigonometry a lot further back in time. Most of what is taught in schools was debatable even when written and now it is purely foolish. No wonder intelligent and aware kids don't pay attention. Neanderthals made refined drugs 90,000 years ago and the psychiatrists who drug society today couldn't refine drugs in most cases, but they give our kids Ritalin. Why all the good alternatives aren't explored until long after they have been proven is a waste of much money and resources because the schools continue to spend their time trying to buffet and support false premises and theories.

Hidden History!

What are the Druids, and what can definitely be said about them? Do we have access to what they really thought about the cultural potential and spiritual reality of mankind and the spirit world? It is OK for scholars to note that Marcus Aurelius was a believer in the cycles or comment of the ages based on astrology from the Hindu system but Druids still are regarded as backward because they could affect the wind and weather or are psychically adept. Astrology was a science of the first level of credibility until very recently because it worked. It worked better than other so-called science and religions or what was called philosophy. The Hindu ages are 2000 years each and a total of 24,000 whereas the Mayan system was very accurate in approximating the sidereal movement of the heavens or the Polar Wander Path. If we don't yet have proof of the energy that is all around us, then whoever says that is so stuck in the Toilet Philosophy they probably don't want to listen. But how these energies affect us is what astrology and divination methods galore try to understand. The shamanistic or mystical sciences are being proven in almost all fields or disciplines of modern science.

Much of the problems are due to the Ussher time line kind of thinking that was promoted in the West. If we had the Puranas of the Hindu as a historical starting point it would have been a lot harder to sell the ignorant and un-cultured humans fiction (cave man). The Puranas talk about millions of years of human habitation and culture. Currently we are seeing the discoverer of Lucy say he makes no evolutionary trees anymore. The possibility of giants like Goliath being a Patagonian 'giant' and all the reports of credible people to that end in South America from the time of Magellan are worth serious consideration. Many hominids appear likely over the 12 million years mystics have said man has been on earth. There is no proof we came from apes and 9 million years is what science tells us we can be pretty sure about. Just a decade or so ago it was 1.5 million years and that human didn't resemble us very much at all. But historians haven't changed their story to coincide with these facts very much, if at all.

Martin Rees is an astrophysicist of the highest standing and he has changed his perspective a lot since the Hubbell photos of the center of the universe became available in 1999. His perception now fits with the cycles and trial and error events except it is on the universal scale. As the Magi say - 'As Above, SO below'. But, how simple such things sound while acknowledging creative purpose at the same time; how can this be real? Wishful thinking would have us believe we are at some god-guided zenith (Professor Lynn White deals with this Euro-centric aspect of our societal make-up.) of science and culture but that must be questioned. It certainly isn't true of our ethics. The Druids new and probably co-existed with other hominids and they may even have been taught by the remnants of the Mungo Man. I think it is likely after reading Fell's work on the pygmies found in a region I know the Adena and Phoenicians were living, as discussed earlier. The use of human bones for aphrodisiacs was most probably done with some of these hominids. Any thing is possible, and I saw photos of a large sea creature on the TV with a fishing ship hauling up a four ton plesiosaur-looking creature in the Tasman Sea. The Yetis is widely seen and one wonders if Neanderthal or these Patagonian 'giants' are still around hiding from those who would use them in unkind ways. Some of these questions will not endear me to normal or conventional readers but I guess these people would have stopped reading a long time before now. There are lots of evidences or artifacts that go unreported or are ridiculed and destroyed.

    The modern skull in Rio's harbor that is geologically dated to a million years ago is just one of many reported by Cremo and Thompson in *The Hidden History of the Human Race*. The scholars who are breaking the Harappan and earlier Ilvarta languages are near to outraged as they write about the colonizing forces that continue to diminish their true history. The date of the RgVeda is off by at least 3000 years in order to make the Aryan European story seem more relevant and keep things in the time frame of the Biblical origins theme. I think 4500 BC as a time that northern peoples displaced and spreading out from the Black Sea a millennium before makes some sense. Despite the fact that they would have been welcomed by their cousins in other places sometimes such a stress or the different bond that existed among the displaced may have led to staying closer rather than integrating in places they went to. Apparently it took two weeks for the Black Sea to fill up and it is quite possible millions survived. When did the northern clan of Rama actually first arrive or make trading arrangements with

Diverse Druids

Ilvarta and the Indus sites now found underwater and when were they inundated? There are many things we may soon know that will shed light on much of this pre-history.

The unification of Egypt seems to have been a meeting of two major cultures and Churchward says this is where Mu and Atlantis formed a union. When was the first time this happened and how long or strong was this alliance? We may never have all the answers and I wonder if the clash of cultures had something to do with the resultant War on Women. The Berbers may be half breeds who became outcasts in the MU culture while the Keltic Brotherhood struggled to keep things together.

Barraclough Fell and the Peterborough Petroglyphs

I have mentioned many things about this issue already and hope a little more interest in seeing what went on and how it relates to Ogham and certain other cover-ups is warranted. This time we have Michael Bradley weighing in and I should point out he is a linguist as well (to some extent, having been retained by the Nova Scotia government to do some deciphering). My Ogham mentor got me to read Fell, and if you haven't read Fell you might not know why the establishment tries to negate or dump on him:

"Because I knew and respected Barry Fell, I wrote a humorous letter to him at Harvard gently suggesting that he should drop his Libyan translations from future editions of his book. He didn't answer that letter, although we corresponded later. One thing about Barry Fell, which everyone who knew and liked him will agree with, is that he never was known to admit a mistake!

And he made a few. But he also, and almost single-handedly, has been responsible for a serious and fundamental contemporary reappraisal of American prehistory. He's been right many times. His opinion commanded, and still does, immense (and cautious) respect.

In 1991, Dr. David Kelley, Gérard Leduc, and I found ourselves at Petroglyph Provincial Park. At that time, all the glyphs still existed. It was easy enough to read the Tiffinaugh - all you need to know is the phonetic value (sounds) of the Tiffinaugh symbols, and all you need is a Norse dictionary, both of which are available. My opinion and Leduc's were worth nothing, but Kelley's was, and is, a different matter. This professor emeritus of the University of Calgary, influential in deciphering Mayan glyphs, published his opinion in the fall 1991 issue of the prestigious 'Review of Archaeology' in the United States: some of the glyphs were Tiffinaugh (Biblio - from page 9 of his article). They told of Scandinavian mythological elements. The ships were identical to the Boslund glyphs.

Further than that Kelley would not go. But, of course, it was far enough. Kelley would not confirm the existence of Ogham, nor would he confirm Fell's long account of Woden-Lithi's story.

'The Peterborough Examiner' ranted about Barry Fell's ideas as 'an insult to Canadian archaeologists and an insult to Native People'. This is a typical example of irrelevant media histrionics. The question was, and is, not whether Fell's opinion is an insult to these groups or whether they deserve to be insulted, but whether it is the truth. 'The Examiner' did not stress the fact to its readers that Canada's foremost linguist also shared Barry Fell's opinion.

Why all this controversy over European glyphs among the aboriginal ones?

Well, if there are European glyphs just north of Peterborough, it suggests perhaps that the Serpent Mound people just south of Peterborough who used copper might have been partly European too. This suggests, in turn, that the culture of Native Peoples around Lake Ontario may owe something to European influence. What's wrong with this?" (5)

Fell's reluctance to remove his interpretations about Libyan (a word for all of Africa in Greco-Roman times) language in the Americas, is not all that ridiculous. Bradley noted turning the letters made them look very English but when we consider the Language studies and alphabet and code work done by the Bards it makes sense. English is derived from the same roots as Libyan and turning letters is

Diverse Druids

just one of the ingredients we see used throughout all Hibernian codes. Many linguists sense a common root for most languages but pronunciation and the living use of languages changes them significantly from century to century. The Druids who would be involved in the missions such as the De Danaan and Megalith Builders would spend seven years of extra study in linguistics. This may have not been necessary after the languages were developed or clear locations that the people would work in were ascertained. The multiplicity of Berber languages and the fact that they were at Carthage to put up the last Classical stand for the Phoenician ethic (although becoming degraded) moves me to think they were a vital and important part of this far more ancient heritage. Fell had a lot less to go on in terms of archaeology relating to Libya and the Berbers.

In the matter of Peterborough and the artifacts gone missing or destroyed by the government and/or Indians, I do not blame the Indians. Even if they knew the whole story it is important that they keep their feet on the ground and get the most they can from the white men who have often broken their treaties. As is commonly said and I observe, there are many among us who speak with 'the tongue that is forked'. But I believe if the truth were known by them (to the extent that I do) they would see many legal improvements in their position.

Fell also has rocks in New England that detail the 30,000 troops who came with Hanno (a common name of Carthage and not the one the academics like to say it was, and thus ridicule) to make the scene in what I believe was a common battleground for millennia. Farley Mowat and *Westviking* were a major part in the proof now accepted regarding Lans aux Meadows and Norse settlements at the turn of the millennium, now he is dealing with Scots who came before that from St. Alban. I believe the Monte Alban Central American people were impacted by these travelers. In fact the Beothuk, are Thuleans from the Ice Age who were part of the copper trade as I will cover again in some detail taken from my research on this culture that is dealt with in far more detail in my book on the Great Lakes.

Orgies and Orpheus
We must endeavor to open the vault to what the Druids knew. Quantum Physics is already doing its part but it is in the area of ethical governance that we need a real kick in the pants. By raising the respect for shamanistic approaches we may be able to travel the same path again. I do not just make a joke when I suggest Affirmative Action for those once deemed heretics, who had bounties put on their heads.

We have dealt with the Keltic god 'Don' and the goddess 'Dana' or the DN. Most of the rivers in Europe are named after Keltic deities whose sprites were often found thereby in the groves that flourish along rivers. In early Keltic times the rituals of worship were held in the open and indeed this was the case with the Druids until their demise. The vascerri of priestly myth makers may well have been part of the deceit that saw Temples built and the things that do on behind walls away from the eyes of those who might complain. It probably varied in different colonies or among different tribes as time went by and some who called themselves Druids would not have been considered so by the real or educated scientists. Dionysius has been connected to Osiris by Sir George Frazer in his landmark book *The Golden Bough*. He quotes many respected scholars who saw other gods of the Mediterranean were also derived from Osiris and his worship that led to the burning of red heads at all their graves. The next quote from Michael Grant might include some of the broader practices that included Scythian, Thracian and the Altaic or Tarim Basin peoples:

"Although Dionysius had been known among the Bronze Age Greeks, their later compatriots were still eager to emphasize that he was a stranger. This was partly because of the wild, shocking irresponsibility which he offered to women, personified by Maenads (Bacchants), whose Dionysiac emancipation from all normal conventions was uniquely alien to Greek religion and life, and a thing apart.

Diverse Druids

In historical times, 'orgies' continued to be celebrated on Mount Parnassus by an official feminine association, but by then the Delphic oracle had toned down the ungovernable excitements of earlier proceedings, . The Sileni and satyrs who surround Dionysius are daemons of fertility, and in choral dances men disguised themselves as animals to assimilate themselves to the god and take on some of his strength. (A weakened shamanistic routine) A phallus, the symbol of this fertility, was carried in Dionysiac processions; but wine, with which he was later universally identified, played little part in his earlier worship.

How many of the vast accretions of Dionysiac cult go right back to its Thracian origins is hard to determine. The second major Greek religion that seems to have been transmitted to Greece by the Thracians (Including the Druid Abaris and Pythagoras' Thracian helper that his will mentions.) was the cult of the singer Orpheus, believed to have been the son of a Thracian river-god Oeagrus (unless Apollo was his father) (Could this name be Oengus and then Angus?) and of a Muse, who taught him singing. (Muse, Oracle and Sibyll are all female Druids or Dryads at one point. Singing is an early tool in the education of the Bardic Tradition).

There were strong, though contradictory, traditions locating the origins of Orpheus in southern Thrace, where his abode was variously stated to be beside the Hellespont, Or (according to the more usual version) in the land of the Cicones (where Mysteries in his honor, for warriors only, were linked with those of Dionysius - which Orpheus was said to have founded). Or alternatively, his origin was attributed to a more westerly region of Thrace, between the Rivers Axius (Vardar) and Strymon (Struma). Medicines were said to have been prescribed on Thracian tablets by Orpheus, for the country was renowned for its healers. And, above all, he was believed to have been able to charm trees, wild beasts and even stones with his song.

But the principal importance of the cult to the Greeks was its latent or expressed promise of immortality (And it amazes me he didn't connect all these things with the Druids and the Kelts who come from the North Black Sea and colonized Greece as the Danaus.). For it was probably this that prompted the later development of similar ideas in

Greek lands, for example, the teachings of Pythagoras, who appealed to the authority of Orpheus and was asserted (though perhaps not accurately) to have circulated his own poems under Orpheus' name.

This doctrine of immortality was linked with the role of Orpheus not only as a god of the underworld, but as capable of dissociating his soul from his body. This shamanistic concept of bilocation had come south from Scythia." (6)

When academics try to study only a certain social group or period of time they end up using the name of the present paradigm or leader. The reality is that all so many of these people are Kelts and they were reporting or respecting both the Druids and the Phoenician traders. In Greece the Phoenicians could dock their ships and stay a long time as if they were the real force and leaders. Some even said they stole Greek women and children. I think if that occurred it was to save those individuals from the growing misogyny that saw Greek women unable to get an education of own land even when it was left to them as the sole inheritor. Who benefits by making a woman the slave and so naïve as to be unable to fend for herself except through a man? Numerous men still think this is the right way to organize the potentials and resources of society. This leads to all of us becoming victims of inane prejudice.

Diverse Druids

CHAPTER ELEVEN:
'Aztlan' - or Atlantis?

Thule, Azores, Sardinia, Lyoness, Mayax (Site off Cuba), Bimini, Thera, etc.

With over 25,000 books published in the modern Western literature dealing with Atlantis and probably more written by the Mayans and Incans or other cultures they traded with; it is some small wonder that Plato's rendition draws so much attention. Plato didn't say it was a continent in the Atlantic that went down as he reported what an Egyptian priest at Sais told him. In fact the design and layout of the city is found in many places around the world because of its cosmological and other organizational efficiency.

The author of a far more recent book on Atlantis, which won an award from the UN, goes a little too far in calling the Azores and the shelf of land around and to the south of it a continent. Berlitz and Otto Muck are well worth reading but I do not believe Atlantis was any one place. These particular sites connect Lyoness to Bimini and then to the site off Cuba. They were important island hopping ways to get to the copper of Lake Superior and then process the ore. Andrew Collins has an excellent book that deals with many facts I do not mention in my books. His *Gateway to Atlantis* predicted (almost) the Cuban discovery through Mel Fisher's work. Was Thule a larger island now called Iceland or the Faeroes and the Shetlands? When the oceans were lower the distance to cover by boat and the landfalls along the way made it far easier to traverse the Atlantic. This was before the formation of the North Sea in 5300 BC.

The deflection of the Gulf Stream into the north of Canada may have enabled some Sequoia type trees to exist on Baffin Island as the archaeologic record shows they most certainly did. The shifting of the Gulf Stream would have dramatic effects on the whole north Atlantic over many centuries and millennia if that happened but I have not seen

Robert Baird

this discussed elsewhere so I must be wrong. Those trees can not live in the place they are without some very weird explanation dealing with oxygen and light requirements or wind shifts that I do not buy into. I cannot cover the work of von Humboldt and Le Plongeon or other seriously involved researchers of note. Indeed I do believe Atlantis is the origin of the Druids and Phoenicians were their people. There is so much I have to summarize that I know it will fall short and be only cursory, at best.

When the Gulf Stream couldn't reach NW Europe due to the Ice Cap, the high probability of Crete being the pre-eminent location for administration does exist. It would have included Thera or Santorini and the authors like Boorstein, and the TV shows are reporting about a late remnant of Atlantis at best. In terms of influence and perhaps in terms of technology the Atlanteans had more than they did at the height of post Pyramidal Crete or Thera. Their cultural zenith probably reached its peak before the great and damaging effects from millennia of glacial turmoil; as well as major catastrophes such as the Carolina Bays meteors that are the cause of instrument malfunctions in the Bermuda Triangle. The Ossianic tales and other legends may only relate to time after that event about 10,500 years ago. But they mention the founding of Egypt by Isis and Manetho says that was 36,000 years ago. The deep mines archaeology finds in Egypt coincide with that timing despite Manetho having pandered to Ptolemy. The whole picture will not easily become clear due to the destruction or robbery of libraries like Alexandria unless the Vatican catacombs yield them up. It was nice of the Gnostic protectors of this library to hide some scrolls we have found but it is unlikely they hid the whole vast collection of knowledge gathered from all over the world.

Why have historians seldom remarked on a plan to destroy all knowledge of these previous times? Yes, they report the specific acts of power-mongering Empire. They do not integrate it with all facts considered together. It wasn't just the Mayan librarians and libraries that the Franciscan burned. They were melting art, trying to destroy pyramids, destroying statues and all variety of culture and crosses throughout the Americas. All this continues as they still try to sell the idea that people all believed in the Flat Earth and none came to America. Each person has the opportunity to find the courage and 'Brotherhood' once rampant on earth.

When Gibraltar was inaccessible as a sea route to the Atlantic and the ice caps made travel to the Cassiterides or Cornwall to get tin they had a land route up the Rhone and Marseilles/Massalia was a vital trading center. At a point before the Mediterranean Sea was really a sea we had mines of Marseilles which have been discovered underwater. There was a series of lakes along the north of the Pyrenees and this was a very key cultural center for hundreds of thousands of years. There are homes found from about 500,000 years ago near Nice and the Magdalenian and other cultures probably knew the caves near Rennes le Chateau very well. The Basque are a people still mostly misunderstood and certainly under-studied. Alexander Marshack's ground-breaking work on an Iberian lunar calendar form a region with up the 30,000 years of artifacts and dating of the notched (like Ogham scratches) calendar to at least 15,000 years ago makes us think a lot about Fell's interest in the Celtiberians and Berber/Libyans or Basque. This was the gateway to the Atlantic between 40,000 and 15,000 years ago. Maybe this was much more recently than that if Lyoness in the Bay of Biscay proves as important as the large megalithic stones of Carnac (not the later one in Egypt with a 'K') nearby would intimate. Michael Grant gives a little input about 6th century Massalia that I think was done in conjunction with Tartessus and the much more ancient culture thereof which Strabo writes had a written history of 7,000 years:

"Thus in the course of the sixth century, Massalia founded a colony at Agathe Tyche ('Good Fortune', now Agde) in Languedoc, near the mouth of the River Aramis (Herault), halfway to the Spanish border. This Council of Six Hundred elected a steering committee of fifteen ('timouchoi') (Which is the number of people necessary to form a Masonic Lodge, perhaps co-incidentally.) from its ranks, under three presidents. A peculiar feature of the Massalian system was that a criminal condemned to death was maintained at the public expense for a year, after which he was executed as a 'pharmakos', or purification of the city. This exploratory voyage by a Greek (Midacritus the Phocaean) (He was probably a traveler to the Americas.) was a rarity in comparison with the much more extensive opening up of the African coast by the Phoenicians. Nevertheless it testified to the wide horizons of Massalia's enterprise.

There has been a good deal of speculation about what the Greeks received in return. Grain and amber have been suggested, and a traffic in slaves is likely. Tin from the Cassiterides in Cornwall, also, may have moved across the Channel and then down the land-and-river routes of Gaul (by way of the Somme, Oise and Seine) through the initiative of the Massalians into whose hands the metal then passed.

Yet, according to the archaeological evidence, these contacts between the Celtic rulers and the Mediterranean seem to have terminated abruptly by c. 500. (The Battle of Alalia that I have done a lot of work showing is central to the founding of Rome by Kelts such as the Brutti or 'Sons of Aeneas' from Britain.) It may be that Massalia fell into temporary economic decline at this epoch, its influence weakened by the Phocaean withdrawal from Corsica (More importantly Sardinia and its 'nuraghi' that Jacquetta Hawkes calls 'medieval' yet date to as far back as 1800 BC.) and, in general, by increasingly successful competition on the part of the Carthaginians, who since the Massalians had blocked their land-route to the British tin mines were developing an all-sea route of their own through the Straits of Gibraltar."
(1)

Academic History of Belief in Atlantis and Debunking Debunkers

I have said that there was a time when a belief in Atlantis was acceptable to most people. I guess a little proof is necessary to support that claim given the current mindset. The quote that follows is at odds with what I reported about the Adena-Hopewell and makes no mention of Thomas Jefferson having studied the linguistic roots of Indians and tied 50 of them in to pre-Cyrillic Russian which is derived (like all Western alphabets) from Phoenicians:

"Thomas Jefferson himself, one of the most important figures in early American scholarship, excavated an Indian mound and reported his findings (Heizer 1960; Greene 1959). The time was 1784. Moreover Jefferson correctly believed that he was excavating an Indian burial site; it was an undertaking aimed at verifying local rumors about the aboriginal purpose of these mounds. However, Jefferson's belief was not shared by others, this because the intense interest in the mounds, other antiquities, and their authors was not rooted in any curiosity about the American Indian. At the time (the eighteenth century), the earthen structures (Including pyramids in some related areas) and the objects discovered were ascribed to the vanished predecessors of the Indians. This belief in a mysteriously vanished race resulted partly from the notion that the Indian was not highly civilized and was incapable of high achievement of any sort (There were many more mounds in places we have built cities.) and partly from an awareness of the fact that civilizations did fall, to be followed by others. Under the weight of a myth of lost peoples, a theme much labored by the popular writers, American archaeology moved generally into the doldrums of romance and wild imaginings from Jefferson's time until the late nineteenth century. The myth, of course, had no basis in the evidence." (2)

This author was writing before the Bering Bridge theory was demolished by the work of Dillehay and others. It shows how crude the ridicule of 'experts' can be in all their smug certainty. This 'expert' would not have accepted the lost tribes of Israel or Phoenician theory for certain, but that was the main theory of the people lingering in "the doldrums of romance". Ignatius Donnelly was a politician in Minnesota who almost ran with Lincoln on his Presidential ticket. His book on Atlantis is still well worth reading even though he bought into the lost continent idea. He identifies the language of Atlantis as Phoenician and the Guanche of the Canaries and such islands are good evidence in support of that theory. The Mormon faith is totally into the lost tribes theory and since the lost tribes are Phoenicians I am in agreement. National Geographic and Scientific American both had early 2001 issues with top stories showing the area Jefferson was working on has settlements of Europeans dated to around 18,000 years ago. Yet still you find most teachers teach the old theories relating to the Bering Land Bridge which was enforced by the Gods of Archaeology called 'Clovis Cops'.

In early maps purporting to be of Atlantis you can see where Thule might have been north and west of Ireland and there is little doubt they would have been on Iceland then as well. (3) The recent finds in Bimini are still not really open to the public and they are obviously connectable to the island hopping routes that many talk about. This route from where the Basque are today might well be from before 10,500 BC. when the Azores were inundated or impacted by meteors. (4) Could the Basque be related to the Ainu in Japan? Recent researchers on Kennewick Man suggest he might be related to the Ainu and it will be some time before the courts allow us to know these things. Nazi Germany was very much interested in all these things and they developed a lot of science that the rest of the world used after the war. Unfortunately there is much of that knowledge that created MK Ultra and programs of a very questionable nature.

The whole matter of a worldwide civilization or Travelers who learned a long time ago about many things we want to believe they did not know, is becoming far more provable at every turn and in all disciplines of science. It becomes

Diverse Druids

increasingly provable as we see Yonaguni, the Indus and a host of more ancient centers than Sumer. Egypt itself has offered a lot of more ancient evidences of advanced culture and the scholars who study it know there was a lot of fudging going on to make kings look more important than they were. Whole eras of priesthoods in Egypt lived off the spoils of grave or tomb-robbing while writing new histories. The Cretan agriculture that had Hybrid grains long before the Fertile Crescent had normal grain harvests may be mirrored in the following data:

"But there was a time in Egypt, about 11,000 B.C., when someone briefly practiced agriculture along the Nile. Radiocarbon dating of grain kernels indicates this activity. But the period was brief, the agriculturalists went away, and Egypt had to wait five thousand years for the Neolithic to arrive in predynastic times, in the Nile Delta, about 6500 B.C." (5) (This ties in to the era shortly before the Carolina Bays meteors.)

There is another factor that relates the Basque and Mayan with a group located in the area between the Black and Caspian Sea. This is our important Iberian homeland that present day Tiflis was the capital of and was also called Iberia until recent history. The factor is not one that journalists can lie about as they write history. It is the blood type Rh factor. Might it also exist in the Ainu, Moriori, Aleutian and Easter Island white people? There are only 300 Ainu left from the last report I saw and they are seldom seen to look like the tall Kelts in the other places I just mentioned as well as the Beothuk. All of those peoples were eradicated in the 19th Century. Is that a co-incidence? Berlitz has an interesting item that ties in with the Julsrud ceramics I have covered in great detail to show Mexican hegemony with American archaeology that seeks to destroy them. They have been carbon-dated to 6000 BC and come from Acambaro, Mexico:

"There exists a possibility that other isolated survivals of a few species of prehistoric animals continued to exist into the time frame of former civilizations on the planet; that is, before the end of the last Glacial Age, 12,000 years ago. On an example of ancient Scythian goldwork from southern Russia a struggle between hunters and animals shows men fighting what appears to be a clear portrayal of a saber-toothed tiger, suggesting that this animal survived to an age in which man was already sufficiently developed in the use of metals to cast this prehistoric tiger in gold as an adornment." (6)

I suggest that the dinosaurs shown in the Julsrud ceramics are a result of advanced archaeology among the Mayan/Toltec/Olmec people of the Brotherhood. However, there is the possibility of 'time-viewing'. Either of these suggestions would threaten the history and academic structure to the point where anyone can see the reason for the outright fraud surrounding their treatment and destruction. Niven also found such work as dolls showing all races in deep digs under Mexico City and Churchward supported his findings in a big way. The Christians used the dinosaur bones to prove the 'monsters at the edge of the earth' fear campaign that fit with the Flat Earth means of keeping serfs at home serving their master's needs.

Do you have any doubt that there was advanced human culture before the Bible Narrative, 'cave men', and the 'hunters and gatherers' theories? We were led to believe Stonehenge was built after Jesus died in Victorian Ussher based time-lines. These cultures were not everywhere advanced to the same level - just as is true today. Much credence grows in support of the research of Churchward even though he made many mistakes. It seems like eons ago that I first learned about the stele made of hematite which I was present at the uncrating of; when it arrived from Peru at the Miami Planetarium. Even though it had been mentioned on radio, I was the only member of the public or media who saw fit to witness it being taken from the truck.

The Planetarium staff who were busy uncrating it had no idea about any of the legends surrounding it. Yes, they knew it had astrological symbology, but why? I told them how a heavenly body had been kept in orbit around earth as a second moon (or perhaps what created the Carolina Bays incident) for a thousand years by the ancient Atlanteans who could attune their collective energy and the Earth Energy then send it through this magnetic rock. Yes, I can understand how weird this sounds to earthbound and well grounded academia. I wasn't saying this was a certainty or that I even believed it. They had absolutely no interest.

Was this really the end of Atlantis or somehow associated with the larger land masses around islands like the Azores and Iceland. Could the meteor of the Carolinas Bay event have caused major climatic changes affecting worldwide water levels? It is estimated that a tidal wave of over a thousand feet was created and the North American horse became extinct in the Americas after this event. I have found a horse in the archaeologic record 5000 years after this in the area of the Copper Mines of Lake Superior that I have a hard time seeing how such a Shetland pony could be regarded as indigenous by those who avoid commenting on it. To me it seems obvious it is part of the Phoenician mining and trading group along with all the processing centers that the experts know none of the normal natives would be doing.

Assuming there is any truth to legends (such as Troy and all the others proven since), what might have the celestial event this stele was used for and when? I don't throw out anything when it comes to facts without giving it some serious consideration. Seeing the etched designs and knowing people spent a lot of time venerating this stele I became all the more interested in the possibilities of pole shifts and catastrophic events that might have eliminated ancient cultures on earth. I had heard about 12,000,000 year old humans or hominids in various accounts and even one of the Leakey's had said something like this was found in Pakistan. That was supposedly disproved later due to some changing approaches to carbon dating. However, the last decade seems to warrant that the 1970s science was about a far off as any field of endeavor when it comes to the age of hominids on earth.

Robert Baird

The 12,000,000 year figure seems to be what we are headed for and yet there could be intelligent species on a far older earth than we have imagined. Just this week I heard they are adding 600,000,000 years to live on earth and last year it was about the same when they went to a Greenland location. So instead of life on earth as protozoa just a billion or so years ago we are up to four billion years of life on earth. When one considers that the Human Genome project says we aren't far removed from the worm in terms of genetic engineering in our genes; and that the worm trails are what led to the recent addition of 600,000,000 years, it can open the field up to a great deal of speculation. I have therefore considered the 2,000,000 year old meteor that caused the creation of the Gulf of Mexico and the Isthmus of Panama as a possible date for the use of this stele. The million year old modern human skull found in the Rio harbor may not be so anomalous.

Russian science is not infected by the Christian god-guided ascendancy of Waspish or Euro-centric history. They think that quantum leaps have a qualitative element as well as a quantitative element. Thus creative input of human or cosmic intelligence and harmonization is more easily accepted there. Pravda reports and various symposium presentations over the last few years bring us a mostly unheard of (in normal media) map that shows the south Ural to Altaic origin of the Tarim Basin peoples. This map may be part of a map of the whole world in three dimensional form with three layers of rock and glass that even modern science may not be able to duplicate. I do not think it is 120,000,000 years old as they speculate it could be. But I think it is older than the Hadji Ahmed map that shows the whole world and the Bering Land Bridge as it was 12,500 years ago - that we didn't know until 1958. This map has been known and kept watch over for 500 years. The Russian scientists who say it could be as old as 120 million years are working from magnetic effects of the location of the magnetic pole that impacts how rocks are formed volcanically. They are also dating component shells in the

Diverse Druids

rock. These things could be included even if it was made last year. I am not able to judge these possibilities fully.

The fact that the language is relatively unknown and undecipherable as well as all other factors does make me think it could come from before the glacial period and the time when the Great Lop Nor of the Tarim Basin was a true middle-earth Sea or Mediterranean. These things must be given serious consideration and the legends of Plato and the Egyptian priest may have merit despite the re-writing of later priesthoods trying to make themselves important. Here are some words from Frank Joseph (of *Ancient American* magazine) as he talks about Otto Muck.

Celestial Communications and Contact

The size of a pollen molecule can weigh enormous amounts and travel 900,000 miles an hour through space to cause earthquakes according to recent astrophysical science. The super dense objects can cause mutations in genes and make a mockery of all the rigid close-minded scientific reasons given to support some evolutionary concept or that of a human-like God who gave us his only Son. Black Holes and the co-existence of matter and anti-matter or all sorts of things including Einstein being right about gravity having a particle of energy associated with it, join all sorts of reasons to alter our perception of reality. Einstein was talked out of many inspired visions of reality and I respect him as much as any great sage of history. He also supported the work of Velikovsky and his catastrophic impacts on the development of man and history in a series of books called *Ages in Chaos*. Many of Velikovsky's assertions thought ridiculous have also since been proven despite the bias of science:

"While the Mid-Atlantic Ridge on which the island of Atlantis perched was and is unstable enough in its own right, one of the finest writers on the Atlantis Question has suggested an even more cataclysmic event touched off the natural disaster Plato described.

In *The Secret of Atlantis,* Otto Muck constructed a fascinating case for the final destruction of Plato's lost civilization by an asteroid's collision with the Earth. Were his arguments put together less convincingly, or his own scientific credentials less impressive, we might be inclined to dismiss his book as another outrageous piece of embarrassing speculation from the lunatic fringe of Atlantology.

But Otto Muck was one of the world's outstanding physicists and engineers before his death, in 1965. Inventor of the 'Snorkel' he was a member of the guided missile research team at Peenemunde that included Werner von Braun. He found that a pair of deep-sea holes in the ocean-bottom off the southeast coast of the United States were created by the fragments of an asteroid that broke apart under atmospheric pressures generated during its descent.

The fragments passed through the Atlantic to pierce its floor, and set off a series of volcanic chain-reactions throughout the Mid-Atlantic Ridge. The celestial object was at least six and one quarter miles in diameter, as it over-took our planet from the north-north west at approximately twelve miles per second. Its impact resulted in an explosive energy equivalent to thirty thousand hydrogen bombs.

Chief testimony for the asteroid that destroyed Atlantis lies among ten thousand craters scattered in a closely packed, oval pattern over South Carolina. They extend over the Atlantic in the direction of its two deep-sea holes. Most of the South Carolina astroblemes are elongated with major axes of the ellipses running from the northwest to the southeast, indicating the path of the asteroid. Circular craters were created by the vertical descent of the meteorites.

Interestingly, the twin holes at the bottom of which lie the meteorite fragments are near the center of the so-called 'Bermuda Triangle'. This is an ill-defined area of ocean wherein numerous instrument anomalies allegedly occur (the least of what happens). Nickel-iron is most notably magnetic, and concentrated deposits the extent described by Muck may be able to play havoc with sensitive compasses and depth-gauges.

Diverse Druids

At a meeting of the American Geophysical Union, in December, 1984, geologist Joseph Kirschvink, of Caltech, presented a computer-generated map which showed a powerful magnetic area on the ocean-floor off the coast of South Carolina, in the vicinity of the two deep-sea holes created by the halved asteroid. (7) Meteor collisions are not as rare as we might imagine." (8)

Is this Heresy? Academia treats it like the Plague. The heretics and nutcases are in charge of the asylums and temples of worship, as I see it. Next up in the matter of Atlantis - we have Michael Bradley again; I do respect this man's opinion and depth of scholarship:

"We will recall that even in Plato's story of Atlantis, it was an Egyptian priest of Sais who recounted the tale of Atlantis to Solon. (An ancestor of Plato, and truly a great historical leader.) We should also remember, that the Egyptian priest spoke of many earth upheavals, not just the huge one that destroyed Atlantis and that has impeded humanity's attainment of civilization. An Atlantean connection with 'Ancient Egypt' cannot reasonably be doubted if we accept the new Bimini and Giza facts, and if we are to accept the implications of the Piri Re'is and Hadji Ahmed maps (and several others), and if we are now prepared to accept Plato's account as, at least, a generally accurate memory of a former Atlantic civilization.

The point of all this, for our limited purposes here, is that much of this ancient. Pre-Christian source of knowledge and tradition making up one part of the Grail religion came from Atlantis. It was preserved in Egypt first. Then it was passed on to other places in the western world, either by foreign conquerors like the Greeks, Romans and Turks who carried off ancient curiosities (like the Piri Re'is map) or more gently by people who preserved ancient knowledge and tradition as religion.

And one aspect of this knowledge was knowledge of America. Plato says that the Atlanteans were great mariners, and the Egyptian priest emphasized that Atlantis held sway over many islands westward to the true continent beyond.

283

Christopher Knight and Robert Lomas discovered that a star called Merika represented these western lands. This name probably came out of Atlantis itself, was preserved in Egypt, and later reached certain religious sects in Turkey and Palestine. Merika or A-merika was thus known from the earliest times of western civilization. (9).

Some of the Bimini discoveries included glyphs, some in animal form, that resembled nothing so much as Magdalenian Ice Age art from Southern France and northern Spain. Since we now know that there was an Atlantis, a glance at the map will show that the shortest route from the Azores Plateau into the Mediterranean is not through the Straits of Gibraltar but to the coast of France at the mouth of the Gironde River. "(10)

The crystal cave that is large enough for a man to sit inside could be a device that allowed for the Fountain of Youth that Ponce de Leon came looking for in the legend called history. Crystals are most important and capable of melding energy to allow great creative force through spiritual and other means. This Bimini cave made of crystal is probably man made although there is little reason in science to believe that prior cultures had such ability. There are pyramids in Bimini that have the same angles of the pyramids at Giza according to Bradley. He is absolutely right to say that these angles are important.

The debunkers who call such things mere co-incidence and don't mention the fact that the same frequency is measured at megaliths in places like the Rollright Stones and the Great Pyramid are never going to get the picture.

They should study the work of Buckminster Fuller on 'icosohedrons' or 'tetrahedra' and then look at the writing of Murry Hope and learn about AL Bielick. I heard an interview with AL on Toronto's CFRB recently. Man alive, what kind of interviewer wouldn't ask if this man has a machine that can send a person physically through time? Fuller details the tetrahedra (two perfect ones inside the Great Pyramid) which create delta wave forms. Bielick says these wave forms are important in the helical structure of time. And though I have seen good interviews with him and know someone who has seen his machine - I still don't know if it does more than 'view' time. The really tough questions have not been asked about disassociation and harmonic focusing of energy. What with alternative and parallel universes and creative potentiality it is hard to imagine a fixed future or past. Hard does not mean impossible, and I really should go no further with these thoughts in this book. I cannot even prove that the Lost Chord and the Druidic harps were connected or that they knew the science of Harmonics better than we do today. The reader will have to draw their own conclusions as to how the Druidic magic worked and whether or not it is real, in the final analysis. Please remember, there is no definite black and white reality.

Administering 'Brotherhood'!
    Some readers may still think magic is an illusion and prefer to class some things as superstition or miracles rather than accepting all things have a scientific explanation even if we don't know it. How could the Pyramids and their designers have kept a worldwide trading empire and Brotherhood together for millennia? Is it really possible that the Ark of the Covenant was a radio or arc transmitter as engineers can now prove? It is a very complex issue to be sure and yet these things appear to be true in conjunction with psychic remote contact that the ether allows minds of adepts to achieve. Modern science takes a different approach but now achieves the same things. Is it so unreal to imagine this kind of magic? Certainly there are worthwhile clues to suggest they did have an international drug or medicinal enterprise that allowed a lot of control and management of the lives of people. Certainly they used belief systems and religions as part of their plan. You can decide if things are all that different today. Many other books are necessary to cover before (I hope) you make your final decision. Bradley is right when he says 'for our limited purposes here' and I must focus on the religions at this juncture:

285

Robert Baird

"The role of the Druids as international arbiters and ambassadors is confirmed from several sources. We have already mentioned the role of female ambassadors (Add the Oracles and Sibylls in later times.) (Druidesses) in negotiating a treaty between the Celtic Volcae and the Carthaginian general Hannibal. We know that about 197/196 BC, citizens of Lampsacos arrived in the Greek colony of Marseilles seeking an alliance. The Massiliots used the influence of the Celts of Gaul with the Celts of Galatia, in this particular instance the Tolistoboil of the Sangarios valley, to persuade the Galatians not to aid Antiochus III of Syria against the Lampsacenians. This is astonishing when one considers the distances in the ancient world. According to Henri Hubert it showed 'that the Greeks of Marseilles and of Lampsacos knew that they would find among Celtic peoples living very far apart a sense of oneness)? It shows the Kelts were still dominant in the Mediterranean as well - see the movie 'Spartacus' and pay special attention to who he gets to take him to Italy, Silesians and Galatians are Kelts, and why.)'.

But what created that sense of 'oneness'? Hubert is in no doubt:

"This solidarity of the Celtic peoples, even when distant from one another, is sufficiently explained by the sense of kinship, of common origin (Practices like sending kids to far off relatives for their education, at fixed prices.), acting in a fairly restricted world, all the parts of which were in communication. But the Celts had at least one institution which could effectively bind them together, namely the Druids, a priestly class expressly entrusted with the preservation of traditions. (The Bards did the history, the vascerri later the religions but the Druids were more above this and scientists or advisers.) The Druids were not an institution of the small Celtic peoples, of the tribes, of the 'civitates'; they were a kind of international institution within the Celtic world." (11)

Thus an Empire like Rome had to deal with the Druids who once had been their own leaders. The Volcae are Kelts

Diverse Druids

of Cisalpine Gaul and include Hallstatt/La Tene people as well as the Bruttii and family of the Brutus who led the navy of Caesar (in Brittany) as well as the one who rose up to defend the rights of people over Empire in the Shakespearean play. Thus I am moved to ask the same question - 'Et tu Bruté'? This is around the time when various Roman Emperors put bounties and proscriptions on the heads of Druids even though they continued to use the Sibylls.

Were the Beothuk our 'Brothers'?

The term 'redskin' or 'redmen' comes as a result of the Beothuk use of red ochre as a spiritual medium and the fact that they wore it to celebrate and witness the arrival of the new horde of white men who were different than the Basque and others that they had been dealing with for many millennia in the St. Lawrence River to Newfoundland. They had a unique watercraft on the east coast just as the mummy people of Alaska had advanced kayak engineering the professional and Olympic athletes of today cannot equal.

The esteemed publication Scientific American ran an article in 2000 that explored the early Aleut people's engineering of kayaks with ivory bearings and split hulls that were made there for at least 9000 years before the Russians finally exterminated these people in the early 19th century. This century saw the British exterminate the Moriori Kelts of New Zealand where they had fled to the Chatham Islands; and the Spanish of Peru get rid of the white men on Easter Island who are genetically related to those Chatham Island remnants. One could also argue that the hegemony was intent on getting rid of other Keltic 'brothers' in Ireland, the Ukraine and even the Jews in the years that followed. The mummies that are in the Smithsonian should be DNA tested (if possible) to determine if they are related to the Chatham Island and Easter Island Kelts as well as the Ainu and Kennewick Man. There was a time when the water from the Great Lakes flowed north and the climate was warmer in the north. This changed as the earth rebounded 2/3rds of a mile after the glaciers retreated. I believe once the water was flowing south and east, the Beothuk Thulean and Dorset Eskimos moved to serve the Copper Route needs of the Phoenicians. In the case of the Beothuk we have digs at L'anse Amour from the 4th millennium BC to bear testimony to them being there at this time. The Phoenicians had a good thing going with their ancient brothers who had decided to live and intermingle with the natives of North America all these millennia. The paid them with red ochre or hematite. Simple red earth that is abundant in places such as Cuba and Georgia.

    I suspect the archaeologists would find my explanation of cinnabar from which mercury is taken in the alchemist's art of great interest. That is a detail I will leave to my book on the Copper Culture of the Great Lakes. Even the Mungo Man has red ochre on his bones. There is at least one burial in the archaeologic record of a tall Beothuk whose bones were disinterred to have red ochre put on them. The descriptions and appearance of the Melungeons like Lincoln and the Adena or other tall (often called 'giganti' and the like in places such as Sardinia or the Tarim Basin) Kelts are touched on by other researchers; if I am entitled to call myself one. After all I was trained as an accountant and do not have a sheepskin or credentials in the field of archaeology. The money trail and power needs are as important as linguistics as far as I can see the nature of academics today. My involvement as owner of a PR firm and meeting all the 'movers and shakers' also gives me a unique perspective that I hope some serious researchers will benefit from. Maybe they can avoid the suppression and band together to get bureaucracy and social engineering out of their profession. Ever since the Palmer Raids in the early 20th Century the whole field has been under funding and other more vile constraints, including the tenured teachers who support their lords and masters as mouthpieces for Manifest Destiny. The Egypt Exploration Fund had similar but more apparent religious purposes.

Diverse Druids

The Beothuk leather skinned craft are reminiscent of Irish curraghs. They beheaded their enemies just like the Kelts and they adorned their bodies as many early Kelts did. The island of Newfoundland and the Grand Banks which are nearby was a key resource through all time. Cartier said you could walk on the fish in the water and his boats had a hard time getting through them. The Basque and other Celtiberians or Berbers and Libyans had a fleet of fishing craft there to meet Cartier. The next author is a 'debunker' and we will debunk him. He does not mention the *Zeno Narrative* that Frederick Pohl and others like Bradley have used to show Prince Henry Sinclair was here a century before Columbus brought the Inquisition and 'colonization' or slavery to new worldwide heights. That narrative tells of his people (who spoke many languages) meeting people who spoke ten languages they did not know when they arrived at what was likely Newfoundland. Not mentioning Pohl's work is not unusual even though he was a respected American historian who wrote before the acceptance of the Norse being here at the turn of the millennium:

"Included in this mythology which over the centuries has developed in the minds of many people are the following 'facts' and theories:

At their peak, the Beothuks in Newfoundland numbered 50,000, and occupied virtually every nook and cranny of the Island. (Viz. Keith Winter.)

They possessed super-physiques, and sometimes attaining a height of seven feet and the women proportionately tall. (Viz. legends quoted by Howley and repeated as fact by Winter, Kelley, 'et. al.')

They were an innocent, harmless people of innate good will, only too anxious to have amicable relations with the European settlers, but learned from bitter experience that no friendship was possible with the bloodthirsty, treacherous whites. (Viz. Kelley, Winter.)

In the early years of European visitation to Newfoundland hundreds, perhaps thousands, of Beothuks were captured and carried off as slaves to be sold in Europe. (Viz. Horwood, Thoms.)

Micmac Indians from Nova Scotia were imported into Newfoundland to wage war against the helpless Beothuks, and French authorities encouraged the Micmacs by offering a bounty for each Beothuk head brought to them. (A legend reported by Jukes, who got it from John Peyton Junior, who got it from a Micmac. Howley did not believe it, but many subsequent writers have.)

The customs and artifacts of the Beothuks - for example, their burial practices, use of red ochre, beheading of their enemies, type of canoe - were all unique to the Beothuks and probably indicated that they had no relationship to other eastern North American Indians but may have been descendants of Viking settlers or, even more exciting, may have been remnants of a European or North African race who reached Newfoundland in the latter days of the Ice Age, either by primitive canoes or by using the ice floes of the North Atlantic. (Viz. Gatschet, Sweetland as reported by Howley, Horwood, 'et. al.')

The European settlers in Newfoundland (mostly English and Irish) undertook a deliberate and systematic campaign to exterminate the Beothuks, a campaign which finally met with success. (Horwood.)

The eventual extirpation of the Beothuks resulted not so much from a deliberate programme as from the prevalence of the sport of Indian hunting, (Not to mention rape) a sport characterized by a strong competitive spirit, with one settler vying with another to carve more notches on his gunstock. (Horwood.) (In my personal experience I know people who went to Indian reservations to hunt for squaws to abuse sexually. The woodpiles of America and the black people or women who were similarly treated is part of a long tradition of repulsive human behavior; enabled by nobles who do the same to feudal serfs as seen in doctrines such as Prima Nocturne which is well displayed, as a major reason William Wallace gave his life in the movie 'Braveheart'.)

Diverse Druids

At Hants Harbor in Trinity Bay the English or Newfoundland fishermen succeeded in corralling some 400 Beothuks, men, women and children, on a point of land subsequently designated 'bloody', and slaughtered them all to the last child. (No white fatalities were recorded, and the fishermen exercised judicious economy with their powder and shot by cutting the throats of the Indian children.) (Reported as tradition by Howley; subsequently given as fact by Horwood, 'et. al.')

The record of the Newfoundland settlers in their treatment of the Beothuks was more brutal and barbarous than anything else to be found in the annals of European-aboriginal relationships. (Winter.)

Those journalists and other writers, who have capitalized on this mythology, building up its melodramatic and sentimental aspects, have created further mythology. The very titles of their articles and booklets indicate their themes: *Hounded into Extinction,* (*Marjorie G. Forrest, 'Atlantic Advocate, October 1974.) *The People who were murdered for fun,* +Harold Horwood, *The People who were murdered,* 'Maclean's, October 10, 1959.), *Murder for Fun - The Rape and Slaughter of the Beothuk Indians.* # (# 'Ernest Kelley, *Murder for Fun,* Cobalt, Ont., Highway Book Shop, 1974.).

The most recent offender in this regard is the well-known Canadian writer Pierre Berton, who in his book, *My Country,* published in 1976, devotes a chapter to the story of the Beothuks, a chapter in which he lists every tired cliché, every allegation of white atrocity, no matter how undocumented - even the traditions and legends that Howley and other Beothuk sympathizers regarded skeptically or rejected outright. Thus he writes of the Beothuks as 'peaceful' and 'innocent', the whites and Micmacs as practicing 'genocide'. He refers to the 300-year record of Beothuk stealing of nets, boats, traps, sails, and other vital articles from the Europeans (The Kelts had a policy somewhat similar regarding unused property to be borrowed and returned.) as 'pilfering', and states 'it did not occur to the Beothuks that pilfering from white men's stores would

Robert Baird

be a crime.' Once more we are told that Newfoundlanders 'set out on shooting parties, as they would do for deer or wolves', that 'Men actually notched their gun butts to tally their kills', and that 'To kill a Beothuk was a matter of pride." (12)

I will take the words of Berton over most all historians who work for governments or have their bread in need of butter. Berton is an independent person of the highest credibility. Scholars who look for legal level proof and do not see the big picture or consider outside interests will never arrive at what is really going on. Mowat gets ridiculed by the same people and his authenticity has been proven over and over again. My oldest brother's first wife was the daughter of a missionary who spent two years with Mowat in the Arctic. Mowat often came to visit our lake, but I never met him. When I recently saw an academic reviewer say Mowat had no experience in the Arctic upon which to base his St. Alban's theories of special watercraft similar to the Beothuk - I knew better. I hope I can trust the reader to make the appropriate decision about the work of this author whose pandering I just laid before you. It is a very good job of skilled debunking.

CHAPTER TWELVE:
B'Hairdic Blarney!

I am a 'Conspiracy Theorist'.
   I might as well say what others call me. Ridicule is ridiculous, but it is the kind of argument I often face when I have the facts and the other side wishes to spend no time looking to see why they wish to keep their ego intact. Everyone is entitled to their own opinion but I respectfully suggest they should look at the facts that others present. Once the facts are agreed upon the possibility of compassionate communication exists in real and useful terms. What good does it do to mouth or pronounce opinions from closed minds? If there is no plan as the 'prevailing paradigmists' wish me to accept - then I tell them - There should be a *plan*! A plan for proactive change and *love*! Each of the points of view may be correct, especially if there are alternate and parallel universes. The important thing is to achieve *purpose* and harmonize or create something more than mere acquiescence to mediocrity and hatred. Certainly there were some among the Beothuk who stole things with no intention of giving them back to people who were raping and killing their women and children, at some point. So what? Why not?!
   The late 50s 'duck and cover' government safety program for the nuclear age was so ludicrous as to be really funny. It spawned another era of fear and that makes people more manageable for bureaucrats it seems. The movie 'Atomic Café' could be used to demonstrate the stupidity of anyone believing the government. That would be a good start for our schools but you know that isn't going to happen, as long as our governments keep doing the same kind of thing. This bomb shelter mentality of people thinking they can hide out in foxholes (personal or global) is the antithesis of Brotherhood. Where is the *love*? How can things change if we are constantly lied to, and public heroes set such fine

examples of how our future generations can 'parse' the language and weasel out of anything including murder; if they have the right mouthpiece, corrupt police, and enough money (O.J.)? Let's not forget Watergate, Iran/Contra, Enron, BCCI, P2 Lodge in Italy, the War on Terra, and all the rest of recent history.

When JFK sought to end the CIA reign of terror after making a deal to end the Cold War with Khrushchev they were both dealt with summarily. He sent them a letter saying they would be disbanded upon his return from Dallas and he never did (return). This is no mere coincidence and I have followed the issue in great depth including a debate with someone who got her Master's Degree who had every newspaper (in the U.S.) clipping and a lot more to work with. She had changed her mind after many years of supporting such idiocy as the 'one bullet theory'. Still I run into people who ridicule me for thinking the Warren Commission was a sanctioned cover up by a higher authority. People used to say the same thing to me when I told them about J. Edgar Hoover being the worst tyrant who ruled in all of history.

Do you think JFK knew his father bought him the Democratic nomination in Chicago from Daly and the Mob? He most certainly did, and so does the Arts and Entertainment documentary on this family and the modern version of Camelot. But how much did Joseph Kennedy agree to give to Sam Giancanna, and what form of barter was involved?

Could the matter of Mob involvement in the whole country or SEC dealings that Old Joe knew about, have had a part in their bargain? The documentary suggests it was a promise that Joe and/or JFK did not keep that was involved. Joe Kennedy ripped off many as any who study the Pantages theatre situation will know. What troubled me most is the possibility that Joe raped his daughter and had her lobotomized and institutionalized to cover his tracks. Now we have another of this clan up for murder.

Diverse Druids

JFK and Jackie are the finest example of American nobility and media management. Deviant behavior, drug use and prostitutes like Jackie (read her marriage agreement with Onassis - another Merovingian) or the common ones brought by truckloads to keep his stomach muscles in shape; these are just a few of the facts his biographers write about. Why did the Kennedy clan go along with the Warren Commission? What layers of skeletons are in their closet? I think it is the Merovingian issue and their part in it that the young Kennedy's were trying to change too quickly. Joe taught his kids about the future of power being in bureaucracy - we need to change that.

In matters deceitful and sublime there is no country or nation that is exempt from corruption. Our sovereign nations are an extension of the evil program that saw kings given Divine Rights. Tammany Hall and the Tri-Lateral Commission join the Eastern Establishment and Beacon Hill Mob along with all sorts of associated groups like the Foreign Relations Council or 'think tanks'. In other places it is the Committee of 300 or the Round Tables of Cecil Rhodes who rise above the normal paladin state of the hoi polloi and become secret supporters of the Merovingians and the Benjaminites of the Priory of Sion or Alumbrados with their Templar to De Medici and Borgia roots in Papal history. The Kuomintang that rose above a Masonic clique in the words of de Gaulle's Minister of Propaganda (Malraux) and the various crime families or religions (is there any real difference) might seem almost second fiddle to whatever really runs the roosts and gooses us in the running of this New World Order.

De Tocqueville and other social commentators like Chomsky make a world of sense to me. Still, I must admit there are intelligent people who deny their perceptions, and say the ends justify the means, while making good arguments against truth and honesty or transparency. How can the average person be expected to take all the time it takes to sift through massive volumes and libraries full of what can often be described as various forms of excrement?

Robert Baird

Why try? Surely it does an individual no personal good to be informed except in matters like medical care. If you see the through line and become able to integrate and see what is about to happen before it happens maybe you can do well as an international criminal like arbitrageurs. Most people will spend most of their lives denying they have any responsibility for what happens as a result of the acts performed by politicians and Armies (of doom and gloom) or bureaucrats. I would sincerely love to see a news program that had Eisenhower's exit speech scroll across the TV screen every night as people sit and eat. Maybe some people would realize the food they struggle to keep down is part of the plunder that ongoing imperialism and oligarchist elitism provides instead of creative resource application.

Knowledge in the hands of the few is power indeed multiplied and often without purpose or real added value. Some people will never get the truth even if it bites them in the 'you know what'. Yes, I am a conspiracy theorist and skeptic who 'thinks'. So what! Who cares? When will there be enough of us to stand up and demonstrate against incessant waste and unethical social administration of our awesome potential?

Gurus and 'Gar- bage' (French)!

I would have to agree there was a point where the Druids were willing to go along with the misogynists. In fact they must have been part of the development of all these oppressive religions we have suffered under for so many years. Clearly some of them did at a minimum. My personal belief is this was generated by the rising number of nobles who sent their kids to Druidic schooling and learned how real or unreal the magic or power really was. I can find this rising kingship got control of the armies of Carthage as a hereditary right rather late in the game and I suspect it happened earlier than the 4th Century BC in other Keltic clandoms including Etruria or what became Rome. To what extent they learned the actual science and knowledge of the

Diverse Druids

best Druids is anyone's guess. Except, I beg you; (!) not those who have lied to you for so long.

The 6th Century BC saw an expansion of religion and a fractionating or greater number of esoteric cults and schools. Clearly the Middle East saw growing misogyny and reduced egalitarianism in the millennium before this, as Hammurabi's Code makes evident. Probably it was something the leaders of what we might call Atlantis saw might happen after the catastrophes and cataclysms surrounding the end of the Ice Age. I think the Giza monuments were designed to leave us all a message or reminder of both what was and what they knew. These are things I have dealt with in great detail in *Neolithic Libraries.* The reduction in wealth associated with the loss of major centers and trading rights was part of this, as well as the loss of knowledge control such as smelting and the trade routes to America. We must loosen the grip of the Flat Earth fiction or lunacy.

I respect the insight of Machiavelli and other whose footsteps follow the nobleman called Plato. Hegel or C.S.Lewis, Nietzsche and other noble radical aristocrats up to paladins like Fukayama are all meaningful and adept observers of how to manage US. They talk about the 'beast with red cheeks' and our need for respect and recognition. Maybe that is how the retirement gifts with fancy words were formulated in the time leading up to labour unions and all the mob control of them. Sick -TRULY FEUDAL (!) and we have been victimized far too long; but in no way can I suggest the Western civilization had a right to rip off all the decent people of other cultures we 'colonized' and upon which our present wealth and power is based. The treatment of women is a large part of what makes me mourn for all humanity. I agree with Virginia Wolff - the world is my country!

Depth psychology and archetypes of conscious Jungian dream states would indicate there is a higher ethic upon which these collective and interiorized archetypes were founded. It may not have been as Golden an Age as I want to believe. It isn't what Machiavelli and these others want you to believe. We are not mere animals! We may be worse than animals in many ways but we have a soul that can make us a powerful force for good and decency - maybe even as good as gorillas, elephants and porpoises. He advised the De Medicis on a plan of social control based on an appeal to 'our base human urges' and they were already well ensconced in such deceit. The use of women as a social bargaining chip that men should aspire to own and manufacture more of, still consumes most of this pubescent world. Will it change without true trade sanctions (etc. - thus no 'oil-lies') and models to demonstrate a better potential for all mankind does exist?

Cayce would have us believe Atlantis had genetic technology just as Gardner and his Rosicrucian uppy-ups assure us they did. Somehow they used crystal implants to control lesser hominids or other humans. Fond as I may be of psychics and mediums, I do not trust Masons like Cayce or mediums who charge for things that empower them even more over their flock; or whatever you wish to call those of us who depend on others for their insight to the soul. Their egos are usually quite evident and the ego does a lot of interfering with true bliss or 'direct cognition' as I can certainly affirm from my own experience. We must all keep an open mind on the road to wisdom and knowledge both 'within' and 'without'. The past that we call history may even have been fooled with by some kind of Time Travelers or even real ET's (God?) for all we really know for sure.

Yes, this chapter will 'dare to go where none have gone before' (a little more). Logical processes of ego and vain comparisons or intellectual diatribes can only take us so far in evaluating the great and diverse ancestry of our race and beliefs. But if the geneticists are right we are all derived from one African hominid or strain. How could man in the present even talk about separate races if that is true? Why talk about it or the Scale of Nature that had European white man at the top of the heap? I find the religions all say pretty much the same thing once you take out the prejudicial dogma designed to appeal to people's needs or base human urges and fears. In this book I am saying the Druids are shamans and alchemists (peryllats) who became Chaos Scientists and learned the keys to Harmonics a very long time before recorded history. But I also admit they may have been taught by other hominid species of far greater antiquity. It wouldn't surprise me if these people were so advanced that they genetically altered or mixed certain strains of hominids like Neanderthal and 'giants', or 'pygmies' and Cro Magnon. I cannot disregard the idea of aliens who set up the human genome project 12,000,000 years ago either.

The brain function processes are not easily adapted to the massive and all-encompassing infusion of cosmic energy and knowledge. The Druids developed a regimen that went beyond ritual, which I have witnessed the best and most advanced adepts today can do. The reason for the codes of symbols and alphabets (that I've tried to give the rudimentary details for) has much to do with Universal Laws or scientific truths. By trying to instill right thought they hoped to increase right action but it would appear people were better off with verbal tradition and that written myths encouraged a proliferation of myths and little discipline. The Druids broke the spiritual truths down. The Ovates administered the situational ethics in well defined laws; which a council of Elders had to almost unanimously agree on changing in any small way. This Council was separate from the lawyers and the system of checks and balances was a good one. The Bairds kept records and all of them taught others to be their best. The Druidic magic is not magic except to those who do not understand. They had the power to curse a person and put a constant projection around him so that all his life would be changed.

"Druids could pronounce the 'glam dicin' or the 'geis' to assert their authority. The 'geis' was primarily a prohibition placed on a particular person and since it influenced the whole fate of that person it was not imposed lightly. Any one transgressing a 'geis' was exposed to the rejection of his society and placed outside the social order. Transgression could bring shame and outlawry and it could also bring a painful death. The power of the 'geis' was above human and divine jurisdiction and brushed aside all previous rulings, establishing a new order through the wishes of the person controlling it." (1)

Pretty heavy stuff, to say the least! It would appear that there was no need for capital punishment or police forces with these 'Dudes' (Druids) around! By knowing how to affect the wind and the rain or through the use of herbs in the early days of shamanistic time these people were the social glue and fearsome leaders. None could challenge this authority and no need to have sophisticated systems and bureaucracies to administer justice was required. Whenever they got the quantum key or ability to use quartz and wands or scepters to affect more directed energy focusing is unknown and may remain unknown unless physical Time Travel in a linear time continuum is real. Most probably the staffs such as Moses and Aaron used in the Bible were one part of this knowledge. The legendary Merlin (Welsh 'Myrddin') was one of their austere elite group that stood apart from kings and was a meritocracy that needed no laws or regulations to empower it. Thus they would not have been subject to the 'wickerman' treatment designed to make bureaucrats like kings ('Rg' as in the RgVeda is Irish for 'king').

There is much debate and confusion regarding this 'wickerman' and how long it may have been part of the culture (if ever) is not within my ability to say for certain. I tend to believe it was used in areas where the Druids were not as plentiful or as well educated and adept, such as the colonial emporiae of the Phoenicians throughout the world. Some compare this practice to the 'sati' in Hinduism. Young women are still thrown on the funeral pyre of their arranged mate in advanced age. Despite having been outlawed this practice and its cousin the 'honor killing' is still in operation throughout India. How anyone can equate the Kelts with the Brahmin caste system or things of this nature is beyond me. I do believe the people of India were affected by the Aryans

Diverse Druids

(Eire-yanns) and that their religions were commonly developed but in this matter and their treatment of women I see no chance that Brahmins or Hindus were the original impetus for egalitarian freedoms afforded all Kelts. Women were not forced into marriages and there was a spectrum of legal associations in Keltic relationships that fairly reflected what all parties did or owned. There was no need for a pre-nuptial agreement because the laws were explicit and fair.

"Caesar claimed it was a custom among the Gauls to cremate the body of a chief and, at the same time, burn his prisoners and favorite animals. In this we are reminded of the Hindu custom which evolved into 'Sati' (from the Sanskrit 'devoted wife'), in which the widow followed her husband into the funeral pyre. It was officially abolished in India in 1829 in those areas under British control. There is no confirmation of this tradition among the insular Celts, and it certainly does not accord with the funeral rituals of the ancient Irish." (2)

'Twisted' Crosses and Cabals

I read with interest about Prince Charles working on a healing garden including Fibonacci designs and the Taoist cosmology to remind people of what is lost in nature. I know what shamanistic pagans will think of this co-opting of their knowledge and I still think it is a good thing. There is an intricate web of plagiarists and usurpers throughout history who really should honor the shamans of all cultures regardless of whether or not I am right about them learning and sharing in a worldwide effort to uplift previous civilizations. We must remember that Jesus and Buddha had to learn a thing or two from somewhere, and the Verbal Tradition or Qabala seems one likely source along with the Magi that even Britannica acknowledges had a major influence on Christianity.

I have quoted the Kabbalah and a host of other roots of the symbolic knowledge that some archaeo-mythologists like Campbell and Gimbutas were able to appreciate. The Gothic crypts and secret societies of many names since Tuthmosis

Robert Baird

reorganized the Mediterranean ones at a point I suspect Egypt was making a move of independence are quite difficult to historically position. They claim roots back to Isis in so many cults and methods that she really must have been a lot of different people. Pythagoras wrote little to nothing but modern researchers in harmonics and mathematics are seeing he knew a great deal. He learned it from the Druids under the direction of Abaris according to good and credible sources. 'Pi' and 'Phi' in the Golden Section or Mean and the 'Singing of the Spheres' is vital for us to understand and I confess I do not fully understand it. It is unlikely that anyone ever fully understood all there is to know about how energy manifests itself and what kind of conscious interplay allows people like his Therapeutae (Jesus was one of their adepts according to many) to heal and perform the near miracles they did. Even those who do these things today can not mathematically and with precision describe it in elegant terms with no confusion.

Maybe I have enough insight to help others see a little more about the 'Mark of Qayin', 'Q' or 'Khu' and all the rest of the geometric representations for the geometric lattice structure upon which energy organizes its interplay of something meaningful if not fully conscious beyond some rudimentary soul. It seems the 'K' had a wavicle of the light or universal harmonic added to it and some say this 'twists' the meaning. Dion Fortune says that about the Kabbalah versus the Qabala. The 'h' or aspirant is just part of the human vocalization and the vowels are perspectives or variations on what words mean in symbolic terms. I do not know what the exact effect of the doubling of a specific consonant or the placement of the aspirant might mean. It does make one wonder about Allah and another system of beliefs called religion, to see it in this ancient knowledge that goes back before the written word. In the beginning (alpha) and in the end (omega) we have circuitous chaos through which forces may appear to be good or evil to one who only perceives part of the realms and planes of dimensional reality.

Diverse Druids

Symbols seem to have more meaning than words or thousands of words strung together in a book. Could ancients like the Mungo Man have known how to chant and cause energy to do their wishes? By placement of the arms and other body parts into specific positions does the mind open itself as Gurdjieff seems to have been able to teach and the mudras and mutras of Greece and India seem to do? Many people like Bernard Baruch who studied with Gurdjieff seem to have gained a lot by it. Deepak Chopra promotes the mutras and makes medical or physiological scientific explanations of how they help.

I can only make a stab at integrating these things at this juncture without having to quote all the people I refer to in books like *Neolithic Libraries.* They are much more able to deal with the formulas and mathematics than I am. The 'h' we saw put after the 'B' at the beginning of this chapter has a possible connection with the B'hai faith. The Hopi Indians seem to have a similar belief system that B'hai scholars say is no accident. B'hai is a very ecumenical system and incorporates the thought of Mani and Zoroaster as I see it. This is the region that saw the Sarman or Sarmoung that can be traced to 2500 BC or so. The Magi of Zoroaster and may be even Zoroaster himself was a teacher for Pythagoras. It is possible from this connection alone to draw the cloak of Druidism around most of the Judaeo/Christian/Islamic complex and other religions of the area.

The cross is very ancient. If one adds spirit to the physical then it becomes the pentagram that Pythagoras used instead of the more secret pentagon-dodecahedron. The dolmen that early Columbus and Cartier missionaries caused to have the arms knocked off, were cross-like representations of man. It is the genesis of the steeple and can lead to many forms of crosses that are all mandalas as we have discussed already. Some say Gurdjieff designed the 'swastika' by making a minor alteration to a Tibetan symbol and all can agree the swastika became a powerful symbol with some kinky customers. By just removing the 'kinks' we get a cross. Too bad we can't do the same with history and thus

Robert Baird

get rid of all radical aristocrats and their brown shirt sheep. Taking a little further look at the *Dictionary of Symbols* might start a thought form or two.

"Gammadion (fylfot or cross cramponnee) denoting the path of peripheral forces." (3)

   This is a description of a swastika turned level. The similarity of the Maltese, Templar and Teutonic crosses (Iron Crosses of Nazis) that endeavor to deflect or cause centripetal outcomes from inputs of the four primary forces should be of interest. Are the Masons and these other gorgon headed Medusas with all so many names able to grasp these energies and deflect them, and our souls? I recommend looking at TracingBoard.com and reading the Kadosh and Plato connections to see how their sometimes claim of having no Jewish connection is not warranted. Jung says the cross comes from primeval sticks that were used to make fire when rubbed against each other and I imagine it might have represented man and woman rubbing too. The I O of I O Torus can certainly be likened to the Phallus and the receptacle.
   "But the predominant meaning of the cross is that of 'Conjunction'. Plato, in *Timaeus,* tells how the demiurge joins up the broken parts of the world-soul by means of two sutures shaped like St. Andrews cross (X). Hundreds of different shapes of crosses have been summarized in works such as Lehner's *Symbols, Signs and Signets,* and it has been found possible, by the study of graphic symbolism, to elucidate the particular meaning of each one. The Egyptian, anserated cross is particularly interesting in view of its antiquity. In Egyptian hieroglyphics it stands for life or living (Nem Ankh) and forms part of such words as 'health' and 'happiness'. Its upper arm is a curve, sometimes almost closed to form a circle. Enel analyses this hieroglyphic as follows:
   'The phonetic significance of this sign is a combination of the signs for activity and passivity (Yin and Yang) and of

Diverse Druids

a mixture of the two, and conforms with the symbolism of the cross in general as the synthesis of the active and passive principle.'

The very shape of the anserated cross expresses a profound idea: that of the circle of life spreading outwards from the Origin and falling upon the surface (that is, upon the passivity of existence which it then animates) as well as soaring up towards the infinite. It may also be seen as a magic knot binding together some particular combination of elements to form one individual, a view which would confirm its characteristic life-symbolism. It may also signify destiny (The Table of Destiny brings us the I O Torus; it is easy to see how the I O and T are in the ankh). Judged from the macrocosmic point of view, that is of its analogy with the world, the 'Ankh'-cross may represent the sun, the sky and the earth (by reference to the circle, the upright and the horizontal lines). As a microcosmic sign, that is by analogy with man, the circle would represent the human head or reason (or the 'sun' which gives him life), the horizontal arm his arms, and the upright his body." (4)

There is another way to spell micro or macro cosmic. Clearly when spelt with the ending 'comic' it seems universal, spiritual and ABOVE. When spelt 'causm' then we can see the other half of the Dictum of Hermes or the Law of the Magi represented by the simple phrase 'As Above, So below'. Each of us is capable of being a flux or conduit through which these forces flow. It is difficult to imagine these things of the 'Spheres' or cosmogony thereof that was still the norm in the day of William Shakespeare. Our material focus and paradigm has caused a lot of disharmony. Do the Masons have many people who (like Pythagoras) heard the 'Singing of the Spheres'?

Pyramid Power, Pottery and Phoenicians

Rather than the 'gods' being 'messengers', or angels and aliens, there were adept humans who taught us our symbols which have so much depth. Would that cause many who would like to be the interpreters for gods to waggle their finger and tongues? Certainly any suggestion that Jesus studied the Qabala or Phoenician Verbal Tradition can get a rise out of those who neatly put the Kelts into some pagan heretical branch of pantheism. Is it obvious to anyone reading this that men (MEN) are threatened by egalitarian Druids? And in this cauldron of alphabets, symbols, and the words or meanings they portend, taken from all corners of the earth, from all the missions for brotherhood, from every science ancient or modern, from divination or the runic root of languages, from chaos to elegant mathematical formula or vectors of earth and cosmic energy flowing through megaliths - in all these places plus our souls - we find a bounty. A glorious bounty, that Keltic culture was able to foster even if it was just one of a series of ancient civilizations from even before the Mungo Man and Timbuktu. Here is the horn of plenty and cauldron of Kerridwen. But instead we apply the *one pie* ideology with elite people gaining their need of power over people.

 The books gathered in the Great Library of Alexandria allowed them to build a steam engine to move sliding doors for priestly impact. Thales (who had a Phoenician parent) also had a steam engine. They made multi-deck ocean liners, slot machines, lighthouses and geared mechanisms. The authors of *Ancient Inventions* say the engineers who made the Antikythera calendrical computer and great ports or statues were capable of doing anything we did until the mid 20th Century. They don't even deal with the Great Pyramid and are conventional scholars. Should we ask our leaders or the esoteric schools if they have more ancient technology they haven't told us about? Gardner certainly has said they knew a lot. The Pyramid is central to some very arcane and advanced sciences according to many researchers, and I am not talking about the alien theorists.

 Is this more Irish or Scottish 'blarney'? You may have watched 'Mystic Knights of Tir na Nog' or felt the *Lord of the Rings* was great fiction. 'Tir-nan-n'oge' was Atlantis and Arthur and Merlin legends probably are part of the Atlantis legend re-done after Christians wished to build upon the old

Diverse Druids

beliefs according to many scholars. Hercules (Herakles) was one of these ancient Keltic people. When Ignatius Donnelly was considered for Vice President of the U.S. after having been Lieutenant Governor of Minnesota, he knew that Hercules was a family ancestor people like Ptolemy wanted in their family tree. He knew Manetho pandered to that desire when he did the Kings List that ended up being used as part of the Bible Narrative. He knew that all the heroes or gods of the Hindus, Phoenicians and Greeks were people who had been great personages in Atlantis. It is known to many that Isis and Osiris are the same and Manetho said she colonized Egypt.

It is highly unlikely that all the linguistic similarities are pure co-incidence as many academics want us to think. 'Bileam' in the Hebrew of today was BLM when it had no vowels. Balaam is the Mayan word for priest and it would be BLM in vowelless Ogham as well. We have dealt with the relationship of BL and BBL (BABEL, BIBLE, Ba'al and Bel) which has perhaps the pre-eminent role in many religions. These knowledge systems and priests thereof are suggested by me to have traveled the world on the sea. The original symbol or letter in most alphabets for 'M' is the wavy line showing the waves of the sea. The Sons of Mil or ML are the 'bees' that I have presented some of the scholar's insights to. The Atlanteans and Kelts were master seamen and there was a king of the Kelts called Finn from whom we get the 'followers' or 'people of' Finn or simply the Phoenicians. BL + M, or the Pelasgi and sea peoples might make one see why Churchward sees the people of Lower Egypt coming from Mayan lands. Cleopatra and all women Pharaohs of Egypt were still honored as Isis Pelasgi, the Queen of the Sea.

The early script of the Indus Valley is only now being deciphered and some think it is not yet that far along. Berlitz shows a chart on page 71 of his book on Atlantis that makes a strong connection between this Harappan or Ilvarta script and the Rongorongo of Easter Island. Sanderson and many others such as Heyerdahl and Russian linguists he quotes are

Robert Baird

onto this and see it in Central America as well. In Easter Island we can see the white people were eradicated quickly after Roggeveen found them hiding out in a number of about 4000. By the time Capt. Cook arrived 50 years later there were only about 100. The use of smallpox given to the people taken to the mainland by Catholics from Peru was the cause of these last few people dying. These people had been in the Amazon mining before 400 AD as many see it. They are Phoenicians or red heads just as the red hair on the Easter Island statues would indicate. Britannica makes no mention of these white people on Easter Island and you have to look somewhere else in their book to find out about what they call 'red knots'. I think these Phoenicians had been here during Pyramid construction periods and the set of Pyramids in Brazil that are laid out like a battery were in fact part of the Earth Energy Grid. I know they were in Peru shortly after that.

Surely every person knows how much Columbus has meant to the 'Manifest Destiny' oriented nations of colonizing European Empires even if they haven't read the Treaty of Tordesillas. What would it be like if those legal tenets and precedents that form the 'unalienable rights' of Americans were shown to have been a plot against our real historical roots in 'Brotherhood'? Could we insist on a re-evaluation of many sacred cows and the special status fro 'Robber Baron' based conglomerates? How about taxing churches that were given one seventh of all the land in Canada? Here is some more proof dealing with a different kind of 'sweat house' than the ones that make more money than drugs for modern criminals involved in human trade. I found a small entry on a review of the third edition of this book that says the Smithsonian regards this book as 'authoritative'. It was originally written before the demise of the Clovis Cops:

"While the pottery of the East, as mentioned, is thought to have diffused from Asia, this is far from being proved. The earliest, or fiber-tempered, may be derived from Vera Cruz, but no precursors have been proved. Kehoe (1962) has rather persuasively argued that the point-for-point similarities between Vinette II pottery and that of the Ertebolle peoples of Scandinavia are far too numerous to be overlooked and that Woodland pottery generally may be a diffusion from Europe. The timing is right; Ertebolle pottery goes back to nearly 3000 BC., with the Vinette comfortably later. Ocean transport from Scandinavia would involve very short voyages, with convenient landfalls at the Faeroes, Iceland and Greenland. Added to this hypothesis about ceramic origins is the appearance in America of mound burial after 1000 B.C., again later than comparable customs appeared in Europe. These reasonable if novel, conclusions are impressively argued, although the compared traits are general rather than detailed. Lacking airtight evidence for the stereotyped explanation of Asiatic origin, I am inclined to accept the Kehoe study as being as reasonable as any of the alternatives. Acceptance is particularly easy in view of Lopatin's (1960) study of the typology of sweat bathing, wherein he shows beyond cavil that one trait, the widespread American Indian sweat-bath technology, is entirely Scandinavian in type (Figure 6.9) (His map shows it is in practice where the Spanish conquerors reported white people in Venezuela and at the mouth of the Amazon and few other South American places. The mouth of the Amazon was a key spot for Phoenicians like those of Solomon and Hiram.). He cannot, however, utilize chronologic argument because the sweat-bath (vapor-bath) data were largely collected ethnographically in recent years, even though the vapor bath was known in Russia before the beginning of the Christian era. There is archaeological evidence in the Maya area showing the vapor bath to have occurred early in the Christian era, according to Lopatin. His conclusions redocument the fact of Scandinavian contact with northeastern North America before 1492 and thus lend some support to the quite-early contacts proposed by Kehoe. Furthermore, adding to these arguments the fact that burial mounds appear to be earlier in the Midwest than in the Southeast, the distribution of this innovation supports a northerly rather than a southern origin of the custom. Such argument conflicts with the possible derivation of burial mounds from Central America. No verdict can be rendered as yet." (5) The Scythian or Keltic burial mounds and the Great Lakes Copper are what are at the root of all these things and many more that I have detailed elsewhere.

He reports on many things he doesn't integrate with other possibilities including 'geometrical earthworks' (pg. 215) that tie in with Stonehenge and the Avebury sites of England. Dr. Robins and the 'Dragon Project' dealing with the ley lines or Earth Energy grid and the astrolabe are all part of a grand and great reality we are still being lied to about. The serpentine mounds and recent proof going on about the Nazca Lines are enough to make one wonder why anyone would ever have been able to sell us this perverse idea of the Flat Earth beliefs that supposed stupid people of human origin once believed. Humans are adventurous and courageous as well as innovative and it doesn't take a degree in some modern university to see that. In fact going to such an institution leads to brainwashing and a lack of integrative thinking skills it seems.

Jennings is an exceptional scholar and his attitude about the 'round shaped skulls' of the Adena and his question about ethnic origins of cranial manipulation (Chanes and boarding kids heads to make them look like Dragon serpents) being the cause, tie in to what we quoted from Frank Joseph. The origins from the north and his doubts about them coming from Mexico are important to the roots of the Iroquois that he senses and we have developed further. They are now tied in with genetics, and so much more.

'The Time has Come'

The Walrus and the carpenter are part of many things.
Of ghosts, ships and all the rest - my dream of culture brings.
I sing to you of heroes great and cover ups galore,
But in the end,

Diverse Druids

You'll have to send;
My missives out the door.
Cause I like Coleridge, portend
Hermetic visions. More.

When I mentioned 'time travel' in an off-handed way it doesn't mean I don't think something of the kind exists or did exist. The NEC labs at Princeton generated 300X light speed in the summer of 2001. I have followed the whole field for years and know that Italy had researchers produce 1.25 light speed when all science still considered it an absolute and sacred cow. That was almost a decade ago as I recall. It is a critical and important aspect of all paranormal reality and thus of great import in our consideration of the 'weird' things Druids did. Yes, Atlantis had some truly extraordinary science and scientists during millennia of good spiritual study. The natural forms and lattices of shapes are somehow connected to these supranormal aspects of Chaos or creative reality:

"The Poverty Point site is also characterized by a vast earthworks composed of five concentric ridges of octagonal shape covering so large an area that it was not recognized as artificial. There was also a possible bird-effigy mound at this site. While the earthworks are reminiscent of Hopewell, they are older than the Ohio works and their relationship is unclear. In fact, the entire Poverty Point site defies acceptable placement in the larger framework of Southeastern prehistory." (6)

Unlike most Indians the Hopewell used copper in breast and head ornaments and sheets were hammered and heated. There are many artifacts not seen elsewhere and fine flint edges that don't fit the Clovis arrowhead theory that ruled American archaeology until 1991. The fact that the Iroquois had a parliamentary system akin to the Masonic design of the U.S. some two hundred or more years before the U.S. even existed is developed by Bradley and was noted by many earlier authors such as Morgan. He has proof of a white settlement on Montreal before Cartier but not

Robert Baird

anywhere near as good a proof as the geologic core sample that confirms Donnacona's report of white men with woolens near Kingston. They were there a hundred years before Cartier and Columbus and the Ministry of Natural Resources data suggests there were 1100 of them. It could be said there is more than enough to sink the academic ship called *denial* and its sister ship *avoidance* in just this one book. But, I know the Admiral of the Fleet is Admiral *arrogant* and his flagship was once *the inquisition.* There is much more data and at least as good detail in two other books I have done, as well as other books with related data that my never see the light of day. But, I keep trying because I *love* mankind and all the great things we did and could still do. If only we could be a Brotherhood once again!

To finish this chapter of what must seem like a totally ludicrous speculation to all who were inculcated with the academic 'norm'; I am choosing some of Michael Bradley's thoughts on the moundbuilders that the Indian legends told early settlers were built by a race of white people from a long ago time. The Chillicothe, Ohio area is central to the Hopewell mound building region, and Monneault is the home of the Methodist minister

Who actually wrote *The Book of Mormon* according to other research I have done. However, that may be (Mormons don't agree), the Mormons and Joseph Smith are major proponents of early white settlement of North America:

"Hunting, gathering, and marginal agriculture cannot support a very large population. The mounds, however, showed that very large numbers of people must have been concentrated in small geographical area while the mounds were being built. And if, indeed, the larger mound complexes had truly been cities, there must have been extensive agriculture of some kind to support the population - a much more sophisticated agriculture than the Woodland Indians exhibited. The sheer number of mounds required a much larger population than the Indians represented at the coming of the white man.

Diverse Druids

Gradually, educated whites, and most educated whites were ministers, began to speculate there had been an ancient North American civilization with a population of millions. With their Biblical orientation, their favorite theory was that the moundbuilders had been the Lost Tribes of Israel who, by gradual assimilation into the Indian population, degenerated into tribal and primitive people with their mounds as monuments to their former existence. The most distinguished American clergymen preached this theory - William Penn, Roger Williams, Corton Mather, Jonathan Edwards, and many others less well known. In 1833, Josiah Priest wrote in his 'American Antiquities': 'The opinion that the American Indians are descendants of the Lost Ten Tribes is a popular one and generally believed.' (7)

Up until about 1900, a person who professed some education could still believe this sort of thing - and perhaps will again be able to in the not-so-distant future." (8)

The lost tribes are actually Phoenicians or Keltic Gaedhils who built the Great Pyramid and part of the Megalith Builder group that traveled the world. They include the Benjaminites at a time even before they were thrown out of Israel even though they had the support of the House of Judah and other Phoenicians like the Arimathaeans who were probably traders in metals all the way back to Cyprus before smelting began. The time has also come to make amends for the horrific treatment of the Irish and most people in Ireland don't even know about the extent of destruction they have suffered. Here is a little tidbit that describes the main point when the plan of removing all memory of the former great Keltic culture was removed.

It was the English Attorney General of Ireland, under James I, Sir John Davies, who was the principal agent in bringing about the suppression of this unique legal system. According to Davies, "There is no nation of people under the sun that doth love equal and indifferent justice better than the Irish, or will rest better satisfied with the execution thereof, although it be against themselves, as they may have protection and benefit of the law when upon just cause they do deserve it."

But having made this observation, Sir John determined that the law the Irish should be made to 'love' must not be their own but that of their conquerors. He went on to denounce the Irish law in general, and the land laws in particular, being so different from the English system and therefore, according to him, absolutely barbarous. A programme to stamp out all traces of the Brehon system (already devolving for at least a millennia) was commenced. According to the Master of the Court of Wards, Sir William Parsons, "We must change their (Irish) course of government, apparel, manner of holding land, language and habit of life. It will otherwise be impossible to set up in them obedience to the laws and to the English empire."

By the end of the seventeenth century, the Brehon system had almost been erased. By the end of the eighteenth century and certainly early nineteenth century, the general population in Ireland had become unaware that a written native law system had ever existed. Yet law manuscripts were preserved in spite of the punishments and persecutions of those found with them. Dr. W.K O'Sullivan, who edited and wrote the introduction to Eugene O'Curry's *On the Manners and Customs of the Ancient Irish (1873)* stated, "During the first part of the eighteenth century the possession of an Irish book made the owner a suspect person, and was often the cause of his ruin. In some parts of the country the tradition of the danger incurred by having Irish manuscripts lived down to within my memory;" (9)

By this time the Potato Famine was aiding the English cause and they taxed and hounded the Irish out of existence almost. It is a very sad thing indeed, because the truth of the Jews, Ukrainians and other Kelts is still not even known to their own 'brothers'.

CHAPTER THIRTEEN:
The Druids of America

The Family of Jesus in Kingston, Ontario
   The bounty put upon the heads of Druids by the Romans and that ever-present Christian sword that followed had made the Druids go to their colonies or 'brothers' in far off places in stages. The Desert had driven the Tarim Basin Kelts to similar places including Barabudur and New Zealand. The Bardic schools were probably greatly diminished but the wisdom still remained in certain small units of people though much knowledge had been lost. If you believe in cycles and take a very long view of history it may have just been another Dark Age. We still aren't fully out of the cycle that deals with violence and misogyny to say the least. There were others who had been assimilated (or infiltrated) into the hegemony itself.
   By the 14th Century the Templars had formed many other offshoots such as that formed by my namesake Robert de Bruges called the Royal Order of Scotland (You can check this out on a good Masonic website called TracingBoard.com if you so desire.). Prince Henry Sinclair and the Stuarts or Jacobins would not be my idea of true Druids but they kept the ideals alive a little and they protected the Family of Jesus or the Merovingian House of Judah, David and Solomon in places like America. There is good reason to show Robert E. Lee is related to Robert the Bruce. The Irish involvement in the American Civil War was far more than any normal person imagines. Maybe these Masons or whatever you want to call the 'octopus' that is inside or outside the Christian complex depending on your point of view, and the particular point in history can be compared to the Brahmins in India. Certainly they include the nobility or aristocracy of this world and have developed a New World Order as seen on the greenback or dollar.
   They were using some good sense and shared a creative and productive bounty with their paladins because they knew

the poverty of pocketbook and soul that feudal government and Empire had wrought. Some of their elite were the very architects of these problems. They were in favor of creating 'Free Trade' like the Physiocrats of Pierre Samuel Du Pont de Nemours. He negotiated the Anglo-American truce or treaty to end the War of Independence and then moved to the United States from his native France where he might have been part of the Priory of Sion. The Duponts are a prime Merovingian family. Their armaments and chemical empire as well as media involvement is classic Merovingian financial and government involvement. The Physiocrats are thought to be the first modern economic school of thought. Quesnay was a follower of Descartes and borrowed the mathematical method used in this 'Tableaux Economique'. It can be likened to 'laissez faire' and all that means for those who are in control.

 The Merovingian Masons who founded the U.S. (including my ancestor Rufus King) were in favor of a system of checks and balances that kept their secret association of 'rogues uppermost' (Jefferson in his 1823 letter to the Mason Lafayette). Many scholars note that Jefferson seems to have picked this theory up while he was in France. It is a trickle down form of economics that we still suffer under but it was far better than the outgrowth of Divine Right of Kings. Thomas Paine writes that his 'association' (Masons and Rosicrucians) are the progeny of Druidic beliefs and knowledge. I say they are different in most ways although it might turn out that they have higher ethics and aspirations that we do not yet know about. We may only have this slim hope if we do not wake up.

 We have seen the Adena may even have been preceded by 'Henge' constructing non-Natives who were able to create a social kingdom of great duration. Donnacona (one of the leaders of the St. Lawrence Iroquois now thought only to be partially Iroquois at best. Is his name a little bit Italian?) may have incorporated some of their legend in his story relating to the white folks he saw in Kingston. He referred to it as the Kingdom of the Saguenay. The Saguenay

River was probably one of the ancient routes taken on the copper transshipment through a lake system over to Allumette and Morrison's Islands where strange re-processing occurred. It is located to the east of where Donnacona and his Stadaconna kin were located, and that might mean the Saguenay Kingdom once covered a very large part of North America. The name sounds as if it is derived from sage and wise people. Certainly we have enough evidence to know that the Iroquois came from the Hopewell through the Megwi and genetics tells us they and their brothers the Sioux who went west were white or Keltic people. I suggest the sage kingdom was the Adena and Poverty Point cultural continuum at some point in time.

Bruce Trigger is the foremost authority on Canadian Indians and he suggests Donnacona was embellishing his story of the Kingdom of the Saguenay; in an attempt to position himself as the middleman in trading relationships such as they had been able to do with the Basque and others. The European lye-based soap found by pure misfortune (for those who wish to keep these things secret or hidden) at Kingston certainly suggests Donnacona had reason to say what he did:

"During the winter, Cartier had been fascinated by reports of a 'Kingdom of the Saguenay', which he was told lay somewhere in the interior of the continent. Donnacona claimed to have visited this place and he described it, through his interpreters, as a land rich in gold, rubies, and other precious things and inhabited by white men who dressed in woollen clothing (200-202;221). Some historians have speculated that this story may reflect knowledge of Spanish settlements far to the south.

It is evident from Cartier's account that the Stadaconans were participating in a trade that had begun in the Archaic period (Before Christ). From the vicinity of Lake Superior, copper nuggets and artifacts diffused from time to time over much of eastern North America.

Historians have been puzzled by seemingly contradictory accounts of how this red copper was reaching the St.

Lawrence. The Hochelagans (Montreal) indicated that one route lay along the Ottawa River, but that this route was blocked by 'agojuda', or 'evil men'. Who were armed to the teeth, wore slat armour, and waged continual war (170-71). (The numbers are references to Cartier's journal.). Some commentators have identified these people as the Iroquois, although this is geographically improbable, unless the story refers to Iroquois attacks on groups living in the Ottawa Valley. Others have suggested that they were the Ottawa Valley Algonkin (Lighthall 1899: 204; B. Hoffman 1961: Fenton 1940: 172). The latter were somewhat acculturated to Iroquoian ways, at least in the seventeenth century, and may have worn slat armour. In the last chapter we presented archaeological evidence which suggests that, in prehistoric times, there may have been prolonged conflict between the Huron and the St. Lawrence Iroquoians. It is also noteworthy that Huron influence seems particularly strong in late sites on the upper St. Lawrence, suggesting a considerable amount of warfare between the two groups at this time (Pendergast and Trigger 1972:284). This warfare may have prevented the Hochelagans from traveling northward to trade with the Algonkians of the upper Great Lakes." (1)

I suggest the contradictory accounts and evidences are not contradictory to the truth, but rather conflict with the Columbus and other fictions that are prevalent through all American history. The Iroquois regarded Hochelaga or Montreal as their spiritual and, no doubt, trading center from time before the more recent white men or Christian colonizers arrived. I have a hard time not referring to them as the Heathen Horde but many were Huguenots in Canada at this earliest of times. They are remnants of the Cathars or at least the Cathar ideology, which I respect a great deal.

At the time of the Dark Ages in Europe the copper trade was almost of no interest due to refined methods of smelting. There was an interest in falcons from Greenland and the Sinclair Castle at Rosslyn shows American maize or corn on an artistic column. Some unique wood has been noticed and gold was still of interest from the North. Emeralds were also being brought out of South America but the need for cocaine had been diminished with the refinement of other drugs. In fact the secret of North American trade was largely kept or made more secret due to the lack o intense need for the rare pure copper. The religious haven aspect of America was quite real but the control exercised by feudal lack of education and the inability for people (other than the Templars) to travel without being seized for ransom made for a complete loss of knowledge in large segments of the population. At what time the Templars and their massive fleet started or stopped coming to America is anyone's guess but Prince Henry (Norse - Scottish) and the Zeno brothers of Venice (Veneti Kelts) certainly brought the special family of the Templarist secret to Nova Scotia shortly after the King of France disbanded the Templars and the Cathars had been genocidally wiped out by the Dominicans in one of many Crusades that made a lot of money.

We have seen Champlain kept the secret while the family of Jesus was making a new home and expanding in Kingston. I think the large number of Métis has a lot to do with this family. The matter of nobles in Scotland is often a case of French nobles who own land in all places. This is the case with the Bruces (Bruges, Bruttii). One could easily make the argument that nations were just a way for the noble families to whip up fear and have their fun with chivalric games because they are all intimately related genetically.

Cultural Celtic Customs in America

We all learned how the Indians treated the French who lost 25 men due to scurvy through boiling white cedar bark when we were in school. Because of the killing agents that subsequently were introduced many Indians died but not quite as dramatically in the North of the Americas it might appear. Whereas 300 whole tribes or cultures were eradicated within 100 years of Desoto's meandering to spread the Plague it seems very few of the northern tribes were decimated. This could be the result of constant contact with Europeans or a better medicine bundle and more shamanistic knowledge. Certainly the Incas had great medical knowledge too. There are many things I would love to see academia spend their time and money researching rather than trying to buffet dastardly designs such as Manifest Destiny and the Flat Earth. But there was a mysterious disease that spread according to Trigger. The Stadaconans were wiped out and the historians like to blame the Iroquois. Could something similar to Fort Pitt have occurred here too? Maybe it was a virulent flu or the smallpox?

The important concepts about medicinal practices, the approach of potlatch, women being equal and respected, elder councils, laws supported by and involving the extended family, and a variety of other Keltic customs seem to be among the Iroquoian and their brothers the Cherokee. The Nipissing were almost Druidic and could be just that, at an early stage, as I interpret the legends.

The practice of giving children to one's hoped for ally or friend is a Keltic custom that includes tolerance and understanding being built in a similar way to the education system the Kelts employed. Trigger makes an excellent stab at explaining the custom as seen by Donnacona when he gave Cartier his children. He describes it as a political and trading demonstration of trust to seal the deal they made. However, Indians were soon to discover deals are seldom kept by greedy materialists. This may have contributed to the saying about 'He who speaks with the tongue that is forked.' Cartier kidnapped the kids and they were mercilessly treated by the French court who found them 'interesting' for a while. Some say that Christ was sent to Cornwall as part of his education in a diplomatic early life arrangement that was related to his relative Joseph of Arimathaea's tin trade:

"Donnacona was obviously not content with the response (2 swords and two wash basins for the children, followed by a twelve gun salute from cannons. At Stadaconna this volley led to two deaths according to some. From Trigger.) he had received from Cartier, and must have grown increasingly distrustful of him as a result of this meeting. Nevertheless,

Diverse Druids

he did not cease to try to dissuade Cartier from traveling up-river. The next day he sent three shamans, with blackened faces and wearing dogskin pelts and long horns, to paddle around Cartier's flag-ship, while one of them delivered a long speech. The shamans landed and were carried into the woods by Donnacona and his men, where they continued their harangue. About half an hour later, Taignoagny and Domagaya appeared, (The two sons who went back to France with Cartier. Later Cartier took his kids by force.) their caps under their arms and their hands folded in imitation of French acts of devotion they had witnessed. They said that one of their deities had informed these shamans that, if the French proceeded to Hochelaga, they would all perish from ice and snow. When Cartier laughed and said his priests revealed the contrary, Taignoagny and Domagaya returned to the woods and soon the other Indians appeared before the ships expressing pleasure at the good news (136-40). Here we see another aspect of Iroquoian behavior that was often to puzzle the French in the next century: the assumption that it is improper to question the beliefs of other people. (They allowed priests to baptize them in the knowledge that any good thing was OK.) Although the French laughed at the Stadaconan shamans' not unreasonable warning, the Stadaconans felt obliged to respect and show pleasure about the French shaman's pretended divination." (2)

These French shamans and their pretended pretensions are the crux of the beginning of the end for many Hurons and other Indians. Cartier returned one of the children when he returned to Stadacona (a boy of three) and the young girl ran away from the French after some abuse. However, Donnacona talked her into returning before he himself was kidnapped and taken away after having saved many French lives from scurvy. Who are the 'barbarians'? He never saw his homeland or loved ones again. Perhaps the issue we should consider in the courts today is that Donnacona told the French to take down their cross and asked them to stop acting as if they owned the land and everything on it. Trigger

Robert Baird

also noted that the Indians had leaders who were answerable to them in the Keltic manner of common consent through a dirfine. Because he intimated many things I have chosen to believe he actually knows the Indians were Keltic 'brethren' but maybe I am reading too much into his words or should I say into the area between the lines:

"Cartier, and most modern historians, have interpreted this as a power struggle between Donnacona and Agona as to which man, or clan segment, should control Stadacona (Trudel 1963:110-11; Morison 1971:420); however, from what we now know about Iroquoian political organization, a personal struggle of this sort seems highly unlikely. Among the Iroquoians, a headman could exercise power only by gaining the support of his followers for each decision that he made. No headman could force anyone to obey him against that man's will, nor would a headman retain the respect of his clan segment, if he were to betray one of its members to strangers. Headmen were elected to manage the affairs of their clan segment and could not, in their own right, control what went on in other clans or communities. The strangers that Guyot observed in the village were probably men who had come from neighboring communities to join in the debate." (3) This is an excellent description of what Aristotle observed in Carthage and called common consent kingship. Many (if not most) Iroquoian clans were headed by women and it is possible that the Stadaconans were only related to the Iroquoians.

The League of the Iroquois that created the forerunner to the U.S. form of government was a step away from the control of women and wise management, towards more Euro-centric ideals. I have never seen a commentator suggest this or the idea that the Iroquois were given muskets to destroy their neighbors and pave the way for a land grab. Rather than the Iroquois teaching the white man about a better form of government Bradley properly observes that the Indians learned this idea from the family of Jesus at Kingston. The Lake on the mountain (Glenora) where they lived is still held sacred by the Iroquois.

Diverse Druids

Lewis Henry Morgan wrote a book in 1851 called *League of the Iroquois* that has a lot of information about them. Unfortunately it is biased and thinks the Iroquois were 'less' until Christianized, or led by Handsome Lake to adopt an Indian religion wrapped around Christianity of that period. But that religion was wiser and better thought out; it had no malice to any other religion. I could even say it was the actual ethic Jesus wanted mankind to adopt. This quote shows a lot of the minstrel stage of the Bardic Tradition was a part of their culture:

"With the Iroquois, as with the red race at large, dancing was not only regarded as a thanksgiving ceremonial, in itself acceptable to the Great Spirit, but they were taught to consider it a divine art, designed by 'Ha-wen-né-yu' for their pleasure, as well as for his worship. It was cherished as one of the most suitable modes of social intercourse between the sexes, but more especially as the great instrumentality for arousing patriotic excitement, and for keeping alive the spirit of the nation. The popular enthusiasm broke forth in this form, and was nourished and stimulated by this powerful agency. These dances sprang, as it were, a living reflection from the Indian mind. With their wild music of songs and rattles, their diversities of step and attitude, their graces of motion, and their spirit-stirring associations, they contain within themselves both a picture and a realization of Indian life. The first stir of feeling of which the Indian youth was conscious was enkindled by the dance; the first impulse of patriotism, the earliest dreams of ambition were awakened by their inspiring influences. In their patriotic, religious and social dances, into which classes they are properly divisible, resided the soul of Indian life. It was more in the nature of a spell (More right than he may have known.) upon the people than of a rational guiding spirit. Their over-powering influence in arousing the Indian spirit, and in excluding all thoughts of a different life, and their resulting effect upon the formation of Indian character cannot be too highly estimated. From the earliest days of the Jesuit missions, the most unremitted efforts of the missionaries have been put forth for their suppression." (4)

Having been with the Indians and Wiccans who celebrate similar things in this regard I am certain there is a Keltic flavour in the Indian dances and rituals. In Sedona, Arizona I observed the similarity of the Keltic and Anastasi music. I heard people more expert in music than myself discuss this similarity on the radio. The Wiccans like to think of themselves as Druids almost, and it is reasonable to say there is a lot of similarity in their respect for nature and sense of oneness and spirit that surrounds us all. Clearly the Jesuits knew the religion of the Indian was in the spirit and in these rituals with fervent dance and music entwined. But most historians have never been to a Sabbat or participated in a Vision Quest. It is in the immortal soul that all people will ultimately find the truth and the Mayan saying I often quote certainly applies, again. 'Do not put yourself in front of your Self.' You would be hard pressed to find such commonality of beliefs as these Druidic 'brothers' shared over a very long time. It was no hypocritical pursuit to say the least; it was as Morgan said, the 'soul of Indian life'.

Taboos, Totems and Toxins

The Western scholar of today may try yet fail to comprehend the silly things that nature worshippers do while they sit in their Ivory Towers removed so much from nature. I love to think there are times I have seen a little of what the 'primitives' knew.

If taboo was associated with fishing, we have little record of it; the only explicit evidence is a prohibition against the roasting of eels, which if violated, would prevent the Indians from catching others. From this and the fact that the Restigouche division of the Micmac wore the figure of a salmon as a totem around their neck, we may surmise that fish, too, shared in the sacred and symbolic world of the Indian. (5) (The Salmon of Knowledge was of primary importance to the Kelts. The salmon's ability to follow energy lines of the earth and get back to the same place they were hatched may have something to do with this.)

Control over these supernatural forces and communication with them were the principal functions of the shaman, who served in Micmac society as an intermediary between the spirit realm and the physical. The lives and destinies of the natives were profoundly affected by the ability of the shaman to supplicate, cajole, and otherwise manipulate the magical beings and powers (They sometimes say with tongue firmly in cheek.). The seventeenth-century French, who typically labeled shamans (or 'buowin') frauds and jugglers in league with the devil, were repeatedly amazed at the respect accorded them by the natives. (6) By working himself into a dreamlike state, the shaman would invoke the Manitou of his animal helper and so predict future events (I think a little confusion exists here. Guide spirits are different than a vision quest. To say it predicts the future is not always true either. The path one will follow can be varied.). (7) He also healed by means of conjuring (Catholic priests or those higher up who do exorcisms are more into that; Healing is one thing, to remove a possessive demon or the like, for healing is more a matter of 'freeing the demon' - within and without.). The Micmac availed themselves of a rather large pharmacopeia of roots and herbs and other plant parts, but when these failed they would summon the healing arts of the most noted shaman in the district. The illness was of ten diagnosed by the 'buowin' as a failure on the patient's part to perform a prescribed ritual; hence an offended supernatural power had visited the offender with sickness. At such times the shaman functioned as a psychotherapist, diagnosing the illness and symbolically (at least) removing its immediate cause from the patient's body. (8)

It is important to understand that an ecosystem is holecoenotic in nature: there are no 'walls' between the components of the system, for 'the ecosystem reacts as a whole'. (9) (A great truth and reason for integrating the soul in healing.) Such was the case in the Micmac ecosystem of precontact times, (That is not known, Norumbega and Old Ireland were here before Christ and the very name Mic and Mac is so like Irish and Scottish prefixes to names for clans.)where the spiritual served as a link connecting man with all the various subsystems of the environment. Largely through the mediation of the shaman, these spiritual restriction and obligations acted as a kind of control device to maintain the ecosystem in a well-balanced condition. (10) Under these circumstances the exploitation of game for subsistence appears to have been regulated by the hunter's respect for the continued welfare of his prey - both living and dead - as is evident from the numerous taboos associated with the proper disposal of animal remains. Violation of a taboo desecrated the remains of the slain animal and offended its soul-spirit. The offended spirit would then retaliate in any of several ways, depending on the nature of the broken taboo: it could render the guilty hunter's (or the entire band's) means of hunting ineffective, or it could encourage its living fellows to remove themselves from the vicinity. In both cases the end result was the same - the hunt was rendered unsuccessful - and in both it was mediated by the same power - the spirit of the slain animal. Either of these catastrophes could usually be reversed through the magical arts of the shaman. In the Micmac cosmology, the overkill of wildlife would have been resented by the animal kingdom as an act comparable to genocide, and would have been resisted by means of the sanctions outlined above. The threat of retaliation thus had the effect of placing an upper limit on the number of animals slain, while the practical result was the conservation of wildlife.

    The injection of European civilization into this balanced system initiated a series of chain reactions which, within a little over a century, resulted in the replacement of the aboriginal ecosystem by another. From at least the beginning of the sixteenth century, and perhaps well before that date, fishing fleets from England, France, and Portugal visited the Grand Banks off Newfoundland every spring for the cod, and hunted whale and walrus in the Gulf of St. Lawrence.

Diverse Druids

(11) Year after year, while other, more flamboyant men were advancing the geopolitical ambitions of their emerging dynastic states as they searched for precious metals or passage to the Orient, these unassuming fishermen visited Canada's east coast and made the first effective European contact with the Indians there. For the natives' furs they bartered knives, beads, brass kettles, assorted ship fittings, and the like, (12) thus initiating the subversion and replacement of Micmac material culture by European technology. Far more important, the fishermen unwittingly infected the Indians with European diseases, against which the natives had no immunity. Commenting on what may be called the microbial phase of European conquest, John Whitthoft has written:

"All of the microscopic parasites of humans, which had been collected together from all parts of the known world into Europe, were brought to these (American) shores, and new diseases stalked faster than man could walk into the interior of the continent. Typhoid, diphtheria, cols, influenza, measles, Chichen pox, whooping cough, tuberculosis, yellow fever, scarlet fever, and other strep infections, gonorrhea, pox (syphilis), and smallpox were diseases that had never been in the New World before. They were new among populations which had no immunity to them. Great epidemics and pandemics of these diseases are believed to have destroyed whole communities, depopulated whole regions, and vastly decreased the native population everywhere in the yet unexplored interior of the continent. The early pandemics are believed to have run their course prior to 1600 A.D." (13) (I think this is true for the whole continent more than the NE portion of North America.)

Disease did more than decimate the native population; it effectively prepared the way for subsequent phases of European contact by breaking native morale and, perhaps even more significantly, by cracking their spiritual edifice (!). It is reasonable to suggest that European disease rendered the Indian's (particularly the shaman's) ability to control and otherwise influence the supernatural dysfunction

- because his magic and other traditional cures were now ineffective - thereby causing the Indian to apostatize (in effect), which in turn subverted the 'retaliation' principle of taboo and opened the way to a corruption of the Indian-land relationship under the influence of the fur trade." (14)

They go on to examine the 'cross-bearing Micmac' which is more than a mythological proof of European involvement from earlier times and the missionaries and their mercenaries who worked under them destroyed these crosses. Bradley documents a large number of Cross of Lorraines that were probably distributed by the Mason/Templarists of Prince Henry, Jarl of Orkney. We can dispense with the innocent use of biologics as these authors suggest because of the knowledge in high places as well as the Paracelsan cures that existed and could have been shared with the Indians. It was as they say, a very effective tool. I wonder why they didn't mention the documented use of the Plague at Fort Pitt?! Could it be something like the same reason historians think Donnacona met Spaniards far to the south wearing woolens? Why would anyone wear wool in the far south? I can see a reason they might want sheep, but not for the wool. There is so much denial and deceit it is hard to imagine the plot being so foul for most people first considering such things.

Melungeons and a Mélange

The Melungeons of the Appalachian Mountains near where the mound builders were once so plentiful speak a mixture of Keltic/Arab or Berber tongues. Columbus brought three Arabic or Berber translators on his third voyage that went near this area. Just as he brought a Phoenician/Hebrew translator on his first visit or invasion, it appears Columbus knew a lot before he arrived. His knowledge came from his father-in-law and papal authorities. His father-in-law was part of the Knights of Christ and they were a reformed or continuing Templar model. This is why he and Da Gama flew the Templar cross you have seen on their sails. The Melungeons are dark haired blue-eyed people in places such as the Pennsylvania Dutch

Diverse Druids

now live. My Wiccan friends who learned the pau-pau from their Indian cousins were from this stock of pre-Columbian white people.

The Pima Indians of the southwest have Berber blood and the Mandans are said to be white people. The list goes on and on. Warfare always includes propaganda and often includes the use of any weapon in reach. Greek fire doesn't explain vitrified rocks unless they really had napalm before Christ - and it would have had to be excellent napalm. There are vitrified rocks in the Appalachians just as there is under Edinburgh Castle. It would seem an appropriate military location where these rocks are found at the juncture of the Allegheny and Susquehanna Rivers. If the ancients were mere hunters and gatherers why can't we build a duplicate of the Great Pyramid or move 600 Ton rocks like those in Ba'albek or in the corner of the great religious temple attributed to Solomon.

How does one make a rock bed such as is called a sarcophagus (no lid) in the so-called King's Chamber. The corners have such a tolerance that Dunn thinks they had to have ultrasound drills. That does fit with my emphasis on harmonics, I think. Can you feel the spirit that comes through the Dervish Dancers or Yamabushi firewalkers?

The Red-Headed League of Megalith Builders and the Tuatha De Danaan are the greatest heroes of human history and they honored the spirit and women. They knew how to attune each part of nature and themselves in ways we are only beginning to understand in science. The Tulkus of Tibet, the Kahuna, the psychic surgeons of Brazil and the Philippines and the Yogis of India are other fine exemplars of these arts and sciences. Tesla and other supposed paranormal or atom-mysticists who invent all the great things our society thrives on aren't heretics as they used to be, so there is hope. The ability of the connected soul is immense:

"A few years ago a hunter dreamed a cow moose kill. A fine, fat cow. He was so pleased with the animal, so delighted to make this dream-kill, that he marked the animal's hooves. Now he would be sure to recognize it when he went on the coming hunt. The next day, when he went out into the bush, he quickly found the dream-trail. He followed it, and came to a large cow moose. Sure enough, the hooves bore his marks. Everyone saw them. All the men around the fire had been told about the marks, and everyone on the Reserve had come to look at those hooves when the animal was butchered and brought into the people's homes.

And not only that fat cow moose - many such instances are known to the people, whose marks on the animal or other indication show that there was no mistaking, no doubts about the efficacy of such dreams. Do you think this is all lies? No, this is power they had, something they knew how to use. This was their way of doing things, the right way." (15)

Right Thought = Right Action! It is more than just a law of people and maybe even this earthly plane. A real thought is more than what Rene Descartes was talking about when he said 'I think therefore I am.' A right or complete thought that includes our soul and its connection to the collective unconscious (Jung's word for what has many names) is a far more subtle, refined and awesome thing or experience. To suggest all Indians or Druids cultures were so wise is not very proper but these authors are right to say it was the intent of most of them. It can include a stillness of the mind with all the busyness it can generate through emotion and ego; and it must be close to the heart and soul. Jesus said it in a saying attributed to him when he said that includes an element of knowing as well. The saying is 'Be still and know that I AM'. In the original saying before he was incarnate the I AM was YHWH the dual gender god that became Jehovah among the followers of Moses.

When rightness is the rule, then civilized actions result in the relationship an individual has with all nature including other people. It is evident in the social construct of many Indians but let us only use the Huron for a simple example of what law, justice, parenting and enforcement today might learn from these people. Even in the case of murder they showed restraint and understanding rather than revenge. The peer pressure to behave according to ethics or rightness is evident in many places of this world but the societal structures don't encourage it. I like to be naïve and think the average person is really not so bad after all is considered. Certainly they are soulfully good and righteous even if they do not know their soul or ever act according to its purposeful prerogatives. I am not the only person who sees the work of what Grey Owl called the 'messengers' in these similar cultural constraints that value freedom and the soul above all the petty things people can spend their time doing to nature (God). These messengers were the Druids not the 'angels' that some priests told the Indians. The Indians were much closer to the spirit world but the priests prevailed upon them through fears including belief in the 'angels', as if they were something more than the Indians already knew:

"The personal treatment that a murderer received was a matter for his clan segment and lineage to decide. Normally, it took the form of verbal rebukes, rather than physical punishment. Nevertheless, since all members of a group stood to lose through the misbehavior of any one member, it was I their interest to bring pressure to bear upon a murderer to make sure that he did not kill again. The guilty person knew, moreover, that if he misbehaved repeatedly, he would gradually alienate his clansmen and lose their support. (Ostracism was the ultimate Keltic punishment) By making tribes, villages, and especially clan segments responsible for the behavior of their members, the Huron were able to secure order without resorting to capital punishment or interfering with the traditional rights of the various groups that made up their confederacy (The fine for killing a woman was higher than for killing a man.). The Huron did not fine or penalize a thief, nor did they permit a man from whom goods had been stolen to reclaim them without first inquiring how someone else had come to possess them. A refusal to answer constituted an admission of guilt. If a man could prove who had robbed him, he and his relatives were socially sanctioned to go to the thief's longhouse and carry off everything on which they could lay their hands. Hence, relatives of a person who had stolen very little might find themselves bruised and despoiled. Again, pressure was put on kin groups to enforce good behavior among their members." (16)

This same kind of communal ethic existed in the Keltic structure. When a person who was in a position of authority took advantage of the trust placed in them this person paid four times the normal fine. I do not see where this extra penalty was needed in the Huron situation because they had fewer public works or officials and the attendant bureaucracy. The Kelts didn't try to make carbon copy reproductions of their homeland and thus colonize the minds of the people they traded and taught or learned from (and so in teaching we are taught). They sought sensible ways to communicate with the wisdom of the people they became involved with. It does make sense that the most 'equal' or blessed among us should be most responsible. Thus the boss was made to pay when the lackey (or foreign student of a Bard) was fined, and both were made to see the error of their ways. I think the fines were used wisely and never became a source of power for the courts to trade upon but I have not found any records to substantiate my possible bias. Perhaps the people who would make themselves powerful need to have an extra incentive to never use that power for personal gain. Do these words of Plato have something to do with what I am saying? "All great things are fraught with danger." Maybe he was advising to be corrupt but careful too.

Kuo Hsi expresses the Chinese point of view about the landscapes of subjective versus objective reality in these words. "If the superior man loves the countryside, why is this so? Hills and gardens will always be the haunts of him who seeks to cultivate his original nature; fountains and rocks are a constant joy to him who wanders whistling among them." I wish Plato had spent more time in gardens.

It is no surprise that history has brought us the Crusades and other horrors if we look to the ethics of our society. We truly have gotten the kind of government we deserve, from that vantage point. However, how are we to know any better if we are kept in the dark and allowed to see only that which someone wants us to know or believe? In my first draft of this manuscript I quoted St. Robert Bellarmine (He sat on Galileo's Inquisition tribunal as a force of reason.) because of an article in the National Post that had news of scientists creating human clones. It is part of my attempt to make history relative and meaningful in the present but it may be a stretch of my fertile imagination, too. Will the sentient robots we dump the contents of our minds into have a soul of their own separate from what ever our brain contained? I do agree with Bill Joy in his Wired Magazine article of March 2000 when he noted such science will not transfer the human soul. Here are the words of St. Robert to end this chapter:

"This is a true mirror of God's existence in created things. God is an indivisible spirit; he nonetheless fills the whole world and all its parts without occupying any place. Rather he is whole in the whole world and whole in every part of the world. And when a new creature is produced, God begins to be in it, though he does not move. Hence, if other heavens and another earth came to be, he would also be in them."

Robert Baird

CHAPTER FOURTEEN:
A World of Wonder - I Wander!

Redskins of the 'Red-Lands'

The Beothuk "skill with the bow - they could shoot four arrows in swift succession and with deadly aim - was more than a match for the clumsy, slow-firing arquebus or even the early flintlocks. On the other hand, it is likely that firearms inspired as much terror in the Beothuk as elsewhere on the continent. Heads of slain fishermen were carried triumphantly back to camp for savage rites of triumph. The fishermen were content to rip off their victim's scalps, with ears and face skin attached, leaving the corpses faceless and bloodily bald. The end approached when eighteenth-century firearms came into use and Micmac were brought in to hunt the Beothuk, matching their skill at surprise and evasion. Nor were the English more humane when they settled the Avalon Peninsula and the outports, As in Australia, hunting the aborigines became an exciting sport in which men, women, and children were equally fair game." (1)

Beothuk canoes were unlike any others in the Americas and were able to travel on the open ocean. They had ballast and larger midsections with raised and reinforced construction. Farley Mowat believes the Dorset Eskimo and Beothuk were descended from or learned from the Irish and Alban Scots who used these variations of the 'curragh'. Admiral Morison who wrote many books supporting the Columbus fiction even notes the Colombian natives used almost exactly the same 'curragh' techniques used in Ireland. These shipbuilding techniques usually vary according to materiel and other factors but to have Morison say that was one of the inconsistencies in his argument. Now that Mowat and others won the day in the Norse debate over their arrival five centuries before Columbus: I wonder what the great Admiral (Columbus and Morison) might say, as to why governments keep flogging the 'No Cultural Impact' theory or fiction.

I still maintain an open-mind that might change if some better or new information comes along from the field of genetics as to who the Kelts are. It seems highly likely that the present numbers of white people are all related to those who came about in the 35,000 to 30,000 BC period from what Gimbutas calls Old Europe. That being the case we must deal with the Basque and Berbers as well as all other fair skinned people being derived from the same people with the Haplogroup X marker. Does that mean the people of the sub-continent were interbred with them? If so it would seem the white people spread quickly to that part of the world just as they did to America to become the Sioux and others, some 30,000 years ago. That makes me wonder if they were helped by a wiser and more ancient people like the Mungo Man. There are many other things that led me in this direction. Certainly we see the Basque fishing in American waters and living in Central America at a very early time. Probably they were there with the Olmec or black people, as well. Timbuktu and the Zimbabwean culture with deep mines dating to 45,000 years ago make me wonder if these people helped them in certain areas like South America and Central America. So the Basque and Berbers are probably the Sea People and part of the Phoenician Brotherhood.

The Mayan connection with the Basque is particularly strong in terms of evidence and it seems the Toltecs and other European whites arrived not much earlier than a thousand BC. They came through Barabudur in the 5th Century AD to BC period and there were some with the Olmec and other Phoenicians who traveled and traded long before that without establishing major settlements. The Mayans themselves are SE Asians and still have the characteristics to the extent they can be mistaken for each other. Churchward says the white men in Europe that established themselves there came from Mayax in the Americas, and I have to consider this though I think there

335

were white people in Europe around the same time they arrived in America:

"These two inventions, zero and the calendar, place the Maya people among the most advanced thinkers in early history.

We know that the first Americans invented the wheel, because many small wheeled objects formed of clay have been found in excavation in Mexico. No one can say with certainty what they were used for, but it is generally believed that they were tops. In any case, the people of ancient Mexico probably did not use wheels on vehicles for transportation like those in the Eastern Hemisphere, because they had no horses of other draft animals." (2)

'Tops'? What about wheel barrows or a time when they had horses or other animals? The logic escapes me. It is true that many American people were not as prone to moving or slash and burn agriculture, like the Kelts of Asia and Europe. The bounty of Central American vegetation and fish makes it so little real need to move exists and the weather is idyllic. What nature provides necessitates and makes for the human adaptive technologies. Snowshoes and birchbark canoes weren't the kind of thing you'd expect to find in Mayan lands. They had rubber and paper of a tree that easily provided the best paper of their era. They had childproof containers for potions according to what is found in Guatemala.

Jefferson was a great admirer of the Indians and it is important to further verify the creed and spiritual manner of all North Americans because we can see the Druids here better than where the propagandists have made their case for many centuries. I sometimes define religion as what one does rather than what one says they believe and this little quote puts the matter simply. "Their only controls are their manners and the moral sense of right and wrong, which. in every man makes a part of his nature." Jefferson made these observations through long contact with Indians he grew up amongst. They certainly had good reason to have lost some of their goodness and morality but he was still able to see

Diverse Druids

these things even though one of his friends was taken to England as a curiosity.

I mentioned the Brazilian pyramids that are arranged like batteries before and it could be that they are the very earliest pyramids made by a culture that Churchward thinks was here when the area of the Amazon was all beneath water before the Andes rose. There is recent proof of a huge volcano that may have brought a major change to the landscape in South America. Let us consider what Berlitz says about these pyramids:

"On December 30, 1975, 'Landsat II', an ERTS satellite, took in its normal course of activities a series of photographs at about 13 degrees S latitude and 71 degrees 30' W longitude, over the jungles of southeastern Peru, from a distance of 550 to 580 nautical miles in space. Close investigation of this series of eight objects has been made by low-flying aircraft. It has been observed that they seem to be tree-covered pyramids and are not eight but twelve, as four additional smaller ones, also arranged in two rows, did not show on the 'Landsat' photographs. Several attempts have been made to get to the area by land, but these have been complicated by difficult jungle conditions that have resulted in the death and disappearance of some of the explorers. These hazards include poisonous snakes, insects, and distinctly unfriendly Indians who are apt to resist intruders with silent blowguns or long arrows and who believe that the area is a sacred city of the 'old ones'.

The difference in the color of the vegetation shows that they are made of different material than that of the surrounding basic jungle floor.

There are two other enormous rectangular formations now covered by trees and two semicircular ones, not so tall as the pyramids. They are to the south but are part of the complex. There are also high semicircular ridges at each end of the complex, which may turn out to be walls. (Could they reflect cosmic energy to join earth energy in the pyramid 'battery' complex?)

Robert Baird

Question: Do you think that they are really pyramids?

They certainly look like it. We sent a request to the Environmental Institute of Michigan, and they suggested that the pyramids might be truncated ridges, like the Devil's Backbone in Colorado. But this would not explain the other structures. I think it is possible that the entire complex is the remains of an ancient city built by some race thousands of years before the Incas.

Fawcett, a colonel in the British army, who devoted years to exploration and boundary survey in the largely unexplored center of the South American jungle, believed that these great cities were thousands of years old and that the 'connection of Atlantis with parts of what is now Brazil. affords explanations for many problems that other wise are unsolved mysteries.'

The presence of non-Indians in Central and South America had been established in earlier times by members of Spanish and Portuguese expeditions, who described encountering white tribes (one living in a city called Atlán) and also tribes of warlike blacks. (3)

David Hatcher Childress writes about a city called Ingréuil and other Brazilian cities that are being researched only within Brazil now. Perhaps they want to do their own 'grave-robbing'; but I think these things upset the Catholic hegemony that takes psychic surgeons to court even though the President took his cancerous daughter to one. Michael Bradley did an early book in his career that detailed the blacks in the Americas and National Geographic reported it as a likely probability 30,000 years before their 2001 article that I frequently refer to. Atlán, Aztlan, the Atlantic and a host of other things and names like Tiahuanaco include Atlantis in them. The 'Red-Lands' may have been Cuba and the spectacular discoveries there that are just beginning 2200 feet below the water. How can that be? Did it happen when the Andes rose or when the meteors we reported hit the Bermuda Triangle? Pretty exciting stuff, to say the least, don't you think?

Diverse Druids

In reference to the Great Pyramid I have been debating the point on the web with a professor of International History and the like. He really doesn't have any specific research other than visiting the Pyramid and accepting the conventional viewpoint, but in response to his comment (in Latin) saying 'A little knowledge is a dangerous thing'. I wrote the following: Yes, A little knowledge is a dangerous thing. The conventional historians built on fallacy without chemists and mathematicians made erroneous assumptions and slapped each other on the back. I have the benefit of a variety of sciences that have done excellent scholarship and demonstrated the actual processes. But, my reading of Pliny and Flinders-Petrie tells me there always were those who saw a bigger picture and that the things they said were called 'maverick' and debunked purely for political and religious propaganda purposes. The miss-translation of Pliny was outright fraud. That would be a word Lactantius might have used just as he did while performing the function of tutor in the home of Constantine as he referred to those 'who lie and forge for religion'.

As to my 'wounded but not beaten' nature - it is true. It wounds me greatly to see the level of ignorance that passes for certainty and the unwillingness of academics to look outside that 'certainty'. I know FAR too many people listen to such 'expertise' and do not think to do their own research to see the extent to which things are neither black nor white and mostly just unknown. At the same time it is exciting to think we now can correct the corruption and disprove the deceitful in order to know the potential man achieved and we could (maybe did) build upon.

Heavenly Maya

"A number of star features that could not be seen without the use of a telescope were given the same names in different languages in both the Old and New Worlds. Such was the Scorpion, a star cluster containing a comet, which reminded both the Babylonians and the Maya of Central America of a scorpion and was called by that name by both races. Greek astronomers adopted the observation of the Babylonians that Uranus regularly covered its moons, an occurrence also unable to be seen by the naked eye, and converted it to a legend that the god Uranus had the habit of alternately eating and later disgorging his children.

The ancient references, which are really astronomical data disguised as legends, to the two moons of Mars, the multiple moons of Jupiter, the five disappearing and reappearing moons of Uranus, the nine moons of Saturn, and even the horns of Venus, suggest that astronomers of former cultures were capable of using artificial sight amplification that was probably a form of telescope. But as far as we know, the first version of the modern telescope was not invented until 1609.

Ground-glass artifacts, however, found at different archaeological sites, seem to indicate that the ancients were able to manufacture an optical lens. In 1853 Sir David Brewster, a specialist in optics with the British Association for the Advancement of Science, produced a crystal that had been found in a buried 'treasure house' in Nineveh. The audience, intrigued by this interesting jewel, was thrown into an uproar when Sir David insisted it was a 'true optical lens' ground in antiquity. The 'lens' was catalogued as a jewel and was put on exhibit at the British Museum with other Assyrian antiquities. Since then, however, other finds of lenses, brought up from under the sea off Esmeraldas, Ecuador, excavated at La Venta, Mexico, and jewel-like lenses found in tombs in Libya, in what was formerly part of the Roman empire, suggest that various ancient peoples used lenses for vision amplification. Some Roman accounts of the arena mention that certain aristocrats used colored jewel pendants to bring closer to them their view of the sanguinary Roman games. According to Plutarch, Archimedes, the inventor genius of ancient Syracuse, possessed instruments able to 'manifest to the eye the largeness of the sun.'

While most of the small artifacts of antiquity have disappeared, a number may be stored in museums throughout the world awaiting further study and classification of what they really were. A survey of some of these previously unidentified artifacts in museum exhibits stresses both the extreme age of civilized man and the scientific achievements of very early, even prehistoric eras." (4)

Solomon was enchanted by more than just the pulchritude of the Queen of Sheba. Her people had the green lenses that allowed them to be the best star-gazers of the Middle East and I love the story of the hermaphrodite donkey the discoverer of her ancient city in Yemen used in his travels. The Moslems thought it was the eighth wonder of the world when they saw it copulate with itself. Archimedes invented the screw that raises water but I know all Central American people have such a thing that grows in their forests and jungles. A tree that winds itself around other trees in a symmetrical manner exists. When the tree would be burned or cut for a stool and pushed into the ground it would have been noticed to bring up earth like an auger. Wood carving was a major craft in the area. In fact Ironwood is better than early iron in terms of a weapon or as a fuel to generate intense heat for ceramics in the natural bellows of a seaside cenote or cave.

Berlitz makes an impressive number of points including the routes of butterflies (Lewis Spence originally) who fly to their death in search of an instinctual homeland that is no longer there. There are roads extending a hundred miles out into the ocean off the coast of South America. I lived in Belize and know it wouldn't take more than a ten foot drop in water levels for the country to become more than twice its size. The Bahamas would be as big a land mass as Florida if the water level dropped a hundred feet. There are numerous sites around the world that are now bringing us exciting news. Yoniguni and Pohnpei join Bimini in providing the kinds of things we have reason to believe shows extensive worldwide cultural community in Pre-Ice Age times. Some of these places may have taken many millennia to become fully covered and there is every reason to believe the things I have laid before you are enough to make the point. However,

Robert Baird

if you want more, the hundreds of books I've quoted will provide thousands of other places to look.

In the eastern philosophies there is a concept called Maya. It is eerily similar to the phrase I often quote from the Mayans - 'Don't put yourself in front of your Self!'. The following description from the *Dictionary of Symbols* should be of interest:

"*MAYA:* The lesson may be read psychologically, as applying to ourselves, who are not gods but limited beings. The constant projection and externalization of our specific shakti (vital energy) is our 'little universe', our restricted sphere and immediate environment, whatever concerns and affects us. We people and color the indifferent, neutral screen with the movie-figures and dramas of the inward dream of our soul, and fall prey then to its dramatic dramatic events, delights, and calamities. The world, not as it is in itself but as we perceive it and react upon it, is the product of our own maya or delusion. It can be described as our own more or less blind life-energy, producing and projecting demonic or beneficent shapes and appearances. Thus we are captives of our own Maya-Shakti and of the motion picture that it incessantly produces. The Highest Being is the lord and master of Maya. All the rest of us. are the victims of our own individual Maya. To liberate man from such a spell. is the aim of all the great Indian philosophies." (5)

Neurophysiological research at Harvard has used MRI/SPECT machines to prove there is a brain lobe shutdown in adept meditation that allows the focus of physicality to be suspended and the contact with spiritual to be enhanced. Parapsychology now has replicable results due to the work of Bearden and others. Acupuncture and the chakra centers of ancient medicine are being proven in many Western Universities to be more effective than pharmacological or other invasive and abusive treatments. Perhaps the most relevant aspect of this modern research (other than the quantum world) is in the area of Thalami research. There we see the work of the Druids and their ability to affect projections and other miraculous things, has a great deal of validity, and a real explanation now exists for those who need to see something before they will let their mind trust their heart and eyesight.

For the people who think ancients did not have any computers or rudimentary devices to navigate by until the relatively recent centuries as well as those who still think ancients believed the Earth was flat I include part of an article found on the web.

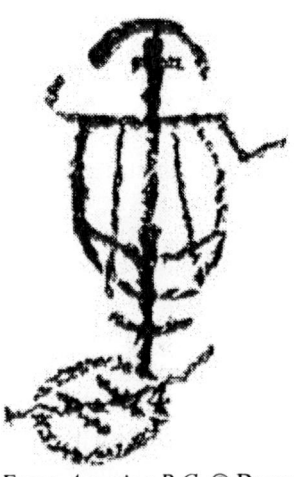

Ancient Navigators Could Have Measured Longitude!
by Rick Sanders
(Full text of article from Fall 2001 21st Century)

Around the year 232 B.C., Captain Rata and Navigator Maui set out with a flotilla of ships from Egypt in an attempt to circumnavigate the Earth.[1] On the night of August 6-7, 2001, between the hours of 11 PM and 3 AM, this writer, and fellow amateur astronomer Bert Cooper, proved in principle that Captain Rata and Navigator Maui could have known and charted their location, by longitude, most of the time during that voyage.

The Maui expedition was under the guidance of Eratosthenes, the great scientist who was also the chief librarian of the library at Alexandria. Could this voyage have demonstrated Eratosthenes' theorem that the world was round, and measured approximately 24,500 miles in circumference? One of the navigational instruments which Maui had with him was a strange looking "calculator" that he called a *tanawa;* such an instrument was

From *America B.C.,* © Barry Fell (New York: Simon & Schuster, 1976), p. 118 *Drawing by Maui of his tanawa or calculator, found in the Caves of the Navigators, Sosorra, Irian Jaya (West New Guinea).*

known, in 1492, as a *torquetum*.
Intrigued by a photograph of the cave drawing of that tanawa in Irian Jaya, western New Guinea, I speculated that Maui must have been looking at the ecliptic to measure "lunar distance," in order to find his longitude. Maui's tanawa was of such importance, that he drew it on the cave wall with the inscription, deciphered in the 1970s by epigrapher Barry Fell: "The Earth is tilted. Therefore, the signs of half of the ecliptic watch over the south, the other (half) rise in the ascendant. This is the calculator of Maui."

The Third Eye and Ark of the Covenant
The Pineal Gland or 'Third Eye' has granular structures or crystals that allow it to be like an old crystal radio receiver and amplifier. The Pyramid adds to energy and focuses it and thus many adepthoods and witches or the Tarim Basin mummies had what people think of as a witch's hat that is now deprecated and called a dunce's cap. Most people who get 'buzzed' feel the vibration of these crystals doing the work that amazing nature has intelligently designed into us. The whole endocrine system or lymph system research that so little was known about a couple of decades ago is making great advances. Sex and the yogic disciplines of Kundalini, Bhakti, and Tantra have been part of the nature of 'working partners' such as Wicca has for at least the 25,000 years they claim to have been around.
These sciences observe factual and observable experience even if the sense of sight is not involved. To say that possessions or ecstatic trance and other real experience are hallucinatory is arrogant, hostile and aggressive stupidity. But if you say these things and call them what they call you then you are branded as some kind of 'quack' or 'nut'. The psychiatrists want to call possessions by the label Trance

Possession Disorder Syndrome so they can drug another whole segment of the society they play a part in controlling. What did they study that makes them so 'expert'? Many have not even taken basic psychology courses and study allopathy or drug-pushing and the anatomy. The spirit is not in bones like the big toe. It isn't even in the buttocks or mass, but it behooves me to suggest they are something that rhymes with mass. If the reader who doubts my assertions reads *Stopping Valium* they might wake up. Sorry for a simple excursion into humor and sarcasm, if it offends anyone as much as this type of vituperative attack on the soul offends me.

For the truly exceptional adept like Murry Hope there are things that happen which only 'black ops' science seems currently aware of or studies in earnest. These things really aren't necessary to discuss in great detail even though they are the essential powers that ancient people were so amazed by and thus would give so much respect to the Druids. The Indian shamans, Druids and Mayans (if there is any real difference) have foretold a time when our civilization will end. The Mayans say it will be in Dec. 2012 and we can only hope all life on earth isn't similarly destroyed by some act of human indifference to ethics. Perhaps it will be a genetic engineering slip or the sentient self-replicating robot. Maybe everyone will be given access to the gene therapy drugs that make people immortal in exchange for an irreversible impotency unless they pay for it. That would lead to a new species called Homo Sapiens Immortalis maybe, but I don't think such and intelligent application of technology is in the political agenda.

Bradley explains another simpler yet interesting object that you might want to hear about. His explanation of the Ark of the Covenant will help people see the extent of technology and the reason for the maps that are so apparently accurate (Portolan) and advanced. There is another associated aspect of mapping and astral possibilities thereof but it is one of those things most people would think I am crazy if I suggested it, here. This explanation is entirely feasible and it illustrates how religious despots used simple technology to woo and empower themselves with the masses. The Isisian Code that a friend of mine is writing a book about is far more complex than the Morse code mentioned here and the Enneagrams are even more mathematically advanced. Both were around a very long time before Christ:

"But every letter and number can be represented by some combination of dots and dashes. That's Morse code. If you have enough electricity to generate a lot of sparks, and if you have a lot of patience, messages of any desired length and complexity can be sent.

So much for what might be called the technical aspects of the Ark. What about its provenance? Where did it come from? The Old Testament tells us that it was constructed shortly after the Exodus by an Israelite craftsman according to instructions given to Moses by God. But the Old Testament is, of course, a Hebrew document. It may well be biased. (!) We will recall that Moses had been adopted into the pharaonic family of Egypt and was, in fact, an Egyptian priest. Could Moses have stolen this artifact? Or, at least, could he have stolen the plans and specifications of some highly venerated Egyptian religious object? Is this why the Egyptians called the escaping horde under Moses 'evil-doers'? Or were the Egyptians just angered at losing slaves?

Considering the dates that have recently been strongly associated with the Giza plateau by geologists and astronomers, and the radiocarbon date for the Bimini organic remains - all about 10,500 B.C. - we must consider the real possibility that the Ark had originally been some sort of Atlantean device for long-distance communication. It was a 'wireless' and less sophisticated and refined example of the basic principles than Marconi's 1901 apparatus. It would have worked - sometimes, with optimum atmospheric conditions - and was both dangerous and cumbersome to operate.

But even with marginal or sporadic operational efficiency, it would have permitted a seafaring culture to establish the accurate longitudes of distant places all around the earth. A signal transmitted at noon, 'Giza Pyramid time' (just for example), could be compared with the local noon where the signal was received. The difference in hours and fractions (measured by sand glass or water-clock) between 'Pyramid noon' and local noon (the sun's highest point in the sky - the 'meridian passage'), multiplied by 15, will give the longitude 'west' of the 'Pyramid Meridian' (Giza) in degrees - and we know that a circle was divided into 360 degrees from very early times, for no obvious reason. (Important to the Harmonic of Light.) This would have provided better accuracy than was available to Columbus - or to any other European mariner - until John Harrison (1693-1776) a Yorkshire blacksmith, invented a practical chronometer in 1749.

My notion is that most large Atlantean trading ships or warships would have carried an 'Ark' on board, and it is possible that large vessels became known as arks (i.e., 'Noah's ark) because at one time they carried arc-transmitters aboard." (6)

He continues to discuss other ancient technologies that we are certain were developed long before history would have us believe. He points out that 'steam engines developed in China' (Thales had one as well.) that were never utilized and pressure bottles that could have been used for natural gas etc., before detailing the difficult issue of when Moses actually left Egypt. He is right about scholarly difficulty with any of the supposed Egyptian 'facts'. As an accomplished marine engineer and map lecturer in universities he is a credible source and he brought engineers in who described the technical aspects and designs mentioned in the Bible. Why is there such a lack of academic willingness to discuss the implications of these very ancient maps?

Ritual Movements

We saw the counter clockwise movement of things in magic and the import of dance; now we can tie a few more esoteric things into view and really boggle the mind of any naysayer who thinks he might be able to grasp the 'waves of the marvelous'.

"Rite in essence, every rite symbolizes and reproduces creation. Hence, rites are connected with the symbolism of ornaments. The slow-moving ritual, characteristic of all ceremonies, is closely bound up with the rhythm of the astral movements. At the same time, every rite is a meeting, that is, a confluence of forces and patterns; the significance of rites stems from the accumulated power of these forces when blended harmoniously one with the other.

Rotation for Roux, in *Les Druides* (Paris, 1961), rotation (the dynamic determining of circumference in rites or in art) generates a magic force, particularly of a defensive order, since it marks out a sacred precinct - the circle - which calls for the projection of the self. For Blavatsky, David's dance around the Ark, like that of the Sabean star-worshippers, was a circular dance or at least a dance that followed a closed curve." (7)

An individual can create their own mantra and rituals to go with yogic breathing and sense the energies. Listening to inspiring music when added to contemplation or a bath is a start. Then, if you have the music arranged to switch to a more or less unobtrusive background sound or natural rhythm as you are standing a more focused approach can begin. Sensing and visualizing the chakras filling and cleansing as the breathing becomes naturally altered in the meditative state allows a heightening of the natural hormonal and neurological firing as controlled and augmented by the Thalami or Pineal Gland (Third Eye). Ideally the superior parietal lobe shuts off the process of the mind body obsession and allows a contact but one should consciously reach out with good intent to all past loves and the totality of creative forces that swamp our soulful existence.

Then twisting the torso from side to side with arms up and out like the dolmen steeple one can feel the palms going through fields of energy. Turning the palms down and up in harmony with the breathing while glorifying and ecstatically enhancing the energy and oneness one feels allows the soul to bounce and burgeon itself in many possible ways that might be directed by your prior intent (present top of mind interests that were formulated and focused upon before the process actually began). It can also allow a tap in to other information and experiences which will be useful in non related aspects of your life. If this is done in the bosom of nature and in harmony with the animals you seek to respect by incorporating their conscious atomic structures with your own (eat) then you may understand the shamans weren't so all fired ignorant. Finally find your eyes closed and turned upwards inside the head to the Pineal Gland after having moved through the mutras. See your body become just a vehicle and perhaps fall to the floor on pillows of sit consciously and naturally before the impending weakness. Do this often for a year and then you will always be able to know its wonder and closeness for the rest of your incarnate life. Share it only in the presence of truthful and like-minded practitioners at a Sun Dance or pau-pau. Know the wonder but do not become enchanted or obsessed to the point that you diminish the awe through over attendance to the buzz and beauty of the soul. Nothing in this paragraph is academic or soundly oriented to the design of this book, I suppose. It may only be my own approach and could even be too much to do all at once. Candles or incense and aromatherapy or objects of power and chanting can also be part of your own ritual.

    The energy that Druids and shamans have caused to be put into the cosmos and our environment may still be with us through the archetypes of human experience. There may well be a genetic function or aspect of this knowledge that imbues our soul. The facts of their philosophy as a legacy we can attune to, or use to ensure the next human civilization is the best it can be, are partially herein contained. Toffler, Ferguson, Naisbett and Campbell as well as the Mayans are telling us the New Age is around the corner if we still wish to see humanity existing as a species. If we don't turn that corner and continue straight ahead, I fear this species will cease to exist. The Druids knew God! They knew he/she/it changes and grows just as all nature does or should do.

Final Thoughts to Hopefully Avoid a Final Civilization on Earth

Martin Doutré has written a book called *Ancient Celtic New Zealand* which is on the same page (soi disant) that I am trying to bring forward. The following review brings up some ugly aspects of the cover up and genocide of true history:

"Martin Doutré's thesis is that New Zealand was inhabited by European-type people for many centuries 'before' the islands were occupied by the Maori, which invasion is said to have taken place around AD 1200-1300. At that time, according to the received wisdom, the islands were uninhabited.

The author has found a large amount of convincing evidence that this is totally untrue. For example, early European visitors and settlers wrote that many of the people were fair-skinned with blonde or red hair, and the Maori themselves have legends of aboriginal inhabitants known to them as 'moriori', 'turehu' and other names, including 'tangeta whenua' (the first people). Some of these were of normal stature and others were of pygmy dimensions. In an early British census, Maori and Moriori were classified separately.

Caves have been found full of human remains, which bear signs of having been massacred with a blow to the skull. A figure of 60,000 skeletons is mentioned. Local Maoris showed no respect for these remains, saying that they were 'not our people'. In fact they were selling the bones to a mill where they were ground up for fertilizer.

In addition to these carelessly-discarded remains, more formal burial sites have been found in which the skeleton is crouched or in foetal position, similar to Celtic burials of northern Europe (A Beothuk similarity too.). Furthermore, the jawbones of these (and the massacre victims) are typically Indo-European. If you are not Polynesian and you

Diverse Druids

run your thumb along the underside of your jaw from the ears forwards, you will feel a slight notch. If placed on a flat surface, your jawbone would sit firmly. But if you are Polynesian, the bottom of your jaw will be rounded, and if put on a table it will rock. These jaw types are easy to distinguish, even in photographs.

Doutré also found evidence of large-scale drainage schemes (Like the Etruscan in South America? I wonder if there were the red, black and white lozenges of Atlantis on the art, too? Is this an indication that at one time all races except yellow were part of Atlantis?) and extensive areas of crop cultivation in addition to the remains of a large city now covered by forest for which access to is discouraged. This, he says, could hardly have been achieved by a few canoe-loads of immigrants in the few centuries between their arrival and that of the British. and indicates a large peaceful population. He suggests that the Maori merely took over what they found and either killed or assimilated the existing inhabitants. Some of the Moriori are said to have fled to the remote Chatham Islands, where the Maori finished them off with the connivance of the British.

Speaking of which, the author reproduces an excellent picture of a Stonehenge-type trilithon in the island of Tonga-Tapu, of which I was previously unaware, and also a Silbury-type mound in Western Samoa.

More research is needed; if that is possible in the current climate of white-washing early Maori atrocities and of stultifying political correctness. Doutré deserves financial support from those of us who deplore the subjugation of archaeology to politics." (8)

WOW! Maybe the truth has a chance?! I must not forget, the facts were even more available before the destruction of the Library at Alexandria and others were put to the sword by the damned hellfire proselytes. If the Father of Biblical Archaeology (W.F.Albright is so named in Biblical Archaeology Review of March 2001) knows the Bible is a Phoenician literary legacy even before the Dag Hammadi finds were translated by 1971 - Why has it taken so long for

Robert Baird

the Phoenicians to be studied in universities? They are not being seriously studied anywhere. I can only hope that some day the egalitarian Kelts will be respected, and that ethics will return to the spiritual realm of humanity.It pains me to see the suffering that results from religious indoctrination and dogma.

Bibliography and Notes:

Chapter One: What (Who) is a Druid?
1) Emory University, The University of Rome and others are continuing the research on Haplogroup X marker identification and tracking of white people in the world. I have seen it reported and commented on in various places.
2) www.phoenicia.org/genoa.html pg. 4 of 13
3) Ibid.
4) Celtic Mythology, by Ward Rutherford, Sterling Publ., NY, 1987 pgs. 79-80.
5) http://home.earthlink.net/-alferian/CONCEPT.HTML pg. 2 of 6

Chapter Two: Hail Atlantis! And The Brotherhood of Man
1) 'Udama', 6.4.66-69; cf. Eugene Watson Burlingame, *Buddhist Parables* (New Haven: Yale University Press, 1922), pgs. 75-6.
2) Primitive Mythology: The Masks of God, by Joseph Campbell, 1959, renewed 1987, Penguin Edition, pgs. 8 & 9.
3) Cf. A. Meillet and Marcel Cohen, *Les Languages Du Monde*, (Paris: H. Champion, 1952), pg.xxiii.
4) Sir Williams Jones, *Third Anniversary Discourse*, (Feb. 2, 1786), 'Works', ed. Lord Teignmouth (London, 1807), Vol. III, pg.34.
5) Franz Bopp, *Über das Conjugationssystem der Sanskritsprache in Ver gleichung mit jenem der griechischen, latinischen, persischen und germanischen Sprache' (Frankfurt am Main, 1816).*
6) Primitive Mythology, op.cit. pgs. 9 & 10.
7) Arthur Schopenauer, Parerga II, par.185, *Werke*, Vol. VI, pg. 427.
8) Primitive Mythology, op.cit.pgs.11-12.

9) Leo Frobenius, *Die Masken und Geheimbunde Afrikas*, Bd., LXXIV, Np. 1, (Hulle, 1898).
10) Primitive Mythology, op.cit. pgs. 12-15.
11) The Norse Atlantic Saga, by Gwyn Jones, 2nd Ed., Oxford University Press, 1964, 1986, pgs. 31 & 32.

Chapter Three: Strabo and the Oak:
1) R. A. S. Macalister, *Newgrange, County Meath*, Dublin; Government Pub'lns., official handbook, no date).
2) J. A. MacCulloch, *The Religion of the Ancient Celts* (Edinburgh: T. and T. Clark, 1911), pg. 63.
3) Primitive Mythology, op. cit. pgs. 430 & 431.
4) HRH N. deVere and Sir Laurence Gardner's books including *Genesis of the Grail Kings* are the source of this disturbing information, connected to the Catholic 'communion', Lutheran transubstantiation, and other blood rituals.
5) Article in 'World Explorer', Vol.1, No.9, by De Anna Emerson who calls it Ea Anna script. 'Ea' is Greek for 'De' and together with Ana is Danu leading to the De Danaan and Homer's DNN; Campbell adds more to the picture. Her script is probably related to a numeric part of Gimbutas' Old European which might be similar to the Tartessus language. Tartessus Iberia and its co-venturers n Casiberia and Ibherniu (Ireland) were in many places of the world. It is one of many key enterprises within the Phoenician Brotherhood. The De Danaan may have developed their adepthoods or they may have had even more ancient hominids teach them, it is hard to know when this happened but I think it happened very early and even before 30,000 years ago as the Old European pre-Black Sea people
6) had a smaller population and had to learn to be better or perish. The fact that they were in Egypt and America around the same time genetics says they came into existence may tell us that they had a helper like the Mungo Man.

Diverse Druids

7) Holy Grail Across the Atlantic, by Michael Bradley, a lecturer and navigational expert, Hounslow Press, 1999 issue, 1989 first edition. The Hadji Ahmed map is part of the illustrations herein and he has many more including the Portolan maps.
8) The Druids, by Peter Berresford Ellis, 1994, Constable, London, pg.174.
9) Phrase of Dr. Janice Boddy from an article in the 1994 Stanford Anthropological Review.
10) The Druids, op.cit.pgs. 16-18.
11) A History of Christian - Muslim Relations, 2000, by Hugh Goddard, New Amsterdam Books, Chicago, pg. 114.
12) Augustine's *Confessions* with the analysis by the American Psychoanalytical Association is covered in another book. Augustine was known to brag about sexual acts he never even did, and was dysfunctional plus motivated by power.
13) The Druids, op. cit. pg.181 - on Pelagius a heretic in the eyes of Augustine because he promoted good acts and Free Will. Pelagius is from the Druidic lineage but sold out by thinking he could change them from within.
14) History of the Franks by Gregory of Tours does an excellent job of chronicling the corrupt church of his time so that we can see where they come from.
15) Early Celtic Christianity, by Brendan Lehane, Constable, 1994, pg. 1152.

Chapter Four: Ogham and the Origins of Communication (Sharing):

1) The Beginning of Language, from the *Great Mysteries-Opposing Viewpoints,* series, by Clarice Swisher, 1989, Greenhaven Press, Inc., San Diego, Ca..., pg.73.
2) Ibid, pgs.69 & 70.
3) Ibid, pg. 100.
4) Carthage, by David Soren, Aicha Ben Abed Ben Khader, Hedi Slim, 1st Touchstone ed., 1991, NY, Simon & Schuster - Albright is the 'Father of Biblical

Archaeology' according to BAR, he says this on pg. 46 of Carthage which is great research for that time.
5) Forgotten Fatherland: The Search for Elizabeth Nietzsche, 1992, by Ben Mcintyre, Macmillan, London, pg. 58.
6) From *Carthage* op. cit. (for Albright's views, see Albright 1956, Albright 1961, and Albright 1968,), pg. 43.
7) The Penguin Atlas of Ancient Greece, by Robert Morkot, 1996, pgs. 16 & 19.
8) Runes: An Introduction, by R. W. V. Elliott, 1959, 1989, Manchester University Press, pg. 53, from page notes.
9) The work of Prof. Robert Schoch of Boston University has been supported by the entire American Geological Association.
10) The Essential Kabbalah, the Heart of Jewish Mysticism, by Daniel C. Matt, Harper San Francisco, 1995, 1st paperback ed., from 1996, pgs. 103-4.
11) The Ego and From Birth to Rebirth, volume 6, from The Notebooks of Paul Brunton (New York: Larson Publications, 1987), Part I, pg. 15.
12) The Language of the Goddess, 1989, by Marija Gimbutas, foreword by Joseph Campbell, 1st Harper Collins paperback, 1991, San Francisco, pg. 3.
13) W. M. Flinders Petrie, *A History of Egypt from the XIXth to the XXXth Dynasties,* 1905, pg. 160, cf. G. A. Wainwright, in F. Petrie, ed. *Ancient Egypt* (1917), pg.iii.
14) Sir Flinders Petrie, *The Formation of the Alphabet,* (London, 1912) from *Peoples of the Sea* by Immanuel Velikovsky, pg. 8.
15) The Peoples of the Sea, by I. Velikovsky, 1977, Doubleday, Garden City, NY, pgs. 7-9.
16) The Language of the Goddess, op. cit. pg. 270.
17) Huna: A Beginner's Guide, by Enid Hoffman, Whitford Press, Atglen, Pa., 1976, 1981, pg. 2.

Diverse Druids

Chapter Five: Greenbacks to 'Wetbacks'.
1) The Secrets of Nostradamus by David Ovason, 1997, Century/Random House, pg. 396.
2) Ibid, pg.149.
3) Ibid, pg. 168.
4) Ibid,
5) Actual Minds, Possible Worlds, by Jerome Bruner, 1986, Harvard University Press, pgs. 53-4.
6) The Theory and Practice of the Mandala, With Special Reference to the Modern Psychology of the Unconscious, by Giuseppe Tucci, translated from the Italian by Alan Houghton Brodrick, Dover Publications, 1961, pgs. 61-2.
7) Ibid, pg. 23.
8) Ibid, pg.143.

Chapter Six: Sumer, Shamans and Silliness:
1) The Tigris Expedition, In Search of our Beginnings by Thor Heyerdahl, 1981, Doubleday, Garden City, NY, pg.11.
2) The Druids, op. cit., pg. 156.
3) The Path of the Masters, by Julian Johnson, M.A., B.D., M.D., *The Science of Surat Shabd Yoga,* Punjab, 15th Ed., 1939, pgs. 121 & 122.
4) The Rise of the Greeks, by Michael Grant, Orion Publishing, London, 1987, pgs. 301-303, *Iliad* II, 814-50 by Homer.
5) From above (Ibid) in notes: In the seventh century the Treres (probably Thracian)who lived west of the River Oescus (Iskar), joined or followed the Cimmerians - which whom they were often confused - in their raids on Sardia and other centres in Asia Minor (Callenus in Strabo, xiii, 4, 8, 627).
6) The Rise of the Greeks, op.cit., pgs. 310 & 302.
7) Ibid, from notes, pg. 356 - on a pre-existing Phoenician Canaanite language of which they 'only indirectly know'.

8) In Search of Genghis Khan, by Tim Severin, Hutchinson, London, 1991, pgs.230-1
9) The Island Race, by Sir Winston Churchill, Cassell & Co., 1956, 1968 printing, 4th Edition, pg. 68.
10) In Search of Genghis Khan, op. cit., pg. 232.

Chapter Seven: The Americas are the Last Bastion of 'Brotherhood'.

1) The Druids, op. cit..., pg. 80, describes the hair style of the Druids, trepanning of the skull to allow access of cosmic energy to the 'Third Eye' is also connected to this, as with Dagobert and the Merovingians.
2) Evolution of Montreal, Under the French Regime, by Adair, pg. 26.
3) Holy Grail Across the Atlantic, op. cit., pgs. 247 -8.
4) Works, by Champlain, Vol. II, pgs. 303-4,. See also the same page for ID of 'rapids of St. Louis' with the Lachine rapids.
5) Ibid, Vol. I, pg. 10, *The Works of Samuel de Champlain,* U of T Press, 1971, ed., H. P. Biggar.
6) Thomas Henry Gilmour, *Knights of Malta, Ancient and Modern,* Kennedy, Robertson Co. Ltd., Glasgow, 1903, pg. 231.
7) Evolution of Montreal, Adair, pg. 36, Canadian Historical Association, Annual Report, 1942, pgs. 20-41.
8) L'incroyable Secret de Champlain, by Florian de la Horbe, Editions du Mont Pagnote, Paris, 1959,
9) Holy Grail Across the Atlantic, op. cit., pgs. 248-254.
10) Ancient American, Issue #33, article by Leland Pederson on Minnesota Mooring Stones.
11) A Dictionary of Symbols, 2nd Ed., by J. E. Cirlot, trans. From Spanish by Jack Sage, forward by Herbert Read, Dorset Press, NY, 1962, 1991, pg. 85.
12) Ancient Mysteries by Rupert Furneaux - also reports the Aymara Indians of Peru knew Tiahuanaco was built by bearded white men. No one believes the Incan attempt (encouraged by the Spanish) to claim they built them. The truth is the Spanish destroyed all kinds of proof that

civilized cultural exchanges existed in all parts of the world for a VERY long time.
13) Scota was a Keltic woman in ancient Egypt who lent her name to the Scythians but all such personages and the time they may have lived is almost unfathomable.
14) Ancient American, Issue # 36, *A Tradition of Giants and Ancient North American Warfare,* by Ross Hamilton and Patricia Mason, pgs. 6 & 7.

Chapter Eight: Egalitarian Doesn't Mean Weak!
1) Zen Buddhism, selected writings of D. T. Suzuki, ed. By William Barrett, Doubleday, NY., 1956, 1996, Image Edition, pgs. 233 & 234.
2) Julio C. Tello, *Chavín, Cultura Matrix de la Civilizacion Andina, Publicacion Antrologica del Archivo,* II Chima; Universidad Nacional Mayor de San Marcos, (1960), 36-37.
3) Rafael Larco Hoyle, *Los Cupisniques,* (Lima: Casa Editora, *La Chronica,* y Variedades S.A. 1941), pg. 8.
4) Muriel Porter, *Tlatilco and the Proclassic Cultures of the New World,* Viking Fund Publications in Anthropology, No. 19 (NY: Wenner-Gren Foundation for Anthropological Research, Inc., 1953): Michael D. Coe, *An Olmec Design on an Early Peruvian Vessel, American Antiquity* xxcii, No. 4 (1962), 579-80.
5) Peru Before the Incas by Edward P. Lanning, Prentice Hall, Englewood Cliffs, NJ., Assoc. Prof. of Anthropology at Columbia, 1967, pg. 100.
6) Ancient America, Issue #35, *Who Mined Great Lakes Copper 4000 Years Ago?* By Jim Grimes, pg. 28.
7) The Hidden History of the Human Race, by Michael D. Cremo, and Richard L. Thompson, Bhaktivedanta Book Publishing, L.A., 1999.
8) The Druids, op. cit., pgs. 93-95.
9) Ibid, pgs, 214 & 215.
10) Mummies of Ürümchi, by Elizabeth Wayland Barber, W. W. Norton & Co., NY, 1999, pg. 68.

Chapter Nine: Sex Magic, Sacrifices and Soulfulness:
1) Zen Buddhism, op. cit., written by a good friend of Joseph Campbell who attended the Eranos Conferences with Campbell, pgs. 97 & 98.
2) Genesis of the Grail Kings by Sir Laurence Gardner, Bantam Press, 1999, back inside flap gives his titles of grandeur.
3) Unknown Man by Yatri, Sidgwick & Jackson, London, 1988, pg. 86.
4) The Secret Teachings of all Ages by Hall, Manly P., The Philosophical Research Society, LA, CA, 1989, pgs. Xxxii and lxxxix. (The Swan if the symbol of the initiates of the ancient mysteries, and of incarnate wisdom.)
5) "The human spine contains 24 individual vertebrae (7 cervical, 12 thoracic, and 5 lumbar) plus the separately fused section of the sacrum and coccyx; which contains 5 and 4 vertebrae respectively. These total 33 in all." This is why there are 33 degrees in Masonry. From *Genesis of the Grail Kings,* Ibid and op. cit., notes, pg. 277.
6) The Secret Teachings of All Ages, op. cit., pg. LXXIX.
7) The Magical Revival, by Grant K., Skoob Books (note reverse of word), 1991, London.
8) Ibid, pg. 142.
9) Genesis of the Grail Kings, op. cit., pgs. 128 & 129.
10) The Druids, op. cit., pgs. 106 & 107.
11) The Magical Revival, op. cit., pgs. 745, 121.
12) Gardner says: "This symbol was used by the hermetic Illuminati, founded on May 1st, 1771 by Jean Adam Weishaupt." This apparent tidbit is MOST illuminating. The majority of people (scholars of the subject included) don't know the Illuminati were hermetical and almost all would not even imagine that Russia's 'May Day' celebration is related to the founding of the Illuminati, because the elite have been presented as opposed to Communism, but what greater control ever existed than in this totalitarian Stalinist Bolshevism the U.S.

supported with armed forces for a quarter of a century? The U.S. Declaration of Independence was signed the same year and some say St. Germain(e) arrived to break an impasse. Though the Illuminati were outlawed they remained a strong influence on Ruskin to Cecil Rhodes and the Russell Merovingian Skull & Bones to Bilderbergs. Hegel outlined the dialectic of playing both ends against the middle.

13) Gardner says: 'This word was first introduced in the Greek *Septuagint* and was retained thereafter." Hermeneuts were seldom hermeticists except in the case of Aquinas, whose name may be derived from 'Qayin' or the ;Mark of Cain' and the aten symbol which along with the ankh is able to encapsulize the I O Torus of the *Ha Qabala* and thus quantum atomics.
14) The Body Electric by Becker, Robert O. and Selden, Gary, William Morrow, NY., 1985, pgs. 42-44.
15) Matthew Henry's Commentary on the Whole Bible, by Church, L. F., Genesis V (19-22) Marshall/Pickering, Harper Collins, London, 1960.
16) Before Philosophy, by Henri Frankfort, H. A. Frankfort, J. A. Wilson, T. Jacobsen, Penguin Harmondsworth, 1951, pg. 160.
17) Genesis of the Grail Kings, op. cit., pgs. 104 & 105.
18) Denendeh, A Dene Celebration, by The Dene Nation, 1984, pg. 9.
19) Jesuit Relations, vol. xliii, pgs. 271-273.
20) The Indians of Canada, by Diamond Jenness, 6th Ed., 1972, National Museum of Canada, Bulletin # 65, Anthropological Series #15, pgs. 162 & 165.
21) The Druids, op.cit., pgs. 152 & 153.

Chapter Ten: Before the Deluge (5500 BC.):
1) The Druids, op.cit., pg. 112.
2) Ibid, pg. 113 from *The Religion of the Ancient Celts*, (1911) by MacCulloch.
3) Ibid, pg. 164.
4) Ibid, pg. 167.

5) Grail Knights of North America, by Michael Bradley, Hounslow Press, Toronto, 1998, pgs. 374 & 375.
6) The Rise of the Greeks, op. cit., pgs. 303-306 brings us other authority like Anaximenes, Aristotle and Homer.

Chapter Eleven: 'Aztlan' - or Atlantis?
1) The Rise of the Greeks, op. cit., pgs. 249 - 252.
2) Prehistory of North America, by Jesse Jennings, McGraw-Hill, NY, 1968, pg. 32.
3) Atlantis, by Charles Berlitz, 1984, G. P. Putnam's Sons, NY, pgs. 32-3.
4) This halved meteor theory of German physicist Otto Muck deserves further explanation that this book allows.
5) Grail Knights of North America, op. cit., pg. 66.
6) Atlantis, op. cit., pg. 178.
7) Discover Magazine, February 1985, pg. 9.
8) Ancient American, Issue # 34, article - "What Destroyed Atlantis?" by Frank Joseph, pg. 12.
9) Grail Knights, brings us, Knight, Christopher, and Lomas, Robert, *The Hiram Key,* Century (Random House), London, 1996, pgs. 76-8.
10) Ibid, pgs. 68-9
11) The Druids, op. cit., pgs. 190 & 191.
12) Extinction, The Beothuks of Newfoundland, by Frederick W. Rowe, McGraw-Hill Ryerson Ltd., Toronto, 1977, 1986 paperback ed., pgs. 4-6.

Chapter Twelve: B'hairdic Blarney:
1) The Druids, op. cit., pg. 140.
2) Ibid, pgs. 137 & 138.
3) A Dictionary of Symbols, op. cit., pg. 68.
4) Ibid, pg. 70.
5) Prehistory of North America, op. cit., pgs. 189-191.
6) Ibid, pg. 214.
7) American Antiquities, by Joshia Priest, Springfield, 1833, pg. 21.
8) Grail Knights, op. cit., pg. 342.
9) The Druids, op. cit., pgs. 196-7.

Chapter Thirteen: The Druids of America:
1) The Children of the Aataentsic, by Bruce G. Trigger, 1976, 1st Paperback ed., 1987, McGill-Queens U. Press, pgs. 196-7.
2) Ibid, pgs. 189-90
3) Ibid, pg. 195.
4) League of the Iroquois by Lewis Henry Morgan, Intro. By Wm. Fenton, The Citadel Press, NJ., pgs. 260-2.
5) As if it is necessary to study whether a part of nature is sacred, this authority if; Denys, *Description and Natural History,* 2; 480, 442; and Le Clerq, *New Relations of Gaspesia,* pgs. 192-3.
6) Ibid, pgs. 417-8 and 215-8.
7) Thwaites, ed. *Jesuit Relations,* 2:75; le Clerq, Ibid, 215-6, George H. Daugherty, Jr. & Johnson also.
8) Le Clerq, Ibid, pgs. 296-9, Denys, Ibid, 2:415, 417-8, Hagar, *Micmac Magic,* pgs.170-77.
9) Plants, Man and the Ecosystem, by Billings, pg. 36.
10) Jesuit Relations, Ibid, 2:75.
11) The Early Trading Companies of New France: A Contribution to the History of Commerce and Discovery in North America, by H. P. Biggar, (1901; reprint NY, 1965), pgs. 18-37.
12) Archaeology As A Key To The Colonial Fur Trade, by John Whitthoft, Minnesota History (1966); pgs. 204-5.
13) Indian Prehistory of Pennsylvania (Harrisburg, Pa., 1965) Pgs. 26-29.
14) The European Impact on the Culture of a Northeastern Algonquian Tribe: An Ecological Interpretation: by Calvin Martin from *Out of the Background* by Robin Fisher and Kenneth Coates, 1988, Copp Clark Pitman, Ltd., Toronto, pgs. 74-6.
15) Out of the Background, op. cit., *Maps of Dreams* by Hugh Brodie., pg. 264.
16) The Children of the Aataentsic op. cit., pg. 61 & 62.

Robert Baird

Chapter Fourteen: A World of Wonder - I Wander!
1) They Shared to Survive, by Selwyn Dewdney, Franklin Arbuckle, 1975, Macmillan, Toronto, pg. 49.
2) Indian Legacy, Native American Influences on World Life and Culture, Hermina Poatgeiter, Julian Meisner, NY., 1981, 2nd Printing, 1982, pg. 120.
3) Atlantis, op. cit., pgs. 111 & 112.
4) Ibid, pgs. 124 & 125.
5) A Dictionary of Symbols, op. cit., pgs. 206.
6) Grail Knights, op. cit., pgs. 164-5.
7) A Dictionary of Symbols, op. cit., pg. 274-5.
8) Fortean Magazine, book review by George Sassoon, April 2001, pg. 55, *Who Were the First Kiwis?*

About the Author

At a young age growing up with a father who had read the total complement of books in a library as a teenager and older brothers who had read Moby Dick by grade two, I had to compete. I learned to love learning and at the age of five I was in grade two because the only grade I skipped was kindergarten (it started the next year where I was living outside Toronto) and they let me in early due to the obvious success of my oldest brother who was already teaching adults in the military while still in grade eight. School bored me and I went from Grade 13 in Ontario into the last year you could get into Public Accounting without a degree. It seems that I was always just getting in under the wire.

After three years of accounting and having been an officer in the Militia which I joined a year before I should have (my only real lie in life) I started my own business with my brother John. It involved traveling all over the States and a lot of learning occurred. We promoted cities in a unique advertising poster and hired my engineer oldest brother. At the age of about 30 I was a millionaire and wrote College Equivalency tests to by pass a BA and got into the best business university through a very exclusive program that required getting over 75%-ile in the Princeton GMAT among other things. Oh, I was written up as a new Horatio Alger and had all I thought I wanted - but it was not good for me, I found. I next got into R & D dealing in a concept that Tesla would have enjoyed hearing how the big boys love to shelve the truly cheap and educative potential that science can offer. I had married a teacher who I loved so much I had given my all for ten years to get married. But she found living with a forever commitment too hard to enjoy and we got divorced but still stayed great friends for 25 years.

About five years ago - I decided I would not play ball in the material world anymore and then began to fight the system. For the past three years I have been writing about a book every six weeks. Most people can't imagine how much it means to create and give your every loving fibre in your soul. Some say I am a fool. It is true! One of my lifelong favorite sayings is 'A fool thinks he is a wise man...'. I don't really care if you think I am a fool - try thinking for yourself - don't follow me - it is hard work - but I love it.

Also Available from The Invisible College Press

Modern Fiction:
City of Pillars, by Dominic Peloso
Tattoo of a Naked Lady, by Randy Everhard
Wieland, by Charles Brockden Brown
The Third Day, by Mark Graham
Leeward, by D. Edward Bradley
Cold in the Light, by Charles Gramlich
MarsFace, by R. M. Pala
Phase Two, by C. Scott Littleton
Utopian Reality, by Catherine Simone
Evilution, by Shaun Jeffery
The Phoenix Egg, by Richard Bamberg
Axis Mundi Sum, by D. A. Smith

Non Fiction:
The Practical Surveyor, by Samuel Wyld
A Treatise on Mathematical Instruments, by John Robertson
The Roscrucian Manuscripts, by Christian Rosencreutz
Proof of the Illuminati!, by Seth Payson, A.M.
Diverse Druids, by Robert Baird

ICP titles are available wherever quality books are sold.

Please visit our website at:
http://www.invispress.com/

Printed in the United States
1415300002B/159